CHARLOTTE Nash

Charlotte Nash began stealing her mother's Jilly Cooper novels at the age of thirteen, and has been enthusiastic for romance ever since. She started writing after medical school, and her enduring stories of courage and love are now published around the world. She writes from a cozy cottage on the east coast of Australia, surrounded by family and chickens. *Iron Junction* was her second novel, now republished in this international edition.

Visit charlottenash.net for all the books and to sign up for her newsletter (comes with exclusive previews and giveaways). She loves to hear from readers through:

 @CharlotteNash79

 AuthorCharlotteNash

 @saxen49

Also by Charlotte Nash:

The Walker-Bell Stories
Ryders Ridge
Iron Junction
Crystal Creek
Great Haven (in 2018)

Stand-alone Romances
The Horseman

Women's Fiction with Romantic Elements
The Paris Wedding
The Lucky Escape (in 2019)

Iron Junction

Charlotte Nash

FLYING
NUN
PUBLICATIONS

First published in Australia and New Zealand in 2014 by Hachette Australia (an imprint of Hachette Australia Pty Limited)

This international edition published in 2018 by Flying Nun Publications, http://flyingnunpublications.com/

ISBN:
978-1-925775-02-0 (paperback)
978-1-925775-03-7 (MOBI eBook)
978-1-925775-07-5 (EPUB eBook)

A catalogue record for this book is available from the National Library of Australia

Cover design by J.D. Smith

For Kev …
from carrier pigeons and dancing on ice,
to trebuchets, Piha, and tomorrow.
My love, my home.

Author's note

I'm excited to welcome you to this international edition of *Iron Junction*, the second book in the Walker-Bell series, stories that blend contemporary romance with family, secrets, and medical drama, featuring the Walker and Bell family siblings and friends in small towns across Australia (though don't worry if you haven't read the first – you can jump in here).

If you're not familiar with Australia, think of both Queensland (capital: Brisbane) and Western Australia (capital: Perth) a bit like Texas – big places full of big characters. There's a bit of colorful language, but also lots of space for ranches and mines (Queensland is about 2.5 times the size of Texas; Western Australia is 3.5 times larger). Perfect to hide from a secret, or to meet an attractive man with a past …

Enjoy!

Chapter 1

Brisbane, November

"Beth Harding, what the hell is going on?"

In the midst of her youngest sister's birthday party, Beth pressed her phone to her ear and crept inside, her pulse racing.

"Hi, Tom." She heard waves in the background. She imagined her former fellow medical resident, Tom Black, a Sydney beach headland rising up behind him. They'd known each other since medical school, and for the past week she'd been sleeping on his couch. She owed him an explanation, but right now she only wanted to avoid telling him everything.

"How's the beach?" she tried.

"Nice try," he said, clearly annoyed. "I called the hospital to swap a shift and instead I find out you resigned yesterday. I thought you were only flying home to Brisbane for Vicky's party. So, what the hell?"

Beth glanced around to see who could hear. Thirty guests crowded her mother's covered patio. Her uncle Jim was grilling the meat, brandishing the long tongs and a tasteless apron printed with a French-maid outfit, the air thick with smoke. Across the tiles Victoria, the birthday girl, radiated charm. Her white sundress, Christmas-bell earrings and blonde chignon were flight-attendant perfect, despite her coming off-shift early that morning. Vicky was in a huddle with Anne, her middle sister, and their mother, while Vicky's boyfriend, Ryan, hovered at the edge of the conversation. No one was looking Beth's way.

Tom went on, "I know you've been frustrated with work, and getting over Richard is going to take a while ..."

Against her will, a strangled sob escaped Beth's throat.

"Beth? Beth?" Tom apologized, backing off the topic. "Look, I'm worried. Why don't we have a coffee when you're back tomorrow and talk about it?"

"I can't, Tom." Beth couldn't help glancing at her case resting in the hallway, its belly stuffed full of *Murtagh's General Practice*, the *Oxford Handbook of Clinical Medicine*, her precious photo album and enough clothes for a long trip. She pushed a wayward length of hair behind her ear and cupped her hand around the phone, the truth spilling out. "I'm going away for a while."

A pause. "Where?"

"Not sure yet. I'm taking a locum job. I'm just waiting for the call to confirm."

Tom suddenly laughed. "Thank god. Finally!"

"What do you mean, finally?"

"Beth, you've been miserably stale for three years. I'd given up thinking you were going to climb out of the rut."

"I wasn't in a rut," hissed Beth indignantly. But he had a point. She was five years out of medical school and still without any direction. No specialty had called her, and the world had contracted around the monotony of her inner-city hospital. And then there had been Richard.

"Are you really sure, though?" Tom continued. "You're a beach girl. What if you end up in the desert?"

"It's only a few months," she said, wondering if that would be true.

Tom sighed. "I wish you'd told me, but I'll hold your boxes. I want to hear all about it."

Beth ended the call and eased back outside, clutching her

vintage camera for comfort, but everyone was clustered at the far edge, watching one of her younger cousins doing tricks on the trampoline. The grill sizzled unattended. She hovered by the doors, not feeling like joining the crowd. She smoothed her blue sundress and checked her phone again, impatient for news.

She jumped as a shadow fell over her.

"Beth! Sorry to give you a fright." It was uncle Jim, grill tongs still in hand, his apron stretched across his belly, a net of broken capillaries over his nose. "Good to see you, love. Where's that fine fiancé?"

Beth evaded neatly. "He's working, Uncle Jim." There, it was just a little white lie.

"Good, good. Well, listen, now the old cooker's under control, can you take a look at something for me?" He cast a glance over his shoulder.

"What have you got?" Beth asked warily as she steered him inside. She'd long ago accepted that being a doctor meant family asked for her advice at odd and sometimes inappropriate times.

Jim pulled up his shirt, displaying angry red skin across his stomach. "Came up all by itself and itches like crazy," he said.

Beth peered at the rash. "Could be an allergy. Have you changed washing powder, or something like that?"

"No, but I was in Thailand last week. Got some new shirts."

Beth raised her eyebrows. "You should see your family doctor," she said firmly. "Promise me you will, Uncle Jim?"

"Okay, okay. But see, there's also this other thing, too," he began, turning and gripping the seat of his pants.

"For goodness sake, Jim, leave Beth alone," scolded a voice. "No one wants to look at your behind, least of all your niece."

Gratefully, Beth found her aunt Judy striding in from the patio. Judy had the same curly, pale ginger hair as Meredith

Harding, Beth's mother, but that was where the similarity ended. Judy smiled a lot, and energy and wit sparkled in her eyes. Jim retreated, red-faced, to the grill.

"That man has no sense of shame," said Judy. "How are you, Beth? Sydney still treating you well?"

"Fine," said Beth brightly.

Judy's eyes fell on the camera, still around Beth's neck. "Oh, you still have your father's camera!" She ran a finger across the lens cap. "I remember when he bought it – he was so proud of it. Are you staying long?"

Beth swallowed, and shook her head. "I just came for the party. I promised Victoria I would."

"You're a good sister," said Judy. "But you'll be glad to get home. I know it's tricky for you in this house."

Beth tamped down all her guilt. *And where was home now?*

Soon, the meat was served and a long line formed around the salad table, hands batting away the flies. Beth waited until the queue was shorter. With spare seats in short supply, she pulled a dining table chair up to the French doors and tucked her camera underneath. She'd just sat with the flimsy paper plate on her knees when a shadow fell across her chair.

"Beth, here." Beth stood reflexively, nearly losing her food plate as her mother thrust a tray of empty glasses at her. "You could help a bit more. These are for the dishwasher. It should have finished the last load. And Ryan needs a fresh beer. They're in the sink."

Beth carried the tray into the kitchen with its familiar worn wooden cupboards and seventies brown tiles. She loaded the dishwasher, and then as she made a move back to her dinner plate her mother reappeared, cross lines circling her mouth. Her sundress was a jovial yellow, a light color for her slender frame. But her eyes were pinched.

"I nearly tripped over this," Meredith said, dangling Beth's camera by its strip, as if it was an oversized mouse. "I don't know why you insist on carrying the moldy old thing around. And how long does Ryan have to wait for that beer?" With a tut, she extracted a bottle from the ice and left.

Beth scanned the camera for damage, all its old-fashioned dials and hand-painted numbers. When she'd tucked it away, Meredith reappeared with Beth's dinner plate. "Someone might have sat on it," she said, moving to tip the lot into the bin.

Beth leapt for it. "I haven't eaten any yet!"

"It's cold."

"I'll still eat it," said Beth, rescuing the plate.

"You're lucky to have such an appetite," her mother went on. "I've barely been able to eat anything. Had horrible stomach pains all week, and my back before that. Must be the stress of the party. I had to go to the doctor yesterday."

Beth glanced up. Her mother leaned against the sink, her ginger curls limp. Beth's heart tightened. "What did he say?"

"Kept me waiting too long, so I left. But doctors are quacks anyway. I'm going to see Anne's acupuncturist on Thursday. He'll sort it out."

"But what if it's serious?"

Meredith's hand flew to her chest. "Did you have to say that? I'm stressed enough already. Christmas is only six weeks away. Everyone's here. I've been packing boxes for the business orders all week and I had to make all the desserts myself. Vicky's only twenty-one once. You should have come up earlier to help."

Beth reached her hand to her mother's arm, desperate to make amends. "I didn't mean it like that." But her mother moved to adjust her bracelet, out of reach. Beth retracted her fingers.

"I didn't expect you to come without Richard," her mother went on. "You might have told me for the numbers."

Beth knew the adult thing to do was to tell the truth, but all bravery left her. "Sorry. I didn't think."

Her mother brightened. "Have you finished your wedding guest list yet?"

"No. Sorry."

"You're not wearing your ring either. Richard's a good man, Beth." Her mother's gaze flickered, her mouth trembling. "Not like your father. No-good deserting bastard."

"*Mum*," Beth said. Even though her father had been gone nearly fifteen years, her mother's loathing of him cut Beth like shards of glass.

"Well, he was," Meredith insisted. "Left us for that mine job, but I stayed. I did the work bringing you all up. I worked hard so you could have things I didn't." Tears gathered in her eyes, and the facade cracked. She fanned a hand over her chest. "I'm sorry," she mumbled. "I don't know why you put up with me."

Beth reached out and her mother pulled her into an awkward, smelling the familiar floral perfume. Beth had always been tall for her age, and now her mother seemed fragile, her shoulders all bones under Beth's hand. "It's okay, Mum," she said soothingly. "I know it still hurts. I'm sorry, too."

Her mother pulled away, dabbing under her eyes. "There, I'm fine," she said. "Now, just … I'll just be outside."

Beth leaned against the bench, trying to assemble the pieces of the conversation into some kind of meaningful order. Her mother swung from criticism to vulnerability so fast it was exhausting. Beth knew she had never quite fit in the family, walking on thin glass around these matriarchal moods, and always feeling the full slug of guilt for not being whatever it was her mother expected her to be. So how could she contemplate going away now and making it all worse?

Like a beacon, her phone rang.

"Doctor Harding? This is Greg at the locum agency."

Beth hung on the words. "Yes?"

"I've confirmed an immediate start position in Iron Junction. It's a mining-town medical center in the Pilbara, north Western Australia. One of their FIFO doctors is sick."

"FIFO?"

"Fly-in, fly-out. You'd do ten days on and four off back in Perth, which they call a swing. Does that sound okay? I know you were keen and we can have you traveling today. It's two flights and a drive, I'm afraid."

Beth's soul surged with joy and uncertainty, hope and doubt. She turned the name of the town over in her mind. *Iron Junction*. A mining town. It sounded remote. She'd been waiting impatiently for this call, and now she wasn't sure why. What did she hope to achieve? Beth bit her lip. The crowd was forming a knot on the patio, now. Maybe it was time for cake. They hushed, and she dropped her own voice. "Yes, but I'm in Brisbane for a family event," she said, feeling herself waver.

"That's fine. I'll see what we can book and call you back."

Beth ended the call divided between apprehension and the first ray of hope in the long, difficult week. She stepped into the hall with its soft pink walls and ornate plaster cornices. This house was such a familiar place. Even Victoria's and Anne's rooms were exactly as they'd been while they were at school. Admittedly, Beth's had become the office after she'd been the first to leave home for Sydney and her old room now smelled of Australian bush pepper and smoked Himalayan salt: her mother's best mail-order sellers. Still, she had roots here. Maybe she was crazy to head off to remote Western Australia. And to a *mining* town; her mother would have a coronary. Maybe she should phone Greg back and call this off.

She slipped out the patio doors, where Victoria's birthday speeches were underway. She might be always at the back of the crowd, but this was a happy day for her sister. Ryan was speaking now, telling everyone how amazing Victoria was, and wishing her a happy birthday. Claps and cheers followed.

Then Ryan hushed the crowd. "That's also why," he continued, "I have something else for Victoria."

Beth took in Ryan's satisfied smile, Victoria's perplexed expression, the murmur of expectation. Her stomach dropped as she realized what was about to happen. Ryan was down on his knee now, offering up a ring box. Victoria's eyes were wide and spilling joyful tears.

Beth couldn't help how her heart lurched. Just a few short months ago, that had been Richard on his knee, and her happiness. Things she no longer had.

She slipped away, found the bathroom and splashed water on her face. In the mirror, her long dark hair was caught behind her ears, but her eyes now had that same pinched look her mother always carried.

"Go," she told herself sternly.

Beth in the mirror refused to budge. Her thoughts turned back to Sydney, circling around how the whole idea had been a mistake, and contemplated calling Richard. She closed her eyes, trying to remember Tom's encouragement. "Please, go," she told herself.

A droplet of water tracked down her face, a tiny sensation that cut a clean path in her thoughts. She must leave now or she would never have the chance. It was time to cast off, and go looking for the self she'd lost.

Chapter 2

First swing

Two flights, a very late night, and a 3 a.m. wake-up later, Beth stood in the graveled parking lot of Paraburdoo airport, square in the center of the Pilbara mining country. "Airport" was a rather generous word, Beth thought, for a single room resembling a lonely highway roadhouse, and the hire car office was even worse: it looked like a security booth. A very tight security booth. Everything was covered in orange dust, including the four-wheel-drive monster truck she was now staring at.

"Erm … I don't suppose you have a small car?" she asked.

The woman beside her laughed. She was the solo employee of the hire car company, and had a tight red perm and a flush of sunburn across her nose and cheeks. Her shirt was damp around the armpits even at six in the morning. "First time up here, huh? This is the smallest we got."

Beth swallowed. In Sydney she'd had a tiny hatch, parking it like she owned the place, never worrying about blind spots. The car before her now had running boards as high as her knee, a bull bar that could hold up a small house, and an orange strobe on the roof like an evil eye.

She lifted her gaze to the post-dawn sky, breathing in the bright air of this new, red-earthed world. She had to admit: the car was probably made for this place. Out the plane's window the land had been a russet smudge stretching to the horizon, wrinkled with hills, streaked with shadows and scrappy trees. From the ground, it seemed just as empty. A great primal landscape, across which she faced a three-hour drive.

The woman pushed the Prado's key into Beth's hand. "Where you headed, love?"

"Iron Junction," said Beth.

"Ah, nice place. It's well signed. But watch you follow the rules on the mine roads – do you know about them?"

"No?"

The woman pointed to the roof. "If you're on a mine road, turn your strobe on. You could be fined if you get caught with it off – safety reasons. Switch is under the dash, but remember to turn it off when you stop. Drains the battery. And if you see a haul truck, you're in the wrong place."

"Um, haul truck?"

The woman laughed. "Don't worry, you'll know if you find one, biggest truck you've ever seen, wheels taller than you are. Run you over easy and wouldn't even notice."

"Right," Beth said, uneasy.

The woman clapped Beth on the shoulder. "Don't worry about it. They're only on the mine sites. You'll be right, love."

"Right," Beth repeated. Nerves tickled her belly. She wasn't even sure how to recognize a mine road. Maybe she'd turn the strobe on at all times.

The woman gave a cheerful wave and turned back to the hire car shack. Beth licked her lips. In the slanting rays of early sun, sweat was already blooming under the dark hair against her neck. She wished she'd worn a singlet, not the stiff cotton work shirt tucked into woolen suit pants, which were sticking to her legs. She became aware of how quiet it was. The flight had been full of hi-vis-clad workers, but they'd vanished in a convoy of dust-stained pickups and SUVs.

"This is an adventure," she muttered as she shoved her case into the back seat and hauled herself up into the driver's seat.

The vast interior swallowed her, roll-bars arching over her head. The engine rumbled to life and Beth eased onto the asphalt strip, feeling as if she were driving an eighteen wheeler. But the steering was surprisingly light, the pedals responsive. Beth sat straighter, a smile on her lips. In the rear view the abandoned airport receded, its windsock lifting a limp end. Just like a scene from the zombie apocalypse. Abruptly, a fist gripped her stomach. Maybe she should have stayed in Sydney. Maybe she should have worked things out …

Stop it.

She set her face, drawing power from the engine's deep grumble. Iron Junction was her safe haven. All she had to do was get there.

Three hours later, Beth rounded a bend and spied a neat township nestled between two rises. All the mental pictures she'd had – of wild, frontier towns – turned out to be quite wrong. Iron Junction's streets were a neat grid hanging from the connecting highway and rimmed by a twin row of train tracks. A large billboard announced the town: *Iron Junction – The Pilbara's Finest Community*, and the company logo in red and green. And when she found the medical center, a new, white, modular building with a cheerful patch of wilting perennials bordering its walls, the company logo was there too.

Outside the center, a man in a suit waited alongside a woman with cropped gray hair, a clinical coat and a coffee mug. Beth's cheeks burned as they watched her two attempts to park, and her careful descent from the cab.

The man strode forward, his broad smile surrounded by a trimmed beard, his hand extended. Beth noticed the perfect Windsor knot in his tie as he squared his shoulders. His teeth flashed white. "Doctor Harding, I presume? Dale King, the mine manager. Welcome to the Junction."

Beth had her hand warmly shaken. Dale turned. "And this

is—"

"Maxine de Wet," said the woman in a brisk South African accent. She tipped the contents of her mug out on the perennials. "How was the drive?"

"Fine, once I made friends with the giant truck," Beth said, holding out her hand towards, she presumed, her new colleague, and trying to make a joke.

Maxine shook briefly, but didn't crack a smile. "Right. Inside out of this heat."

Dale gave her a sympathetic smile, and gestured ahead into the clinic. Through a large door was a pristine cool-blue waiting area, with white chairs, water cooler and kids' play area. The seats were thickly padded, and a receptionist clicked away at a sleek monitor behind the desk. The whole set-up looked like a private inner-city clinic.

"Jennifer, this is Doctor Harding, the locum," said Maxine to the receptionist, not stopping as she marched towards into the corridor.

Dale King stopped by the desk and Beth lost sight of Maxine. "Well, Doctor Harding. Elizabeth?"

"Beth's fine," she said.

"Beth." He smiled again. "I'm very glad you could come. Three years at Royal Sydney, second in your class at medical school. Your CV is very impressive."

His grin was broad. A pink glow spread across Beth's cheeks. "I didn't expect to meet the mine management," she said.

"Of course! I'm across everything in our operation, and I wanted to personally welcome you and give you a quick run-down on our procedures. Did the agency give you our information packet?"

"Yes, I looked at it," said Beth carefully, aware Dale was watching her reaction. She had looked at the brochures, briefly on the plane. She remembered sheaves of glossy photographs and bold headlines on sustainability and community engagement, which hadn't meant much to her. It hadn't had much in it about the clinic, but she smiled anyway.

Dale grinned back, all charm. "Excellent. So, you understand the medical center is a partnership? I personally make sure everything is top notch. Any issues at all, you just let me know. I'd like us to be on good terms. Doctor Gregg normally handles all the company cases and paperwork, runs our education programs, does a lot for the mine. With all the contractors in town for the expansion, his illness has really left us short. But I'm sure I can count on you to fill the gap."

Beth was searching for a reassuring reply, despite some alarm about education programs – the agency had never mentioned that – but Dale was already moving on.

He grabbed two forms off Jennifer's desk, one pink, one blue. "Fill these out for any company worker. Then, put them into this internal envelope to come back to me. Clear as mud?"

Beth peered at the forms. "Okay …"

Dale patted her shoulder. "Anything you don't understand, just call me directly. Here's my card," he finished, pressing the white oblong into Beth's hand. "And make sure you come to the company Christmas party this Saturday, down at the creek. Everyone will be there." He stuck his hand out a second time. "Maxine will show you around. I'm sure we'll speak again soon." He winked.

Beth stared after his departing back. She'd never had such a personal welcome from high management anywhere. She raised her eyebrows at Jennifer, who shrugged. Then Beth noticed Maxine waiting in the hallway.

"Minor procedures in there, eye room there," Maxine said, striding on as Beth caught up. "Vaccination fridge. Supply room …" Beth tried to keep up as they rushed around the U-shaped hallway, Maxine outlining in detail the contents of every cupboard. "The tea room's on the other side," she went on as they circled back. Finally, she stopped outside a door.

"And this here is Doctor Gregg's room, where you'll be working. You heard what happened?"

"He's sick?"

"Pancreatitis," said Maxine, ushering Beth into Doctor Gregg's desk chair. "He's in the Royal Perth Hospital. We had to evacuate him down there last week."

"Sounds serious." Beth glanced around. Standard exam table behind a curtain, bookshelf over the desk, slimline computer monitor, pot of tongue depressors, a smaller one of jelly beans. She could survive the length of a pancreatitis bout in this place. What would it be, six weeks? Eight?

Maxine shrugged. "I'm sure he'll recover. I just want to know that you can stay until he's back." Beth assured her she would, but Maxine lingered, giving Beth the once-over. "You don't look like the sort we usually get in here."

"What sort's that?"

Maxine folded her arms. "In it for the money. Broken by what they've been doing before and looking for a holiday. People like that. The roster soon sorts them out."

"Oh?" asked Beth, her stomach squirming. She might be a little bit broken. But she wasn't looking for a holiday, just a chance to familiarize before she started work tomorrow.

Maxine plowed on. "We run on the mine's schedule, which is twelve-hour shifts, except Friday, which is a half-day to allow for flights out. You can get your key to the apartment across the road from Jennifer when you finish tonight. Your first appointment's in an hour."

Beth's jaw was still open as Maxine disappeared.

By ten the next morning, Beth began to breathe again, but only just. The previous afternoon had been chaotic with all supplies in unfamiliar places, appointments running behind. But Jennifer had been helpful, especially when a mine worker called Stuey had appeared with painful urination and a nasty discharge, which needed swabs and the overnight courier to a pathology lab. Given what she'd coaxed out of him about a wild holiday to Bali in the last off-swing, Beth suspected the problem. She'd seen it plenty of times back east. Finally, she'd escaped to the apartment she'd been provided, and spent an exhausted hour unpacking and fiddling with the knobs on her air conditioner before falling into bed. At least there'd been no time to think about Richard.

Now, with Stuey back in the waiting room, she clicked through to the lab results and found she'd been right. The gods had certainly delivered a wonderful first case for her. Well, this wasn't at all awkward.

"I'm afraid you've picked up an infection," Beth began. "The results came back positive for gonorrhea."

She watched big, burly Stuey turn red. "That's bad, right?"

"It's certainly serious, and you can also pass it to other sexual partners. We can treat it – you'll need an injection and an oral antibiotic. But I also need to make sure we trace anyone else who could have been exposed. Can we go through that now?"

Fortunately, Beth discovered that Stuey had been working a crammed roster since his holiday, and had no other partners to trace. "And I want you to come back in a week and get re-tested," she said.

"Won't the shot do the trick?" Stuey said, squirming in his seat. He clearly didn't want to come back. Beth couldn't help thinking of Uncle Jim's rash. Had that really only been two days' ago?

"The diagnosis is just a preliminary result," she tried to explain. "There's also a culture for antibiotic resistance, which is becoming more of a problem. I want to make sure it's definitely gone."

After she'd organized the shot and script, and gently led Stuey through prevention, Beth wearily filled out government notification forms. The long day was exhausting. As she returned from handing them to Jennifer, she found Maxine standing in the doorway of her office. Beth was yet to make any progress with the older doctor, who seemed reclusive and standoffish.

"Sniffles, aches and refills," Maxine said now with a sigh. "You seen anything actually interesting?"

Beth moved closer, hoping to start a conversation. "Yes. Gonorrhea."

Maxine raised her eyebrows. "Let me guess, holidaying in South-east Asia? There'll be more. You wait." Then she disappeared into her consulting room. Beth was about to follow when Jennifer trotted down the hall. "Got a walk-in with an eye injury," she said. So, Maxine would have to wait.

Two minutes later, Beth found a man in beaten blue overalls sprawled on the exam couch and holding a wad of white surgical gauze over his eye, his hair a nest of snared greenery and twigs.

"Brian?" she asked, after taking the details from Jennifer. "I'm Beth Harding, one of the doctors. You want to tell me what happened?"

Brian's one good eye swiveled. "Tree branch whipped me across my face," he said. "Hurt like hell."

"Show me, then." Beth braced herself, but when the dressing came off, all she could see was an inflamed, weepy eye.

"What were you doing when this happened?" she asked, to distract him while she asked him to look up, left, right and down.

"Clearing trees."

"At the mine?" asked Beth, pulling down Brian's eyelid, looking for debris and finding none.

"Ah, yeah."

Beth regarded Brian, who seemed uncomfortable as if he was keeping something to himself. "How's the pain?"

"Not too bad right now."

So, she tested his vision. Acuity was slightly reduced on the injured side, but that might be explained by the weeping.

"I'm going to need to look at your eye with some

magnification. Can you sit there, please?" She faced him across the slit lamp, a table-top device for eye examination. "Just put your chin on that rest. Great. Now try to look over my shoulder."

Beth fiddled with the dials, buoyed by the challenge of finding the elusive injury. The eye was red and angry. Time to pull out all the tricks.

"I'm going to need to put some fluorescent dye in your eye. It'll help me see if there's any damage."

After squeezing in the drops and switching to the blue lamp filter, Beth spotted the problem.

"Aha! There it is. You've scratched your cornea," she said. In fact, Brian had done rather a good job. Under the slit lamp's glow, she could clearly see a ragged mark across his eye, the edges glowing green with the fluorescent dye. If she'd been back in Sydney, Brian would be referred straight to an ophthalmology department. But even in this well-appointed company town, there was no such thing. She'd have to make her own plan.

"Here's what we're going to do. I'm going to make sure there's no foreign matter left in there to do any more damage. Then, I'll put in some antibiotic ointment and a patch over the eye. You'll have to wear it for a few days."

"What about work?" asked Brian, eyeing the form Beth had started.

"I'll give you a certificate until the patch is off."

Brian shifted in his seat. "Shit," he said softly.

"What?"

Brian went to rub his eye and Beth caught his hand. "Try not to rub it. Is there a problem?"

"We're short-staffed, that's all. They don't like us having days off."

"Is there something else you can do for a few days?"

Brian perked up. "I can drive forklifts."

"No driving," said Beth sternly. "Two eyes for that. But

anything else should be all right."

As Brian was leaving with his certificate, he turned back. "What about playing volleyball? We've got a big game tonight."

"Cheer squad only," she said.

When the last appointment finished, Beth tiredly knocked on Maxine's door, remembering their interrupted conversation.

The older doctor had glasses pushed down her nose, feet up on her desk, a medical journal in her hands. "How was your eye victim?" she asked, not looking up.

"Keen to get back to work," said Beth. "Do you want me to run the case by you? Or the earlier one?"

"No need," said Maxine, intent on her journal.

Beth lingered, feeling the loneliness of isolation if all the days continued like this one. She wanted a better rapport with Maxine. "I hear there's volleyball on tonight," she said, despite her exhaustion. "Can you tell me where?"

Maxine clucked her tongue. Finally, she sighed and threw down the journal. "Yes. Technically, I'm supposed to go."

As Maxine pushed open the door of Iron Junction's impressive sports club, Beth had to stand back and admire. The place smelled of wood polish, clean bathrooms, and sport-shoe rubber. The foyer boasted a trophy cabinet, and the main floor opened out into a full-size multi-purpose court, different colored lines crisscrossing the floor. Tucked down the far end were two squash courts and an open equipment store, full of mats where a bunch of kids were playing. For the match tonight, a high net stretched across the court.

"I haven't been down here in a while," Maxine said. "We give the games medical support, but the center's just around the corner. Doesn't seem necessary to be here in person."

Maxine led the way towards the stands, which were already dotted with a mix of hi-vis mine gear among the jeans and T-shirts. Someone on the far side was fiddling with a banner that said, *Go Iron Spikes!* On court, two mixed teams lofted a ball around, half of them in company colors. To the side, three men clustered at an AV equipment table and Beth recognized Dale King among them.

Beth cast her eye over the assembled players. "Is Iron Spikes the local team?"

"One of," said Maxine, finding a pew in an unpopulated corner and pulling out a battered paperback. "The opposition tonight are from Karratha. It's very competitive."

"This is impressive," said Beth. "How does such a small place have such great stuff?"

Maxine shrugged. "The company pumped in a lot of money. It was a test case for an agreement with the residents and the Indigenous landowners. The company consults them on everything it does, and they get shares in the mine and support for the community. It's a compromise, but you can't argue with the quality of the medical facility. And we have far lower rates of alcoholism and disease here than just about anywhere else you can name. I guess it's good for everyone."

Beth was amazed.

"Don't be too impressed, it's not all roses," Maxine went on. "It's still remote. We find it impossible to keep a physiotherapist, or a nurse. Jennifer's good at helping out with minor procedures, but she's not registered. Teachers are always rolling through the school. Then there's this expansion at the mine, and all the FIFO contractors in town that come with it." She nodded towards a group at the far end of the grandstand, who sat a little apart.

"What's wrong with contractors?" asked Beth.

"Depends who you ask. The locals would say they take money out of the town, and bring an … unfavorable influence. Housing prices go up, drinking goes up."

"And what would you say?"

Maxine gave a rare smile. "We see some interesting patients, as you saw today."

Within a few short minutes, the stands filled and the teams lined up. An announcer began to whip up the crowd. Beth pulled out her camera; she wasn't really a fan of sports but she could test out the fast shutter. She then spotted Brian from the clinic, eye patch still in place and wearing a team shirt. He waved and made his way over. Maxine buried her nose in her book.

"Two docs tonight," said Brian. "You come to check on me?"

"You're not playing, right?" asked Beth.

Brian shook his head and sat beside her. "You play?"

"Not since high school. It's a really nice court, though."

"Yeah, fantastic. Best one around."

Down on the court, the announcer handed over to Dale King.

"Hi, everyone," he began. "I won't take much of your time, because I know we want to play, am I right?"

A cheer erupted from the stands. Dale continued, "I want to remind everyone about the company Christmas party on Saturday afternoon – we'll have buses running from town and a big surprise for all the kids. And the music festival line-up in a few weeks is looking fantastic. Carols, fireworks and bands, so tell all your friends. We want the whole Pilbara community here. Now, let's play! *Go Spikes!*"

"There's a music festival?" asked Beth.

"Bigger every year," said Brian.

"Used to be on in February, but it was always rained out," put in Maxine. "So, they rolled it into Christmas."

"Well, better get back to the barracking," said Brian, standing up. Beth returned to her camera, turning the shutter speed knob.

As the first serve streaked across the net, Maxine didn't look up, even when a photoflash went off to the side of the stand. Beth glanced over and saw a dark-haired woman crouched with a long lens lining up the match, a battered professional camera bag alongside.

In the company of another photographer, Beth became self-conscious. Maybe she was in the wrong position, too high to frame the action. So, after the Spikes scored fifteen points and the players broke before the next set, she apologized to Maxine and scrambled down to the floor.

The photographer had moved right against the stand and had her attention on the screen of her camera, shifting through photos. Beth couldn't help admiring the hardware.

"Is that a Canon 650D?" she asked, before she could stop herself. She'd spent too much time ogling cameras online.

The woman looked up, her dark eyes searching for the person who had asked the question. Beth couldn't help noting the clinical details. The photographer's chest was barrel-shaped, her shoulders hunched, and where her fingers worked the camera's buttons, Beth noted the blunted ends. Finger clubbing. Her doctor's brain computed: although this Aboriginal woman was young, maybe in her early twenties, she had lung disease, and a bad one at that. Beth hoped her summation didn't show on her face.

"Yeah," said the woman, warily, before her eyes lit on Beth's camera. "That looks vintage. Minolta?" she asked, incredulous.

Protectively, Beth held it up. "Yes. I know I should make the transition to digital, but this is such a nice lens." She didn't mention what else the camera meant.

"May I?" asked the woman, dropping her own camera onto its neck strap.

With a flutter of attachment, Beth handed it over. The woman handled the body expertly, hefting the weight, putting the viewfinder to her eye. Finally, she held it out to admire it. "This is the original case and lens cap. How long have you had it?"

"A long time," said Beth. "It, ah, was my dad's."

The woman handed it back with care. "Did you come in for the game?" she asked, rummaging in her lens case. "Haven't seen you around before."

"No, I'm working here for a while," said Beth. "I'm a doctor at the medical center. One of the regulars is sick."

The photographer paused in her search. Beth hoped the woman wouldn't think she'd sought her out because of her obvious condition. "You look like you're working," Beth said quickly, as the whistle blew for the next set. "I'm Beth, by the way."

"Nice to meet you, Beth by the way," the photographer said with a cheeky grin. "I'm Caitlin." Then before Beth could leave, "If you need your film developed, see Mack at the store."

Beth smiled back, pleased. When she climbed back to her seat, Maxine was scribbling in a pocket notebook. "Meeting the local talent?" she asked, her pen pausing.

"You mean the photographer?"

"Yes. Caitlin Murray."

Beth's eyes drifted back to where the photographer now stood on a chair, her lens angle down into the play. "Is she from a paper?"

Maxine shook her head. "She works with the school, mostly. Her photos were really good – the mine even sponsored her to do a course down south a few years back. Looked like she was going places. But she had a bad time with her health, so here she still is."

"Respiratory disease, right?" Beth asked softly.

"Bronchiectasis," said Maxine, putting her pen in her teeth.

Beth had to swallow her surprise. Bronchiectasis was usually a disease of much older people, or secondary to severe illnesses such as cystic fibrosis. Caitlin likely had quite a story, and not a happy one.

A shout from the court interrupted her thoughts. A rally had reached an exciting length; each time the opposing team saved the ball from the court, and lofted it back across the net, a new cheer went up. The ball set high; a spike was hit and blocked; the ball went long. Then, as a second spike streaked past the net, two players leapt to block at once. As they came down they collided, and with a squeak of sneakers, both fell to the floor.

Beth leapt up. One man remained down, gripping his knee. Beth pushed towards the court and through the gathered players. "Clear some room," she said, helping the injured man to sit up. "What's your name?"

"Steve," he said through clenched teeth. Then Beth realized everyone was staring at her. "I'm Beth Harding," she said. "I'm a new doctor at the clinic. Let's get Steve off the court, huh?"

Maxine met them at the stand's edge, a mobile kit in her hand. "Hello again, Steve," she said. "Told you not to play, didn't I?"

"Yeah," said Steve sheepishly. "But we were short because of Brian."

Maxine turned to Beth. "Since he won't listen to me, he's all yours," she said.

Much later, after Steve's knee had been iced and elevated, Beth hummed as she walked back to her apartment, still buoyed from the game. Her mobile phone rang as soon as she closed the door, and her heart tripped as she saw the caller ID. She still hadn't told her mother the truth about Richard.

"My back's been terrible today," was her mother's greeting. "How many of these tablets can I take?"

"Paracetamol? No more than eight a day," said Beth, sinking down on the bed, ready for the familiar routine. "Mum, will you see a doctor, please?"

"No, no. It's all the extra work from the party last week. And orders are still up, especially those flavored salts after *MasterChef*. If you'd just stayed and helped clean up I would be fine."

This continued for a few minutes, Beth's mother listing more tasks Beth ought to have helped with. Beth listened with growing guilt until she found a break. "I'm sorry I couldn't. I had to go to work." At least, that was true. "The business must be doing well if orders are up? You've worked so hard on it."

A beat of silence. "Of course. I've had to, haven't I?" But her voice was less sharp now. "Beth, can you put Richard on? I want to talk to him about something for the wedding. It's a surprise."

Panic lodged in Beth's throat. She mumbled that he wasn't here right now. She really was digging herself in deep, not mentioning where she really was, let alone that she'd left Richard to be there. This was going to come back to bite her.

Amazingly, her mother's mood remained bright. "Well, tell him I send my love, and I'm looking forward to the next visit. When are you bringing him up again? Tell him those pictures he hung for me last time are perfect."

Beth's limbs were leaden as she hung up. Her secret was safe, but it hung heavy in her heart.

Seeking solace, she pulled her long-abandoned album from her case. It had lived with her camera in a cupboard in her Sydney flat, remnants of her childhood that she'd taken when she left. She opened the pages. The last photograph was from Ireland: a luscious green meadow around a white-watered stream, a romantic stone ruin far in the background. Beth hadn't taken it; a friend had sent it as a postcard, from a holiday just after graduation. Beth had so loved the idea of going there, and adding more pictures like it.

She fingered the empty slots that followed. She'd never made good on her desire, but perhaps she could start, especially after Caitlin had admired her camera. Carefully, she pushed the release and wound the used film back into its roll. Now, all she had to do was find a new one, here, in the middle of nowhere.

Chapter 3

Six hundred miles south the next morning, Will Walker opened his eyes, saw white curtains and imagined he was back on Ryders Station. Beyond those curtains was the endless plain filled with golden grass and cattle. His brother, Mark, would be up already, and would give him a hard time when he came out late. And his father …

Will panicked. Then his gaze shifted. No, wait, this room had carpet, not floorboards.

Reality returned. Perth. A hotel. He'd arrived back on the late-night flight from the east coast after three days at the company's mining conference. Three days of restlessness. He ached to be back north, where real work happened. Where his hands turned red in the dust and he made his own way in the world. Back on-swing.

The sheets shifted beside him and Will spied long fair hair on the next pillow. Oh, yes. If Sarah was in his bed, he was certainly in Perth. Silently, he rose and escaped to the shower, then dressed and packed his bag. His flight to East Angelas, in the Pilbara's red center, was still three hours away, but he didn't want to linger.

Sarah caught him when he was just through brushing his teeth. "Did you say you were flying north today?" she asked, sleepily.

Will glanced at her in the mirror. She was leaning on the

doorframe in just her underwear, her hair all tumbled about her shoulders. She was certainly beautiful, and when he arrived in Perth, fresh from two weeks on-swing, her company was always appealing. But they didn't talk much, and now he wondered what he was doing.

"Yeah," he said, slotting his toothbrush away. "I'm a day late because of the conference."

"How was Queensland?" she asked. "You didn't say much last night."

"Three days of sitting in a meeting room and schmoozing with the management," he said, remembering the number of suits he'd been introduced to. No need to mention what else he'd done when he was there. The Queensland city of Mackay was a tricky location, one that brought back all kinds of bad memories. The accident might have been five years ago, but it never retreated into his past. The blame was always riding on his shoulder, so close he could almost see it in his rear view. "I better get going."

She drummed her fingers on the doorframe, then disappeared. Will heard the bed being rifled for clothes. He zipped up his bag, then slipped out and nabbed the newspaper from outside the hotel-room door, scanning the headlines as he re-entered the room and picked up his shoes. A story about a new mining tax. The Eagles skipper was injured again. A politician in court for punching a reporter. *Perth man to ride camel to the Pilbara.* Geez, the things people did. He flipped over and ran his eyes down the sports page. Cricket. Footy.

"Will."

"Mmm?"

"Will." Sarah's tone changed, losing patience.

Will dropped the paper on the sideboard. She stood before him, pointing one long finger into the center of his chest. "Look, Will. I'm fine with this being casual, right? I'm not your girlfriend. You and I don't owe each other anything. But you don't have to act like you need to get away so fast. I'm not going to cling onto you and ask you to stay. So, can you behave like a human being, please?"

Dammit. He couldn't afford to miss her, but he was acting like a jerk, and he didn't want to be hurtful. He put his arms around her. Her hair smelled faintly of shampoo. "I'm sorry," he said.

After a heartbeat where she held tight to him, she gently pushed him away. "It's fine. I might see you in a fortnight, might not. Take care, Will."

After she left, Will ran a hand through his hair. Christ, what was he doing? This was just going to get complicated, and he didn't want Sarah to be part of any destructive trail he left behind him.

So, it was good to be heading back to the mine, to long working hours, building something that counted.

And that small voice inside him that said work was the place where he could avoid thoughts of home – of his brother, Mark, sister, Cat, his father, and all the bad things – well, Will knew well how to bury all that stuff. And he did it best alone.

Five hours later when Will made it back to the East Angelas mine, the senior engineer, Dan, hauled himself up from his desk, sporting a chunky chopper moustache, his face red and merry. "Mate, how was it in Mackay, then? Rubbing shoulders with the upper echelons?"

"I've got a packet full of business cards and a sore hand," said Will, noting Dan looked worse for wear. The man had a reputation as a solid drinker, and none of the appeals from his wife seemed to shift the habit.

"I bet," laughed Dan, maneuvering his bulk back into a seat. "Better than a sore ass, though. Do you know how rare it is to find a junior who knows what he's doing? They were probably falling all over themselves to recruit you."

Will suppressed a smile, but the glow of approval lit inside him. He'd spent years as a tradesman in a mine back east before earning his engineering degree. He liked that the seniors now respected him for his early practical experience, especially Dan, who was generally dismissive of anyone educated after computers had entered the curriculum. Will missed the physicality of being a tradesman, but being an engineer gave him more responsibility, more opportunity. He might have come from a farm, but this, here, was his own world. One he'd made for himself.

He pulled out the design drawings and the punch-list – to-be-completed items from recent upgrades – and checked his watch. "I'll go down and see the shift and start marking up the new work. They'll be doing the changeover right about now."

"Drinking coffee and Red Bull, you mean." Dan levered himself out of his chair again and jerked the venetians up with a gust of orange dust. He stared meditatively out over the plant.

Will leaned back in his chair, a moment's respite before he headed outside. Through the window of the engineering office, which was in a stack of demountable offices alongside the heavy-machine shop, he could just see the edge of the plant. Will's mood always lifted being here. The plant rose five levels, all the way up to the hopper, where the haul trucks dumped the ore. It might look like a tangle of steel, but it held crushers, screens and conveyors, all critical to the mine's purpose. And all of it he'd helped build.

Dan's voice sharpened. "Wait … where the hell's he going with that nut fucker?"

Will was on his feet in an instant. He saw what Dan was talking about: one of the plant technicians was striding across the dirt road, a massive shifter wrench balanced over his shoulder, its head almost as big as the man's hard hat. "There's nothing in the plant that needs a shifter that big," said Will. "Must be planning on belting something with it."

Dan narrowed his eyes. "Better go find out what."

Will sped out the door, collecting his hard hat on the way. He jogged across the road, the plant consuming more and more of the sky.

He caught up with the wrench wielder on the mid-platform, heading towards the conveyor drives.

"Mick," he called. No response.

"Mick!" he roared.

Mick whirled, guilt written in the red dust on his face. The big wrench over his shoulder looked more like a medieval mace. Will wanted to laugh.

"Where the fuck are you going with that thing?"

"The new chute," yelled Mick, trying to brazen it out. "Not a big deal."

Will put out his hand. "Give it over." After Will had confiscated the shifter, he followed Mick to the new chute, part of the not-yet-commissioned upgrade. He found half the guys from the night shift still there, scratching their heads.

"What's going on, boys?" he asked as pleasantly as possible.

Rob, one of the night shift, jerked his finger at the chute. "Flange misalignment. Just needs a bit of encouragement."

Will looked; they were joining the chute outflow with the bin below, and the two halves weren't quite lining up. "Dammit, that looks out of square," he muttered.

Will felt every tradesman's eyes on him. He understood where they were coming from; taking the chute apart would cause a massive delay. But if it had come to whacking things, he had to step in.

"Leave this and go on to something else," he said.

He returned to the office five minutes later to find Dan on the phone and looking thunderous. "Yes, I understand that," he was saying. "No, no. But we need him here. I didn't go to all the trouble – all right. Fine." The phone rocked on the desk as Dan slammed it down.

"What the hell did you do in Mackay?" he asked.

Will felt the blood run out of his face. Then he realized Dan probably meant at the company conference. "Why?"

Dan paced around the office. "I've just had to hear from

some big boss in Perth that you're being reallocated to Iron Junction, when we're right in the middle of things here!"

"Come again?"

"That's what I said. But there's no mistake – the manager's asked for you specifically."

Will shook his head and collapsed in a dusty chair. "Why do they want me? I don't know anything about Iron Junction."

"Oh, you'll love it," said Dan. "Proper town with a pub and everything. It was a company flagship a few years ago – real pioneering stuff. Win–win agreements with the community, shares for the traditional landowners, whole shebang. They're upgrading the site at the moment, big two-stage project. They'll love you too – you cost less than a senior like me. And with your skills, you're a bargain. Dirty bastard move, though, pinching you from under my nose."

Will scrunched his fists. It wasn't that he minded going to other places; he'd built a career on it. But he'd only just warmed to East Angelas; he'd settled into his travel pattern, found his vantage points, and the people he hung out with. It was comfortable for now, and he didn't want to leave on someone else's terms. He dug in his pocket for the business cards from the conference and found the Iron Junction one. "Dale King," he said, flicking the card onto the desk and searching his memory. "I only met him once. Big talker. Not much substance."

"Yeah, I know," said Dan.

Will caught the tone. "There a problem?"

Dan shrugged. "I worked with him once, long time ago now. He hated it on-site, actually. I picked him for an office bloke. But he was always a real charmer; the big bosses liked him."

"I don't go in for charm," said Will, thinking about the long drive on that empty highway. "Do I get a choice?"

"Not if you value my ass," said Dan. "This is over my head. But keep in touch, okay?"

By Friday morning, Dan and Will had run all the numbers, and solved the chute problem. The boys were starting on the work, but Will wasn't going to see the end of it, a fact that made him cross as he prepared to leave.

"I've logged the journey with mission control," said Dan as Will threw his duffel bag in the back of his Pathfinder. "Make sure you call them when you get to the other end or they'll be sending out a search party, and you know how they love that. You'll get a royal pineapple."

"I know," said Will. "And Dan? Ease off on the drinks, okay?" With Will going off-site, there'd be no one to bully Dan to go to the gym instead of the wet mess, where he could drink away the off-shift hours.

"Deal," said Dan.

Will shook his hand, then drove out of the mine gates and swung onto the road west. When he was out of sight, he pulled onto a wide shoulder, alongside the sign that boasted the mine's working days without injury. From here, it was a long drive. He took out his phone.

"Mark Walker."

"Hey, little bro," said Will automatically.

"Will! Good to hear from you, mate. I was going to ring you today." Down the line, Will could hear the lowing and shuffling hooves of cattle, and the buzz of a dirt bike. Sounds of Ryders Station. "How's everything out there?"

"It's all right," said Will quickly. "How's Daniella?"

Mark's voice warmed when he spoke about his fiancée, a doctor from Brisbane who'd met Mark back in Ryders Ridge. They had a long-distance relationship, but seemed to be making it work. "She's wonderful. She's in Townsville at the base hospital at the moment. I'm going to see her this week."

"That's great," said Will, cheered at Mark's happiness. His brother was a good man, deserved good things. Will played with the stitching on the steering-wheel cover, the vanishing strip of bitumen in his peripheral vision, unable to avoid the contrast between Mark and himself. "Yeah, well, I'm just about to do a long drive between mines, so I wanted to let you know. In case, you know, I get eaten by camels."

Mark laughed.

"Dad all right?" Will asked quickly.

"He's still doing really well after the stents. Taken ten years off him. It's amazing," said Mark.

Will felt himself smile briefly. "He's tough. He was always going to do well."

"Yeah. Look, Will, like I said, I was going to call you," said Mark. "A letter came for you. It's got a Mackay lawyer's logo on it. Looks important. Do you want me to open it?"

Will's heart kicked against his ribs. Three seconds ticked by before he could answer. "No. Just forward it to me care of the Iron Junction camp."

"Sure. Everything okay?"

"Yeah, it's nothing. Don't worry about it."

Mark took him at his word. "Well, look out for the camels. Safe trip."

Will set the phone into its cradle on the dash with a trembling hand. His feet itched. He wanted to throw the gears into first, balance the clutch and let the engine have all the revs it could take. Turn the dirt with his tires and bury his shame in a roar of mechanical noise. His knuckles were white against the frayed stitching of the wheel cover, his whole body a mess of anticipated dread.

He stumbled down from the cab. The Pilbara silence soaked him; earth and grass and sky, red and green and blue. He paced once around the car, breathing hot air with each step. Nothing stirred, but that long-ago night crouched like a wild animal, ready to chase him. It didn't matter that he'd been young and stupid. There had been three of them in the car. One dead. Two who knew what had really happened. And he couldn't take back what he'd done.

Will climbed back in and kicked over the starter, then

cranked up the air conditioner. All he could do was push on to the next thing, keep himself in check. So, with cold air on his skin, he hauled towards the horizon.

Chapter 4

After the excitement of the volleyball, Beth's week sped past. A bad batch of curry at the camp mess kept her busy with scripts for Imodium, and the long days filled with workers, tourists and farmers from out of town. Through all this, Maxine remained scarce, seeing her share of the patients but making little contact, even when Beth offered mugs of tea or coffee. And when Friday's half-day appointments ran out just after one, Maxine disappeared like a ghost. Beth was disappointed, having planned to invite the doctor for dinner. She quizzed Jennifer.

"No, she keeps to herself," said the receptionist. "I've never even seen her place." So, defeated, Beth now faced the afternoon with no plans to fill it. That was how she came to be on the main street, in a pair of cargo shorts, a singlet and a baseball cap, with her film roll in her pocket and searching for Caitlin's suggested store.

It didn't take long. Iron Junction's businesses lined a long central boulevard with industrial workshops and suppliers on one side and commercial places on the other. Beth spotted a small used-car lot, windscreens sparkling under the sun, and workshop across from an accountant, a pharmacy and a coffee shop, whose tables dotted the sidewalk. She found the general store nestled between the coffee shop and a butcher, and not much bigger than a convenience store in any suburban Sydney street. It was decorated with a motley crew of posters and A-frames for phone cards and ice-cream. Beth pushed inside, and discovered a Tardis, offering all kinds of services. Post office, newsagent, roast chicken purveyor, DVD supplier and stationery vendor. She stepped around open-carton displays growing from the walls of the aisles like fungi.

"Can I help you with something?"

Beth turned to find a man in his sixties with a pair of reading glasses pushed up on his head, a pencil over his ear and a kindly smile. The man's expression shifted. "You're the new doctor," he said, holding his hand out. "I'm Mack. Like the truck. I saw you at the volleyball the other night, helping out Steve. You settling in?"

Beth assured him she was. When the pleasantries ran out, she took a breath. "I heard you might process film." She held the roll out on her palm.

Mack took the canister, tipping his glasses down as though the film were some kind of gemstone. "Well, now, haven't seen one of these in a while." He chuckled. "I'd have to send it away. Are you wanting another one?"

"Is that too much to hope for? I have a half-day off and wasn't sure what else to do with myself."

Mack nodded sagely. "Just like the boys in camp. They come up here and do the long hours, then can't switch off. Except at the pub. Better to head outside, I think."

He ambled towards the counter, a narrow gap in towering stacks of candy. Beth noted his limp. His right leg was the problem, his knee stiff, his hip lifting with each step. He pulled up beside three shelves of books, stuffed under a rack of torches, batteries and candles. Digging around behind, he pulled out a dusty box of film canisters, their packets sun-bleached yellow.

"I can't guarantee what treatment they've had," he admitted. "Most folks around here use digital now. It's quite possible these are some kind of relic."

Beth sorted through the box, selecting two rolls still within expiry, not believing her luck.

"So, where are you heading now?" Mack asked.

"I really don't know." She'd spent the whole week in a one-block radius of her apartment, restricted by the roster. The outside world seemed so vast and unpopulated.

"Let me show you something," he said. He led her through to a dim, windowless room at the back of the shop, where a desk groaned under stacks of papers, a chunky laptop and piles of catalogues. Bookshelves stuffed with folders and archive boxes ran to waist height on every wall. From a small kitchenette wafted the scent of coffee, the kitchen counter propped up at one end by a brick.

"I know it looks like a hoarder's paradise, but I'm the unofficial town historian," Mack explained. "Got newspapers, reports, photos – you name it. Though sometimes I wonder if it's an affliction rather than a hobby. I'm even working on a book. I thought you'd like the gallery."

He flicked a switch. Spotlighting chased the dim away and illuminated walls of spectacular photos. Mack pointed to a frame nearest them, showing a rugged rock formation in black and white, its columns thrust against an unforgiving steel sky.

"That's Iron Bluff, where they first surveyed this area," he said. "I took that one myself, back when I first came through here in the eighties driving trucks. It's changed a lot since then, though."

"Oh yes?" she asked, moving around the room, inspecting each photo. Most were red landscapes cut with scraps of highway. One of a camel train. One of a railway gang, rough faces etched with character, in seventies short-shorts, taking a break on a gravel siding.

"It wasn't always a mining town," he said. "Used to be a rest stop and supply area, plus the Indigenous community. But when the mine came, they threw a lot of money in. We needed the medical center, and we're better supplied now. But I can't keep staff in the shop anymore, they're always off to the mine."

Beth glanced at Mack, sensing the divisions that could run through this place. "That sounds tricky."

"I guess you can't be too harsh. The mine's what makes the money. Of course, now there's the FIFO camp. We haven't seen anything like the expansion before. So many people. The mayor doesn't know how the water treatment will handle it, but I'm yet to see more business in here, to be honest."

Beth was about to ask about the water when she came to an enormous framed photo over the desk and forgot the conversation. "Where is this?" she asked, transfixed. She was staring at an azure pool, ringed with red, layered rocks. Clinging to each strata were mosses and grasses and ferns in every shade of green. Water, white in the long exposure, cascaded like pale cream. And beneath the water surface, the colors shifted through jewel blues and greens, reflecting the world above. Surely it couldn't be somewhere in the dry expanse outside? It wasn't merely the colors. Somehow, the photographer had captured the soul of the place; the way the pool echoed the curving rocks, the weight of the water they cradled, the loft of the sky overhead.

"That's Karijini," said Mack. "It's a couple of hours east of Paraburdoo. That photo was taken by one of the locals. Caitlin Murray. I send prints away for her sometimes. She's very good, don't you think?"

"Wow, really? I met her at the volleyball. Maxine said she works with the school."

"Yeah. She's one of those liaison people. Keeps the local kids coming to class and helps develop programs. She uses her photos a lot for that, talking to the kids about the land and the mine and how they feel about it. She's pretty special."

Beth digested this, wondering at the paradox of prosperity, that the mine could bring both wealth and problems. But she also saw how Mack was kneading his fist against his hip.

"Leg hurting?" she asked gently.

"Oh, yeah," admitted Mack. "Bad accident, years ago. Aches in the summer with the rain. Lucky the monsoon's late this year."

Beth put a quick hand on his arm. "If it's troubling you, make sure you come in."

He smiled. "There's a nice drive through town and over the ridge, takes you along the old creek and the railway. That's near where the Christmas party is tomorrow. Bound to take some good photos there."

Beth gave her thanks and left, her thoughts still with that blue pool and its red-and-green garden.

The Prado's engine coughed once, then caught and roared to life. Beth ran the air conditioner while she scrutinized the town map. Mack had said there was a drive through town, but all she could see was a collection of streets, the highway, the train lines and the road out to the mine. Beth traced its snaking length, which stretched out beyond the town limits. Curious where her patients worked, she decided to start there.

Five minutes later, she turned east onto the highway, and before long found a big arrow pointing down a south turn: *Iron Junction Mine*. She flipped on her strobe. After a few hundred meters, the bitumen ran out and the Prado hit dirt.

Beth grinned as the car bounced on the undulations. Suddenly, the cramped world of her working week expanded around her, ripe for exploration, full of possibility. A silver flash went by on her left.

Beth hit the brakes and pulled up in a cloud of dust. She jammed into reverse and backed up, peering over the wheel. As the air cleared, she spied a leaning wooden sign with peeling silver letters: *Iron Bluff*. A dirt track wound off to the left, disappearing down a slope, a knobbly hill rising in the distance. Mack had mentioned something about a survey point; the bluff probably had a good view.

Soon, she was rattling down the track, two deep wheel ruts in the dirt. The hill crept closer until the road ended in a crude car park: just a clearing in the knots of grass.

Beth eased out of the cab and grabbed her water bottle as the heat descended, making her sweat. Nothing stirred. She gazed upwards. It didn't look too far, and despite the bluff being bare of vegetation, she saw an overhang beside a red knobbly column; the possibility of shade.

She found an easy trail that curved up around the bluff with only a small scramble using her hands at the end. Soon she stood on a great west-facing flat rock, flanked by two weathered columns. The sun was sinking, a bright patch in the thinning clouds, and the land between stretched like an endless red blanket. To the north, across the highway, was the town, perfect and efficient in the shallow cup between the ridges. To the south, she could see where the mine had opened the blanket in two great pits. She could just make out vehicles, ant-like in their slow progress along a hairline road. Buildings made pale squares and a complex structure of steel and odd shapes hugged a precipice. She had no idea what any of it did.

She sipped at her water. By the mine, she could see a yellowish water pond corralled behind an earth mound on one side of the pits. Everything else was red. No rivers, no lakes, no ocean. She sighed; the only evidence of water was a streak of green, north beyond the town and the eastern ridge. The sun baked into her skin, and she suspected she was burning already. To her surprise, the overhang covered a shallow nook, a retreat from the sun and sky. Beth sank silently into the cool shade. The light breeze caressed her skin. This place had a rhythm, a wavelength that was longer and deeper than her usual thoughts. With reverence, she raised her camera on her fingertips.

Beth thought about going back to town when her water had

nearly run out. As the sun had slipped lower and lower, she'd crept into the retreating shade, turning her lens out, up and within, making her limited shots count. She didn't want to leave; for the first time, she felt at peace with her decision to leave Sydney. But would that last when she returned to town?

She eased up and stretched her stiff legs. Her backside had gone numb on the hard rock and she moved from foot to foot as sensation returned. Her fingers smelled of sunscreen. She peered down over the edge, where the Prado waited in the car park below, its cheerful red flag limp and its roof slowly flashing with the orange strobe. Very slowly.

Oh, *shit*.

Beth scrambled off the ledge and down the path towards the car, her chest twisting with panic. *No, no, no.* She'd forgotten to turn the bloody strobe off. She skinned the heel of her hand against the rock and, when she nearly catapulted herself off the cliff, had to slow down. When she finally reached the Prado, the strobe was barely turning. She threw the door open and flicked the switch off, then stood waiting, biting her lip. She remembered, long ago, her father telling her that power could trickle back into a battery. How long should she wait? Five minutes? Ten?

She hauled herself back into the seat, but left the door open; the cab inside was a plug of hot air that stank of vinyl. She threw the ignition. The starter gave two kicks before it died. Beth dropped the key. *Shit.* She waited another minute. *Please, please, this time.* She turned the key. The starter sounded once. Further turns of the key produced only clicks.

Beth pulled her phone out. No reception. Of course. Even after scrambling back up the hill, her throat sucked dry and her insides coated in dust, her mobile proclaimed no service.

She was keenly aware she hadn't told anyone where she was going. And from the condition of the road and the car park, she suspected no one came up here much. The sun would be down soon. She peered at the town across the landscape, wondering if she could follow the road all the way back. It only looked a few miles. In the distance, she spotted a truck on the mine road. *There.* She could walk to the turn-off and flag down a passing car. She rubbed her fingers across her dry lips, knowing she had no better solution.

Soon she was back at the Prado. She downed the last of her water and then rifled through the vehicle. She found another half-full bottle hiding under the driver's seat, so she stuffed that in her bag, twisted her hair under her cap, and turned towards the road.

The horizon swallowed the sun before she reached the end of the Iron Bluff track. Her singlet was wet through by then, her sneakers full of sandy earth.

She stood at the intersection as the light faded through brilliant pinks and golds and reds, but no vehicle came. Beth rubbed her arms. Her lips stuck together now; her throat burned. She recognized her dehydration: not dire yet, but her water was gone. A spark of fear lit in her belly. The track had been longer than she'd expected, and now she faced the rest of the mine road and the highway back to town.

She took a long breath and started to walk towards the last blush in the darkening sky. Maybe someone would come.

Chapter 5

Will Walker spotted the twinkling lights of Iron Junction just on dark with a mixture of relief and sadness. He'd pushed the envelope on the trip over, taking longer than he should have with frequent stops to stretch his legs, not feeling like returning to civilization. He admired the red-earth hills and their green hides, rugged and enduring, like the beauty of hard work. Back home, the country was all golden-edged gray-green grass; it had a softness about it that the Pilbara never did.

He checked his watch. The mine office would expect his call soon. If he left it much longer, they'd start sending out searchers; not the best way to start a new job.

The mine road turn-off appeared in the distance. Good, that meant he was only a few minutes from town. He'd just make it. Then, his headlights caught a movement, off to the side of the road. Instinctively, he took his foot off the accelerator, expecting wildlife that might throw itself across his path. But then he realized it was a person. A woman, her back towards him, dark hair sweat-tangled down her back, trudging towards town.

Will slowed. He hadn't passed any vehicles, and she was too far from town to be just out for exercise. She stumbled around as he pulled in behind her, a bewildered look on her face. The red dust clung to her long hair, and her legs were orange from her sneakers to her knees. She looked to him like a woman in an adventure magazine: tall, ready for action in cargos and a singlet, with determined eyes and broad shoulders. He felt an unexpected twinge of desire. Then she caught her foot on a rock and pitched forward.

Will was down from the cab in a heartbeat. "Hey, you all right there?" he asked as she righted herself and leaned on his bull bar.

"My battery died," she said, her voice dry and hoarse. "How far is it to town?"

"A couple of miles yet," he said.

Her unfocused gaze wheeled determinedly back to the road. "I can make it," she said. She tried a step, then wavered.

Will caught her arm. He now saw how her lips were cracked into tiny rivers, and the dried salt marks on her singlet. She wasn't thinking straight. He guided her towards the passenger side and up into the seat. "Here, sit down." He grabbed a bottle of water, cracking off the cap.

She steadily emptied half the bottle and tipped her head back. Her focus sharpened. "That tastes so good," she said. "I ran out back there. And I lost my hat."

"How long have you been walking?" he asked.

"What time is it?"

"Ten past seven."

She scrunched her eyes, as if trying to calculate. "An hour? Maybe more."

Will whistled softly, wondering if he should take her straight into the town's medical center, if it was even open. "Where's your car? I don't remember passing one."

She pointed vaguely over her shoulder. "Down there. Iron Bluff. Off the mine road."

Will scrutinized her face as she returned her focus to the water bottle. She had the soft skin of someone who took care of themselves, probably spent her working life indoors. From her cargo shorts and singlet, he guessed she was traveling across the Pilbara. Will pushed aside thoughts of the time and his need to check in with the company. "Can you show me back to your car? If it's a flat battery, I can start it again."

"I'm so sorry," she said, as if aware of him for the first time.

"Don't worry about it. I'm Will," he said, offering his hand.

"Beth," she said, and her hand felt smooth in his.

He climbed back into the driver's seat and hooked a U-turn, heading for the mine road. He glanced across. Beth was staring out the window. He sensed her embarrassment in the long pause.

"Where are you from?" he asked.

"Sydney."

"That's a long drive."

She missed the joke and rubbed her eyes. "No, just to the Bluff. I was taking photos."

"You know, you should maybe think about stopping in Iron Junction for the night," he said. "Get some rest and water and keep going in the morning. The accommodation must be expensive, but it's not worth driving on when you're tired. I'm heading to the camp, so I can show you the way, once we get you started."

She sighed. "I'm not going anywhere. I *live* in town."

"Oh," he said, with a flutter of interest. "Are you working at the mine?"

"No. I'm a temp doctor at the clinic. I'm filling in for one of the regulars. I only see patients from the mine."

So, she was a doctor. She glanced out the window again, and Will saw the pale outline of her reflection, like an echo of her in the glass. He wondered how long she was staying.

The headlights made two tracks into the gathering darkness, the cabin mercifully cool. Beth massaged her temples with her thumbs. The dirt had worked its way under her singlet and between her toes. She longed for a shower. She was developing a headache now, which she figured was partly from the dehydration and partly the remorse for this whole situation. She turned her frayed focus on her rescuer who was negotiating the night road. Dark blond hair cut short, the angle of his jaw glinting with stubble, fit looking with a muscled torso in a polo shirt tucked into blue hi-vis trousers. Definitely a mining man. He had a command about him, a self-assurance he could handle whatever was in front of him, which obviously included a flat battery.

Soon, they were back on the mine road. Beth sat forward, looking for the bluff's turn in the headlights. "There," she said when the wooden sign finally came into view.

"Good eyes," said Will. "I nearly didn't see that." He swung neatly, his hands sure on the wheel, finding a smooth path. Beth polished off his water, her empty stomach demanding dinner. A few minutes later, her lame Prado came into view. Above, Iron Bluff was now just a dark shadow on the sky, a patch lacking stars.

Will pulled his bonnet in close to hers. "You weren't out here all day, were you?" he asked as he killed the engine and climbed down.

Beth tried not to stumble as she followed. "About two hours, I think, after work. I forgot to turn the strobe off." She pointed to the offending beacon, then unlocked and felt under the dash for the hood-pop.

"Thanks," said Will, hoisting the bonnet with one arm and sliding the catch into place. "Your battery must be on the out. A few hours wouldn't normally be enough to run it down."

He turned and rummaged in the back of his own vehicle. Beth rubbed her arms. The landscape that had seemed so full of possibility was now heavy with night, weighing on her with its heat and distance. "I'm so sorry about this," she said, for the fifth time.

He gave her an easy smile. "It's no trouble, really." He

popped his own hood. "Can I give you some hints?"

Beth raised her eyebrows, prepared for a lecture about whatever it was she'd done wrong. But he just stood by the engine bay, thick hands curled around the jumper cables, shoulders stretching his polo, the work pants worn with use but fitting perfectly. The Pathfinder's engine ticked softly. She realized he was actually waiting for permission.

"Sure," said Beth, wondering where he had acquired such consideration. If he'd been one of her consultant supervisors, they'd be halfway through a lecture by now.

Will clipped the leads onto her battery terminals. "If this ever happens to you again, especially out there—" he gestured to the world beyond Iron Junction, "—put your hood up, like it is now. It makes the car more visible, and it signals there's a problem."

Beth edged towards him, watching what he was doing with the leads. "Positive to positive," he explained, pointing to the red terminals on both the batteries, which were marked with a "+". "Negative to negative." The second lead clipped on.

Beth tracked him, interest piqued. "What else?" she asked.

"Stay with the vehicle," he said. "Especially out there. It's the most visible thing, and it's shelter. Plus, if you've got any fuel in the tank and the engine's running, you can get water out of the air conditioner."

"Really?" said Beth. "Hmm, I really screwed up."

Will shrugged. "That's the survival stuff. Today ... well, the town's visible from here. It was probably a good idea to head for the mine road. But I guess you missed the shift change. You just got me instead."

"I'm really sorry to put you out," she repeated, pressing her fingers to her temples.

"Beth, really, it's fine." She glanced up; he was taller than her by a few inches, and the headlights' golden glow outlined his broad shoulders. As their eyes met, a tiny crease pulled between his brows. "Headache?" he guessed.

"Yes. Need more water."

"Let's get you going, then."

With his Pathfinder running, restarting hers was easy. Beth never thought she'd feel such joy at the sound of a beefy engine turning over, even while the noise primed her pulsing temples. Will wiped his hands, then let the bonnet go with a satisfying thunk.

"Follow me back to the shop," he said.

"The shop?"

"The mechanic. There'll be one in town. Your battery's probably cactus. If you drive home, you'll just have the same problem tomorrow."

And so Beth followed him along the track, the mine road and the highway until they pulled into the dark parking spaces outside Iron Junction Auto, on the west side of the main street. She got down from the cab with a wave of weariness. Across the road, Mack's shop was still open, its light warm and inviting. But she couldn't contemplate anyone seeing her right now; she only wanted a shower, and bed.

Will tore a page from a notebook and scribbled. "I'm telling them to replace the battery and to call you in the morning about it. Do you want to write your number there?"

He handed the paper across. Beth fixed on his long, strong fingers. She had to concentrate to make her handwriting legible. The pen moved like a log. Finally, she handed the note back and he tucked it under the windscreen wiper. "Leave your keys in it," he said.

Beth hesitated.

Will chuckled. "It's fine," he said, gently steering her back to his vehicle with a hand on her shoulder. "No one would touch it. Even if they tried, it's not like it's going to start for them."

"It just feels weird."

"I know," he said. "It's a city thing. You'll get used to it."

The drive back to her apartment took less than two minutes. Will shut off the engine.

Beth twisted in her seat. "I can't thank you enough. I don't know if I'd have made it."

Will's smile was warm. "Glad I came along at the right time."

Gratefully, Beth climbed down and walked around to his open window. Her hair stuck to the sweat and dust across her forehead. "Are you in the mine camp?" she asked.

"As far as I know. They told me it's the temporary buildings across the oval, but I just came in today. I've got to go and let them know I'm in. They'll be getting ready to send out the search parties." He said this, and yet made no move to start the car again.

Beth blinked at him, her mind sluggish from the heat and dry, her emotions an unpickable knot of shame and gratefulness. "How far did you drive today?"

"From East Angelas, about six hours." Will tapped the steering wheel with his thumbs. "Well, Beth, it was very nice to meet you." A warm smile spread across his lips, and she held his gaze longer than expected for someone she'd just met.

"You too," she said finding it impossible not to smile in return.

He reached for the ignition and then pulled his hand back. "Listen, I'm new here. How about a drink on the weekend? You could tell me about the town."

"I don't know that much. Just the sports club, and the main street. I've only been here a few days." She searched his face: honest, open, and something about how he looked at her made her stomach disappear. "Well ... maybe you could tell me about the mine? I have no idea what goes on out there."

"Sure thing. I'll give you my number."

After he had pulled away, Beth hauled herself up the stairs to her apartment, feeling the day evaporating like a bad dream. She could hear instrumental guitar music seeping out from under the facing apartment door, but once inside her own white box, the atmosphere was cool and still. She twitched the curtains aside and peered down to the intersection at the end of the street, wondering if she'd see Will drive past. No, he was long gone.

She should have headed straight to the shower, but instead she paced into the bedroom, thoughts muddled. Was this incident a sign? That she wasn't suited to this place, that she had been crazy to leave Sydney. To leave Richard.

She sank down on the bed, and wrapped her arms around the emptiness in her chest. Her album was still on the covers from the previous day. She opened it, not to the pages of photographs, but to the back cover where a photo was wedged in the spine. Richard and Beth, on the balcony of their Sydney place on the cliffs at Freshwater, the beach behind, both of them smiling into the camera. And even though she'd been the one to end it, she'd been the one who decided this couldn't go on, those smiles tugged on the shards of her heart and pulled her to pieces.

Beth sobbed with the photo pressed to her chest. She had no one to tell about this pain. No one could rescue her from the fear that she'd been wrong.

Time was what she needed. It healed all things, didn't it? So, when her tears had made tracks in the red dust covering her cheeks, Beth finally headed to the shower, to wash away the dirt and the pain. This uncertainty that was trying to grow would wither and be no more if she just stuck it out.

Chapter 6

The next day – just for irony – Beth saw two workers from the mine who were woozy with dehydration and covered in dust. She'd had great difficulty in extracting from them how they'd ended up in such a state and both escaped back to work as soon as they were pronounced rehydrated. As she was elbow-deep in paperwork for the two of them, Jennifer appeared in her doorway. "Beth, a guy's come in with a laceration on the thigh. Circular saw. I've put him in minor procedures."

The words *circular saw* filtered through Beth like a cold drip. How bad was this going to be?

She found a burly man on the couch with a wad of white gauze pressed onto his thigh, below which a dried blood trail ran over his knee and halfway down his leg. His graying hair was sweat-slicked and some recently removed head-gear had made a furrow above his ears and a red indentation across his forehead. Beth noted his hands and arms were flecked with tiny red spots.

"Hey there, doc. I'm Wally," declared the man, offering the cleaner of his two hands. Beth shook it, mentally noting to scrub extra carefully before she started any work on him.

"I hear you've had words with a circular saw," she said.

"Grinder, actually. But it had a saw blade on it." He then recounted the whole story, which involved cutting pipe they were running at the mine. From his hand gestures she worked out that the saw had caught, jerked and bounced down into his thigh.

The wound was neat, and deep. It was still bleeding, but only at oozing pace. Amazing. Nothing critical had been hit.

"It doesn't look as bad as it could have been," she told him. "But it's going to need a very good clean and stitches. Then we'll make sure you're up to date on your shots and there'll be some antibiotics and painkillers. I'll ask Jennifer to come and give me a hand."

It wasn't until after Beth had scrubbed in, administered the local anesthetic and started on some mattress sutures that Wally said, "So, the hire company gave you a dead battery, huh, doc? Got you stranded out at Iron Bluff yesterday?"

Jennifer's eyebrows shot up. Beth sighed. After yesterday's misadventure and subsequent turmoil, she'd woken feeling more level. Now, the memory thrust itself forward again. Had Will told his workmates what had happened?

"News certainly travels fast," she said carefully, looping the suture to make a knot.

"You know if you get stuck like that, you really should stay where you are," said Wally. "Put your bonnet up, too. And remember to turn that strobe off."

"Thanks. Yes, I realize that now," said Beth, pulling the knot tight as a liquid heat of mortification flushed through her. She didn't suppose she deserved to keep the escapade a secret, but she didn't want to look foolish – the out-of-place city girl – in front of everyone. The mechanic, Graham, had already called; the Prado was ready to be picked up. The hire company was covering the cost. She'd hoped that would be the end of it.

"Good, good. You know people have died walking away from their cars. It happened the year before last, over in Queensland. That's usually where I work. I'm just here for the contract."

Maxine was standing by the front desk as Wally limped

back to reception. "Did you have trouble with your car?" she asked Beth.

"How did you know about that?" she asked, handing Wally's patient file across to Jennifer and wondering if the receptionist had relayed the story in the few minutes since she'd left minor procedures.

Maxine sipped a steaming cup of tea. "I saw it parked at the mechanic's this morning."

"Flat battery," said Beth, escaping to her room and hoping to avoid further details.

A moment later, Maxine appeared in her doorway. Trust this to be a time she wanted to converse. Beth threw up her hands. "I drove out to Iron Bluff and left the strobe on. It seems the battery was on the way out and that finished it off."

"How did you get back?"

Beth balled up a company form she'd filled in incorrectly and threw it towards the waste basket, considering how much to say. "A nice man helped me out."

"Where did you find one of those?" said Maxine wryly.

"Coming down the highway. A guy from the mine."

Fortunately, Maxine didn't launch into any lectures, just thrummed her fingers on her chin. "Well, we're never short of those," she said.

With that, Maxine disappeared and Beth pushed on to her next appointment, a portly haul-truck driver in the early stages of diabetes. Carefully, Beth stepped through a number of tests and checks, trying to sort out how he was going to manage his diet, working long shifts and eating from a camp kitchen. She didn't hold out much hope; the guy made it clear all he had to do on-swing was work, eat and sleep. Beth massaged her temples, feeling last night's headache returning, and wondering if she'd get out of the clinic in time to pick up her car.

But as her patient left, a flash of sun from the car park announced her Prado bouncing to a stop. A moment later, a man in grubby blue overalls strode inside, *Graham* stitched in white on his breast pocket, her keys dangling from his fingers.

He spotted Beth in an instant. "Ah, you must be Beth Harding," he began, his eyes falling on the stethoscope around her neck. "Graham. All ready to go. Will I show you the new battery?"

Beth was aware now of the waiting patients, craning their necks to see what was happening and Wally still hovering at the desk with a grin on his face. "That's all right," she said quickly.

"Lucky break," Graham continued. "You know, people have died getting stranded out here."

"Maybe you could show me that battery," Beth added hastily, drawing Graham outside and feeling six pairs of eyes track her as they went.

Out in the car park, the mid-afternoon heat bounced off the bitumen, striking her face like a blast wave. Graham popped the hood to reveal the shiny new battery. "Like I was saying," he went on. "You know, you need to put your bonnet up …"

Beth listened as Graham went through the same list as Will, but far less patiently. Finally, exasperated, she said, "I don't understand how people found out so fast. I didn't tell anyone!"

Graham shrugged. "Will Walker rang me this morning. Nice bloke. I got the story out of him. It's a good one. Everyone'll enjoy it."

When Graham left, Beth pulled her shoulders straight and marched back inside the clinic, though she still felt like a fool.

Jennifer handed her the next file with a grin. "Don't forget about the Christmas party. Bus leaves here at five."

Beth thought about all the people that might involve, and whether she'd in fact like to strangle Will Walker.

At that moment, Will was standing in the middle of the half-complete Iron Junction plant extension with the leading hand, Matt, trying to make sense of a curling plan stretched between them. Across the expanded mesh deck, a bunch of tradesmen milled around a tool chest. The Pilbara sun beat down in earnest. Under its glare, Will was just realizing what a pile of shit he'd been dropped into.

For a start, he wasn't working *with* a senior engineer. He'd learned that this morning when Dale King had met him with an apology. "The man let the whole lot get in a state. He had to go, obviously," King had said, clapping him on the shoulder. "It's a lot to ask, but you're a capable bloke. Push ahead with my full support."

The schedule wasn't the only problem. The work was so bad in places it would have to be redone. A critical pump order had been delayed. Other orders had been delivered and vanished. Equipment needed repair. All signs of poor management. Will could feel the frustration and ill will dripping off the men, a potent mix that could ignite at any moment. Having talked with as many of them as he could, and removing all the outdated drawings he could find, he was now scrambling to make a viable plan.

"So, we're right up to here," said Will, tracing the drawing's structural supports underneath the primary crusher. "Except these water pipes are in the wrong place."

"Yeah," agreed Matt. "And this part's gotta change. The equipment's disappeared out of the lay-down." He shook his head. "We've been so short on managers, it's no wonder things are behind. No one's been signing off on the work since the last guy left and there's about ten drawing revisions floating around. King doesn't know what he's looking at. About time he got someone in."

Will grunted, glad to have found an ally in Matt, who was in the same job Will had held back east. They understood each other. But Will now had greater responsibility and, knowing how engineers were generally viewed, an uphill battle to win the crew's respect.

Will threw the plan onto the temporary work bench. "All right, here we go," he said, grabbing a carpenter's pencil. "Take this section off here at the flanges." He arrowed in on the diagram. "When that's done, recheck these pipes." He circled the offending lines and put a two in a circle next to them. "When we get through that, I need the welders on the ground and we're fixing that section. I'm going to the office to handle the hot work permits and make copies of this plan, so be ready when I come back. Are we square?"

Grumbling assent. The tradesmen had done this work already, and they weren't happy about doing it again. Matt was onto it like lightning. "Embrace the suck, boys. Will's going to keep the heat off your asses."

Will was glad of the few smiles that drew, but his heart was hammering. Pulling this job back onto any kind of schedule was a huge ask. After setting the crew to work, he was soon back in the office, scrutinizing the original program and looking for ways to make up time. After that, he'd have to find out what had happened to the missing equipment and the late deliveries.

Two hours later at break, Matt brushed his boots at the door of the office and collapsed into a grubby desk chair, the dark skin of his face touched with red dust. "What's that?" he asked.

"Beginnings of a new plan," said Will, still scribbling, feeling Matt peering over his shoulder.

A minute later, Matt leaned back in the chair with a look of approval. "You fish, Will?"

Will stopped writing and looked up. "Around here?"

"Nah, on the coast near Dampier. I'm taking the boat up there on the off-swing. My brother's in the army there. Him and pilot Troy are gonna catch some big ones. Maybe one-eye Brian'll come, too." He chuckled. "Wanna come?"

With difficulty Will shifted his thoughts from the new plan to the next off-swing. Sarah naturally entered his mind. And then, abruptly, the doctor he'd met out on the highway. Will stubbed the tip of his pencil. In the chaos of the workday, he'd pushed her to the edge of his mind. Now he couldn't think of anything else.

"I thought your brother was on a farm?" he said, groping for his last thought about work.

"That's my other brother. So, fishing?"

"Maybe."

Matt laughed. "Yeah, after all, it's good to have search-and-rescue along."

"Come again?" Will abandoned the lost thought and looked up.

"I heard you rescued a doc out at Iron Bluff. Or was that a different Will Walker?"

"Yes, that was me," he said. "But it was just a flat battery. No rescues."

Matt leaned forward. "Is it true she walked back to town?"

Will stifled a groan. Being a FIFO worker put him on the edges of the communities in which he worked and lived, never a part of either one. He'd almost forgotten how good small towns were at spreading gossip. Iron Junction was like being back in Ryders. Beth would have everyone asking her about it before long. And she'd probably think he'd told them all.

Matt raised his eyebrows.

"Yeah," Will conceded.

"Hmm," said Matt. "How far do you reckon a wajala girl could make it out here?"

Will got up from the desk. "Probably not a good idea to test it. Shall we go see these pumps?"

"Sure. You coming to the party tonight?"

"What party?" asked Will.

"Company Christmas party," said Matt. "Oh, right. Sorry. You're in the camp? It's only for the townies."

Will shrugged it off. "One of the joys of being a temp."

"You'll miss another sighting of the famous doctor, then, eh? Brian and Steve said she's all right."

Will gave Matt an exasperated look. "Go easy on her, okay? She just got here."

"Wasn't gonna say nothing."

The shift end came too soon. Will had a long to-do list, and he needed to talk to the other crews, and sort out the supply problems. Despite this, as soon as he left, thoughts of Beth intruded. He had a picture of her in his mind, dust-coated and determined, telling him she'd make it back to town. She had spirit, and he liked that. He chuckled as he turned out the mine gate.

He found the Iron Bluff track easily this time. Long shadows made the bluff into a harsh palette of dusky blush and inky black. Will could still see the tire tracks in the earth from Beth's car, and her footprints in the dirt. Soon, he was climbing. Up and up, until he reached the great flat rock and its knobbed columns. The Pilbara spread out beneath him, the town and the mine etchings between the ridges of an ancient riverbed; the road just a crease, clouds gathered on the distant horizon bleeding sunbeams into pink and indigo. As he watched, the mine became dotted with tiny lights, like a waking nocturnal creature.

Will suddenly shuddered. It was all so endless and empty, like that space in his chest, and he didn't want to be here alone. He scrambled down and into the car, hooked a turn and bit the Pathfinder's tires into the soft shoulder. The diff slipped and he eased the wheel while balancing the clutch. Muscle memory; it never left. He had a shot of longing for his sports truck, which had been sitting back east for five years, with good reason. The fishtail evened out and he tore up the track.

He'd just reached the turn to town when his phone rang.

"Yeah, Will? Matt here. Got a problem before the next shift starts and we need a sign-off. You still here?"

Will looked at the welcoming lights of Iron Junction spread before him, with its promise of food, a shower and maybe Beth, all things that came second to work.

He sighed. "I'll come back."

Beth rode to the Christmas party in the back of the company bus, a blast of cold vent air on her face, listening to the din of excited children. "I had no idea it would be such a big thing," she said to Jennifer, who was sandwiched in beside her.

"Oh, it's always huge," she said. "That's why they have it down at the creek where there's lots of space for cricket."

"And where's that?" asked Beth, already lost as the bus made another turn.

"It kind of skirts around the mine and the town," Jennifer said. "Runs into the Ashburton River, eventually. Not that it's much of a creek at the moment. Not enough rain this year."

Beth saw what she meant the moment they were off the bus. The children took off in a dozen directions like a disturbed ant nest, but the creek was a patch of rounded red stones coursing through a landscape of delicate grasses and tougher trees, all backdropped against the Junction's northern ridge. The company, however, hadn't let the lack of water deter festivities. Several grills were already sizzling, filling the air with the smell of sausage and onion. A waterslide – made from a heavy-duty plastic strip – had been set up on a gentle slope, supplied from a vast mine water truck. Beth also spotted ponies being led around for rides, face-painting and a magician entertaining a cluster of children. Hovering overhead were four mobile flood-light towers, each stenciled with *Iron Junction Mine*, ready for when the light finally gave out.

Beth turned to ask Jennifer if Maxine was coming, but found that the receptionist had vanished. She sighed. Among the cavorting children and the ready-made community who knew each other, she was aware of being an outsider, and a temporary one at that. She paced around the edges, unsure where to begin and conscious of the vastness of the land pressing back beyond the gathering. She seemed caught in between – not brave enough to venture out, but understanding nothing of the lives and community before her.

A hand landed on her arm. "Doctor Harding, I'm so glad you could make it."

Beth spun, and saw Dale King. She felt a small kernel of disappointment. "Dale, hello. I was just trying to find my way around."

"Allow me," he said, steering her towards a food tent, where Mack sat on a high stool behind the sizzling grill and a woman with graying hair was savagely buttering bread slices. "Mack and Nancy here will fix you something."

Mack raised his tongs in acknowledgement and soon Beth had a steaming, saucy sausage wrapped in bread. Dale drew her on further, pointing out the activities. "Now, it is focused on the kids, of course," he said. "But we've got a big surprise soon that everyone will enjoy. Can I introduce you to some people?"

Beth didn't really want to be social, looking at the dozens of people in company colors standing in groups, but she allowed Dale to lead on.

"Everyone here is an employee from town. The contractors do their own thing in the camp." He leaned in with a wink. "Keeps the riffraff out."

Aware she could very easily be seen as part of that riffraff, or be the target for more survival advice, Beth stepped back. The sun had sunk low now, shafts of apricot and blue spilling over the ridge and onto the creek stones.

"Maybe later," she said. "I'm going to take a few photos."

As she escaped, she was conscious of a flash of annoyance in Dale's features, but kept going. Risking indigestion, she inhaled her sausage, licking the sauce from around her mouth as she found a narrow path up behind the slide's water truck. A perfect vantage, and safely in view of civilization. Unpacking her camera, she settled against the ridge.

A shutter clicked behind her. Beth snapped around and gazed into the wide black circle of another lens.

"Nice photobomb," said Caitlin, emerging from the bend in the track, her voice husky. "You following me?"

"I'd go with 'great minds think alike'," said Beth.

Caitlin chuckled and slipped in beside her. She nodded at Beth's camera. "Don't let me put you off."

Beth lined up a shot but she sensed Caitlin watching her movements. "I can't with you there," she said as she lowered the camera.

"Why not?"

"I saw your photo of Karijini in Mack's shop. It's amazing. I'll never function under the scrutiny of someone so talented."

Caitlin laughed, then coughed thickly. Finally, she said, "You're using film. I'll never know."

Beth had to admit this was true, and finally, she took a few pictures. Alongside, Caitlin did the same, her digital shutter working overtime. From time to time, Beth caught Caitlin watching her, an appraising look on her face.

Finally Beth frowned. "Am I doing something wrong?"

"Light's going. What settings are you using?" asked Caitlin, keeping her eyes on the crowd below.

Beth felt as though a consultant was grilling her on a case. "Ah, f-stop at two-fifty. But the film's ISO four hundred, too. I know it'll be mostly blur, but the crowd's in focus ..."

Caitlin was silent.

"What?"

Caitlin kept her hanging, then cracked a smile. "You know enough about what you're doing. So, shoot like you mean it."

"What are you, Yoda?" complained Beth.

But Caitlin only grinned, and Beth took her tongue between her teeth and tried to do whatever *meaning it* looked like.

After a few minutes, Caitlin said, "Try using the cliff edge as a tripod. You done that before?"

Beth told her she had, a long time ago, when she'd first moved to Sydney. After that, she found herself talking about the places she'd photographed in the eastern states. Caitlin parried with the best spots around Iron Junction.

When Beth finished her roll and was winding the film back, Caitlin finally said, "Of course, Iron Bluff's the best of them, but you already know that, hey?"

Beth served Caitlin a sharp look. "Are you going to give me a lecture, too?"

"Nah. But it is one of the best places to take shots of the mine." She gave Beth a coy smile. "Haven't walked out there in a long time, though."

"Yes, well, I dare say I won't be doing it again either," Beth said, extracting her film.

"Pity. No one walks much around here. Land's different when you walk in it."

Beth nodded in acknowledgement; the land had been beautiful, even when much of it had been trying to get into her shoes and hair, and pull sweat from every pore. She was thinking of what to say about that when an engine rumbled overhead.

"Here comes the surprise," said Caitlin, raising her lens again.

The next moment, a small plane streaked low over the ridge, the pilot waving to the crowd. The distorted PA system made an announcement, which Beth could make no sense of, but the meaning was plain enough. Santa appeared below on the back of an ATV, a trailer filled with a giant sack. Already excited by the plane, the children rushed into the center of the space, where Santa pointed up. Caitlin's shutter whirred. Beth tracked dozens of faces, all following the plane as it made a slow turn and came back over the ground.

"Uh oh," murmured Caitlin, tucking her camera under her knees.

Suddenly, it was raining candy. Below, the children streaked about, arms outstretched, eyes skyward. Beth saw the impending disaster a moment before it happened; then it was too late as two sets of children collided, face first. Both pairs fell, stunned, the tears erupting after a long moment of shock.

Other children carried on, oblivious, scooping up candy, as the parents surged forward.

"I'd better go," said Beth, scenting blood.

She reached the fallen children quickly. One pair had lumps on their foreheads but stopped crying as soon as the sweets were handed over. Another boy of six had a bloody nose; his partner in collision seemed to have bitten his tongue. Beth escorted them both to the first-aid tent, where she found Maxine in a deck chair, a first-aid kit waiting on the table.

"Hello, first victims," Maxine greeted the children.

The boy with the bloody nose sat down woozily, and Maxine directed Beth to see to the other child, Trent, who was now playing with his tongue with some concentration. "Can you show me your tongue?" Beth asked.

When Trent stuck it out, Beth saw it was bloody but uninjured. "Is it sore?" she asked, perplexed.

Trent shook his head, then proudly pulled his lip up, displaying a fresh socket. "My toof fell out."

Much later, when the children had been patched up, Beth sat back in a chair, happy to have found a moment to speak with Maxine.

"That might not have been the best party idea ever," Beth commented, plucking a candy from under the tent edge.

"No. Maybe Dale thinks he has to try to outdo the last manager."

"Mmm," said Beth, crunching on a peppermint bullseye.

"Someone say my name?" asked Dale, appearing at the tent opening.

Beth swallowed rapidly, but Maxine was unperturbed. "I was just saying what a hit the plane was."

"Yes, well, hmm. I'd rather it hadn't come to actual hits, but everyone's okay. It's rather a shame, really. It was definitely more exciting than last year." Dale shifted his weight.

"Something we can help you with?" asked Maxine.

"Actually, I'd like to speak with Doctor Harding, privately."

Beth followed Dale outside. The lights had come on,

obscuring the stars, but a campfire had been stoked and two guitars were tuning up, promising songs. Dale leaned against a parked truck. "Not going to run off on me again, are you?"

Beth frowned. "Sorry?"

"Poor choice of words. But I heard you had a flat battery yesterday," he said.

Beth gave a short laugh. "Dale, I've had about ten different people already give me advice about that. I hope you'll understand if I don't want to hear it again."

"I understand. But." He paused, scrutinizing Beth's face. "I may need to report it. Officially."

Beth's stomach flipped. She dropped her voice. "Why would you need to do that?"

"Well, it was a company-hired car, and technically on the mine's lease."

"But I don't work at the mine."

Dale sighed, leaning in, a bit too close. "I know. It's a gray area. Look, I'll see if I can let it go this time, all right? But the company takes safety very seriously and I have to make a note that you didn't log a travel plan. That generates a warning on your record, and you have to be careful not to get another one. It would look really bad if we had to fire a doctor who'd only just arrived!"

He laughed, and put a hand on Beth's shoulder, but his tone bit into her pride and she didn't like his touch. A flush of embarrassment crept up her neck and she wrapped her arms around herself. She tried to smile but her insides shriveled.

"Now, you'll have to excuse me." Dale straightened his collar and stalked towards the dinner tables. Beth watched him go, stopping to ruffle children's hair and shake hands with their fathers.

By the time Beth arrived back at her flat, her mortification had honed an angry edge. Dale would never have known if Will hadn't told everyone. Bold in her ire, and with one too many beers from the company bar, she found the number he'd given her.

"Hello?" On the phone, his voice was rough.

"I'm annoyed with you," she began.

"Who's this?"

"Beth Harding. You know, the doctor you apparently rescued out at Iron Bluff?"

"Oh, right!" His voice warmed. "Uh oh, what have I done?"

"I'm getting a hard time from everyone."

Will took a breath. "I swear, I only told the mechanic."

"You sure about that?"

"Yeah. Look, I'll make it up to you. Have a drink with me at the Re-Bar this week."

With effort, Beth held onto her anger. "All right. But at the rate you're going, you better buy me dinner, too."

Chapter 7

Around seven-thirty the following Tuesday evening, Beth wandered towards Iron Junction's main strip, looking for the Re-Bar and not entirely in a good mood. Two more patients had heard of her misadventure, and the story had acquired some alarming variations – in one, she'd been collapsed on the side of the road and in the other, nearly run over by a haul truck. Beth's molars were wearing thin. The worst thing wasn't the advice and cautions, though, it was the doubt that the whole episode had injected into coming here. And that doubt made her think of Richard and wonder if she'd done the right thing. Again.

She passed Iron Junction Auto, its roller doors down for the evening, then Mack's convenience store, closed but with a yellow light inside. Otherwise, the main street seemed deserted. A warm breeze ruffled the skirt of her blue dress, the one she'd been wearing at Vicky's party. She thought it would be cooler than jeans, though if she had to walk much further, the fancy sandals would give her blisters. Then, in the distance, she spotted a ring of four-wheel drives and pickups around a wood-clad building on the corner, a row of rainbow party bulbs strung under its wide awning. Hanging from the awning was a welded sign in bent steel, thoroughly rusted, that read *The Re-Bar.*

A few men lounged outside smoking, their voices a low

rumble. One nodded in her direction. Beth wondered if they were talking about lost doctors on the highway. She didn't see Will anywhere.

Inside, the bar's walls had been stripped back to raw brick and exposed beams with all the fittings on top, like a trendy city pub. She smelled the tang of beer and rum mixed with frying oil. The place was thick with men in mining gear or jeans, faces every shade from pale white to deep black, crowding around the bar and the pool tables. She spotted a few women, similarly dressed and involved in the conversations. A banner above proclaimed a company pool competition.

Everyone ignored her.

She smoothed her dress, aware she stood out. The only familiar person she spotted was Mack, balanced on a stool in the far corner, wolfing a counter meal. The occupants of a few other tables could have been backpackers, sporting zip-off pants and trekking shirts. A crack sounded from the pool table as someone broke.

She kept moving, trying to appear purposeful, scanning the crowd for a sandy head. After one trip around the floor, she came to the conclusion that either she'd missed him, or he wasn't here. Beth took out her phone, wondering whether to tell him she was leaving. If she stayed much longer, someone would come and ask about her flat battery, and she wouldn't be held responsible for the consequences. She'd already noticed some unsubtle pointing; the attention felt like a blowtorch.

But as she pressed the keys, she sensed a shift in the air. She looked up and there he was. Head of thick hair, eyes dark in the low bar lighting, in a fresh pair of jeans and a slim-fitting gray T-shirt.

A sheepish grin spread over Will's face. "I'm late, I know." He nodded down at her phone. "You telling me to piss off?"

Beth's bad mood faded. "Maybe. Depends how good your apology is."

"Fair enough," he said, steering her gently away from the

wall, and parting the crowd like celebrity security. He found a corner table and pulled her chair out. After a slight hesitation – no one had ever done that for her before – she managed to sit down. As Will walked around to slide into the opposite corner, he trailed a hand on her shoulder. It was only the briefest touch, but the last of Beth's tension bled away. Soon, Will had snagged a passing waitress and they ordered.

He leaned forward, his face sincere. "I'm very sorry the story got out."

Beth rolled her eyes. "What story?"

Will grinned. "Well, there's several versions. None of them include camels, yet, so that's a plus. And I mean it, I know what it's like to have everyone talking about you. But they'll forget it soon."

"Are you sure about that?" Beth asked. "You're not from around here. Maybe they'll give me a nickname I'll never shake."

Will raised his eyebrows innocently. "Intriguing ... we've already got Cyclops Brian out on-site. You could be—"

"Don't you dare!" she shot at him, but she was laughing.

"Hey, don't worry, there'll be a bigger story next week, you wait."

"As long as it isn't to do with someone getting hurt, I'm happy. I've had a few too many of those in the past few days."

"Rough days at work for you too, huh?"

Beth nodded, but she didn't want to talk about the clinic. The paperwork was getting her down. Instead, she picked up her glass. "I guess I've never lived anywhere this small before."

He gave her a sympathetic glance. "And this isn't just anywhere, remember. It's a mining town. Different beast."

"What does that mean?"

"Well, the town itself isn't much different, I guess. But there's a camp here too. Usually I work in East Angelas where there's only a camp. Lots of guys, not many women. Everyone works swings – on and off between there and somewhere else.

It's a different life, different culture to a town. It can bring some problems when they're both in the same place."

Beth raised her eyebrows in question, remembering Maxine's comments. "Like what?"

"Well, the camp puts pressure on the town's water processing. But that's just engineering stuff. Mostly, I guess it's the high-pressure work. Long shifts. Drinking and drugs aren't a big problem because everyone gets tested in this company, but people still find outlets, which doesn't go down so well with the locals." He paused, eyes dipping, as if he was going to be more specific and thought better of it. "Plus, people fly home and take their money somewhere else."

Beth looked around the crowd, trying to see the ills that these people could bring each other, just in the way they worked. "Why do it then?" she asked.

"The money's really good." Will's grin broke again, then faded. "Of course, that's fine if you're young and single. If you've got a family, the money might not be worth it. My boss, Dan, he's on his second marriage. It's a life that breaks people sometimes."

Beth frowned. "You sound like you know a lot about it."

"By observation, sure. I started working mines back east, when I was still a tradesman. I did jobs here and there, so I've been all over. Mount Isa, Moranbah, Emerald. Then I got my degree and came west."

"What was that like? Working all over, I mean. I always wanted to travel."

Will tipped his head, considering. "Exciting. I've always loved traveling from place to place. It makes the world seem bigger. There're downsides, too, I guess, but I've met a lot of interesting people." He smiled. "Like you."

Beth blushed at his smile. "So, how did you end up here?"

Will raised his voice as the bar music stepped up. "I got roped in from the site I was working at. I was supposed to be a junior engineer, but I got here and found the senior had left. So, I'm doing his job instead."

"I wouldn't have picked you for a junior."

Will raised his eyebrows. "No? Too old?"

She laughed, letting the smile that had been building break across her features. "No, too confident. In med, it takes a while before someone gets enough experience to look like they know what they're doing. You just seem so assured. You didn't even blink the other night."

"Ah. Well, cars are my thing. It wasn't my first time with a flat battery. I can even change tires and everything."

Beth rolled her eyes, but found she was enjoying herself. "Tell me more about places you've worked."

And so Will laid it out. How he'd been a leading hand in Mount Isa, where the town and the mine faced each other across a road like two disparate hemispheres of the same world; how he'd worked a development in the Bowen Basin, going underground into the hot, black tunnels of a coal mine repairing equipment; how he'd driven to Carnarvon Gorge on his days off in Emerald, camping beneath singing currawongs and going platypus spotting at dusk. Beth listened, enraptured as dinner arrived and they drank down another pint.

"Don't get me wrong, I love Queensland," Will finished. "But it was time for a change, and Perth is great. It still feels small, and the beach is to die for."

Beth sat back, tiny threads of longing weaving among her thoughts. "Sounds amazing," she said carefully trying not to envy his adventures.

"What about you? You said you were from Sydney?"

"Ah, no, actually I'm from Brisbane." She hesitated; next to his stories, her own seemed so paltry. "But there's nothing much to tell. I moved to Sydney for med school and never left. I always wanted to travel further, I just never did." Wistfully, she looked around the Re-Bar, wondering if Iron Junction might satisfy those yearnings.

"Where do you want to go?" he asked.

"I could name a dozen places …" Beth paused. Usually,

that's exactly what she'd do, but something told her she could be honest with Will.

"But the place isn't so important. I just want to go. See what happens."

Will gave her a knowing smile. "Those are the best trips. I've never been to Sydney. What's it like?"

Beth tried to explain what it was like to climb the cliffs at North Head after a night shift at Manly hospital and watch the sun rise, or trek from Bondi to Tamarama and look out on the glittering Pacific Ocean. Will listened with careful attention, even when he ordered another round. For the first time, Beth's adopted home seemed like a special place.

Conversation flowed on to hospitals she'd worked at in Sydney, and then comparing the med center in Iron Junction. Will parried back, detailing the camps he'd lived in, from the quality of the food to the rosters they worked. What seemed like only minutes later, it was ten-thirty. "I really better think about heading back," Beth said reluctantly, stretching.

Will slipped out of his seat and guided her outside under the rainbow lights, the balmy air heavy on Beth's skin. They'd drifted closer together over the evening, and now he walked in step with her, until they reached the corner. She stood on her toes to glimpse the rows of the camp's white temporary buildings, just visible across the broad oval. "You heading back?"

"Yeah, I'm walking," he said. And with casual grace, he bent and kissed her cheek. Beth let it happen in a dizzying moment. His aftershave touched her senses and his lips left a warm flush on her skin. His fingers caught in hers, and he dropped his voice. "Do you ... want to come for a walk? Maybe find somewhere quieter?"

Beth's gaze locked on Will. Her stomach disappeared as she took him in: his skin dappled with the colored lights, the strength in his shoulders, the lingering warmth from his kiss. Something about him made the request gentle and so easy to accept. Her face flushed, imagining him taking her in his arms, her tangling her fingers in his hair.

Then, the cool check of reality crept in. Slowly, she disentangled her fingers. "Will, ah. I broke up with someone, just before I came out here. I'm … I can't."

He squeezed her hand and let her go. "I'm sorry about that. Bad break-up?"

She laughed, without humor, Richard's face in her mind. Had it even been a break-up? Or had she just skipped town? "Bad enough," she said. She rubbed her arms, feeling foolish.

Will touched her shoulder. "Beth. I enjoyed tonight. And I'm sorry if I was a bit forward. Friends?"

Beth scrutinized his face; no trace of mocking. "Okay, friends."

"Good. I'm sorry again about the gossip. Maybe we can do this again sometime," he said as he walked away.

Slowly, Beth regathered herself and turned towards home. It could have been so awkward, she reflected as she left the Re-Bar's bubble of noise and light behind. But Will hadn't taken it personally.

Only when she'd closed her apartment door did she pull out her phone and find two missed calls. One from her mother, another from her sister, Victoria, who'd left a very excited voicemail asking Beth to *call now*. Being in Will's company seemed a week ago.

"I've got such a *great* idea," Victoria said a moment later. "You have to clear some time this weekend. I'm coming to see you!"

Beth quailed under threat of discovery. "Ah, I'm not in Sydney this weekend," she said, then wished she'd just said she was working so she'd have some kind of excuse.

"Well, where on earth are you?"

Beth bit her lip. "Perth."

Victoria laughed. "You and your bloody conferences and things. That's fine, though, I can be on a flight shift to Perth."

"You really don't have to do that—"

"But I can, and it will be totally worth it. You'll see!"

Around lunchtime the next day, Will sensed the mood change on-site that signaled the run-down into off-swing. The crew occasionally whistled; one big Maori guy even struck up a song. Walking through the latest rework with Matt, Will shook his head. For the first time, he didn't share the elation. He'd begun to make a difference, but issues were hardly sorted. Work was still behind, they were short-staffed, and reorders had to be made and confirmed. Drawings checked and re-issued to the crews. His off-swing fill-in was another junior with no experience, so Will felt as though he should stay across the off-days to keep an eye on things. He wouldn't be allowed on-site – fatigue was a serious issue – but he could still take calls.

Then, there was Beth. She kept returning in his thoughts. He'd spent the evening feeling bad for propositioning her, then rampantly curious to know who the jerk was in Sydney. He wondered how long he should want to call her.

As he unwrapped his camp-mess lunch, he thought about facing his four days off. Just a matter of driving back to Para and getting on the flight. Usually, by this point in the swing, he'd want Sarah's company. Not so this time. Instead, he was wondering whether Beth was heading to Perth. He toyed with the idea of calling her and seeing if she wanted to come with him to the beach.

Now who was being a jerk?

He'd just bitten into his first sandwich when the phone rang, *Mark* on the caller ID.

"Mark," said Will, swallowing quickly.

"Hey, Will." A pause. "Did you get that letter?"

That thick fist in Will's gut curled again. He'd forgotten in the excitement of flat batteries and work chaos. It was still where he'd left it: unread, stuffed into his site locker. "Yeah. Thanks."

"A guy from that Mackay lawyer came by here yesterday looking for you. You want to tell me what's going on?"

The fist drummed Will's insides. Letters were one thing; people turning up at the station in the middle of nowhere was quite another. He and Mark might have been apart for much of the past five years, but the time and distance had done nothing to lessen the bond. Will chose his words carefully.

"It's just a work thing," he said. "Dad didn't get pissed off, did he? He okay?"

"He wasn't here. And yeah, he's good." A pause. "You want to talk to him?"

Will's breath snagged. The idea of speaking with his father was as incongruous as a snowflake falling in the Pilbara. He'd steadfastly avoided conversation for more than five years, even in Brisbane when Mark had been injured after a chopper crash last year. It was easier that way.

Mark tried again. "You know, Dad's changed a lot. After all the new work on the station, he's completely different. I know you guys had your problems, but I think you should speak to him."

Will rubbed a hand over his mouth, the desperate thread of home dangling, just out of reach. "Not this time, Mark. Sorry. I'm off-swing tomorrow."

Mark paused. "Listen, Will – we've been thinking about coming out there. You know Daniella's brother, Aiden? He's been posted to Perth and she'd love to see him."

"Maybe after Christmas," Will said quickly. He loved his brother and Daniella, but he didn't think he could face visits right now.

When they hung up, Will forgot his lunch and went down to his locker. Pulling the rumpled and unopened letter from inside, he went out to his Pathfinder and braced against the rear door to read it.

Then he read it again, sweat trickling down his spine. Finally, he took a long breath, full of dust and heat, and called

Bruce Turner, the family's lawyer in Townsville.

Bruce listened while Will read him the letter. He had to work hard to keep his voice steady; all he could think was that it had finally happened. The accident had caught up with him.

"I don't usually deal with this kind of thing, Will," Bruce said finally. "I'm really a corporate guy. Do you want me to recommend someone else?"

"No," said Will. "I know what happened with the station last year and what you did for Mark and Dad. You're the one I want."

"Leave it with me, then, and I'll come back to you when I know more," he said.

"And not a word to Dad or Mark, yeah?"

"Of course not, I'd never discuss a client's business. And try not to worry until I know more."

But a black pool was already spreading in Will's gut. All thoughts of time off-swing had dissolved. He needed something to do. The whole shift would change tonight; he didn't want to end up in town or in Perth with time on his hands, especially not when Sarah was there.

He paced back to the office. He found Matt in his chair, hard hat tipped back and his fork buried in a salad. "Girlfriend's idea," he complained, chewing with disgust.

"Matt, you said your brother's on a farm up here."

Matt nodded, chewing the green stuff with clear distaste. "Yeah," he said from the corner of his mouth.

"How far away?"

"Coupla hours."

"He's busy, right? Do you reckon they want some more hands out there for a few days? Free labor while I'm off-swing."

"Thought you was going to Perth."

"Nope."

Matt rested his fork against the plastic container. "I'll give him a call, eh?"

"Thanks." Will about-faced.

"You avoiding someone down in Perth?" asked Matt. "Or you just need the land in your fingers?"

Both, thought Will. But he said, "I just don't feel like going city-side this time."

"Sure you don't wanna come to the coast?" said Matt, digging back in. "Good fishin'. I'm leavin' right after shift. Boat's here." He nodded towards the window. Will glanced towards the car park where a sleek fishing boat sat under a shade cloth, tethered to Matt's LandCruiser truck. Will knew he couldn't spend a weekend in such a small space.

"No, I'm good," said Will.

If he said it, it must be true.

Chapter 8

Saturday morning found Beth back in Perth, exhausted from the long swing. After the Iron Bluff incident, the idea of the three-hour drive back to Paraburdoo for her flight had been too much. Instead, she'd appealed to Mack, who'd booked her on the Friday-morning coach, and a few clicks online had changed the flight. Arriving at the city hotel in the late afternoon, she'd suffered with insomnia until after midnight. If the routine disruption wasn't enough, she was due to meet Victoria at a cafe soon.

Beth hurried, knowing Vicky was always early, a quality that went with unstoppably social, energetic and driven to succeed – qualities Beth admired in someone eight years younger than herself, but which could be exhausting. She spotted the smooth back of Victoria's head across the cafe.

"Hi," Beth said brightly, touching her sister on the shoulder as she slid into the opposite seat.

"Oh Beth, you're here," said Victoria, jumping up to hug Beth hello. She wore a thin, gauzy top against the summer heat, her hair freshly straightened, her eyelids glowing with green pigment. "How's the boring conference?"

"Fine, fine," Beth said, faking a smile and feeling awful for lying.

Victoria's eyes fell on Beth's camera case. "You had that at the party, too. Very retro."

Beth pushed the camera protectively under her seat as she flagged down a passing waiter and ordered a flat white.

Victoria took a sip of water. "So, guess what, guess what?"

"What?" asked Beth.

"I got the ring!" Victoria put her hand out like a sore paw.

"Oh my ..." Beth finally managed, taking in the huge brilliant-cut rock set on a white-gold band. "But I thought you already had it?"

"No, that one was just a stand-in. Show me yours again," she said.

Beth clamped her hands under the table. Her ring was back in Sydney, in the hands of the man who'd given it to her. And knowing how much Richard had meant to all of them, she wasn't ready for this conversation yet.

"Not wearing it, sorry. I have to wash my hands so much at work, it's easier not to."

Victoria's lips compressed. "But why wouldn't you want to wear it? You should put it on a chain around your neck."

There was a lovely thought. Beth nodded weakly, struggling to rein her mind back from reliving Richard's proposal, or imagining his face when he'd found the ring returned on his bedside table.

Victoria turned her hand in the sunlight, making the diamond sparkle. "So, what are you going to get me for an engagement present?"

"What do you want?" asked Beth, remembering the enormous juicer Vicky had given her less than a year ago. Beth hated juice.

"I have an idea." Her eyes twinkled.

"So, it's a shopping day?" asked Beth, her energy draining.

"I know how much you don't like it, but you will love this. You and I are going wedding-dress shopping! It's all organized. Mum promised me money for the dress and everything. They're expecting us at this little boutique."

Beth's heartbeat quickened. A coffee slid onto the table in

front of her. "Oh, no, Vicky, I really don't feel like it."

"Oh, come *on*, Beth. Be a normal human being for once and come. You can get back to that important job of yours on Monday. Besides, I want to talk dates …"

Beth let herself be blown along. She followed Vicky to the boutique, where bejeweled models in white stared down from framed wall photos, and two attendants ushered them towards the gowns. Not a single man, anywhere. They had it backwards, thought Beth. Everyone wanted to celebrate the day, but it mattered what happened when the guests went home. No one would photograph it, no one else would care. But it mattered the way no dress or cake or shoes ever would. And it was that realization that had driven her from Sydney.

But she made an effort for Vicky. She made the appropriate noises as her sister tried a fairytale full skirt, a clinging mermaid fishtail and a short beach-style dress. When Vicky was in the change room Beth trailed her hand down the rows of ivory lace. She stopped at a simple A-line with a sweeping skirt and plain bodice in rich cream silk. It was what she might have chosen. She didn't hear Vicky come back. "Try it on, Beth," Vicky insisted. "Mum said to make sure you were looking as well. She wants to see a photo."

"Oh, that's perfect," said Vicky, a few minutes later. "You should stick to the plain ones." Beth had to agree. It was a beautiful fabric and a classic design. The bodice emphasized her waist and made her neck look long and slender, almost making up for her dark wind-tossed hair. Perfect, if she'd still had a wedding to dress for.

Vicky breezily aimed her iPhone at Beth and snapped a photo. Beth tried for a smile that covered her turmoil. Creeping in to whispering distance, Vicky continued. "Beth, Cara says she'll sell this one at half price if we buy both our dresses today."

"Don't you want to look around a bit first?"

"What *for?* You said it was perfect. Richard will love you in it. *And* …" Victoria's eyes sparkled. "Since this is half price and I still have to buy all the bridesmaids' dresses, you could help me buy mine as an engagement gift!"

"Ah, I don't think so, Vicky," Beth said, escaping back into the change room. She tugged her jeans on with shaking hands.

When she emerged, Vicky was still in her dress, facing the mirror, smoothing the skirts. She lifted the heavy mass and caught Beth's arm, her eyes wide with concern. "What's wrong?" she asked, dropping her voice. "Is it the money? I know Mum promised me some and not you, but that's only because you've got such a well-paying job, Beth. And Ryan and I are saving for a house. You've got Richard's place, and you're older. Please? Pretty please?"

As gently as possible, Beth pulled away. "It's not that," she said. "There's still lots of time. Maybe you'll see something you like better and you'll be sorry you bought this one. It's so much money."

Beth sank onto a waiting chair, but she saw Vicky's furrowed brow, suspicion and hurt mingling in her features. Vicky knew something was up. Beth knew she would have to broach the truth, but not yet. She had to be prepared before they found out.

With a deep breath, Beth paced back across the boutique. Beside Vicky's blinding white, she looked shabby. Her jeans loose and faded, her dark hair lank around her face. "Come on," she said. "I'll take you out for lunch."

Vicky's mouth lifted, but only just.

Vicky was quiet as they walked back through the Perth streets towards Beth's hotel.

"Are you staying the whole weekend?" asked Beth.

"Not if you're not in this mood, after I came all this way."

"Look," said Beth, trying again to defuse the situation. "It's been a bad few weeks. Do you want to come upstairs? Have a cup of tea."

Vicky gave a sigh. "Yeah, okay."

In the hotel room, Beth splashed water on her face and took five minutes in the bathroom, regrouping. Then Vicky disappeared while Beth made the tea. She rubbed at her temples as the kettle growled its way to a boil.

"So, I've been thinking," said Vicky, emerging from the bathroom, her voice sporting a reasonable tone. "What if you just lent me the money? I could take my dress home with me, and I'll get the money off Ryan somehow. It's what I really want, Beth."

This was the point at which Beth normally caved in to Vicky's persistence and big blue eyes, and then regretted it later. "Paying back" didn't have a literal meaning for Victoria Harding. But now, sitting on the edge of her bed in the hotel room, a strange sensation brushed across Beth's skin. Dust. She rubbed the back of her neck. Nothing there, but it felt just as it had when she'd trekked along the highway near Iron Junction. Putting one foot in front of the other. Determined and unyielding.

"Vicky, I'm not going to spend that kind of money today," said Beth.

"Half price, if you bought yours too," corrected Vicky, her voice slippery now. "Please, Beth."

Irrational tears gathered in Beth's throat. Why was this so hard? "No, Vicky."

"You know, you weren't very enthusiastic today. I mean, even for you. And your phone's got no history of calls or texts from Richard in a month. What's going on?"

Beth nearly knocked her tea over. "You looked in my phone?"

"Stop avoiding the question." Vicky had the flint in her now, that streak of quartz that came straight from their mother. "Did you tell Richard you were just here for a conference, too? Who's this Will Walker in your call history?"

"No one." A hot flare burned through Beth. "It isn't like that."

"Then what's it like? Because it looks really bad to me. Richard's lovely. Don't do something stupid, Beth."

Beth got up and poured her tea down the sink. With her vision blurring, she kept her back to Vicky as the truth leaked from her lips. "Richard and I are over," she said. "I came here to work up north for a few weeks to get away. That's it."

"*What?*" Vicky's tone cut like surgical steel.

Beth braced her hands on the sink. With a great effort, she turned. "Please don't tell anyone. Not yet."

Vicky was hastily scrolling through her phone menu. "No. No. No. Richard is *perfect*. You love him. And what about the wedding? You can't do this to Mum. Whatever you did, you have to fix it. I'm calling him now."

"Jesus Christ, Vicky," said Beth. "This isn't for you to fix. It's done. Leave it alone."

But Vicky kept fiddling with a bully's determination. A moment later, she put the phone to her ear. Beth broiled with panic. The raw wound that was Richard was ripping open. She felt like she was burning up. She had to shut this down. She couldn't end up on the phone with Richard, upset and needing comfort, but she was frozen by Vicky's gall.

Beth closed her eyes. And for a split instant, she was back on the rock at Iron Bluff. The whole world spread out in a stretch of red canvas, old and weathered, beaten down and beautiful. She blinked, and it was the hotel room again, and Vicky opening her mouth.

"Richard, hi—"

Beth snatched the phone and dropped it into the tea cup in Vicky's hand, hot liquid erupting like a geyser.

"Jesus, shit!" said Vicky, leaping up and spilling more before she ditched the cup on the side table. She rushed into the bathroom and ran her hand under the cold tap.

Beth sucked her breath in and out, not knowing what had come over her. She let Vicky run the water for the burn, but only for a minute. Then, with her last ounce of mettle, she pointed a finger at the door. "Out," said Beth. "Out, out, out!"

"Crazy bitch!" swore Vicky. Beth bundled her into the hall. Vicky then banged on the door while Beth fished the slimline phone out of the tea. She stared at the screen, now black. Dropping it to the floor, she kicked it wet and dripping under the door. The banging stopped.

Beth stood rigid, heart racing, shocked at herself. She had never behaved like this. She was always the mediator. Vicky seemed equally surprised. Five long minutes ticked by before a timid knock came.

"Beth?" Vicky's voice, muffled and cautious.

Beth pulled the door open. "I'm sorry about your phone. I'll get it fixed," she said.

Vicky suddenly laughed. "Don't worry. I dropped it in the bath two months ago. It'll dry out again. It's almost worth it for the crazy story."

"Please, please don't tell Mum," said Beth, hating herself for begging.

"Why? What do I get?"

Beth felt sick. "Please."

Vicky sighed. "All right, fine. But you owe me, Beth. And I don't see the problem; she's going to find out anyway." She looked at her watch. "I'm going to call my shift coordinator and see if I can get on a flight tonight." She gave Beth a one-armed hug, exemplifying the woman in control. Of her hair, of her emotions, of everything. Beth tried very hard not to envy that, and failed. "Make sure you come back for Christmas," Vicky said as she left.

A minute later, Beth was alone, a stain on the carpet the only evidence of the conflict and its strange resolution. It may as well have been blood. Beth waited long enough for Vicky to be far away, and then, leaving her phone in the hotel room, she went down to the street.

She picked a direction and walked, her camera bumping against her chest. The rhythm of her feet was the only thing saving her now. Her skin trembled with what she'd done, not only to Vicky's phone, the dress … but what she'd left behind in Sydney. Maybe she couldn't do this. The world without familiar things was a spindly branch in a great wind. Could she hold on long enough to balance again? And so she forced her thoughts back to the red land around Iron Junction, vast and enduring. She had to go back.

Chapter 9

Beth returned to Iron Junction the following Tuesday with a sense of relief. She muscled into work, ticking along through blood pressure checks and script refills until mid-morning when a Garry Browne appeared on her appointment list. "Walk-in from the mine," explained Jennifer over the internal phone.

Beth knew as soon as she came out to the waiting area what Garry's problem was. He was standing in the corner by the water cooler, like an accessory to the potted jade tree, even though five seats in the area were vacant. Classic back pain. And there, sitting next to him, was Dale King.

Dale rose. "Doctor Harding. Seems Garry's done his back – can you take a look?"

Beth wanted to say, *No, really, that's just my job*, but she detected the tension licking between Garry and Dale. "Come through, Garry," she said, making sure to give Dale a hard look that said *stay there* when it seemed he might come along.

In the consult room, Beth helped Garry to lie on the couch, and then ran through the history.

"I wasn't really doing anything, just bent down to grab my wallet," he said.

"Have you ever had this kind of thing happen before?"

"Not really …"

Beth looked up. "You can tell me if it has."

After some chewing on his lip, Garry admitted he'd had the same problem three weeks ago, when the truck he'd been driving on-site had hit a huge pothole. "It was like going over a cliff," he said. "My seat spring hit the stops and I felt something go in my back, then I hit my head on the cab roof on the rebound. I was laid up for a week."

"Did you see a doctor?"

"I, uh, no. It was just after Doctor Gregg got sick and appointments were backed up. I had to get back to work."

Beth pursed her lips. She made sure Garry wasn't experiencing any sinister symptoms, then completed a full physical evaluation. Garry's pain was localized in his lower back, with extension down the back of his right leg. Beth let him stay on the couch while she went through her findings.

"We could be dealing with a disc in your back, pushing on the nerves," she said. "To know for sure, you need to have a scan, which we have to do in Perth."

"Can you just give me some painkillers?" asked Garry. "It usually comes right in a few days if I lie down, then I can get back to work."

"Garry," Beth said gently, "I don't want you to end up with a big problem here. If it's happened before, it's likely to happen again. What you really need is physical therapy, rehabilitation for what's going on now, and a plan to help it stop getting any worse. Now, I know there's no physiotherapist in town at the moment—" This was a major point of frustration according to Maxine. Many of the patients the medical center saw could use a physiotherapist, but the town had lost its last one six months ago with no replacement. Paraburdoo offered the service, but at several hours' drive away it was impractical for the long days of on-swing workers. "—but when you're off-swing down in Perth, I want you to see one. I'll write you a referral letter, and you'll need a few days off for now."

Garry was quiet.

Beth gently touched his shoulder. "I don't want you to have to see a surgeon, and that's where this could end up, and much faster than you might think."

After Garry finally agreed, Beth wrote out a medical certificate to cover him for three days, and insisted he come back to see her again before it expired. Then, Beth escorted Garry out to the desk to ask Jennifer to organize a physiotherapy appointment in Perth.

"No bending over to pick things up, I don't care how light," Beth reminded him. "Take it easy and I'll see you in a few days. Call the medical center if you have any problems, or if the pain meds aren't working. One of us can always come round."

"Thanks, doc," said Garry.

Dale strode over to the desk. "Garry all good to go, then?"

Beth glanced at Garry, who was pointedly staring out the doors into the car park. "I'll let him tell you about it," she said.

"Actually, could I have a word?"

She glanced at her watch. "A quick one." She led him back to her consulting room, but left the door open. "What can I do for you, Dale?"

He held up his hands. "I know you can't discuss any of the particulars with me, Doctor Harding. Beth. But I want to ensure that all my workers get back to their jobs as quickly as possible. How can we make that happen for Garry? I know he can't go back to driving immediately. But he could do something else for his next shift, couldn't he?"

"Garry can't even comfortably sit right now. He needs some time for the acute inflammation to pass, the pain to be properly managed and then he needs physical therapy to recover and have a chance of avoiding the damage getting worse."

Dale tapped his fingers against his lips. "Look, here's the thing. We've got performance targets to meet. If Garry doesn't work his next shift, it drags our stats down. He can do *something*, surely. It would help everyone."

Beth had the uneasy feeling of being adrift in a world she didn't understand. But she thought about Garry; she suspected he would put himself in physical danger if it got Dale off his back. No one deserved that.

She walked to the door and pushed it wider. "My recommendation is as I've given it. I can't change my clinical opinion; that's not in anyone's interest, least of all Garry's. I hope you understand."

Dale held up his hands, as if he'd gone too far, but Beth could see a red flush creeping up his neck. "Understood. I'm just looking after everyone. Speaking of which, I wanted to make sure you're all fine for the first presentation tomorrow."

"What presentation?" asked Beth, crossing her arms reflexively.

"For the mine. I mentioned it when you arrived. Doctor Gregg does an educational series for the workers, twice a year. It's in your calendar."

Beth slowly walked back to her desk and brought up the calendar. Indeed, there was a red appointment the next morning. "I'm sorry, I didn't see it. I don't know how I'd even put something together—"

"No need. All of that was already done. It's just a matter of presenting the information, with your medical expertise of course, and answering questions. There are a few more next week, but they're all the same. So, can I count on you?"

Beth scanned Dale's face, his well-combed hair and efficiently trimmed beard. He seemed so earnest now, the trouble of a moment ago forgotten. "I suppose," she found herself saying.

"Excellent." He rubbed his hands. "I have full faith in you. Doctor Gregg's illness left us in a real spot, so you have my thanks."

Beth sighed. "Fine. But send the material soon so I can

look at it tonight."

Beth let him show himself out. As she watched him go, Maxine appeared in the door of her room across the hall, peering like a meerkat.

"What did he want?" she asked.

Beth tried to relax her face. "I think I just let myself get railroaded." When she explained what had happened, Maxine made a face. "Doctor Gregg got on well with Dale."

Beth chewed her lip, thinking about Dale's earlier attempt to change her treatment. "You sure about that?"

"Well, that's how it seemed," said Maxine, and disappeared inside her room. Beth remained in her doorway. Dale King had stomped on her turf, and now she was doing him a favor. But if she was going into that world ... maybe she needed to understand more about the mine. And the only person she knew on the inside was Will Walker.

Will was not entirely sure he was going to make it through the day. Between the work he'd done off-swing and Matt's chatter, he was already knackered. He'd spent his down time on the station with Matt's brother, Ernie, vaccinating their herd before summer, which had meant mustering into the yards that fed the crush, and operating the neck stock.

But even with muscle memory, it had clearly been too long since such physical exertions. All his time in the gym and surfing the Perth beaches was no match for the raw bone-grind of station work. And then, on Monday, when they'd been nearly done, the herd had surged. Will had been shutting a gate and he'd caught a kick in the ribs. It had been enough to bend him over for half a minute getting his breath back, and had left him with a fifty-shades-of-blue bruise down his right side. The sucker was still throbbing, and pain ebbed his energy worse than sleep deprivation or frustration – and he'd had a bit of both on those fronts, too.

"I mean barramundi, this big!" said Matt, holding his hands the width of the plans they were currently going over.

"Yeah, pull the other one and it plays 'Jingle Bells'," said Will, hoping Matt would let the glory of weekend fishing rest. The midday sun was shining off the new metal, drawing perspiration from all in buckets. So, when his phone rang, Will answered it with uncharacteristic irritation.

"What?" he demanded.

A pause. "Is this a bad time?"

Beth.

Amid the chaos of the plant, her voice was like the calm of midnight. "No," he lied. "Sorry about that."

"So, it turns out I have to give some kind of presentation at the mine tomorrow and I don't understand what goes on there at all. Can you help me out?"

Will's thoughts raced into pleasant places. Since the Re-Bar, he'd thought of a dozen excuses to call her, and then reminded himself to leave her alone. "I might be able to do a sort-of tour, if you're up for it."

"Yeah?" she replied, sounding pre-emptively grateful.

"There's just one catch …"

"Which is?"

"It's too late to get you on site, signed in and all that stuff." He paused. "You'll have to meet me at Iron Bluff."

And so Beth found herself, for the second time in two weeks, sending the Prado down the dusty track to Iron Bluff, the memory churning in her stomach all the way. When she arrived, Will's Pathfinder was parked perfectly square against the rising cliff. After scrambling up, Beth found him at the top with a pair of binoculars, facing the mine, which lay in the basket between the ridges. With his back to her, she admired the cut of his torso into his blue work pants, the straight-backed authority of his stance. She wondered at the wisdom of this meeting after the other night. Then a rock dislodged under her foot and he looked around.

"You made it." He grinned. "Strobe off?"

"Don't you start," she warned, tentatively moving next to him. But her worry quickly abated; Will showed no trace of discomfort, and seemed on-purpose, facing the jumble of the mine's complex, which glinted in the falling sun before them.

"We're losing the light," he said, passing her the binoculars. "What do you want to know?"

"How about everything," said Beth, sweeping the binoculars over the mine, wondering which part of it Dale King inhabited, and whether Iron Bluff would be a good launching point for an air strike.

"What's the presentation about?" he asked.

"Knowing my luck, dehydration," she said. "No, really, I haven't got the slides yet."

Will chuckled. "All right, I'll start at the beginning. Over there—" he pointed far to the south, "—are the pits. That's where the ore is. To get to it, we use massive excavators and sometimes explosives."

"That's comforting," Beth said wryly, lowering the binoculars.

"Not really, those shotfirers are crazy," Will said with a perfectly straight face. Beth looked at him, imagining carnage. "Kidding," he said finally.

"Not funny."

Will just laughed. "Okay, I won't talk about explosives." He sat down on the lip of the bluff with a wince.

Beth was onto him like lightning. "Something sore?"

"Yeah," Will admitted. "Ribs."

"Show me?" She meant it as a medical question, concerned for him, but as he lifted his shirt showing her the mottled bruise covering his side, she could be forgiven for thinking about him with his clothes off.

"Nasty," said Beth, trying not to admire the way his oblique muscles stood out against his ribs. Oh, her looked better than she'd imagined. "How did this happen? Not at work, I hope?"

Will let his shirt go. "Nah. I didn't feel like commuting to Perth on the off-swing, and Matt – he's the leading hand at the site – his brother works on a cattle station out here. They're flat out getting prepared for the wet, so I went to help. I copped a kick from a steer."

"A cow kick? Seriously?"

Will shrugged.

Beth shook her head. "Well, I guess, on the upside, I don't have to fill out any forms about it."

Will laughed. "Too true. Now, where were we?" He faced the mine again.

Beth braced the binoculars on her knees as Will continued. "So, the ore gets put onto big haul trucks – that's them moving on the haul road, see? – and they take the ore to the big hopper at the top of the plant. And you see the half-finished duplication alongside? That's what I work on."

Will gently turned her shoulders, pointing out the plant, which rose under a high wall. Beth watched as a loaded truck, tiny in the distance, reversed to the edge and emptied itself, a soundless cloud of dust spilling skywards.

"So, what does the plant actually do?"

"Takes ore, crushes it up and puts it on a conveyor to a stockpile."

"That's it?" said Beth. She glanced at him; pride shone in his eyes, and she sensed how much complexity lay beneath his statement. Similar to her saying, *Patients come in and I treat them.*

He caught her looking. "Sounds simple, but it's on a huge scale. I mean, just look at it. If you've never stood under a reclaimer or a haul truck, or gone down the highway alongside an ore train … it's still amazing people can do this. Gives me a thrill every time."

Beth nodded, a smile on her lips. "All right. What's next?"

"Stockpiles." Beth traced the arc of his finger along the conveyor to the great piles of yellow-tinged ore, set in parallel lines.

"Are those cranes?" she asked, pointing at the giant machines chaperoning the piles.

"Stackers and reclaimers," said Will. "They put the ore down, then pick it up again for the train conveyor." He pointed at another bin straddling the great loop of train line. A train was nearly loaded, its hundreds of wagons snaking around the loop, ready to head towards the coast. "After that," Will continued, "it's onto a ship and away, though the port itself is just as big as this."

"What about over there?" asked Beth, pointing to where she could see a flash of movement beyond the pit, flanking the mine's dam.

Will squinted. "Um, no idea. Can I borrow those?" After looking for a minute, he shook his head. "Looks like heavy equipment working. Could be a new road, maybe, or grading. I'm not sure."

"What about all the rest of the stuff?" she asked, pointing to the huddle of buildings and sheds.

"Mostly support. Workshops for the haul trucks and the light vehicles. Admin. Temporary offices for the construction. Water treatment and pipes, that sort of thing."

He went on in more detail, describing how the departments worked together, and how the site formed part of the company overall. Beth let the binoculars rest in her lap, thinking. "How do you feel about doing this kind of work?" she asked. "I mean, mining gets a bad rap sometimes."

"Pretty much everything we use comes from a mine, at least in part. I don't really care about the politics. I do think they should pay more back to the country we're pulling it from. The profits are pretty obscene. But my job's about what's going on here, on the ground. We've got good regulations for safety in this country, which is more than a lot of places can say." He leaned back on his hands. "Most of the time, it seems like making impossible things happen. That's what I like, really. The challenge of it." He glanced her way, a small frown creasing the corners of his eyes, and his eyes searching her as if there was something to find. "No one's asked me that before," he said. He sounded touched.

The light was turning through purple now, the day's heat leaching from the rocks. Beth drew in a breath of the faintly dusty evening air as she thought about what Will had said. She could hear the satisfaction in his voice, the pride in his own capability. She wanted to find such certainty for herself.

"Thanks, I really appreciate it," she said after he'd led the way back to town. "I know you're busy, but I didn't know who else to call." She didn't want to admit to him that driving back out to Iron Bluff had taken a lot of self-convincing, and she'd been glad he was there to follow home again.

"Call me any time. I'm happy to help. And I like talking about it, especially with you." He smiled, glancing away, as though he shouldn't have added the last sentiment. But Beth hardly minded. For the first time, in his company, the empty space inside her had disappeared.

Chapter 10

Unfortunately for Beth, Dale didn't send the slides through until eight-thirty, when she was picking at a takeaway dinner from Mack's. Around nine, she'd just finished eating and opened the presentation when her mobile rang. Answering it with trepidation, she saw the call was from Jennifer.

"Oh, Beth, good, I can't raise Maxine. The paramedics are bringing in a woman in respiratory distress. Can you come in?"

It took only a few minutes to put her shoes on, grab her stethoscope and jog across the road. The ambulance was just unloading, Jennifer opening the center's main doors.

"All right, fill me in," said Beth, then she stopped cold as she recognized the woman on the stretcher.

"Caitlin Murray. Advanced stage bronchiectasis. Acute shortness of breath, worsening since last night. Oxygen sats ninety-one per cent. Worsening lung function over the past few years. Regular courses of antibiotics," she heard from the paramedics.

Once they were inside, Jennifer went straight to the file room, calling over her shoulder. "I need to pull up the file. And I'll keep trying Maxine."

Beth took a deep breath and focused on the task. Caitlin's attention was directed solely on breathing behind an oxygen mask, but she looked more annoyed than anything. "Caitlin, it's Beth Harding," she began. "Maxine's on her way, but let's check you out."

Caitlin gave a single nod. Beth unslung the stethoscope from around her neck and kept an eye on the sats monitor. She heard crackles in both lungs, and a wheeze. Caitlin's temperature was also up, enough to be suspicious of an infection. And she had a hacking cough that brought up foul gunk. Grimly, Beth collected it for pathology.

When the fit settled, Beth pulled up a bedside chair. "How long have you been sick?"

Caitlin spoke between short breaths. "A. Few days," she managed. "Worse. Last night."

Movement caught Beth's eye and she turned to see an older Aboriginal woman with gray, curling hair slip into the back of the room. Watchful eyes. Worried. Caitlin exchanged a few gasped words with her that Beth didn't understand, then said, "My mum."

"I'm Beth," Beth supplied, then spoke to both of them. "I'm going to watch your sats, and pull up some records. Won't be long."

Jennifer produced a set of Caitlin's lung tests from several months ago now, showing long-deteriorating function. And after ten minutes, although Caitlin's oxygen sats improved, Beth wasn't happy. An infection in someone with already compromised lungs was serious, and Iron Junction was not the place to deal with it. Caitlin Murray needed to get on a plane to Perth.

Just as she'd sent Jennifer to organize evacuation, Maxine came in the back door. "Caitlin Murray's in with acute dyspnea," Beth said, quickly running through the presentation and management. "Jennifer's just gone to organize an evac. That all right?"

Maxine gave a humorless chuckle. "Sure, organize whatever you want. She won't go. We've been trying to get her down to a tertiary hospital for months for a tune-up. Last time, the plane sat on the runway while we looked all over town for her. The only way she'll go is in a body bag. Here's my mobile number if you need it, but otherwise, I wash my hands of it. You want to try, go ahead."

Beth was left in an eddy as Maxine walked away, an unfamiliar despair settling on her shoulders. Alone with a difficult patient. Beth found it hard enough to reconcile the passionate, talented photographer with the sick woman down the hall. Worse to carry Maxine's words back with her. Heavily, Beth pushed back into the room. Two sets of dark eyes tracked her. The older woman's gaze was still watching and worried. Caitlin's expression seemed tired, but set against what she obviously knew Beth would say.

Beth sank back into her seat. Caitlin's breaths broke the constant oxygen hiss. "No," she said between them. "Not going."

"Why not?" It made no sense to Beth why someone so ill wouldn't want to be treated.

Caitlin's breaths sucked the skin down above her collarbones. "Too far."

"The flight's a couple of hours."

But Beth knew she really had nothing that could win Caitlin over, chiefly because she was sure Maxine had tried them all. Friendly doctor, explaining and reassuring. Passionate doctor, imploring and stressing importance of the treatment. Then the nihilist; the point where you said, *Do what you want, it's your life*, hoping that reverse psychology would work.

The fierce desire to help beat inside her chest with no words to make it happen. Beth knew there wasn't anything special about her that would make this time different. She let the seconds tick by in counterpoint to Caitlin's breaths, which weren't any easier. Perhaps she would pass out and make the decision moot.

"Look," Beth said finally. "I've seen your work. You take amazing photos. And I know you work with the school, too. I don't want today to be the end of all that. You need to take care of this infection. You'll be back before you know it."

Finally, the older woman broke the silence. "Caitlin says you were walking back from da bluff? Car broke down, eh?"

Beth sighed. "Yes, that was me."

The woman's face broke into a grin. Beth gave Caitlin a look of exasperation: had the whole town heard? And for a bare instant, Caitlin's smile flickered, but the effort to breathe caught her. Enough was enough. Beth would make it happen somehow. She excused herself and found Jennifer at the front desk, holding the phone between her chin and shoulder as she dug through the top drawer.

"On hold," she said. "Is she going to go this time?"

Beth stared out the front doors. The car park was a gray expanse under the moon. A white four-wheel drive lumbered past on the road, its flag swaying, its strobe turned off. "Ask them if they'll take her mother, too."

Beth paced as the evacuation coordinator came back on the line. Finally, Jennifer cupped her hand over the receiver. "Yeah, they'll take her too. But are they going?"

"Hold them for two minutes," said Beth. She strode down the hall, where she found a changed atmosphere. Caitlin was sitting back against the pillows, her mother leaning forward with a hand on each thigh.

Some exchange had occurred, and Beth hung in the doorway. "What if I could send you both?" she asked.

Caitlin's head rolled to the side. Beth couldn't bear the idea that she might die here, an accident of geography and circumstances. And she was sure that this would happen soon if Caitlin didn't go.

"Please," she said, mustering her last hope. Caitlin's hand moved, and Beth looked up. The older woman gave her one quick nod.

After the drama with Caitlin, Beth found herself unable to

sleep, and then she had to haul herself up, gritty-eyed and nervous, at five a.m. for the presentation. She dressed in trousers and her only long-sleeved shirt, having seen all the workers wearing their ankle-to-wrist uniforms. The sun's low angle threw Iron Bluff into a sunken blue as Beth steered herself out to the mine's gate, where a guard directed her to a shadecloth-covered gravel car park, already bristling with orange-tinged trucks, emblazoned with identity numbers on their doors. Beth was struck by the place; it spoke of dirt and business, and hard work, lacking the inviting feel of the town and the medical center.

In the administration block, a bright receptionist rushed Beth through an induction, and then took her two doors down to the meeting room.

At ten to six, Beth tried to douse the butterflies. She'd had barely enough time to run through the information once, but now the computer was set up and the presentation title screen glowed blue on the wall behind her. Two air conditioners rattled in the far corner. The receptionist had put bowls of candy in the middle of the tables, and now the room was filling with men in blue work pants and orange shirts. Loud voices, sweaty bodies, dust-crusted boots shedding on the floor. They all found people they knew and started chatting. Beth felt invisible. She recognized no one from the medical center, and Will wasn't among them.

She had them for two hours. Then a second group straight after. Beth took a breath as the minute hand passed through six.

"Let's make a start," she called. The rumble of chatter continued. Beth wasn't the best public speaker, but she'd had her share of standing up in front of people. Presentations at grand rounds, conference papers. Playing a part in the medical-school revue. The only difference now was the audience.

The conversation buzz checked itself with inexorable slowness. Thirty sets of eyes turned on her, one after another, until only one man was talking. Then his neighbor slapped him on the arm and Beth had silence. One of the men down the front was still wearing his sunglasses and a defiant grin. She wondered if he was planning to sleep through the session.

"All right." She cleared her throat. "I'm Beth Harding, and I'm a doctor currently working in Iron Junction. This presentation is about some common medical problems that affect workers on mine sites and is part of the company safety initiative."

This was script straight off Doctor Gregg's notes. But already she could see the glazed expressions on the guys at table two. One of them was shredding a mint wrapper. As she continued, first into some slides about dehydration, the tuned-out look spread like a virus. Only now did Beth realize how dry the material was. Doctor Gregg's presentation slides were mostly long text dot-points, his notes delving into detail that would probably only interest a medical professional.

So, when ten minutes later, she said, "Now, let's move onto skin cancers," the whole room was already lost. Beth flashed the next slide up, a chart of different sun spots. But even a picture failed to get much reaction. One guy tipped his lolling head to the other side. Beth tried asking questions to involve them. She flashed up Doctor Gregg's melanoma slide. "Does anyone know what this is?"

She knew some of them must. Silence.

"My ex-wife," said a wag down the back.

Beth pressed on. Through to the end of skin cancers, into basic first aid for wounds. She thought about Wally, the guy who'd caught himself in the thigh with a circular saw. A case story could help, but she could hardly break patient confidentiality.

The session limped to the one-hour mark. There wasn't supposed to be a break, but at the rate they were going she would finish early. Beth sighed inside. "Let's take a ten-minute break."

Ten minutes stretched to fifteen, then twenty. When some

of the men still hadn't returned, Beth started again, only to have them straggle in through the next ten minutes, interrupting her rhythm each time the door creaked open and clunked closed. She persisted, right through recognizing a heart attack and the effects of alcohol and drugs. With ten minutes to spare, she handed out feedback forms with the churning feeling that no one would check the "good" column, and probably half of them would be unanswered.

She fared no better with the later group, in which she was surprised to see Wally, still limping after his incident with the saw. But even the familiar face didn't help. The candy were exhausted early and fidgeting reached primary-school proportions. Two men down the back corner passed a note back and forth. By the time the last session was half-done, plenty of the guys were looking at their watches. In a rare moment of temper, Beth asked one of them, quite politely, if he had somewhere else to be. The guy was unapologetic. "We got taken off the job to do this," he said. "We're behind and we just want to get back to it."

"Seriously?" she asked.

"Bloody oath."

As she finished the final slide, there was a stampede for the door. Beth was left in the upturned room. Chairs were abandoned at skewed angles and candy wrappers littered the floor. Beth sank into a chair. A hand touched her shoulder.

"You okay, doc?"

She looked up to find Wally standing over her, weight on his uninjured leg. "Just tired," she lied. "How's the wound?"

"Oh, it's coming along," he said, sitting down across from her. After a minute, Beth realized he was trying to work out how to broach a topic.

"Leg hurting?" she asked, to give him a start.

"Oh, no, it's fine," he said. "Just, I know I'm not supposed to say any of this stuff, but I figured you're my doc, right? So, I can tell you."

"Tell me what?"

Wally rubbed a hand over his face. "There's stuff happening out here on-site that no one's real happy about. Work's getting pushed ahead fast. Paperwork's dodgy. Procedures are bad, and I've seen some bad ones. Guys are getting hurt." He gestured to his leg.

Beth frowned. "I noticed. What can you do? Report to management? Your union?"

Wally shrugged. "Everyone wants to stay employed right now. It's tricky. Easy to get disappeared if you're a contractor. Some of the guys aren't even coming in to the med center if it's not too bad—"

He broke off as the meeting-room door cracked open. Dale King appeared, fresh in a crisp blue shirt.

Wally scrambled up. "Gotta go, doc. Thanks again." He limped out as Dale strode over.

"All went well, then?"

"Actually, I'm not sure it did," said Beth, her thoughts still turning on what Wally had said. "I think it might have been a bit heavy going. Too much to take in."

"I'm sure it was fine. These guys don't do well in a classroom. You just head on back to work now."

Beth chewed her lip, choosing her words and trying to ignore the patronizing tone. "Dale, can I ask you something?"

"Of course. That's what I'm here for."

"I've seen a lot of injuries these past weeks."

Dale showed no reaction. "An unfortunate reality of this job."

"Well, I'm concerned. I'm also wondering if we're seeing everyone who needs treatment."

"It's not something to worry about."

Not something to worry about. Odd. Beth's thoughts turned to Wally, and Brian, and Garry. "What happens to the injury forms when they come back here?"

A spot of color appeared on Dale's cheeks. "They're filed for reporting to the mines department."

Beth kept her voice level. "Can I see the records?" Then, when the spots of color spread, she hurriedly added, "I just want to understand the system. To get a better idea of patterns. Maybe I can help."

"It's confidential information. But, Doctor Harding, if you have concerns, or if anyone reports something that worries you, I should be the first to know about it." His gaze drifted to the door.

Beth let it go, concerned he'd overheard something from Wally. Besides, she did have to get back to the medical center. Six hours of appointments to go.

In the long shadows just after dawn the next morning, Will paced outside the workmen's crib room, looking at his watch. All around, the rich red earth was silent, the air still, the tufts of vibrant green grass unmoving. Too still. Where the hell was everyone?

Finally, he heard footsteps and Matt appeared, jogging back from the plant. "I know where they are," he said. "Night shift got sent up the back."

"What's up the back?"

"New dam and earthworks. Stage two."

Will frowned. "Since when?"

"It's been running for a while, but all contractor work. Nothing to do with us."

"So, why are they taking shifts off the plant, then?"

Matt shook his head, twisting his lips. "Must be trying to push something through. There's a bigger problem, though."

"Christ, what now?"

Will followed Matt through the buildings and out into the red expanse of the lay-down yard, where several plywood containers were lined up on palettes. "These are the new water pumps," said Matt, shifting a lid aside. "Take a look. They're all like this. It's not the first time, either. Last week it was damaged pipe. That's still on order."

Will peered into the box, the body of the pump dull gray in the shadows. It didn't take long to spot the damage: the motor turned off at a strange angle, and an intake line was dented. "We can't use that," said Will, thinking of the thousands of dollars and lost time the pumps represented. He snatched up the dockets, groaning when he saw that the company had accepted the shipment from its depot in Paraburdoo. "Leave it with me," he said.

Eventually, when the night shift arrived back at the crib for hand-over, and Will had set the day crew to work, he marched to the office, looking for Dale King. King would have to authorize the pumps being reordered, and someone would have to check them properly this time. But as Will rounded the office, he heard raised voices. He slowed, his boots still silent on the dust, an argument issuing from the open doorway.

"I want it in writing this time," said an unfamiliar male voice. "No more handshake agreements. I want all those work orders written down. I'm not having more trouble with the next progress claim. You're already in danger of the union getting a strike going. No pay would give them license."

"If anyone downs tools, you're in violation of the agreement." This was King. Will rested his fingers on the dusty wall, listening. "And you can't get high and mighty with me, with your record this past year. You're lucky to have the contract at all."

"What's signed is signed," argued the man. "We're holding our end. You hold yours."

Booted footsteps stalked out of the office, and a gruff-looking, gray-haired man in hi-vis gear appeared. Will let him pass before knocking on the door.

King swung around in his desk chair; his site shirt still clean. Will eyed the spartan office: desk perfectly tidy, unpacked boxes stacked against a filing cabinet.

"Mr. Walker, how are you doing?"

Will cleared his throat. "Not good. The pump shipment's damaged. It has to be re-ordered. And our shift was moved out of the plant last night. Nothing got done."

King stood, his hands on the desk, bent over like he was thinking, a muscle tightening in his jaw. "If the pumps are damaged and need reordering, that's your time and budget problem now," he said. "You're the engineer responsible for the plant. It's your job to work out the schedule. If I need a shift to do something else, you need to work that out. Or is that too much for you?"

Will sucked a deep breath, recognizing a familiar feeling. If he'd been in a bar right now, this would be the point where the other guy suggested they go outside. Will knew he had to stand his ground. He'd worked for hard bosses before. He could recover this.

"No," he said finally, "it's not. I'm just making sure we understand each other." He tried a smile he didn't feel.

King wavered, an intense concentration crossing his face. Then he smiled back. "I like your spark, Will. I know you won't let me down."

Will shifted on his feet, uneasy. "Dale, I know I'm only the acting senior engineer, but the shift change last night has screwed my planning. Do I need to know about these earthworks up the back? Is it going to happen again?"

"No. Focus on the plant."

Will turned to go.

"Oh, Walker? Since you're here, we need to talk about the incident the other night."

"Incident?" Will couldn't read anything in King's expression.

"Yes. You were supposed to check in with company reception before seven on the night you drove in. You didn't."

"I told them I was helping Doctor Harding with her car. They said it was fine."

"It's not fine. A report had to be filed and preparations made for a search."

Will had no idea what to say. He felt the pressure of King's gaze. Finally he said, "I didn't realize."

"Well, now you do," King said, coldly. "You can go."

Will left, unsettled. When he reached his desk, he stared at the schedules and plans for an hour before he got up and walked into the drawing room.

Slowly, he thumbed through the filing system looking for stage two, but he found nothing beyond concept designs; early stuff. He went back to his desk and opened the network drive. Fifteen minutes and three searches later, he found a feasibility study, a concept design and planning reports. All running to several hundred pages. He skimmed. Stage two was a dam and a wash plant, but the scheduled dates for that part were next year and beyond.

Will spun on his chair, thinking. Then, before he went back out to the dusty plant, he dashed off an email to Dan, his supervisor in East Angelas. *What do you know about stage two starting early at Iron Junction?*

Chapter 11

When Saturday, mid-swing hump day, rolled around, Will suspected things were going just a bit too well. The damaged pumps had been reordered, and would arrive on a truck at the Paraburdoo depot next week. The plant had caught up a week's worth of work. Dan hadn't known anything about stage two starting, but in the midst of the plant progress, Will figured it didn't matter for now.

Matt was the one who jinxed it. "Doing good, Will. Nearly back on schedule. Grinner, get over here!"

Grinner was a surly man with a shaved head and a thick neck, who never broke a smile, nor used words as far as Will could tell. But he was a first-class welder, and he worked fast despite his ambling walk. The whole crew were working more smoothly. Will could see ahead to when he'd be able to go back to East Angelas.

"Look, out – white-shirt," Matt said, nodding his hard hat towards the temporary buildings forming the office. Will glanced over to see Dale King striding towards the plant stairs.

"Boys," King greeted them as he came up. Even though he was dressed in the same company hi-vis and issued safety gear, he stood out as an office type. Too clean; too good to be out in the plant.

"Mr. King," returned Will. He waited, keen to get on.

King looked around the plant with distaste. "I need a word

with you, back in the office."

Will caught Matt's raised eyebrows as he followed King.

"You're doing well," King began, going straight to the point. "I think we can move the tie-in schedule up, don't you?"

Will hesitated. The tie-in was a critical time in the plant extension when they'd shut the existing plant to link it up to the new equipment. Coordination had to be perfect, and a detailed series of checks needed to be completed before everything could be brought back online. The complex process was set to run at the start of the next swing. "It should stay where it is," Will said finally. "Next week we've got the new pumps coming in and I have to go to Para for that. Half the procedures still need writing and I'm off-swing on Thursday anyway. If anything doesn't flow, I want to be here to sort it out."

King rubbed his chin. "Don't trust the people in Para, is that it?"

"They did accept a damaged shipment last time. I know containers fall off trucks, but I need working gear. I want to sign them off myself." He paused. "Does this move up have to do with stage two?"

"Do you have trust issues, Walker?" King had that flat expression again, the one Will found impossible to read. But the threat was there. "Well, do you?"

Will tried not to let his frustration show. "I'm just trying to understand my job."

King pushed a piece of paper across the desk. One glance and Will felt the blood leave his face. It was a copy of the email he'd sent to Dan. "I need to know I can trust the employees here. We have a policy of not discussing our commercial endeavors with parties outside this mine. Do you need to be reminded?"

Will knew he'd never printed the email. And while it was common to discuss projects, King was a prick who would obviously ride the legal line whenever it suited him. This was the point of retreat. "No, I don't," he said, while mentally lining up King's mouth with his first two knuckles.

"Excellent. Safe trip, then."

The same day, Beth found herself groaning under additional appointments as Maxine made a house call to an outlying station. Two town kids came for vaccinations, one of them four years old, the other, eighteen months. Then, an elderly woman with a beaten Akubra pulled down on her graying tangled hair arrived with a broken left wrist after having fallen on a sidewalk. Beth recognized her from the Christmas party: Nancy, who'd been helping Mack with the grill.

Refusing all help from onlookers, Nancy had driven herself to the medical center – "What? The car's an automatic," she told Beth – then refused to be seen until the other waiting patients had gone in. Jennifer muttered something about her being as tough as an ironbark fence post.

Finally, Beth coaxed Nancy into the treatment room. With the break not displaced, Beth set about wrapping the wrist in soft gauze before applying the plaster. Nancy scrutinized her every move.

"Not bad," she commented, turning the arm over, the stringy muscles of her upper arm bunching under the extra weight.

Beth was bemused. "You're a connoisseur of casts?"

Nancy cackled. "Seen enough of them in my time. Out here, everyone's always breaking something. Kids or men. I grew up over in the Northern Territory; I saw my first broken arm when I was five. My brother trying to help my father. And a few kids at schools, too."

As Beth cleaned up the plaster materials, Nancy launched into stories about her school-teacher days, shipped to tiny places and tinier classrooms. By the time Beth finally washed her hands, Nancy was onto Iron Junction. "Came down here when they first opened the place up," she said. "My husband ran the mechanic's place, then the produce. Sold them both, though. I was principal at the school up until last year. Now I'm trying to be retired, but the teachers keep coming in for a year then buggering off again. So, I find myself going back."

"Do you still enjoy it?" asked Beth.

"Love it," said Nancy. "Don't understand people who want to work in the mine. I drove haul trucks for a year, just to try it. But it's not my thing. These days, I leave the mine to Caitlin and her photos. Isn't it terrible she's so ill? She's great at keeping the community kids involved. We've never had such good attendance."

Beth listened while Nancy went on about the school program, how the students discussed the impact of the mine in their lives, what they thought about the landscape and the wide world outside the town.

"They're lucky to have you," Beth said finally.

Nancy waved her good hand, not caring for praise. "I suppose I'll have to stay out of the pool for a few weeks now? I coach the kids' swimming," she explained.

As Beth was answering, Jennifer stuck her head into the treatment room. "Your next appointment's here," she said.

"Right, then," declared Nancy, slipping off the bed and heading for the door.

"Wait. Have a seat for ten minutes at least, Nancy. You might not feel too steady."

"That's all right, love. Done worse to myself before and no problems. You've got more important things to do."

In the end, Beth was only able to hold Nancy long enough to print the scripts for the painkillers, and to say she'd call about a return appointment to check the cast. "And Jennifer's going to drive you home," she said firmly, confiscating Nancy's keys to the beaten pickup in the car park. "You've just had a shot of morphine and I'm absolutely not letting you go alone."

"Fine," grumbled Nancy. As she and Jennifer disappeared

out the glass doors, Beth found Garry Browne alone in the waiting room.

"Well, you're looking a bit better," she said.

He grinned and followed her down to her consult room. "Yeah, been laid out and not getting the spasms anymore."

Beth was able to do a much more thorough examination than she had four days earlier. When she finished, she sat down and went through everything with Garry. "You're past the acute phase," she finished. "So, now it's really important to keep on top of it and get that rehab happening. You're still seeing the physiotherapist next off-swing? Good. And how do you feel about work?"

"Itching," admitted Garry. "I'm bored in the camp and the project's getting back on track. Glad I didn't have to work when it was real sore, though."

"Well, I'd think you could do something non-physical. And half-days. You might find it hard to sit for long periods."

Beth wrote up her recommendations, thinking how Dale King should be satisfied, too. "I'd like to see you again after your physio, or earlier if you've got any problems."

Because Jennifer was still out with Nancy, Beth flicked to the appointment calendar, skipping ahead to the next week. She'd find an appointment for Garry, and one for Nancy before she forgot.

Then she noticed Tuesday, Wednesday and Thursday – right up until the end of the swing – were blanked out with the light-blue "busy" color. "Weird."

She hovered over the title block. "Presenting safety initiative training," she read, and then realized. The other presentations Dale had mentioned. But someone had made a mistake and blocked three entire days. She apologized to Garry and said she'd call him about the return appointment when the diary was sorted. As he left, Jennifer was back at her desk, and Maxine appeared a moment later, her cropped hair windblown from driving with the window down.

"Jen, I think there's a mistake with my calendar next week.

These training sessions are booked all day.”

Jennifer’s brow furrowed. After a minute clicking into the calendar, she said, “This says in Paraburdoo, Tom Price and East Angelas.”

A cold pool gathered in Beth’s stomach as she recognized two of the names. “Wait, are those other mines?”

Maxine peered over her shoulder. “Is it presentation time again?”

Beth’s hands tightened against the reception counter. “But he never mentioned anything about other sites,” she said.

It took over an hour to get Dale King on the phone.

“Well, of course they’re at other sites. It’s a companywide initiative. This is how it’s done. The presentation is just the same as the one you’ve already given. No effort on your part. Just go through the script.”

“But these sites are miles away,” she said, having scrolled through Google maps to find out just how far.

“It’s not a big deal. As I told you before, just make sure you log those travel plans. And allow yourself enough time between sites. Jennifer can help you with that.”

But all Beth could think of was the time she’d been isolated at Iron Bluff. She’d still been in the town limits, then. There was no way she wanted to drive hours across country to strange sites, just to give the same, awful presentation. “I don’t think I can,” she said. “We’ve got so many patients to see.”

Dale let the silence stretch, as if Beth were being unreasonable. “The time’s booked,” he said finally, and coldly. “Doctor Gregg committed to this, and you’re his replacement. This is part of our company responsibilities. I don’t want to have to tell your agency you were uncooperative. You want another job to go to, right?”

Beth’s stomach curled with annoyance as his words sank in, but Dale had moved on. “It’s not a big ask. Just a few days, and it’s a great way to see the region. I’m counting on you, so don’t let me down.”

"All right," she said. But she looked at the map, still open on the screen. Miles and miles of empty landscape.

"Shit," she said, once she'd hung up the phone.

The afternoon appointments dragged on and Beth found herself sitting in the office long after the sun had gone down. She hadn't spoken to Will since Iron Bluff a few nights ago. But he had said to call any time …

When he answered, Beth could hardly get a word out. Her throat seemed occupied with her beating heart. "Hi, Will."

"Beth? I was just thinking about calling you. Long day?" She heard a rumble in the background.

"You could say that. I have a small problem. You know about my little walking adventure the other week? Well, since then I haven't been keen to drive anywhere. And that would be fine, except I have to drive to some other sites next week. Can you convince me I'm being stupid?" She tried to laugh, but her heart was heavy.

"I'm heading back to town now," said Will. "Where are you?"

"I'm at work."

He pulled into the car park five minutes later. Rugged and filthy after a long day, he still managed to look appealing in his worn blue trousers and heavy boots. She showed him the schedule. "I'm supposed to be in a different place each day. I feel ridiculous saying this, but what if I get stranded again? I didn't even want to drive to Para last off-swing. I … I took the bus." Beth bit her lip, embarrassed to admit it.

Will straightened. Next to the clean sheets of her exam couch and the white walls, he was a shock of life and color. He didn't make fun of her. "It's not stupid," he said. "What if I drove you?"

"Don't be silly," Beth said, even as her hopes leapt.

"I have to go to Para to inspect deliveries," he said. "And the rest of the week I'm writing procedures for the tie-in, which I can do from anywhere. I'd only have to change a day from what I'd planned. I can run you out to Tom Price from

Para, and I can put you in East Ang the next day if you don't mind driving at night. I want to see Dan anyway. And you can catch the off-swing flight from there."

Beth looked at him in amazement. "Are you serious?"

He gave her a winning smile. "Absolutely." Then he looked down at himself and around the clean office. "There's a lot of white in here. I better back out slowly and head to the shower. I'll call you about the details."

After Will left, Beth leaned back in the chair, her heart rate returning to normal. But one problem solved still left another. "I need to do something about this bloody presentation," she said aloud.

Beth tipped open her sleeping laptop intending to work, but her mind wandered. She checked her email. Nothing from her family. Her friend Tom had sent her a collection of LOLcats, and another message asking her what her plans were for Christmas. Beth checked the date. Only three weeks away. An ache sprang into her heart.

Last year she'd been in love with Richard, and he'd proposed a few days later. Now she faced the idea of this year without him. Without decorating the tree together. Without him as a refuge at family gatherings. Maybe she should pretend there was no Christmas this year. Work would keep her busy. She straightened up and opened the presentation notes. To hell with Dale and his script. She took out an imaginary scalpel.

Chapter 12

By Monday afternoon, Beth had more reason to be grateful for Will's offer. An overnight call for chest pain – another long-hours worker knocking on heart-attack's door – followed by a full day's work had left her exhausted. Jennifer noticed her yawns as Beth dropped her bag by the front desk then ducked into the store to grab a Styrofoam box.

"Geez, Beth, you look done in," she began. Then her eye caught on the white Pathfinder that had pulled up outside. "Oh, who's that?"

Will was striding towards the front doors, sunglasses setting off his angular face, the fading sun glinting in his hair. With his work-shirt sleeves rolled up his forearm revealing thick muscle and strong hands, he looked serious and capable. And a heartbreaker. Beth's stomach squeezed. "That's my ride."

Jennifer gave her a wicked eyebrow. "Lucky you."

Will pulled off the shades as he reached the desk. "All ready to go?"

At her nod he grabbed her bag and marched it out to the car. Beth followed, feeling Jennifer's envious gaze behind her. Will threw the bag onto the back seat.

"What's that for?" he asked, sliding the foam box in beside her bag.

"Can we make a stop at the butcher?" asked Beth. "Then

I'll explain."

"You need a pie? Travel food of champions."

Beth laughed. "No, for something else, and I need to duck into Mack's store for ice, too."

Will paused. "Ice? You know, this thing has air-conditioning," he said, patting the dash as they climbed inside.

The stops didn't take long. Beth picked up her order from the butcher, throwing the bags into the foam box. When she'd emptied a bag of ice over the top and firmly shut the lid, Will raised an eyebrow. "Are you going to tell me what you're doing now? Barbecue?"

"It's for the presentation. I'll tell you all about it later, if it works."

"If it works?"

"After the last one, I had to make some changes."

"The first one didn't go well?"

As they drove, Beth told him about it. She tried to make it funny, impersonating the guy who'd tried to sleep through the whole thing, and Will was soon laughing. But she could hear the frustration in her own voice. "I would have been bored, too, so I had to do something," she finished, staring at the asphalt and suppressing a yawn. Fatigue was dragging her eyes closed.

Will gave her a sympathetic glance. "You know those things are always boring, right? Don't take it too hard."

"I'm not," she protested. "But what's the point if no one remembers anything? I can't abide something so mediocre."

"Fair enough." He chuckled.

"What?" demanded Beth, through another yawn.

"Nothing."

A smile twitched onto Beth's lips; she was suddenly glad to have Will's company as she stared at the car's long shadow, sweeping beside them down the highway. She hadn't counted on how isolated things were out here. She'd expected an adventure, but it wasn't like a movie montage. It was long stretches of work. Long stretches of being alone. She was just a temp, skimming the surface of a giant pond she'd never swim in. But through Will … she'd touched the fabric of the world out here. His company was safe, inviting … and strangely exciting.

Beth tipped her head back on the seat, savoring the cool cabin air, not quite sure what to do with these feelings. "Maybe I'll just close my eyes for a bit."

"Beth." Will touched her shoulder. "Beth."

She opened her eyes. Through the Pathfinder's streaked windshield, the dark sky outlined rows of buildings and silhouettes of gums. Beth breathed in clean bush air tinged with diesel. Will pushed a key into her hand. "We're here."

The next morning, Beth woke clear-headed in her motel room, which smelled of industrial cleaner and stale airconditioned air. The early light, filtered through the long leaves of a gum, made a dappled pattern on the bricks. She could hear boots on the cement path as men left for the day.

No nerves, yet.

She showered and dressed with time to spare, then tipped open her sleeping laptop and checked through the slides again. A knock came at the door and she jumped. Scrambling up, she found Will outside, in a clean pair of site clothes and with his hair damp from the shower. He held a takeaway cup. "Caffeine for you," he said.

"Oh, you're wonderful," she said, seizing the coffee.

"You might want to save that judgement until you've tasted it. The machine looked like it should apply for benefits."

Beth sipped; scalding hot and strong, just how she liked it.

Will drove her out to site and Beth stared out the window at the massive processing plant, stockpiles, a looping train line and a cluster of tiny administration buildings. Will carried her gear into reception. "I'm busy with these pump tests all day, but good luck," he said. "Tell me all about it later."

Once in the assigned room, Beth took a few deep breaths. By the time the workers started to file in, she had everything laid out, and the PowerPoint fired up. This time, the workers looked at the desks curiously: every second one contained a plastic-covered lump, which she asked them not to touch.

At the appointed hour, she flipped a slide forward, a *Far Side* cartoon of an operating room. "Hi, everyone," she began. "I'm Beth Harding, a doctor from Iron Junction." But that was as far as she stuck to Doctor Gregg's notes. "This presentation is part of the company safety initiative and we're going to talk about some medical problems relevant to you on-site. I know you are all busy, so I'm trying something different today. Could you all now reveal your patients, please?"

The workers looked at each other, then pulled the plastic off the lumps on the tables. "What's that?" asked one guy.

"It's a ham," said another.

"You're half right," said Beth. "This is definitely pig skin. What I want to talk about first is sun exposure, and more particularly skin cancer. And you're going to cut out a skin cancer. Has anyone ever had this done?"

A few hands raised around the room, mostly older men. Beth then produced the hastily assembled kits. She'd decided against syringes to simulate a local anesthetic, but she'd managed to conjure up several dissection kits, unearthed from a box in the back of the Iron Junction pharmacy, which contained all the essential pieces. She'd also swiped a bunch of sutures from the med center.

"In case you're wondering what the point of this is—" She looked at their faces. They didn't really care. They were practical people. She sensed she had a narrow window to make use of their attention. "Never mind. This is how you do a basic excision."

She quickly drew on the board, then broke the class into groups.

As they worked, she approached each group, finding out

what they already knew and filling in gaps. When they'd all successfully removed the skin, she called a halt. "I think you probably know the most serious skin cancer?"

"Melanoma," supplied a few people in unison.

Beth flashed through a few slides of aggressive-looking black skin growths. "Right. That one is a big worry. And you'd have a much bigger excision than the one you've just done. Remember that. But ultimately, for all cancers, you want to be on the lookout for skin spots that are new, changed, or worry you for other reasons, like bleeding. Now, let's look at stitches."

On it went, Beth keeping their hands busy while she gave information and tested what they knew. The session took the whole first hour, but everyone had been engaged. She felt a wave of satisfaction as she moved on to her next topic: injuries and recovery. She talked about muscles and joints, which ones were critical in their physical jobs; how to minimize injury and maximize recovery. Then a role play about heart attack, during which several workers got serious about their acting.

"No, doc, really, my chest hurts, right down my arm," complained one guy, grimacing so convincingly that Beth actually sat him down. Then he laughed, delighted to dupe her, and she couldn't help but smile.

At the end, she finished with a *Dilbert* cartoon of engineers in a hospital, which drew a few laughs. "Thank you, all. I'd appreciate a few minutes with the feedback forms if you can."

The room emptied. Beth's bones ached, but her heart was light. Another group would follow, but she was confident they'd be fine. By early afternoon when Will came to collect her, Beth knew she had a satisfied grin on her face.

"Do I take it things went much better?" he asked as they carried gear back to the Pathfinder.

"Indeed," she answered, depositing her laptop on the back seat, followed by a plastic bag full of the dissection kits.

As she climbed into the front, Beth glanced across. Will had rolled his sleeves up, his forearms bunching as he reached for the wheel. He gave her a shrewd look. "Are you going to tell me what you did now?"

Beth grinned. "I made a few adjustments. People were bored just listening to a bunch of details written on slides. So, I turned it into more of a practical."

She told him about the pig skin, at which Will laughed. In an expansive mood, Beth admired the red crust separating the road from the scrub. With the presentation sorted, she could see her way clear through the week. She was actually looking forward to her days off; she planned to find a cinema and see a movie or two, have a haircut, and shop for Tom's Christmas present. Maybe she would even find one of these famous Perth beaches and take her swimsuit out. And for now, she was enjoying Will's company.

"What sort of day did you have?" she asked as they made their way back into town.

Will rubbed his hair. "Ah, a tricky one. I came here to inspect a pump delivery, and some other gear we need for the plant, but the supplier's unhappy."

"Why are they unhappy?"

"Because they're not getting paid on time and they won't deliver on credit anymore. I've got to get on a teleconference back to the Junction and try to sort out the accounting."

Beth felt a wave of sympathy. "Oh, that doesn't sound good. I was going to suggest we have dinner."

"I should be able to sort it out, and I'll grab something at the mess when I get back, but that will probably be late. However …" He cut off, as if trying to calculate. "Beth, it'll take us an hour or so to reach the Tom Price site tomorrow morning. I'll try to make it back in the afternoon. There's a good place there I'd like to show you. We could get takeaway from the mess and have dinner there, if you like, and head to East Ang after." He gave her a sidelong smile as if testing her enthusiasm.

"Sounds great," she said, smiling in return.

Beth sailed through the next day. Apart from a few complaints – from people she came to realize had wanted an excuse to sleep for a couple of hours – the participants seemed impressed. She was packing up, humming to herself, when Will reappeared.

"How did it go?" she asked.

"Much better," he said. "Pumps are sorted. I'm counting it as a win."

Soon, as promised, they'd collected takeaway meals from the camp mess and Will turned the Pathfinder south. The town of Tom Price rose gently up the hill at their backs, flanked by imposing hills. The sun was dragging its heat down below the horizon, the shadows throwing the landscape into stark relief. She itched to reach for her camera.

"So, where are we going?" she asked, conscious of Will's purposeful turns of the wheel. He'd clearly been this way before.

"Well, I survived the bench testing today, and you're past halfway, so a celebration's in order. *And* since you enjoyed Iron Bluff so much …"

Beth gave him a mock glare. "Careful where you're going with that."

After a few minutes and a long, upward-sweeping bend, the Pathfinder halted at the edge of a lookout, the town spread out in front of them. In the fading light, they clambered out. Below, the blood-red soil thrust between the sage and emerald tree tops, steely bitumen and white stones. Beth used the bull bar to haul herself up on the bonnet, breathing in the dusk.

She pointed. "Is that a golf course?"

Will climbed up beside her. "Yeah. I've even played there." He laid the dinner containers in a row between them. "When I first came out here and I didn't know anyone, I used to spend the off-swing just driving from place to place. So, I found a lot of spots like this. Up there—" he pointed to a peak rising above the town's ringing hills "—is Mount Nameless. It's beautiful, but I didn't want to head up there after dark."

Inspired by all these hidden treasures, Beth edged closer to him. "What else?"

"Out on the coast, north of Dampier, there's this amazing park full of Aboriginal rock carvings, the most anywhere in the world. Dates back to the last ice-age. I drove there, maybe six months ago. You can see how the carvings changed when the sea level last rose."

"Yeah?"

Will nodded. "The oldest ones are land animals, and then they became fish and turtles. I saw a documentary on it once. There's flood stories in oral tradition all round Australia. Can you imagine?" He shook his head. "My family's been on the station for a long time, but nothing like that."

Beth smiled. "Pity it's not closer," she murmured.

"Well, there's Karijini," he said, pointing off to the darkening arc of horizon. "Gorges and rock pools. Amazing."

"Really? How far?" said Beth.

Will looked up, calculating. "A couple of hours from here."

"When I first arrived," Beth said, "I saw a photo from Karijini in Mack's shop. One of my patients took it. It really made me want to go." She snorted. "Actually, that's what inspired me to go to Iron Bluff."

"Well, why don't you go in the off-swing?" asked Will.

Beth shook her head. "Oh, yes, that would make a nice matched pair. Get stranded in a gorge next and need another rescue. I might even make the news. Maybe another time. Do you have plans?"

"Going over the tie-in plans and being on-call for Iron Junction."

Beth paused. "You'd work on your days off?"

"I did last time."

"Oh, yeah. How're the ribs?"

Will grinned. "Just about recovered, doc. And don't worry,

you'll get your driving confidence back."

"Thanks, but I'll stick to shorter trips for now."

They sat in silence as the hills bled into purple and blue in the fading light. Will didn't break the moment with words, and yet Beth sensed the space between them close. They'd only known each other for a short time, but she trusted him. She'd been able to rely on him, and – just like now – he had a way of bringing pleasure into her day. Not wanting to let the moment go, Beth gently slid down and took out her camera, then balanced it on the edge of the hood to take a long exposure. Will watched her work, and under his attention Beth's cheeks glowed red, like the last of the sun.

With the photo taken, she climbed back into place on the bonnet, the camera in her lap.

"Was it a good one?" he asked.

"No idea. That's the surprise when the prints come back."

Will smiled. "Nice to have a little mystery."

Beth stopped herself before she could act on the sudden impulse to rest her head against his shoulder. "Was growing up in Queensland like this?" she asked, looking down on the town's clutch of buildings within the hills.

Will leaned against the windscreen. "Nothing like this. Cattle station in the north-west. All sweeping grass plains. Mark runs the place now. That's my little brother," Will said. "He and Dad are turning it around after nearly losing it. I'm really proud of him. I don't think I could have done that."

"Is it just you and Mark?"

"I've got a sister, too. Cat. I used to see her a lot when I lived in Queensland. It's been a while, now."

Beth leaned back beside him, feeling the draw and connection of family. "Do you miss them?"

"Yes." Will took a breath. "Not far from here, there's another lookout full of memorial stones. People write the names of their departed loved ones on the stones. There're thousands of them." He paused. "I ... put one there for Mum last year."

Beth was taken aback. "I'm sorry. When did she die?"

Will cleared his throat. "Nearly two years ago. Anyway. I wanted to put one there because Mum loved to travel, too. She would have liked it, I think."

Beth rested a hand briefly on his arm, touched at Will's gesture, and the intimacy of his telling her about it. "I'm sure she would have."

The night was becoming blue now, the heat slipping away. "What about your family?" Will asked.

"Ah." Beth's words stopped against an invisible wall. She looked for a way through. "I've got two sisters, Anne and Victoria. Both younger. Vicky's a flight attendant. Anne and Mum run a mail-order business. Vicky's just got engaged." Beth bit her lip as the sting of that particular fact dug into her heart.

"Yeah? Mark's engaged too. Daniella's lovely. I'm happy for him. You know, Daniella's a doctor, too," he added.

Beth laced her fingers together. She felt the urge to confess. "Vicky and I aren't what I'd call close. I wish I could be happier for her. But it's hard."

Will studied Beth's face. "That sounds complicated."

"I love her to bits," Beth said quickly. "It's just ... my family can be difficult."

"Difficult how? I mean, Mark, he used to get me in trouble all the time, nicking Dad's scotch and then pretending I took it. I got a whipping I didn't deserve more than once."

A smile crept over Beth's lips. "Not exactly like that, no." Briefly, she relayed the shopping experience.

Will laughed, but his expression then turned serious. "What else?" he asked gently. "I know there's more to it. Does this have to do with your break-up?"

"What makes you say that?"

He shrugged. "Sixth sense."

Beth turned her gaze on the town. Streetlights pinpricked the dull land, an echo of the early stars above. In the easy quiet of this place, in the warm night air cupped by the sky and earth, she wavered. "I was engaged, too. Then Vicky got engaged just after it all ended."

Will absorbed this; Beth could almost see his thoughts turning. "And now you have to watch her doing things you were going to do."

Tears prickled behind her eyelids. She pushed her food away and hugged her knees into her chest. Will sat stoically, watching her, his face saying he was ready to hear more. But Beth wanted her thoughts as far away from here and now as possible, to purge the feeling of being stripped to her skin.

Slowly, he put an arm around her. Beth let it rest on her shoulders, a comforting weight. She sniffed. "The thing is, I can't bear to tell anyone else. I don't know how to. When Vicky found out, I made her promise to keep it a secret. But she thinks I made a big mistake and I should make things up with him."

"What do you think?"

Beth shook her head. "I don't know. When I left Brisbane for med school in Sydney years ago, I knew what I was doing. I had a plan. This time ... I'm not sure why I'm here at all."

Will hugged her to him. After a brief hesitation, Beth hugged him back, taking the comfort she needed before pushing away.

"I think it's fine not to know," he said. "Something made you leave and brought you out here. Maybe you just have to follow through until you work it out."

Beth wasn't sure about that at all, but Will's words burrowed inside her anyway. She felt them changing her, threading a connection between them.

Finally, Will gave an unrushed sigh. "So, what was it like studying medicine? You must have some good stories."

"I'm not sure you'd like to hear them. Are you good with blood?"

"Come on, I grew up on a cattle station," he said.

"What about strange things in various orifices?"

Will put on a face of mock horror.

Beth found herself laughing again, the sadness of moments ago forgotten. "There was this one consultant everyone had, and we were scared of him," she began. "He used to quiz students to breaking point in front of everyone. The med school revue did a terrific send-up of him with sock puppets. He was horrible." She paused. "Actually, he reminds me a bit of Dale King."

"He is a challenge."

Beth turned towards him. "How is work, really?"

Will's pause told her enough. "Chaotic. There's lots of problems. But I've worked for difficult managers like King before. It's part of the job sometimes. Let's talk about something nicer, all right? How about the new *Thor* flick?"

"Ah, Tom Hiddleston," sighed Beth. Will rolled his eyes with a grin.

And so the evening drifted towards midnight. Not once did Beth have to talk about her family or Richard again, as Will steered the conversation between movies and music. Only when Beth felt she must get to bed to be fresh for the next day did they leave the lookout behind as Will guided the Pathfinder back to town.

As they parted by the stairs to her room, Will called her back. "Wait, Beth. Don't worry about your sister. You're just cutting a different path. Lots of us do that. Otherwise I'd still be in Queensland." He looked at her intently. "You know, I could tell that you were different, that night I found you on the highway. When I told you how far the town was and you said you could make it. That's determination."

Beth laughed. "Come on, Will. I was probably delirious."

"Still, I mean it." He caught her hand and squeezed it. "Sleep well."

And Beth had to turn away so he wouldn't see the tears in her eyes.

Chapter 13

The next day, Beth cleaned up from her final presentation in the East Angelas mine. The afternoon had a lovely end-of-semester feel. The sessions had gone smoothly; tomorrow morning, she'd be on a flight for the off-swing in Perth, and Tuesday, back to her work in Iron Junction. She itched to see patients again; she'd felt a stab of envy this morning when Will had been in obvious high spirits to be back on his familiar home turf.

Beth glanced out the meeting-room window. East Angelas was a middle-of-nowhere place, a town-less mine flanked by distant hills. The sky seemed a vast ocean on which the harsh sun floated, the mine rising up from earth the color of blood. Just outside the gates, the green grasses and trees formed a ring as if ready to reclaim the territory. From the little Beth had seen, she had a sense this place ticked along like clockwork, a den of activity amid the great expanse of land. This even included the camp accommodation – a clutch of white temporary buildings in the red landscape. Even Beth could appreciate the different atmosphere from Iron Junction.

Will appeared a few minutes later, his site clothes beaten, orange dust stuck to his face.

"You look quite the part," she said, closing her laptop.

He gave her an easy smile. "Dan put me to work. I think he's pissed."

Beth had met Will's boss briefly when they'd arrived this morning. "Why?"

"He's annoyed I'm going back to the Junction next week, and that I've spent most of the day with my head in the plant drawings, writing procedures for the tie-in. We did one here a while back, so it was good to be here. Actually," Will continued, "it gave me an idea."

Beth arched her eyebrows.

"It's a surprise," Will said. "But I promise the best view on site."

Half an hour later, Beth – in oversized gloves and a borrowed hard hat – squinted out of the windscreen as Will drove them around the mine. She'd already been to the crow's nest above the pits, to see the massive operation spread out below. Will had proudly pointed out the automatous trucks crawling along the carved roads, a pioneering project for the site, and the loaders scooping yellow-tinted ore. Beth found it impossible to appreciate the tiny trucks had wheels taller than she was, until Will drove them out to the vast symmetrical stockpiles, silhouetted against the approaching night. When they climbed out of the cab, Beth stood under a gargantuan structure stretching its heavy arm protectively across the pile. At the end of the arm was a bucket-wheel, but Beth spied others with plain ends, each machine resting on tracks that shot off down the length of the stockpiles.

"Stackers and reclaimers. This is what you saw from Iron Bluff," said Will. "The stackers build the stockpiles. And when they load a train, the bucket-wheel pulls the ore and the conveyor takes it to the load-out. This is what everything is about."

"It's huge," said Beth. Never had she felt so tiny than under the eye of the bucket-wheel, and so awed that people built these machines.

As the sun sank, they drove back to the plant and Will led her up a metal stairway, which opened on to a narrow mesh deck along the wall of a giant hopper. Beth faced the sprawl of the site and the distant hills, now blue with evening against the apricot sky.

"I wish I'd brought my camera," she said, admiring.

Will parked himself against the hopper, removed his hat and ran a hand through his hair. "Yeah, shift change is done, and the plant's shut for now, so we're not going to have two hundred tonnes dumped into the bin behind us."

Beth slid down beside him, shaking off the gloves, feeling part of this dusty, machine-driven world. But despite being content in Will's company, the longer she stared out at the Pilbara's vastness, the more the distance she'd come from Sydney spread a lonely ache in her heart.

"When's the last time you were home?" she asked.

Will looked skywards. "A long time. Five years, maybe."

"Why so long?"

"Dad, mostly."

"Did you have a falling out?" Beth's experience with her mother hung in her mind; even with all the unpleasantness, she couldn't imagine staying away for so long.

"Of sorts." He hesitated.

"It's all right, you can tell me," she said.

"I love my father," he said simply. "And I respect him. He's a hard man in a hard business. But I was always a disappointment. I knew I wasn't staying on the station; I never wanted that life. It's … too hard to face his expectations."

Silence descended, in which Beth thought about her family wanting her to marry Richard. A gentle breeze blew through the plant, setting off the soft tinks of falling dust. Finally, she asked, "Will you go back for Mark's wedding?"

Will made a noise in his throat. "I hadn't even thought about that. I guess I'll have to."

Beth's fingers itched to take his hand. It didn't matter how caked they were with dust; she wanted to let him know they shared the experience of a difficult family. And yet at the same time, when she had these thoughts, her heart would kick with reproach, reminding her of Richard. It was like a broken foot that only hurt when you walked on it, and so Beth made no move. Instead, she said wistfully, "I admire you for going out on your own like that. It can't have been easy, and look at all the places you've been. You said your mum liked to travel; I bet she'd be proud of you."

Will said nothing.

"Sorry, I didn't mean to upset you."

"You didn't." He reached across and squeezed her hand.

Beth's breath caught. "It's just I wish I'd been brave enough to do things like that, too."

"What about coming out here?" he asked. His fingers were still around hers.

Beth looked away, but his touch was sending pleasant shivers through her whole body. "Hasn't exactly been what I imagined, what with driving misadventures, Maxine, and Dale."

"So you had some false starts. That always happens."

"Or maybe I shouldn't have come."

Will gave her a strange look, a frown colored with disbelief. "You remember the other night when you were telling me about med school? You moved to Sydney for that. It must have been tough, too. But here you are, a doctor." He shook his head with a soft laugh. "Your family must be so proud of you."

Beth stared. He really meant it. A deep and unexpected sadness unwrapped inside her. She swallowed a sob and removed her hand from his.

"You okay?"

"Fine," she sniffed. Then she realized she wasn't fooling anyone. "It's stupid. It's just … no one's ever said that before. Mum hated me going to Sydney, even for med school. I know I made things hard for her. I've always felt bad about that."

"You feel bad? Seriously?"

Beth shrugged helplessly.

"Well, *I'd* be proud of you," he said.

Beth sighed and leaned back against the bin, their shoulders touching. Beth listened to Will's breathing; he seemed to know it was time to be quiet. Gradually, the first stars pricked the sky's canvas.

Will finally got to his feet and offered a hand. Beth took his warm palm and he easily pulled her up. He extracted his phone from his shirt pocket. "Before it's completely dark, let me take a photo in all the Pilbara glory. Then you can remember the adventure." He gave her a wink.

The plant's railings were hard under Beth's hand, family memories immovable in her head. But as she moved into place by the outer rail, she looked up into the sky's curve and sensed the endless red dirt, stretching out under the night. So much land must mean many roads; and maybe there was one for her. Will's flash lit and she blinked. "Too much flash. All you'll have in that shot is me and the railing!" She laughed.

"All right, fine, Ms. Photographer." Will smiled and carefully balanced the phone on the bin's edge and pressed a button. Then, he ducked forward and slipped in beside her. "Countdown and no flash," he whispered. "Don't move."

So, Beth held still against him, absorbing the scent of his skin until the shutter clicked, not wanting the moment to end. Will scrutinized the result. "Ha, that's pretty good." He tilted the screen towards her.

The shot had caught the fading sky light, the mine buildings spotlit far below, and Will beside her, their faces a few inches apart. A perfect fit.

Beth smiled up at him. Will slid the phone away but didn't move. His lips parted slightly, his gaze intent on her. Beth was aware of a space about them, a cushion of air and land and sky. She met his eyes, her breaths coming faster. Feelings that had been trying to gather surged forward.

Then, deliberately, Will reached for her. His hand gently pulled her against him. An electric excitement lit inside Beth. The air warmed as his lips met her cheek, sliding smoothly down, seeking her mouth. Her heart thundered, the immediacy crashing against reason. She tipped her lips up to meet his, soft and sublime. Then his arms drew her in and the kiss became deep. Beth slid her hands across muscle and through his hair, lost to him in this moment.

Then, like a black aftertaste, doubt pinched at her heart. What the hell was she doing? This wasn't Richard. She tripped on unfamiliarity, on the pace of change, stumbling onto the broken foot of her heartache. She slackened in his embrace, then pushed away.

"No, I can't."

Will removed his hands instantly, one drifting across his mouth, his breathing heavy. "Shit. I shouldn't have done that."

Beth wrung her hands, flushed with the heat and shame of wanting him and yet smarting from his regret. "I, ah … I just …" She couldn't say she didn't want him, that would be a lie. "It feels wrong," she managed finally. "I was with Richard for a long time."

Will rubbed a hand across his forehead. "I didn't bring you up here so I could hit on you, really. You already told me to back off once." He dropped his head. "I just … you do something to me. Not that that's an excuse. I should know better." He gave her a quick smile. "Can we forget it?"

Beth knew that would be impossible, but she held her tongue. He meant far more to her than just an attractive man. He'd given her a window into a new world, given her the sparkling hope that coming here hadn't been crazy after all. She took a deep breath, the air sweet with night, her cheeks burning. "Listen, Will … I meant what I said about being friends. I'm out here by myself. Even false starts aside, it's been … lonely." She allowed herself a glance at him. "You put some life back in it for me, really. I don't want to mess that up."

Will took her hand and squeezed it. "It's fine. I wouldn't be much good for you anyway, not with the kind of work I do."

Beth sat back under the railing, dangling her feet off the

edge, and patted the space next to her. With obvious relief he sat. "So, shall we talk about the weather, seeing as I just made it uncomfortable?"

Beth laughed with him. Will had a way of speaking the obvious that took the weight out of awkwardness. "I don't know, I thought perhaps sports. How about those Swans?"

Will chuckled. They sat companionably in the light-dotted night, until Beth's phone began vibrating in her pocket. She was still smiling as she retrieved it, then her mirth turned chilly.

"Mum," she said, flipping it open.

"I'd been wondering why you hadn't called," Meredith began. "But now I find out you've walked out on Richard, and you're off in Western Australia. What on earth are you thinking?"

Beth was acutely aware of the volume of her mother's voice, and Will nearby. "I can't talk about it now, Mum."

Meredith paid no attention. "Oh, of course you can't talk about it. Don't bother to tell your mother anything. I called Richard after you didn't reply to my emails and the next thing I know he's telling me you've walked out. And making Victoria keep it secret, too. I was so embarrassed. Last to know, like you don't trust me … your own mother."

"I didn't know how to tell you," said Beth, helpless.

"Didn't know how to tell me? After all I've done for you. I sacrificed to give you opportunities. Your father—" She broke off, and Beth heard a tissue being plucked from a box "—this is just like when he—"

"I know, I do," she said, desperate to avoid this well-worn track.

"Don't tell me you've taken off with some other man?" Her voice was full of tears now. "Don't do what he did, I couldn't bear it."

Beth closed her eyes, shame dripping through her after Will's kiss just moments before. "I'm just working, Mum. I'm doing a temp job."

"Richard's waiting for you to call him, Beth. You owe him

that."

Tears gathered in Beth's eyes that she rapidly wiped away. Will had moved away to give her space, but he must have heard everything, must have seen her distress. Beth tried to regain control.

"How're Vicky's plans coming along?" she said.

"You should ask her yourself. What day are you back for Christmas?"

"I'm not sure yet."

"I need to know this week, Beth. Don't make me call again."

When the call ended Beth felt like the pile of old tires they'd seen by the mechanical shed, deflated and shredded on the edges. She eased herself onto the top step beside Will, her stomach churning.

"How much did you hear?" she asked.

He glanced across, his voice rough. "Enough."

Then Beth realized he was angry, the taut lines of his face and arms evidence of holding himself back.

"What's wrong?" she asked, alarmed.

He took a breath. "I don't like seeing you upset like this," he said, not looking at her. "Or someone talking to you like that. I don't care who they are."

"That's just how she is."

Will remained unconvinced. "You're going to have to explain that to me."

Beth searched for the words, but she couldn't find any that captured the gravity of her family dynamic. "It's difficult," she began. "Mum had a really hard time after Dad left. He was working on mines and construction sites. One day he went and didn't come back. She brought us all up by herself. Then she started this business that took a long time to make money. So … I guess I understand why she's not … kind."

"Not kind? Beth, you're still shaking."

Beth looked down at her hands. She could feel it inside her, too, the awful sinking sensation that lingered after her mother's reprimands. "I just didn't want her to know about Richard, not yet. I knew she wouldn't like it."

"Isn't that your business?"

A tear tripped down Beth's face. "Look, it's hard to please her. I know that I don't have to, but she's my mother. Vicky and Anne are different, they're more like her. It's easier for them. You have to understand: she liked Richard. They all liked him. I felt I was on a different plane until I found him. He'd made things easier with them. I've felt lost without that."

"Ah." Will glanced away and Beth couldn't see his expression. "It's not my business, Beth. I just … don't like you being upset."

They drove back to the camp in silence. Beth's thoughts were consumed with Richard, the turmoil of her feelings for him, and the gentle simplicity of Will's kiss.

Will walked her to her room then said goodnight, and told her he'd collect her early for the airport drive. Beth closed the door, needing some distance, then felt bereft without him. She lay awake for a long time, and in the darkness, familiar doubts nestled against her heart. What was she doing with her life? Beth screwed her eyes tight and gripped the pillow into her chest. She missed Richard's arms around her, missed his assurance for what was right for her. Then Will's kiss intruded, and his confidence that she would find a way through. God, she was so muddled; how would she work it out?

Will pushed his way through the camp buildings thinking about going back to talk to Beth. There was more to this family situation than he understood. Even for the difficulties he'd had with his father, it was nothing like what he'd sensed from Beth. He'd just circled back when his phone buzzed. Looking down, he saw Matt's number on the screen.

"Mate, I hope you're having a good holiday out there,

because I can change all that," Matt began.

"What's going on?"

"King's pushing the tie-in ahead early. We have the orders for a Saturday start."

Will thumped a fist into the side of the storeroom. "I only just sent the draft through to King today. It's scheduled for next week. We're not ready."

"That's why I thought you'd want to know. Are you coming back? The crew's edgy. They don't want King running it."

Will mentally calculated the distance. It would take him a whole morning to drive back, even with an early start. "Yeah, I'm coming back. Just … Christ, try to hold it off."

He was still inwardly cursing when his phone rang again, this time with a number he knew well. Will's stomach clenched, and he looked for a corner where he wouldn't be overheard.

"I'm sorry to call you so late, but I'm in meetings all day tomorrow," his lawyer began, sounding tired. Will reached the camp's games room, empty except for a well-used ping-pong table, and shut himself inside.

"Here's what I can tell you at this stage," Bruce continued. "The girl's parents are bringing a wrongful-death suit against Michael Hodges, and calling you as a witness to the accident. It's a civil case. The court will determine whether there's any merit. If Mr. Hodges is found responsible, the court will award damages to the parents."

Will digested this like it was a meal with spikes. "Why so long after? The coroner finished with it years ago."

"The statute of limitations on these kinds of cases is three years after the death. It seems they waited until the last possible moment to file and the system is really slow. They'll have spent time gathering information, finding experts, that sort of thing. Why they waited so long to file, I don't know, but the case will probably be set down for the end of January in the Mackay

District Court. You'll be served a subpoena to appear."

The weight of the word "subpoena" fell on Will like an anvil. The room contracted. He pulled at his collar and stumbled outside. Even there, the Pilbara night coated him, hot air and cool fear. He braced himself against the building, his legs trembling. He couldn't go under oath and lie.

"There's one more thing," Bruce was saying.

Will forced his voice out. "What's that?"

"Michael Hodges has asked to be put in contact with you. But I really don't recommend it. Any correspondence should come through this office."

Will thought about that, thought about his position, standing behind his lawyer while Michael wrongly took the blame for the accident. A trickle of orange dust escaped from the awning and vanished into the air. "No, give him my number," said Will.

"I don't think—"

"We were friends," Will said shortly. "Give it to him."

Bruce was silent, and Will heard scratching as the lawyer made a note. "All right. So, let's set up a time to discuss this properly. And if I don't speak to you before, Merry Christmas and a happy New Year."

Will ended the call and paced towards his room on autopilot. He'd never understood how lawyers could be so disconnected from the enormity of the things they must tell people every day. Bruce could go straight from details of a wrongful-death case to "Merry Christmas". Will couldn't turn his thoughts so quickly.

All around were the familiar sounds of camp – the silence of the big land punctuated by bursts of conversation and booted footsteps – and yet he felt adrift. Even the problems in Iron Junction paled in comparison. What the hell was he going to do? And worse … had they found something new?

Gradually, the panic subsided, but his good mood was polluted. He thought of Beth and groaned. She was sincere, kind, determined. And she'd been through a lot. So, why did he have to get caught up in that moment and kiss her? He wanted to smack himself in the head. No, he wouldn't cross that line again. He could be the friend she clearly needed. That would have to be enough; he couldn't burden her with his problems.

When he fell asleep that night, Will dreamed he was back on the homestead at Ryders Station. The hall was the same creaking wooden floor, with the VJ board walls and the old-fashioned light fixtures. The place was deathly quiet, and he felt like an intruder. He snuck between the rooms, peering into each empty bed, searching.

Then, when he reached the end of the hall and opened the heavy door, the veranda with its wrought ironwork disappeared. He found himself standing under the hot Pilbara sun, on the road, bare feet on the bitumen. A shock of fear ran through him: he would melt. The asphalt folded, becoming a ravine with crumbling sides. He looked over the edge and felt that black place in his heart bloom – the place that knew he was still running from the accident. He stumbled backwards, and the ravine vanished. The bitumen divided the red bluffs. And Will found himself facing a large animal.

A camel, its eyelashes hooding a penetrating gaze.

The next morning, Beth opened her door to find Will about to knock.

"Morning," he said, overbright.

"Morning," returned Beth, holding up a hand against the sun's outdoor furnace.

Will took her remaining presentation materials and silently loaded them into the Pathfinder, moving bags and a pile of drawings around with unnecessary force. After last night, Beth hadn't been worried about awkwardness, but she had clearly been wrong.

When Will slammed his door and stabbed his key in the ignition, Beth jumped in. "Will, I know you said things were fine last night, but you're obviously upset."

Will gripped the wheel, then slowly unclenched his hands and let them fall. "It's not that," he said. "Matt called last night. King changed the schedule and I have to go back to Iron Junction."

Beth breathed out. "Oh."

"I'm worried about what's going on at work. There're crews depending on me and I don't want to let them down." He exhaled heavily, giving her a sidelong glance and a smile that seemed sad. "I meant what I said last night. I shouldn't have put you in that position. It's better for both of us."

"Good." She sounded convincing, but disappointment still flickered in Beth's heart. Which she knew was unreasonable. This was what she'd asked for. She was still working herself out, he had moved too fast. They agreed. Move on.

Beth adjusted the air vents, trying not to dwell. She had things to do this weekend. Christmas presents, for a start ... and thinking about her next job. Doctor Gregg wouldn't be ill forever. The only problem was, she couldn't make a decision. She let the land rush past in a blur of green and red, and contemplated asking for her old job in Sydney.

Just as she was giving the idea room, Beth spotted a dark dot on the horizon.

"What's that?"

Will slowed as they approached. "Might be someone broken down."

But as they drew near, Beth saw the shape was actually a camel, no, two camels. One was pulling a hollowed-out van, the other tied on behind. And walking before them was a figure swathed in khakis: long pants, shirt, boots, and broad hat trimmed with a fabric skirt. As they slowly glided past, the figure raised an arm to wave. The camels plodded on as if they couldn't care less.

"Amazing," said Beth. "There's nothing for miles. Where do you think they're headed?"

"Probably to the coast," said Will.

"But that's hours away, and it's so hot out there."

Will drummed his thumbs on the wheel. "I've seen those camels before. The first day I ever came to the Pilbara they were on the road near Newman. I heard from a few people that the guy travels all over, so I've expected to see them again and I haven't until now." He glanced in the rear-view mirror. "That's really weird."

"Why?" asked Beth, adjusting the air vents again to blow more directly up her shirt sleeve.

"Because last night I dreamed about a camel."

Will took the turn off the highway and the low building of the airfield crept into view. He pulled in alongside the other vehicles dropping off, and unloaded Beth's bags onto the dusty concrete path.

"Thanks for all your chauffeuring," said Beth, as they faced each other.

"No problem," said Will. "What are you going to do in Perth?"

"Probably Christmas shopping. But I want to see a patient, too."

They hovered in an electric arc of uncertainty. Beth imagined his arms sliding around her, the right kind of goodbye. But neither of them moved.

Another car tooted to be let into the drop-off zone. So Will gave a reluctant half-wave, and pulled himself into the Pathfinder's cab.

"Don't work too hard," she called.

A moment later, she was alone, sweating in the sun with her bags and the dissipating tendrils of what could have been. Beth sighed. Without looking back, she trekked towards the terminal.

Chapter 14

On Saturday morning, Beth strode into the Prince Harry Hospital in central Perth and breathed a lungful of the familiar hospital cleaner. It seemed an age since she'd set foot in a medical facility large enough to warrant elevators and a directory board. Her body fell into the old rhythm: she found the lift and punched the floor number. But as she rode up to Respiratory Medicine, that same feeling of habit nagged at her. It was just like Royal Sydney back home, where she'd become stuck in a pattern that had led her nowhere. Thank goodness today she had a specific reason for being here.

At the nurses' desk, she introduced herself as Caitlin's doctor from Iron Junction.

"That's fine," the nurse said warmly, after inspecting her ID. "Tricia Forrest is one of the registrars. She'd be happy to talk to you."

Five minutes later, she found herself in an office with Doctor Forrest, a petite woman with fair hair tied in a ponytail and an eager expression behind her glasses.

"Thanks so much for taking the time," Beth said. "I know how busy the ward can be. But I was really concerned about Caitlin's lung function and I wanted to see how she was doing."

"Of course," said Doctor Forrest. "The first few days were

tough. Her respiratory capacity is a fraction of what it should be at her age, and the infection was extremely refractory. She deteriorated and spent two days in intensive care. It was touch and go, I have to tell you. Fortunately, she's over the worst."

Doctor Forrest clicked on the computer and brought up the lung-function test results, and the X-rays from Caitlin's first week in the hospital. Beth felt an immense relief that she'd managed to get Caitlin on the plane, and simultaneously, the sinking realization of how serious her condition was.

"What does it mean for her when she goes home?"

"She's extremely susceptible to further infections, and she doesn't have much capacity to deal with it. She might not survive another infection like that and she's requiring some oxygen support now. She needs to be on the transplant list, and to hope to have one in the next year."

Beth accepted this. "Why isn't she on it already?"

Doctor Forrest tipped her glasses onto her head. "Our discussions haven't been very productive. She does seem to want to get better, but she wants to go home. We're doing the pre-transplant work-up and education, but she isn't committed to going ahead. I'm not giving up yet, though."

When Beth left Doctor Forrest, she wandered down the ward to a four-bed room. Two of the curtains were closed, and one open with an empty bed. Caitlin occupied the fourth bed, closest to the window overlooking central Perth. She sat on the edge, her barrel chest hunched.

"Knock, knock," said Beth.

Caitlin looked around with a weary expression that changed to surprise. "Beth," she croaked. "I thought you were one of the nurses."

Caitlin looked a different woman from when Beth had seen her last; she still had nasal oxygen prongs but her eyes were unclouded, her lips no longer dry. Beth saw a small camera in her lap, just a point-and-click type that people took on holidays. "Missing your Canon?" Beth asked.

"Yeah. The nurses lent me this one."

Beth sunk into the visitor's chair under the window. "Is it any good?"

Caitlin shrugged. "It works, but it's limited. Film would be better. Where's your Minolta?"

"I left it at the hotel, but I was thinking of taking it out tomorrow."

"Where to?" asked Caitlin, her eyes lit with interest.

"I'm really not sure. I don't know Perth at all. I'll have to get a tourist map or something."

Caitlin sighed and looked out the window into the fierce afternoon sun. "I'd do awful things to get out of here."

She keyed through a few buttons and passed the camera to Beth. "Here."

Even on the three-inch screen, Beth could see the artistry. Caitlin had lined the sun up behind one of the city buildings, casting its face into near blackness, while sunlight beamed out from one edge, a pillar of light above the hazy streets below. "Great shot," Beth said.

"Nah," said Caitlin. "Light's all wrong here."

Beth sighed. "I guess that's the difference between you and me. I can't see what's wrong with it."

But Caitlin waved her hand for Beth to be patient, took the camera back and changed the SD card. "Look, here, you'll see." She handed the camera back.

Beth flipped through the images. They were similar ideas: the sun caught behind an object in view, but vastly different pictures. In one, a wattle caught the sun, its rays blazing through yellow blooms and falling on a black scorched mass of timber in the foreground. In another, the sun danced between a natural rock fissure, the foreground rock thrown into ripples of red and ochre and black.

"Took them after a fire," Caitlin explained. "I had the card in my pocket."

Beth looked up. She could see the satisfaction and pride in Caitlin's eyes. Caitlin tapped the camera. "Place makes a difference. Up north, I can work. I feel right. Don't connect here."

Beth bit her lip. "Caitlin, if you had the transplant, you'd have a much easier time. You'd feel much better. You'd be able to do so much more."

Caitlin silently looked down at the bed, fingering the crisp white sheets. Beth couldn't help feeling how stark and clinical this room was, how it had not a shred of the emotion and passion she saw in Caitlin's pictures.

Caitlin took the camera back and unloaded the card. "I had a picture picked up once, a while back. It was of a protest, when the mining tax was new. Not my thing, but Reuters got it and it impressed people. So I thought maybe I could really make a go of it." She paused to cough, then gazed out the window. "I *do* want to be well again. Stop the coughing and the antibiotics and all of it. But I feel sicker here than when I'm up north. That's my country. I want the transplant, yeah. But I hate the city. And everyone needs me back there. My family, and the kids in the school. Don't know if you can understand that."

Beth leaned back in her chair. She thought about her own idea of home, what it was for her. Neither Brisbane nor Sydney, right now. And she'd come out here to get away. She experienced a wave of envy that Caitlin had a connection to one place and its people over another, that it meant so much to her that she would put her health second to it. "I don't know if I can really understand," she said finally. "But I can see the difference in your pictures. That one of Karijini got me the moment I saw it."

Caitlin smiled. "Karijini's in Banjima country. That's my dad's mob. My mum's white and I grew up in all these different places around Australia. But I never liked it. I went back up there as soon as I could."

Beth looked at her in surprise. "I thought your mum came with you down here?"

"Nah, I call her 'Mum' but that's really my aunty. I live with her up there in the Junction because that's where there's work. But my country's east. I want to get back there."

Beth saw the look in Caitlin's eye. "Promise me you'll stay until you finish the treatment."

Caitlin coughed a few times, then made a face. "I can't promise what I might not do. Sorry, Beth."

Beth left the hospital, pondering Caitlin Murray. She had never considered how much place meant to patients. She'd always thought a hospital was a hospital; you were sick, you went in, you got out and went home again. But maybe for some people home was too important to leave.

But her lack of influence made Beth uneasy. Despite the fact they had some kind of rapport, Caitlin wouldn't yield to what Beth saw was medical sense. And that might be the end of her.

The idea dogged Beth's steps back to the hotel. There, she pulled her shopping out onto her bed. The coffee machine for Tom, a silk bathrobe for Anne. She had nothing yet for Victoria or her mother. Before, she'd thought this was a sign she wasn't trying hard enough.

Now, Beth sat heavily beside the discarded bags and crisp new plastic, and rubbed her face. These things seemed paltry compared with what she wished for Caitlin.

Beth had settled into glum contemplation by the next morning, when she lay awake in the dark of her hotel room, flashes of the muted television playing on the sheets. A paralysis had crept into her thoughts. What was her next move? Should she go back to the hospital and talk to Caitlin again? Leave it alone and hope?

Go back to Sydney and sort her life out there?

A shrill ring jolted her upright, and she fumbled for her phone.

"Hello?" she said tentatively, sounding half-asleep.

"I seriously hope you're at the beach."

Will Walker. Beth felt a burst of nerves and quickly pulled herself together. She squinted towards the thick hotel curtains, tightly shut, and affected a groan. "No, seems I'm not."

Will sounded scandalized. "It's a *perfect* day. And you're wasting it where … oh, god, don't tell me you're watching TV in your hotel room."

Beth grabbed the remote and flicked off the offending set. "I was weak," she admitted. "I think it was on all night."

"Tell me it wasn't home shopping." In the background, Beth heard a surge of power-tool noise and male voices.

"Worse," said Beth, putting her head in her hands. "I've watched a *Miami Ink* re-run marathon on cable. I almost went and got a tattoo myself."

Will laughed. "I should have warned you. You have to look out for the trappings of the FIFO lifestyle, right?"

"What do you mean?"

"If you find yourself buying a jet ski, a performance car and a big-screen TV you never watch, it's too late," he said.

"Uh oh," said Beth. "Why do I have a receipt here from Kawasaki?"

Will laughed. "You are a lost cause. So, you went to the beach yesterday?"

Beth plucked at the rumpled bed sheets. "Actually, I went to the Prince Harry to see a patient."

"Working; bad as me," said Will. A burst of mechanical noise screamed down the line.

"What on earth are you doing?" Beth asked, scooting out of bed.

"I'm back in Iron Junction, dealing with the plant tie-in. It's not pretty. Why are you seeing patients and not going to the beach?"

Beth flung the curtains aside and winced as the Perth summer sun struck her night-adapted eyes. "She's a photographer, too," she said. "And besides, I want to see how soon she can come home."

"Is that Caitlin Murray?"

Beth paused. "How did you know?"

Will's footsteps came down the line, boots on metal. "Matt knows her family. He mentioned she was sick and in Perth. How's she doing?"

"Better," said Beth, not knowing how to capture the complexity of Caitlin.

"Good. But you didn't answer my other question," he said.

Beth took in the view. The sky was a perfect summer blue, the clouds lofty and soft, just enough to prevent over-exposure. Her fingers rested on the window glass; she was trapped in here. Her eyes roamed for the bedside table, where her Minolta rested, a fresh roll of film in its belly. Her mood lifted.

"I'm leaving soon," she said.

"Excellent. My work here is done. At least, I wish it was. Make sure you get to Cottesloe. It's amazing."

Beth paused in rummaging for her shorts. "Will?"

"Yeah?"

"Is everything okay there?"

"Nothing I can't handle. Enjoy yourself. Show me a picture."

Beth stopped, shorts and T-shirt hanging from her hand, aware that even over the distance of the phone, their connection was now firm. "Will. Why did you call?"

"That's what friends do."

Chapter 15

Third swing

On Tuesday morning, Beth found herself deep in catch-up appointments but glad to be back in clinical territory. All the while, Caitlin was in her thoughts. No further progress had been made about the donor list, but Beth was still hopeful. She'd caught the coach back to Iron Junction with a new perspective, camera in her hands as the Pilbara's splashes of red earth, spectrum greens and blue sky streaked past. It seemed more alive than she'd noticed before.

Maybe it was the time of year; the medical center was now thick with Christmas decorations, complete with fake snow ludicrously lumped in the sills of the windows. Beth hummed carols about reindeer as she showed a burly patient down the hall.

"You know it's thirty-five degrees outside," said Maxine as she passed. The older doctor had already informed Beth of two more gonorrhea cases while Beth had been away, and seemed to be in a bad mood.

"It's all right, love, I'll teach you the Aussie version," said her patient with a grin.

But even Maxine couldn't dent Beth's enthusiasm. She hadn't sorted what she was doing for Christmas yet, but she was back in love with her camera, back doing the work she enjoyed. Even two cases of hemorrhoids this morning couldn't get her down, so what could go wrong?

The answer showed itself soon after midday when Jennifer appeared in the tea-room doorway, just as Beth had finished for lunch. "Dale King's here to see you, Beth."

Beth sighed. She'd hoped to be done with Dale after the presentations.

"I don't have long before my next appointment," she told him as he came into her consultation room.

He braced his fingers together. "Well, I'll get straight to it. I'm disappointed the presentations didn't go to plan."

Beth frowned. "I'm not sure what you mean."

"The presentations were developed with very specific ideas in mind, to meet our corporate goals, and Doctor Gregg's content was approved. You didn't have the authority to change it."

He glanced towards the open door. Beth had an inkling that Dale very much wanted to tell her off but he was calculating who might hear. She was glad to be on her own turf, but anger prickled her cheeks. She'd been in a good mood, dammit.

"I had to make some changes. No one could pay attention. I retained all the critical information and I think there's more chance the workers did, too," she argued.

"You obviously don't appreciate the situation. You might think that you've done a good job, but how do I know that? The company spent money to do these talks to achieve specific aims. How do I know that's happened? That we haven't just wasted resources?" Dale's neck was bright red now, his words angry while his face remained curiously still.

Beth hesitated. She'd been pleased with the presentations; the workers had reacted well. They'd learned things.

Hadn't they?

"But I've got a folder full of positive feedback."

"But from who?" Dale demanded. "I'm sure anyone would give you a tick if they were entertained, and that sounds very much like what went on. You're here to fill in and you haven't done what you were asked. I should report you."

Beth's stomach clenched, but something wasn't right about this – report her to who? She wouldn't allow him to treat her with disdain. Slowly, she stood. Her hands shook as she stepped into the hall. "I have patients to see," she said. "I'm sorry you're unhappy, but there's nothing I can do about it now." And with that, she walked away, heading to the desk for her next file.

Dale collected himself and stalked out, ignoring Jennifer's goodbye.

"What was that about?" asked Maxine, appearing at the tea-room door. Beth wondered how much she'd heard.

"I changed the presentations and he wasn't happy."

Maxine looked Beth up and down. "Come and have a talk with me at the end of the day."

Beth then had to apologize to her next patient – an attractive young woman looking for a pill script refill. Beth checked her blood pressure and, noting she was a new patient, started on other opportunistic checks. With the other STI cases in the back of her mind, she said, "While you're here, there's a couple of other things I'd like to talk about around sexual health. Would that be all right?"

The woman smiled. "Okay."

"Have you had a pap smear in the past two years?"

"Oh, yes, I'm all up to date."

"Great," Beth smiled. "And what about an STI check-up?"

"Yes, I had one last month. All clear."

Beth nodded. "Good. Well, you certainly are proactive."

The woman smiled again. "Of course. You have to be in this industry."

Beth tilted her head. "Which industry is that?"

A pause. "Escorts. Sorry, I thought you realized. You know, with the questions. Usually the town doctors work it out when there's contractors around. Too much good business."

"Well, no. I'd ask those questions of anyone who'd come in

about the pill. Especially a new patient." She paused, considering. "But it's an isolated place out here. Do you ever feel unsafe?"

"These sorts of places are usually all right," the woman said. "There's less time wasters, actually. But honestly, this town's getting a bad vibe about it."

"Bad vibe?"

"Yeah. Lots of people are aggressive. And the motel's getting nosy. I reckon it's going to be a hassle soon, so I'm moving on."

Beth told the woman to look after herself. But, as she moved to the next appointment, she couldn't help but wonder about Dale, and these tensions leaking from the mine.

After the long afternoon, Beth flicked off her consult-room lights and knocked on Maxine's door. The other doctor was focused on her computer screen, one hand on her chin and only her eyes moving as she clicked through the pages. Her graying hair stuck out from her head in different directions.

She turned to face Beth. "So, you've made good friends with Dale King."

"Hardly." She leaned against the wall. "I don't understand. He got angry because I changed the presentations, even though the feedback was excellent. Two weeks ago, he tried to change the treatment I recommended for a patient with a back injury. I've seen quite a few injuries. And one of the workers mentioned that things were being rushed, that some workers' injuries might not even be coming in. But when I asked him about it, Dale said injuries were nothing to worry about."

"Anything else?" Maxine pressed.

"When I said I didn't want to do the off-site presentations, he intimated he'd give a bad report to my agency."

Maxine scowled and leaned back in her chair. "Sit down, Beth."

Beth dutifully sat.

"King's been here less than a year," Maxine said. "A lot of the town think he's charming. But I've heard about people leaving the mine. And that never used to happen. I've seen managers like him before. He wants to be in control of everything. Anyone who gets in his way either gets in line or gets out."

Beth frowned. "Great. Which are you?"

Maxine scoffed. "I stay out of the way. But don't worry … if you can get Caitlin Murray to Perth, you can handle King while you're here. I'm just waiting for him to move on to something bigger. That's the best thing for everyone."

"Speaking of Caitlin," Beth started, "I visited her in Prince Harry on the weekend. She was looking much better. She was taking photos out the window."

Maxine tucked a pen behind her ear. "That's more than I've got her to do in two years. I'm impressed."

Beth felt only a moment's satisfaction at the praise. "She hasn't agreed to go on the transplant list, though."

"Don't hold your breath."

"She said she felt sicker down in Perth," said Beth. "That's why she doesn't want to be there."

Maxine sighed. "Yes, of course." She glanced at Beth, who knew she looked incredulous. "What?"

"I'm just surprised," Beth said slowly. "I didn't think you had any sympathy for Caitlin."

Maxine shook her head, her South African accent thickening. "Oh, I've got bags of sympathy. All those blacks up here have been uprooted and shoved around. Displaced and broken up and put back together in new places. Caitlin isn't from this town; her family come from further east. Her father got moved here years ago, before the mine, onto stations. Then her mother dragged her off to the city. Think about what it's like to lose your homeland like that."

Maxine's face was lit with fire. "I know what that's like. It changes you inside when other people take what's in your soul. I've got sympathy in plenty." She paused. "But sympathy doesn't help. It's a long line of awful things. Her lungs are broken because of who she is and where she lives. Because she's black and she had terrible pneumonia when she was small. If she were white and lived in a city, everyone would be outraged. It's the same in lots of places. Misogyny and racism and every other ism. But I'm a doctor and I have a doctor's tools. And for her that means going to Perth or onto a transplant list."

Beth took a breath, glimpsing the deep pool under Maxine's demeanor. There was more to this woman than she knew.

But the fire dimmed as quickly as it had flared. "I'm glad she decided to take a positive step, even if it's only one." Maxine turned back to her screen, the discussion over. "I don't suppose you called in on Doctor Gregg while you were down there?"

"No. I don't know him at all," said Beth.

"Oh well, no great loss there." She stood up and gestured to Beth that it was time to go. "Not that he isn't competent, but you're much more interesting to have on the staff."

Coming from Maxine, Beth wasn't quite sure how to take this. "Thanks," she said finally, deciding it must be praise.

"He's supposed to be recovering," added Maxine as she strode towards an ancient Ford Laser with a missing hub cap. "You'd better make the most of Friday night."

Beth stopped in the gathering dusk, the heat radiating upwards from the day-cooked earth. "What's Friday night?"

"Music festival, remember? See you tomorrow."

As Beth watched Maxine tear off down the street towards the house she must have somewhere in town, she wondered what had happened to Maxine; why she too had chosen to leave her home and come to live in this place.

Beth sighed as she trekked towards her flat. She may never find out. Her days as Doctor Gregg's replacement were shrinking with every moment.

Chapter 16

By Friday afternoon, Beth wondered just how gargantuan this event was that the company was putting on in town. Steadily through the day, trucks had rumbled past the medical center bound for the showground, and the atmosphere was charged. Every child who came through the center's doors chattered about the carols, which from the flyer Beth understood was the family event before the full extravaganza kicked off at nine.

"Are you going?" Beth asked Jennifer, who was standing near the glass doors watching the trucks.

"Sure. Wouldn't miss it. Did you know they had Keith Urban last year?"

Beth, who had no appreciation for country music, tried to look impressed. "What about Maxine?"

Jennifer shrugged. "Unlikely. But come by the bar tent if you go, we'll probably be in there before the fireworks."

Beth considered calling Will, but knowing how busy he'd been at work, decided against it. So, around eight, in the same singlet and cargos she'd worn out to Iron Bluff, she wandered towards the showground. Iron Junction's tidy streets were choked with parked cars, many sporting mine insignia and the bug-peppered windscreens of long-distance travel. When she reached the showground, tucked between the edge of the mine camp's temporary buildings and the town's houses, Beth found it dotted with company tents and teeming with people. A big stage drew the heaviest crowd, all holding lit candles, and the final strains of "Silent Night" were being sung in various melodies, accompanied by a string quartet on stage.

Beth made her way to the edge of the crowd and stood beside a tent wall so she could watch the children wave candles and sing along. The melody soaked through her, evoking a nostalgia for Christmas quite unlike one she'd ever experienced. One that was soft and gentle, that soothed her heart. The bar tent was nearby, all its occupants in twos and threes, laughing with each other. Her first and brief thought was what a great shot it would make: the mix of mining blues and country checks, steel caps and cowboy boots. She wanted to share that with someone and again, Will entered her thoughts.

"Doctor Harding," said a voice.

Beth turned to find Mack ambling over, his limp making the beer in his cup slosh with each step. "Hi, Mack."

He stopped and leaned against a speaker pole. "Great, isn't it? Some of the families drive for hours to come."

"I had no idea it would be so big," Beth said.

"Well, the mine's good at following through on things like this. They've got a reputation and goodwill to uphold, eh?" Mack chuckled. "The manager plays Santa every year."

Beth tried to smile, but the thought of Dale in such a role seemed distasteful.

"Anyway, doc, your latest lot of photos came back today. Come and pick them up tomorrow."

Beth said that she would but Mack hovered, concern in his eyes. "Listen, one other thing. Can you tell me anything about how Caitlin's doing?"

"I actually saw her on the off-swing," said Beth. "She was looking much better. I'm sure she'll be back before long."

"Good," said Mack. "Well, I'll leave you to it."

Soon, Beth was alone again. She rubbed her arms, wondering whether to stay for much longer. The carols were wrapping up now, the performers on stage taking their bows. The volume in the bar tent rose and fell.

Then suddenly, a wave of gooseflesh ran up Beth's arms.

"Hello, stranger."

Will appeared beside her, tall and handsome in fresh jeans and a white T-shirt, and smelling unidentifiably amazing. "Hey, Will," she said. The way he looked at her, she almost regretted agreeing to only be friends. The night immediately took on a distinctly sparkly quality.

Will leaned in beside her. "So, you came for the fireworks?"

"I don't know why I came, actually."

"Are you waiting for someone?"

"Not anymore," she said, then wished she could take it back as the conflict over how she felt about him unfurled within her.

Will only looked pleased. A boom sounded, and the first firework streaked skyward behind the stage, a glittering trail lit in red and green and gold. Cheers erupted, and excited clapping. The display went on for ten minutes, all to an upbeat Christmas soundtrack, which finished with "Rocking around the Christmas tree". When the final strains ended and the children were being ushered out, Will leaned in. "Drink? Come on," he said, and led her towards the bar tent.

Inside, the crowd was thick and lively, Jimmy Barnes pumping from the speakers. Will tried to draw her with him, but looking at the jostling bodies, Beth pulled up near the entrance. "I'll wait here."

"You sure?" Will's brow furrowed. "Okay, won't be long."

Beth seriously doubted it, but she sat on a stool and watched the crowd. It was different from the Re-Bar in town; there, most of the men looked as though they belonged to the town, or at least to the mine. They knew their way around. Here, a restless energy coursed through the gathering. Beth couldn't know for sure, but most people seemed to be from out of town, sizing each other up. Or maybe they were just more contractors. She became aware of a body alongside her, a young man with a stubbled jaw and a blue shirt, beer-crossed eyes and a cap sporting the company's logo.

"How's it goin'?" he asked, leaning in to compensate for the music.

"Fine, thanks," said Beth, catching breath like an old bar mat.

"Havin' a good time?"

He was too close. "Yes, thanks," she said, edging away.

He edged along with her. "Buy you a drink?"

"No, thanks," she said.

He backed off muttering, "Typical in this fucking town."

Beth suddenly wished she hadn't let Will go ahead. Eventually she spotted him, struggling out of the crowd with two beers. Seeing her face, he glanced over her shoulder. "What happened? You look white."

"Fine," she said brightly. Will fixed his gaze back over her shoulder; she saw the way his body shifted, like a lion bristling before competition. He let it go, but Beth sensed tension. An atmosphere was developing in the tent like a thundercloud.

"Why does it feel all weird in here?" she asked.

Will shrugged but after ten minutes of conversation made impossible amid the noise, their beers not even a quarter finished, he shook his head. "Screw it. Let's go somewhere else."

It was then that a glass smashed outside, and raised voices ripped through the canvas.

Will stiffened, listening. "Stay here," he said abandoning his beer and heading for the exit.

Beth obeyed for five seconds before she followed him, and walked into a different world. A loud ring of men jostled in the bar's courtyard, with two at the center – the man in the cap who'd hit on her earlier, and a burly-looking guy in a company shirt. Beth was struck by the animal energy in the group, how the mood had turned savage. Danger signals pulsed in her brain. She spotted Mack in the circle's center, hands raised, failing to settle them down.

"Typical!" cap man was saying. "These fuckers come in for the good money, strip the guts out of the place, then piss off somewhere else when it's all done. Local guys can't get a look-in."

The burly bloke thumped cap man's chest. "Fuck you, mate. Your pissy mine can't pay its bills, couldn't organize a root in a whorehouse. Not our fault you locals can't do the work."

In response, cap man threw his fist. Mack was shoved aside and slammed into the ground. Beth then watched as Will shouldered his way in, shoving cap man backwards. "Break it up," he yelled. Beth's heart leapt in her throat, conscious of the number of men, of how outnumbered Will and Mack were, and of the fact that Mack hadn't risen.

"Fucking contractors," spat the cap guy, lunging towards Will, elbow first. But Will dropped his shoulder and shoved back like a one-man scrum, then straightened out, using his voice like a sledgehammer. "I said knock it off!" he roared. "I don't care how this started. I mean it, Grinner. I'm your boss, so pull your head in. Do you all want to get fired?"

Chills crawled over Beth's skin. Will had always been easygoing with her; to witness this power display, a man who would go alone against a fight circle, was to glimpse dimensions within him she'd never seen before. He had courage, or maybe it was stupidity.

Whatever it was, it seemed to work. The crush dispersed. Half the crowd went back to the tables, the others stalked away towards town. Beth rushed to Mack, who'd pulled himself onto his side. At that moment, a new band counted themselves in and music roared from the outdoor speakers. Beth had to raise her voice. "Are you hurt?"

Mack grimaced, holding his hip. "Nah, just having trouble getting up."

"Here." Beth glanced up to find Will, blood running from

the corner of his eye, offering Mack his hand. Her stomach lurched. When Mack was on his feet again and protesting that he was fine, Beth and Will guided him towards an upturned log seat.

After five minutes it seemed Mack was fine, so Beth pulled Will aside and gently turned his chin. "How bad is it?"

Will gave her a small smile. "You tell me." Beth inspected the split skin high on his cheekbone, trying not to shake. She never shook looking at an injury. "I need better light and some equipment. If you come with me to the medical center, I can patch it up there," she said.

Will's eyes were flat in the dim light. Around them, the bar crowd murmured in an undercurrent to the music. Beth sensed the unnatural calm and spotted three blue-clad security people at the other end of the tent. "Nah, this way," he said. "My place is closer."

Beth followed Will around the edge of the showground, and then into the passages between the mine camp's temporary buildings. Each block was the size of a shipping container, the same as Beth had experienced in the camp in East Angelas. Here, the rows were wider, the buildings less well established. The noise from the showground fell away behind them. In one of the dark passages, Will's fingers found her hand, guiding her around a bend, which set Beth's heart racing. When the path lights kicked in again he released her, leaving only his warmth on her skin.

In the next row, he inserted a key and pushed open a door. Inside, a large bed, neatly made, occupied the short wall, facing a flat-screen television, a desk and a small bar fridge. The desk was stacked with motoring and travel magazines. Will's room.

He pulled a duffel bag from under the desk and rummaged through. "Here," he said, passing over a field first-aid kit. "Always prepared."

"Right," said Beth, closing the door as Will sat in the desk chair. She took a good look at the cut under the light. "What was all that about, anyway?" she asked, trying to ignore the silence and proximity to him in the intimacy of his room.

Will shrugged. "Townies and contractors striking sparks off each other. The site work's rough and a lot of people are fed up. Morale's low. It just takes a few beers and someone to start shooting their mouth off."

Beth rifled through the kit, extracting steristrips and antiseptic. "Would you really have fired them?" she said.

"I can't. That was just a bluff. Lucky it worked."

Beth paused and caught his eye, her stomach twisting in concern.

His lips curved in a smile. "Don't worry. I thought it would work."

Beth returned to cleaning the cut. Will winced.

"Sorry," she murmured.

"It's okay. I'm tough," said Will. But he looked relieved when she packed the medical supplies away.

Beth leaned against the desk, her insides still tangled, trying to reconcile the new image she had of him. "You feel fine?"

"Sure. In fact, I'm hungry. Did you eat already?"

"No. But I don't really feel like going back down there."

Will stood up. "No need. As long as you can tolerate kettle cooking." He produced two sets of cup noodles and two beers from the fridge.

Soon the noodles had steeped, and they sat on the edge of the bed. Beth poked at the rehydrating chunks of carrot with her fork as Will demolished his. She managed to match him by half, distracted by his proximity, spending too many thoughts on wanting to kiss him again. But then, where could that lead that wasn't complicated?

Will soon put the spent cup aside. "Are you going home for Christmas?"

"I don't know yet."

He stood up and dropped his empty bottle into the bin. "Another one?" he asked, opening the fridge.

"I should leave you alone and let you recover," said Beth, although going home to her flat wasn't appealing.

"I'll recover either way. Stay for a bit and finish eating. Now, can I tempt you?"

Beth allowed herself to smile. "You know, drinking won't solve my problems."

"No, but it does solve being sober," said Will, twisting the cap off. He grinned. "Joking."

Beth laughed.

"That's better," he said, sitting back down beside her. "In fact, do you know what? I have a surprise for you."

Beth raised her eyebrows.

"Behold." He flicked on the TV, cruising through the satellite channels until the opening credits of *Tattoo Nightmares* splashed across the screen.

Beth groaned as she scooted back onto the covers. "Oh, no … I can't watch this," she said with glee, resting the noodles between her knees.

"Yeah, you are addicted, aren't you," said Will, moving up beside her, but keeping some careful space between them. "It's bound to be a marathon, too."

"Stop it," said Beth happily. "I have work tomorrow."

By the end of the second set of credits, Beth was yawning. Will muted the TV as the news came on, the bulletin beginning with a cross to a reporter outside a courthouse. The ticker scrolled: The prime minister had been on a surprise visit to the troops in Afghanistan; a heat wave was forecast for the Christmas week.

Beth sighed. "I have to go." If she didn't, she could easily end up doing something she would no doubt regret.

Will prodded the dressing on his face.

"Try not to touch it," she added, sliding her shoes on.

"I'll walk you back."

Beth paused, wavering. He looked so appealing in his jeans

and T-shirt, his long legs over the side of the bed, hair ruffled where he'd had his hand behind his head. Definitely a bad idea. "No, I'm fine. I'll stay clear of the bars."

She slowly opened the door into the evening air. The strains of a banjo floated from the showground. She hesitated. "Hey, Will?"

"Mmm?" He was still sitting on the bed, watching her. Her stomach fluttered.

"How do you do it?"

"Do what?" He rubbed his hair, a warm smile breaking on his face.

"The traveling thing. You said your dad didn't want you to leave home, but you did anyway. How do you not second-guess yourself?"

For a second, Beth saw a strong emotion fly into Will's features. "You remember the first week you were here, and people were talking about you getting stranded?"

Beth groaned. "Yes, of course."

"Stuff like that used to happen all the time when I was growing up – people talking about other people like it mattered so much what anyone else thought. You can't let them pull you down." He stood and leaned on the wall beside her. "I knew I wanted to get away from the farm, that I wanted to do *this*—" he waved a hand generally at the camp "—so I did it. Who's life is it, anyway?"

Beth rested her head on the doorframe. "And what if I don't know what I want?" she said quietly.

Will gave her a knowing smile. "Yes, you do. You just have to admit it."

Beth wanted him to be right, but delving into all the muck of how she'd left Sydney and what she was doing here – not to mention her feelings about Will – made her feel sick. "Okay. I'm going now."

"Hey, Beth?"

She turned in the doorway. "Yeah?"

"This was fun. I'm glad we met." He met her eyes, sincere and unembarrassed.

A wanting unfurled in Beth's chest. She wanted to say she was grateful for who he was, for respecting her wishes, for being gentle with her feelings, but none of that captured the intensity of what she felt. "Yes, it was," she said finally.

"But I do think it's a good idea you go now." His eyes were full of longing.

Beth had to drag herself away. She returned to her flat through the still-crowded streets, retreating from the distant rise and fall of the music. Once inside, she leaned against the closed door, thinking, trying to rationalize the impulse to call Will. Restless, she woke her computer. Ten messages. She deleted the spam, and "We miss you" emails from five Sydney businesses. All that remained were two messages from Tom, and one from Vicky, whose subject line read *Engagement Party*.

Beth clicked on it with a twinge. *Hi Beth!* it began. *I hope you're okay. Mum was pretty mad but I swear I held off telling her for as long as I could. Anyway, we decided on our engagement party – it's going to be so much fun you MUST come, see attached!! Vicky*

Beth rubbed her temples and opened the attachment – a flash party invitation to a restaurant at Brisbane's Riverside. Then Beth's eyes fell on the date: 31 December.

New Year's Eve. The date Richard had proposed.

And Victoria knew that.

Numbly, Beth closed the laptop. She waited for the emptiness to consume her, for the familiar loss and guilt to claw at her insides. But it didn't. She flipped to the back page of her album and extracted the photo of Richard. He was as familiar as ever, a part of her life she remembered well. But the pain when she looked at him was dull.

Well, that was new.

The next day Will's shift dragged on – tools were missing, equipment down for maintenance. The tension from the previous evening between the town miners and the contractors remained on low boil. But eclipsing all of this were thoughts of Beth Harding.

A dozen times, he considered calling her. Playing it cool and easy, just the friends they were supposed to be; not showing any sign he could barely keep his hands off her last night, and that it was far more than a shallow attraction.

He recognized the symptoms. First, he was too curious about Richard and what had happened between them. He wanted to cheer her up; wanted her to confide in him. He wanted to be special to her.

She'd been very clear last week that they could only be friends. But he couldn't take back the memory of what it had been like to kiss her.

At lunchtime, he grabbed his phone. There was only one person he could call.

"Mark Walker."

"It's Will."

Mark was typically happy to hear Will's voice, which put a lump in Will's throat. "How's everything?" he asked, a little impatient.

"Great," said Mark. "Daniella gets here tomorrow for a week off. You in Perth?"

"On-site," he said tightly. He didn't know how to start this conversation. A long, obvious silence stole upon them.

"Something's up," Mark said finally. "Is it about that letter? Spill it."

"I met this girl, Beth Harding. She's a doctor working out of Iron Junction. I found her on the side of the road when I drove in. She had a flat battery."

Mark laughed. "Seriously, she's a doctor too? Nice going. That work out well for you?"

"Yes and no. I had to drive her around sites on this work thing last week." He explained the job to Mark, but he was avoiding the heart of the issue.

Finally, Mark said, "I'm sensing a question in all this. What's happened? You obviously like her. What's the problem?"

"Wants to be friends. She's just broken up with someone. And I've been seeing this other girl off and on down in Perth."

"Who?"

"Some dick called Richard."

Mark laughed. "Not who's she broken up with. Who've you been seeing?"

Will regretted mentioning it. "Never mind about that. My point is, I don't know what to do."

"She's going to get over this other bloke eventually, right?"

"Yeah," said Will, pressing his face into his hand. "But I … don't feel good enough for her."

"Why the hell not?"

Will paused. "I just don't."

"Maybe you should let her decide that," said Mark. "You know, Will, this really doesn't sound like you. You sure this working FIFO isn't getting to you?"

Will tried to laugh. "Maybe."

"You remember last year when I was losing my shit over Daniella and you gave me some good advice?"

"Yeah?" said Will, feeling hopeful.

"Well, you're my brother and I love you, but let's face it: you're usually the one for good advice. What would you say if it were me asking you this?"

Will rubbed his face. "I'd probably say go with what feels right, or some shit like that."

"There you go, then."

Will had a sinking feeling. What felt right was selfish on his part. He'd been hoping for some kind of magical insight that would tell him how he could settle this upheaval in his chest: of wanting Beth against her wishes, and even with all the bad history he had pressing down on him. A little voice tried to speak to him in that moment, one that whispered of righting wrongs, of home and history. He pushed it aside.

"Okay," he said finally. "Dad all right?"

Mark paused in the face of this question Will asked, every time. Will could not have explained it to Mark; how he could love his father and yet be incapable of speaking to him. How the years had stretched the estrangement so wide Will could no longer see across it.

"He's fine," said Mark wearily. "I don't suppose I can convince you to come home for Christmas? Daniella and Cat will both be here. Everyone would love to see you."

"Thanks, but no," said Will firmly. No other answer was possible. They said their goodbyes and hung up.

Will thumbed through the menus on his phone. Sitting in messages were two week-old texts from Sarah, neither of which he'd answered. Man, what a mess. He stepped out of the office and onto the dusty walkway. The clear Pilbara sky greeted him, the plant calling for attention. A month ago, it was all he'd needed.

Now, he wasn't so sure.

Chapter 17

Late on Sunday afternoon, just as Beth had finished her appointments, the phone rang. Maxine had already left for the day, and Jennifer raced back to the desk to pick it up. "Medical center."

Beth waited by the doors, just in case, and a moment later Jennifer put her hand over the phone. "It's the mine. They want you to come out."

"Why? We don't do calls out there. We're not supposed to."

"They said a guy's broken his arm and he's refusing to come in here."

Beth frowned. "Well, let's hope it's not actually broken."

Beth remembered her way to the mine from the ill-fated presentation day, and she was greeted at the door by a man she hadn't met before.

"Doctor Harding? This way," he said.

Beth followed him down the hall and out a back door into a patch of long shadows.

"Can you tell me what happened?" Beth asked after him.

The man slowed so he could talk to her. "One of the contractors was welding a rail on top of a dozer and slipped coming down. We think he broke his arm 'cause it looks funny. But he doesn't want to go in."

"Why not?" Beth said.

"Ask him," said the man, shrugging. "Here we are."

They came to a room that was obviously some kind of first-aid station. The guy lay on the bed, his thick arm protectively cradled across his wide chest. Beth recognized him as the man who'd thrown punches at the music-festival bar. Another man in work gear stood over him, and two others hovered by the end of the bed, one of whom was a short, dark-skinned man. The other was Will Walker. Beth and Will exchanged a brief glance, his concern obvious.

"Grinner, this is the doctor," Beth's guide announced. "And that's our first-aid man, Scott."

Beth made a quick assessment. Scott was trying to persuade Grinner to have his arm put in a sling, but Grinner's face was pale, drawn and belligerent.

"Everyone out for now," she said. Scott gratefully stepped back.

Beth introduced herself and reached for Grinner's uninjured wrist. "Is Grinner your real name?" she asked.

Grinner's eyes flickered. A trickle of sweat ran down his face. "No. It's Mike," he said finally.

"How bad's your pain, from zero to ten?" asked Beth.

"Nine." Grinner swallowed. "It's bad."

"Okay, I want to take care of that." She stuck her head out the door and found Scott and Will hovering. "Where are your painkillers?"

"Like Panadol?" Scott asked.

"No. Like morphine."

"Ah, it's in a locked box in one of the cabinets. We're supposed to ask the assigned responsible doctor before we can give it out," he said.

"That's her, you tool," said Will.

Scott flushed. "Right."

After Grinner's color had returned, Beth said to him firmly, "I need to check that everything's okay in your hand, which means feeling your pulse and checking you haven't got any numbness. I'm not going to move your arm and I'll be as gentle as I can."

Grinner nodded, though the whites of his eyes were wide. Beth felt for his wrist pulse; it was there, fast probably because of the pain, but strong. Sensation was another matter; his middle three fingers were numb.

"Are you having any pins-and-needles in your hand?" she asked.

"A bit, soon after it happened," said Grinner.

"Okay. Stay where you are."

Scott was nowhere to be found, but Will was still waiting in the corridor. "Call the center's after-hours number," Beth said, "and tell them we need an evac. I don't care whether it's a private contractor or the Flying Doctors, but Grinner needs to go off site."

Will took the orders like a soldier and strode off. Beth then went back to Grinner and tried to explain that his elbow was likely broken, that it might need surgery.

Grinner blanched afresh. "I need this job, doc."

"What does that mean?"

"I can't get injured. Can't I stay here?"

"You're already injured. Is that why you didn't want to come in?"

Grinner would say nothing more, and Beth could give him no choice. "Sorry, your arm's at risk, and that's more of a problem."

Grinner eventually acquiesced. Beth then had to stabilize the arm, and meet the community ambulance, which would ferry Grinner to the airstrip.

Finally, she watched the transfer ambulance lights disappear down the road. All beyond the mine was black now, not even the ridges visible against the sky.

Will's hand touched her shoulder. "You want a coffee?" he asked.

In the kitchenette, Beth stirred her milky brew. Will sat across from her, dusty from his work day, his long legs stretched out, meditatively stirring his own mug.

"Why would he think he's going to lose his job over this?" she asked.

"It shouldn't happen," he said. "But as a contractor, if you can't work you might just be let go. It doesn't show up in the statistics, then."

Beth mulled this over for a minute. "Another worker mentioned something like that to me. He was worried about 'being disappeared'. I thought things were meant to be great here. What's going on?"

Will shook his head. "I don't know. It's weird. The expansion's behind schedule, I think because we've lost staff and had equipment problems. But we should have been able to get back on track. Problem is, every time we've made up ground, our resources get diverted to the next stage of the project. Grinner's supposed to be on the plant, but here he is working on something else tonight. I don't understand what King's doing."

They sat in silence. Beth picked up a stale biscuit and dunked it until she lost it to the bottom of the cup. She pushed the lot away. "Dale King gives me the creeps," she said finally. "He threatened to tell my agency I was uncooperative. When I mentioned the injuries I've been seeing, he didn't care. And he told me off when I made those presentation changes, saying he should report me, which was weird."

"He threatened you?" Will's eyes glowered.

"Not directly. Just to give me a bad work report."

But she could see Will's expression darkening. "This job so isn't what I expected," she said hastily.

"It never is." Will leaned forward, fatigue pinching his eyes. "You were great today, you know that?"

"Thanks. I just wish I understood what was going on."

"Leave it with me." He offered his hand. Beth took it and he pulled her up.

In the car park, under the glare of a spotlight, she faced

him. "Thanks for your help."

He shrugged. "Have you decided on Christmas yet?"

Beth groaned, the strength going out of her arms. "No. You?"

"Well, I'm going to be off-swing, and I'm planning on staying in Perth. How about spending it with me?"

Beth's pulse accelerated. She should probably get on a plane and make the dash back to Brisbane; that was expected. But Will's allure had its grip on her now. "What did you have in mind?"

He looked into her eyes. "Just taking it easy. Go to the beach. Stay in the aircon … maybe play Mario Kart."

Beth swayed. "Don't taunt me. I used to love that. There was an old Super Nintendo in the student common room and I used to beat Tom all the time."

"Who's this Tom?" demanded Will. "And you can't scare me with victories past." He gave her an enticing eyebrow.

Beth bit her lip. Christmas in Perth with him was dangerously attractive, but she couldn't quite let go of the obligation to do what she did every year. "Can I let you know?" she asked.

"Offer's open," he said.

Before Will left the mine, he slipped into his desk chair. He brought up the incident database, which listed all the injuries that had happened on site. He scanned back through the entries, thinking of Beth's comments. With all identifying information removed, he couldn't tell who was who, but no entries had been made for a month. So, Garry and Wally hadn't been reported. Data entry might just be behind. But now there was Grinner, too.

He went back to the reports he'd found on stage two of the expansion and scanned them again. Executive summaries, proposed programs, resources … then, after half an hour, his eyes fell on a short paragraph of text. *Hydrology studies are incomplete, but recommendation is that works are undertaken outside the wet season, or a comprehensive analysis with modelling and risk assessment should be completed.*

Will frowned. Hydrology studies meant someone was concerned about water flow. Will grabbed his hard hat and gloves and strode down to the light-vehicle shed, snatched a set of keys from the rack, and scratched the number into the log-out book with a stubby pencil. He guided the pickup out into the dark mine night, swinging the headlights across the light-vehicle road, the truck's strobe casting a dusky splash across the bonnet. He drove for ten minutes, climbing steadily, passing only rumbling trucks on the adjoining haul road. Eventually, he reached the end of the access road, and when he climbed out, he found the dust dancing under massive spotlights below. There, scrapers and dozers lumbered, shifting earth under the glittering sky. So, this was stage two.

Will couldn't see the edges of it. He rubbed his mouth, astounded by the extent of the works. This was far more than getting started as King had implied; this was running full tilt. Something very strange was going on.

When he got back to the office, Will picked up his phone, then paused as he considered what he was about to do. King had made it clear that Will shouldn't involve outside parties. But, enough was enough. He had to figure out what was going on, or he feared the whole project could eat its budget in mistakes and time penalties.

He keyed in a number.

"Dan Beecham. I hope you know what time it is."

"Beer o'clock," answered Will. He could hear the roar of the East Angelas wet mess in the background. "Dan, no shitting around. You remember I told you there were problems here? It's bigger than I thought. I need you to sober up and think about getting in a car."

"Wait a minute."

Will heard the scuffling as Dan hauled himself out of the wet mess and shut the noise inside. "What's going on out there?"

"Something weird. I told you the plant expansion was behind. But King's mucking with the program and cutting corners, even when we don't have enough staff. And all the while – you remember me asking about stage two? It's running at full steam. I can't understand why. I'm way out of my depth."

Dan groaned. "I *knew* this was going to be a bad gig. But it's nearly Christmas and I've got some stuff going on."

Will caught a tone. "What kind of stuff?"

Dan tried to brush it off. "Family stuff. Wife reckons she wants a divorce."

"Christ, Dan. I didn't know."

"Oh, well. It's been coming for a while. But don't worry, that's what beer's for. And anyway, I want to find that senior engineer who was there before you. I'll ring you next week."

Will ended the call, concern for Dan and Iron Junction swirling together. He hoped next week was soon enough.

Back in her flat, as the air-conditioning clicked off, Beth paced the carpet. The evening's events stirred within her, refusing to settle. Part of it was about Grinner, but the other was Will and his invitation.

Slowly, she calmed herself. She flicked the television on, then off again. She opened her computer. In her inbox sat an email from her sister, wanting to know why she hadn't RSVP'd for the engagement party. With a noise of disgust, Beth shut the laptop lid. Energy itched under her skin, demanding to be let out. She had an irrational desire to rush off into the night, not caring where she went as long as it was somewhere else.

Clearly, time for a cold shower.

She was half undressed when her mobile rang. Her heart

skipped, wondering if it was Will. But on the phone's screen she saw a different familiar name.

"Tom!" she exclaimed as she shut off the shower.

"Doctor Harding, I presume," he joked. "How's that adventure of yours?"

"It's going all right," she answered, surprised that she almost meant it. "It's good to hear your voice."

"Are you drunk?"

"No," she said, flopping down on the bed.

"Hmm. You sound like you do after we've been to a keg. And you haven't answered any emails in a week."

Beth put her hand over her face. "I know, I know. I got distracted with ... stuff."

"Family stuff?"

Beth glanced at her laptop. "Not exactly."

"Oh, you're going to be mysterious?"

"Work stuff," she clarified.

"Boring. But fine, you're forgiven. It's Christmas next week. Are you coming to Sydney? You know my family would love to have you. I promise the beach and a metric ton of shrimp."

The offer was sorely tempting. Tom was fun and Beth had met his family on a number of occasions. But they were still his family, with their own traditions and connections that she could never share.

"Please don't go to Brisbane," said Tom, a rare act of begging. "You always feel awful about yourself afterwards."

"I do not," protested Beth. She didn't like having someone point it out.

"Yes, you do," insisted Tom. "Think about it."

Beth paced the carpet again; she'd wear a track in it soon. She tried to imagine jumping on a flight to Perth, then catching another one through to Sydney. Tried to imagine Christmas near her beloved Freshwater without once bumping into Richard.

It didn't feel right. Will's invitation returned to her, over and over again.

When she had said goodbye to a disappointed Tom, she glanced at the time. Ten-thirty; Will might be asleep. So, she typed him a text: *Were you serious about Mario Kart?*

To her surprise, a message quickly came back. *Deadly serious. Will there really be a metric ton of shrimp?*

Of course. It's Christmas.

Beth paused. *I'm in*, she wrote.

She turned her phone off. All the problems of Iron Junction could wait.

Chapter 18

"Why are we leaving so early?" complained Beth. "The flight's not until evening. Aren't we just going to be waiting around at the airfield?"

Dawn had just broken the following Friday, and Will had been unrelenting on the pick-up time. Now, finally, after turning up in board shorts and a T-shirt, he gave her a sly grin. "It's because I have a surprise for you."

Beth gave him a mock scowl. "Am I going to like it?"

Now, his smile was sweet. "I certainly hope so."

It wasn't until they missed the turn for Paraburdoo airport two hours later that Beth suspected that something was up. "Where are we going?"

Then, as they passed Tom Price, Will slowed for a left turn and Beth read *Karijini* on the brown-and-white direction sign.

"Karijini?" she asked.

Will kept his eyes on the road as he smiled.

Beth felt her face split into a huge grin.

The sun hadn't climbed far by the time Will took the turn-off into the park. Through the drive, Beth had watched the long morning shadows contract across a landscape of sunlit grasses and blood earth. She had never seen such color – soft gray-greens and bold emerald-greens, warm reds and harsh blacks, a landscape painted in richness. As they slowed into another turn, a flock of parrots streaked across their path:

green wings, yellow bellies and turquoise tails.

Soon, they passed a red, flattened airstrip and pulled into the visitor center, designed to look like a sculpted black ribbon flowing from the earth. "The center's not open yet," said Will, "but I figured we could come back here later if you like." He pointed to their location on a map.

"It's huge," said Beth, tracing her finger from the visitor center to where they'd entered the park. She turned it over and scrutinized the list of walks and gorges.

"Oh, I think I have an idea of where to start," said Will.

They drove east for fifteen minutes on a horribly corrugated road; Will expertly navigated around the worst section until he pulled off into a loop. Beth counted a few tents in the distance, but no life stirring. In a white singlet and shorts, warm air licked her arms and shoulders, but ahead, a deep crack in the earth promised cool.

Will opened the Pathfinder's rear door and pulled Beth's bag to the edge.

"What are you doing?" she asked.

"You'll want to bring your swimsuit," he said. Beth dug for them with a thrill in her veins.

Will led the way down a path. Over his shoulder Beth saw the gorge edges: like great stacked plinths of iron red rock, formed into giant stairs, each tread crowned with green. Nestled down in the gorge was an azure pool, and white water tumbled down the cliff sides towards it.

Beth consulted her map. "Fortescue Falls?" she asked, scrutinizing the trail down. She glanced at Will. He'd pulled on a beaten cowboy hat that she hadn't seen before, and looked comfortable in his T-shirt and shorts. Beth grinned and set off at a jog.

Soon, she had to slow her pace. The trail dropped along the gorge walls, and she had to be careful not to slip. The deeper they went, the cooler the air became, and ferns began to replace grasses on the rock walls. Finally, they stood beside the water. Beth had her hands on her camera and Will patiently waited while she took several shots. Then, as she moved to sit down, Will shook his head. "A bit further."

They followed a track upstream, Beth's fingers tingling with anticipation. Then, they reached a wooden platform and a scene from her mind opened before her. Here was another pool, nestled within rock figs and gums and cadjeput, and lined with grasses and reeds. Two water streams trickled in over a jutting rock. The air cradled them, cool and silent.

Beth was speechless. It was Caitlin's photo, and the picture had captured it perfectly. Beth felt the same soul she'd seen in the image, the same restfulness, the same love. Awed, she put her camera away, knowing she could never capture a worthy image and feeling wrong about trying.

Without a word, they stripped down to togs and slipped into the icy water. After a few minutes, Beth was certifiably numb. She climbed out and sat in the sun, warming herself until Will also gave up freezing and clambered out. It was then Beth noticed an angel tattoo in black and gray on the back of Will's left shoulder. "All those cable ink shows and you didn't tell me you had a tattoo?"

Will gave her a quick smile. "Didn't think about it. So, how do you like Karijini?" he asked, sitting beside her.

"It's perfect," she said, her voice soft. "Have you been here before?"

"Once," said Will. "Months ago when I first took the job out here. It was nice then too, but it's even better to come with you."

Beth caught his eye, desire for him making her stomach disappear.

"I mean, not a good idea to go walking here by yourself," said Will quickly. "This gorge is fairly shallow as they go, but some of the others are deep. It can flash flood here, too. That's why it's better to come before Christmas."

"Mmm," said Beth, leaning back on the rock. "Do you think I could just run away and live here?"

He turned his head, a small smile on his lips. "Wouldn't you miss your work?"

"Well, you said people fall down the gorges, right? And surely there are snakes. I think I could find some work."

He chuckled. "True. What about the great features of Iron Junction? Wouldn't you miss those?"

Now Beth sighed. "It's only temporary. Though I do like the pies in Mack's shop. And you're there ..."

Will's smile broadened. Beth was aware of him beside her, the droplets of water on his skin.

"Though I guess not for long either, right?" she added hastily.

"Yeah." But he held her eye, and Beth had to remember to breathe, aware of the thin figure-hugging swimsuit she wore. It would be so easy to slip her arms around him. Finally, she looked away, but his smile stayed in her mind.

They left reluctantly and started back down the trail. As they came back alongside the larger falls, Beth caught a glint up in the gorge, then again a few paces later. She squinted towards the spot.

"Just a sec," she said, as Will turned to the climb. She edged along the pool until she could plainly see a person, mostly in the shade of a gum, aiming a lens down the gorge. Beth nearly fell over in surprise.

"Caitlin!" she exclaimed.

She waved. Tentatively, Caitlin waved back. Beth scrambled down the remainder of the path to where Caitlin was set up on a rock, a battered short-legged tripod supporting her camera. She looked better again than she had in the Prince Harry just two weeks ago, but Beth was shocked to see her out here so soon after her illness.

Caitlin turned her head to cough, one long-fingered hand gripping the camera. She came back with defiant eyes, as if daring Beth to tell her she shouldn't be here.

Beth sighed. "Did you escape?"

Caitlin gave her a half-smile. "I felt much better. I had to leave."

"Did they discharge you?"

"Sort of."

Oh dear. That probably meant "no". Or, at least, against advice. Beth listened to the rush of the waterfall and tried to decide what to do. She hadn't been the treating doctor in Perth, but she had been the one to send Caitlin down there.

"Don't worry," said Caitlin. "I'm taking all the pills and I have this." She tilted her backpack so Beth could see the bright edge of a small medical oxygen cylinder poking out the top.

Beth raised her eyebrows. "Seriously?"

Caitlin shrugged, as if it wasn't a big deal.

"How did you get out here?" Even if Caitlin had flown back to Para, or Newman, it was still hours of driving to the park.

"My aunty drove me in. She works with the visitor center. She's never far away."

"Shouldn't you wait until you're completely back to normal?"

"I'm as normal as before," argued Caitlin. And despite her exasperation, Beth had to admire the kind of passion that drove Caitlin to do things other people thought were stupid, because she loved what she was doing. Then Caitlin tipped her head. "Who's that?"

Beth glanced around. Will had taken up residence on a rock at the foot of the path, well out of earshot. "Will Walker. He's working in Iron Junction and drove me out here," she said.

Caitlin unscrewed her camera from the tripod and put him in her shot, but didn't push the shutter. "I like how he's sitting there," she said, between breaths. "Right in the way of my view." She gave a small smile, quickly replaced with a tiny frown of concentration.

Beth laughed and Caitlin smiled again. "I went on the register," she said a moment later, as if they'd been talking about something else all along.

"You did?"

Down the path, Will stood and wandered towards the water.

Caitlin shifted the lens. "Yep." Click. Click. "They told me it can take a long time. Maybe never."

"True. But there's always a chance," said Beth, tracking Caitlin's shots.

Caitlin pulled the camera down, scrutinizing the display, then handed it to Beth. On the screen was the water pool, a blue eye dominating the frame. And in the left corner was Will, bag and hat cast aside, his gaze into the depths. It had been taken precisely, as he'd stepped forward; Beth could see the lines of muscles in his legs echoing the pool's smooth stone. She was struck with a sudden certainty: he was as deep as that pool. She knew so little about him really, and yet, it hardly seemed to matter.

Caitlin pushed some buttons. "I can't keep it," she said, moving to erase the image.

Beth stopped her. "Why?"

"I didn't ask him."

"Don't delete it. I'll ask. I'm sure it will be fine," said Beth.

She caught Will's attention and beckoned him up, then introduced him to Caitlin.

"Beth's told me a lot about your pictures," he said. "She said you're very talented." He inspected the shot she'd taken, and smiled. "That's really good. Can I buy it off you?"

Caitlin dug in her bag for paper and pen. She took Will's email address and promised to work something out with him. Then, she headed back to her vantage point, stopping to suck on the cylinder for a few breaths. Reluctantly, Beth felt she ought to leave. Caitlin wasn't in any immediate distress, and stubbornness was hardly a treatable condition, so there was nothing she could do. "Can you come to the medical center next week?" she asked, before they walked away. "I'd like to see the photos."

Caitlin promised she would, and Beth made a mental note

to call Doctor Forrest in Perth if there weren't any discharge notes waiting for her back in Iron Junction.

She followed Will out of the gorge, sweat running down her back as the morning sun struck. They retreated to the Pathfinder where Beth had a hard time forcing her thoughts back to the present. She tilted her head towards the driver's seat, and Will searched her face with a curious expression. The whole day seemed to fly together in this moment. She wanted to lift her hand and touch him, let him know how much it meant that he'd remembered she wanted to come here.

"Thank you," she said softly.

He smiled and straightened up. "I think we have time to go down the gorge to Circular Pool. Or, we can go west and find something different?"

Much later, when they finally rolled into Paraburdoo airport, Beth felt almost fond of the low, unassuming terminal, accepting the long strings of miners, all bound for somewhere else, their own private adventures that touched a common base in the dirt and work of the Pilbara. Even if all the Christmas traffic meant she and Will hadn't been able to change their separate company-booked flights.

"I'm heading into town to wait," he said. "But I'll pick you up from the hotel tomorrow morning. Bring your beach stuff."

"You better turn up," she warned him playfully.

With a grin, Will grabbed his Akubra from the back seat and slipped it onto her head. "I promise," he said.

By the time Beth caught a taxi from Perth airport, she was thoroughly in the Christmas spirit. The streets were full of twinkling lights, the taxi driver was wearing a Santa hat, and when she reached the hotel, there were free candy canes on the reception desk. Beth was in heaven. It was Christmas Eve tomorrow, and for the first time she could remember, the idea of it came with joy.

For his own part, when Will arrived in Perth much later that evening he wandered around his flat, clearing up. Two swings' worth of newspapers went down to recycling and he shoved a stack of old site plans in the desk drawer. All evidence of his toys – the kite-surfing line he'd been repairing, his half-finished Blackhawk model, the surfboard – he carted down to the garage. He stuffed all the clothes from the hamper into the washing machine, only separating the red-dust-stained work shirts, and let the machine cycle while he ducked out to the supermarket. Returning later with supplies, including a mega pack of colored tinsel, he put Joe Satriani on the stereo and set about making things festive. An hour later, he stood back, satisfied. The place was now presentable for female company.

But for one thing.

And without thinking too much about what he was doing, he went down the hall and remade the bed.

Chapter 19

Beth was waiting by the hotel loading zone the next morning, wearing Will's hat, when he pulled up in a tiny yellow convertible. For a second, she blinked, not believing what she was seeing.

"A Mini Moke? Are you serious?" She laughed as she threw her beach bag and the hat onto the back seat.

"No making fun of the Moke," said Will. "It's a cultural icon. But that door doesn't open, so you'll have to climb in."

Beth giggled as she stepped over the Moke's running board. A thick strip of green tinsel had been shoved between the dash and the windshield. Will's knees divided around the steering wheel and his shoulders extended beyond the narrow driver's seat; Beth had to squash herself in.

"Sorry about the room," said Will, spinning the wheel and taking to the street. "I don't usually have passengers."

"Of all the cars I expected you to have, this wasn't it," said Beth.

Will gave her a look. "What did you expect?"

"I don't know. You said cars were your thing. I thought you'd have something, you know, grunty."

"Grunty?"

"Yeah. It's a technical term."

"This has grunt," said Will, revving the engine as they stopped at the lights.

Beth listened to the tinny whine. Alongside them, a streamlined black sports car pulled up, its growl drowning out any sound from the Moke. Beth could see the driver and the passengers looking and pointing. "Well, I guess it attracts attention in its own way."

The lights changed to green and the sports car sped into the distance. "Don't you listen, girl," Will told the Moke, patting its dashboard. Then he looked over at Beth. "When we were kids, we used to go to Magnetic Island sometimes for holidays. These things were everywhere. This one came up for a steal, and I had to have it. I have got another car – a special sports truck." He stopped suddenly.

"Is that here?"

"No," he said quickly. "It's back home."

They drove west. Finally, they turned onto a road that ran flush to the thin strip of grass and sand that separated them from the ocean. Beth drew in the sea air. For a heartbeat, tears prickled her eyes as a rush of longing – for Sydney, for Richard, for what was lost – surged through her. But then the breeze dried her eyes. Her hair floated against her cheeks, her heart lifted.

"Marine Parade, Cottesloe Beach," said Will with satisfaction.

"Are you doing this just to taunt me? I thought we were going to your place first."

Will slowed the car, and Beth sat up. "You're kidding, right? You live here?"

He said nothing as they made a left turn into a concrete driveway, which led under a red-brick building with white-framed windows and ocean-facing balconies. Will pulled the Moke into an open car bay and killed the engine. "Here we are."

Beth grabbed her bag and followed him, speechless, up three flights of stairs where he unlocked the door to apartment three. He stood aside and gestured for her to go in. Beth could hardly believe what she was seeing. The short hall opened into a large lounge room, all in polished wooden boards. Tinsel hung above each door. The furniture was sparse – a deep, comfortable-looking couch, a shaggy white rug and a coffee table – and opening off the side of the lounge room was a balcony. From there, she could see the long line of the beach, the water that deepened from azure to the indigo horizon, and the sky streaked with brilliant white clouds.

"It's not too bad," said Will, standing beside her.

"Not too bad, huh?" she repeated softly. In fact, Will's place was homey in a way she had never expected. The beach reminded her of Freshwater near Sydney, of the flat she'd shared with Richard. But here, the furniture was worn-in rather than IKEA-fresh, inviting her to sit, to linger, to enjoy … as if she had transported to a parallel universe; and she was a different Beth from the one who'd left Sydney.

"I can't believe you live here," she managed finally.

"Well, I don't most of the time," said Will. "And I'm only renting it. The furniture came second-hand. Though if one of these apartments ever came on the market I'd give it serious thought."

Beth stepped away from the railing. She needed to touch base back to reality, otherwise she'd start having fantasies about moving to Perth and buying a place like this, preferably with Will in it.

"So, we can do whatever you want," he said. "Just north there's a golf course, or you can run the dunes with the army boys just up the beach. My soon-to-be brother-in-law is posted here, apparently. It's clothing-optional up there, too." Beth glanced at him, and he winked. "Or, the beach right here isn't bad either."

"Smartass," said Beth, but she couldn't wipe the silly grin off her face.

"Bathroom's down the hall if you want to change."

Beth's eyes fell on her bag, and Will grabbed it to pass to her. He pulled up short, hefting the canvas. "What on earth do you have in this thing? It weighs a ton."

"Um, textbooks," Beth admitted. "I kind of forgot to take them out."

Will looked scandalized. "You brought textbooks on Christmas holidays? No, you're messing with me."

So, Beth hauled the overstuffed backpack up on the couch and unzipped it. "Look, here, see?" She dumped *Murtagh's* and *Harrison's* on the cushions.

Will picked one up, measuring its weight. "God, you could kill someone with this. Worse than high-school science."

"You didn't have thick books in engineering?"

Will grinned. "We did. I really was trying to forget that. And some of them got used as door stops. What's that?"

Beth's eyes followed where he was pointing. "That's my album," she said.

Will raised his eyebrows.

Beth hesitated. She hadn't shown anyone her album, ever. Not even Tom. From the outside, it didn't look like much: its edges were tattered from so many years of being handled, and it bore coffee stains on the plastic sleeve edges from before she'd made a rule of not having drinks around it.

She sank onto the couch and pulled it into her lap. "I bought it when I first left Brisbane, when I was learning to use the camera. I started sticking other things in it, too, though."

Will settled beside her, interested. "What kinds of things?"

Beth held the cover closed. "Um, things I liked."

"Pin-up boys?"

She laughed. "No, not like that." She opened a few pages in. These pictures were all of one house, a post-war timber place, high-set with cream walls and on a sloping block so that the upstairs opened onto a patio at the back. Different times of day, different angles. "Mum's house in Brisbane. I took them on my first visit back after I left for Sydney," she said, flicking on past shots of Sydney. Manly, Circular Quay, one of a young man pulling a face outside a sandstone building.

"Tom, my friend from med school. We worked together,

too," said Beth.

"Ah, the famous Tom," said Will.

Beth moved on.

"I like that one," Will said suddenly. He pointed to a house with stone walls facing down a long paddock of grass. The photo had been taken at dusk with buttery light reflecting in its windows.

"Mmm," said Beth, running her fingers over the shot. "I took that at the end of first year, out west on elective."

"Looks like home," he said softly.

"Ryders Ridge, right?" said Beth, keeping her gaze on the photo. She felt the warmth of him, just a few inches from her shoulder. She turned the page. Abruptly, she encountered a full-page fantasy art poster in brilliant reds: a fierce dragon fighting a woman in armor with a shield and a javelin. The dragon's fire met the shield in a spray of sparks, as the female knight with scandalous cleavage thrust her spear towards the beast's neck.

"That's a bit different," said Will, with a soft, cheeky whistle. "Not bad."

"Yeah, I remember that one," said Beth with a laugh. "I'd had a big fight with my mother because she wanted me to move back to Brisbane. I found that picture really soothing at the time."

She quickly turned the page. Her entries were sparse in the later years of her studies. She'd been so busy, and the shots became more aspirational: operating-room scenes, promo-type shots for hospitals and healthcare centers. "I was a bit obsessive," she explained.

She flipped past graduation. After this, Beth's own photos ceased and instead, she'd inserted cut-outs from the wider world; startling landscapes, a few that were captioned from the Word Press Photo Exhibit. These had all been after she'd moved in with Richard, when her camera had mostly stayed in the cupboard. All things she'd wanted to see.

The photos ended, and she flipped back to the front.

"Is that your family?" asked Will.

Beth looked down. The first photo in the album was one of her mother and sisters, on the patio in Brisbane, clustered around a picnic table. Beth remembered the day well. Summer was just beginning, the light pouring in through the green of the garden. Her sisters were smiling; her mother too, looking uncharacteristically relaxed. Beth had taken it only days before she told them she was going to Sydney.

"Yes," she said simply, pointing out Vicky and Anne. "And that's Mum."

"Why aren't you in the photo?" asked Will.

"I took it," she said. But the truth was, she'd always been an outsider. Even if someone else had taken it, she wasn't sure her face would be there. She closed the album. "So, anyway, enough of that," she said.

Beth reached for her bag to put the album back and something fluttered out of it. Will leaned forward and retrieved a photo from the floor. Beth's heart skipped as he handed it back.

"Richard?" he asked after a pause.

"Yes," said Beth tightly, accepting the shot of the two of them against the backdrop of Manly beach.

Will chose his words. "I won't pry. But if you want to talk about what happened, I'm happy to listen."

Beth bit her lip as she looked at the photo. The feeling was no longer the pain she'd felt for losing him. It was something far deeper … a longing for what Richard should have represented but never had, a yearning for something she didn't have. She looked at Will.

"If I tell you, will you make fun of me?" she asked him.

He didn't joke now. He didn't laugh or smile or make light of her feelings. "I would never make fun of you."

Beth took a breath. In that instant she noticed tiny things. How soothing the rug was under her toes, the gentle scent of Will's aftershave, the way the sunlight shone through the table lamp, casting rings across the wall. Small things that composed the room. So, she began with the small things, the details at the beginning, because those were easier.

"We were together for five years," she began. "We met at a party I didn't want to go to. He's a dentist and we'd both been to the same university, so we started out chatting about that. He was a nice guy, steady job, no annoying habits." Beth allowed herself a brief smile. "I liked him, and he asked me out the next week. Neither of us had a lot of time the first year. I was busy at work and he was in a new practice. So, we ticked along. Sometimes I wonder if we'd spent more time together early on, it might not have gone as far as it did."

"How do you mean?" asked Will.

Beth pushed herself back on the couch so she could face him, grasping for the right words. "After a year, I felt we had a certain … inertia. We never had arguments. And my mother and sisters loved him, which was amazing. They'd always disdained my dates before him. He was immune to all their drama, too; it just washed right off him. So, when I went home for birthdays or Christmas, I wasn't always worried what they'd be thinking of him, and vice versa." She sniffed. "My friend Tom reckoned I was just substituting, though, that I made Richard my Sydney family. Mind you, Tom and Richard never liked each other, and Tom's in psychiatry now, so he would overanalyze it."

A frown passed across Will's face. "All right, so what happened?"

"We bought a unit together a year ago, and he proposed on New Year's Eve." Beth took a breath. Emotion was threatening to break in and ruin her composure. Will's arm gently settled around her shoulders. She leaned into the pressure and held herself together.

"My mother was ecstatic. Well, you know, in the way that she is. She said she'd never thought I could manage to hold onto someone like Richard."

"Nice." Will snorted, which made Beth smile.

"But the thing was … I couldn't shake off this nagging feeling that something was wrong. I had nothing to put my finger on, though. We had a perfectly pleasant life."

"But that doesn't sound like you at all," said Will. Beth glanced up at him. His expression was serious. "Beth, I haven't known you that long, but you've got the determined fire. If your job wasn't enough, then walking back to town from Iron Bluff? Leaving Sydney to work across the country? Coping with rooms full of miners and Dale King? Jesus."

Beth shook her head, but Will pressed on. "I can't imagine you settling down with a dentist in the suburbs. No offence to dentists … some of them must be party central. But it sounds like you were bored."

"No, not bored." She was searching for the words that would express what she'd never before been able to. "I began to notice … how I was compromising. I'd pick and choose what I'd tell him about my day because I knew his tastes weren't the same as mine. I'd agree to do things he liked, but he wouldn't often do that for me. I'd want to do something different – go away for the weekend on a whim, or dive or learn to fly – but I'd let it go because I knew he wouldn't be keen. He just wanted to read the paper and drink coffee. It was like we could never quite connect. I tried to talk to him about it, but he couldn't see that there was any problem. I guess from his point of view, there wasn't. I just let it go on that way."

"So, when did it change?"

Beth remembered that morning so clearly now. A Saturday morning. The carpet had been soft under her toes like now. She'd smelled coffee from the machine in the kitchen. The sunlight had been coming through the blinds, making bands across the wall. "I was on leave from work. We were sitting at the table near the windows. Richard was reading the paper. I was stealing parts of it, which I knew he didn't like because he always wanted to keep it all in one pile. Anyway, I saw an ad for a temporary position. I didn't know where I wanted to go, career-wise. Richard wanted me to choose something that had regular hours, like general practice, or dermatology. And buy a proper house, and a dog." She wrinkled her nose. "I was panicking at the thought of those things, but the ad gave me a bolt of enthusiasm. I showed it to Richard."

"And?" asked Will.

Beth could see it as if the whole thing were happening before her again. "And, nothing," she said quietly. "He read it, and he put the paper back together. And he gave me a look. He knew I wasn't going to take a job like that. That was when I realized I had changed myself for him. So slowly I almost hadn't noticed. It … terrified me."

Beth closed her eyes, remembering the night that had followed. Creeping through the dark apartment, her heart twisting, her hand sweaty on the handle of her bag. Knocking on Tom's door at midnight.

Beth blinked, and sucked a deep breath. "I don't know what was different about that night, why I left then. I was so unsure I was doing the right thing." The doubts crept upon her again, their weight crushing her voice and her reason. Beth still had the photo in her hand. She didn't want to put it back in the album, but she didn't know what else to do with it. Idly, she folded the picture in half, running the crease right between their faces, and slipped it into her backpack.

Will watched her, his arm still protectively behind her on the couch. "Was he upset?" he asked.

"I don't know," Beth admitted. "I haven't seen him since. It took a week to organize all the locum details. I stayed with my friend Tom, but all he knew was that I'd left and I didn't tell anyone else. I'm dreading when I finally have to face Richard. I feel like such a coward."

Will drew Beth towards him, hugging her against his chest. After a moment's hesitation, she turned her cheek into him and rested in his embrace. Disclosure had rubbed the wound raw.

"I'd just like to know one thing," he said, finally releasing her.

"What's that?"

"Why on earth did you think I'd make fun of you?"

Beth shrugged. "It's hard to explain when there's nothing overtly wrong. My family think I'm mad. If Richard had been violent, or been cheating, then maybe they could understand. But throwing away a perfectly good relationship that I could have worked on? No. That's what Mum's always said my father did."

"Is that what you think?" asked Will.

Beth shrugged; the conviction didn't quite reach every part of her, but relief came from the admission. It stayed with her as she changed into togs and a sarong, even when Will confiscated the textbooks, reassuring her they would be released when Christmas was over.

Then, just as they were about to walk out the door, Will pulled Beth into a quick hug, dropping a kiss on her forehead. "I think you made the right decision," he said against her hair. He stood back. "Of course, my opinion's biased, because otherwise you wouldn't have come to Western Australia, but still. You never have to apologize for being yourself."

Then, Beth had trouble remembering Richard at all. Even as Will went ahead, her forehead sparkled from his kiss.

Chapter 20

The day was scorching, the beach packed, but Will managed to find them a shaded spot, under a pine tree flanking the Indiana Tea House, its green roof and pale stonework perfectly suiting the sand and sea. The water was thick with swimmers, and surfers competed for the best waves further out.

Any trace of Beth's lingering doubts disappeared in the sun. She studied Will, still trying to process him without blue work pants and a hi-vis shirt. In a pair of board shorts, a surfer singlet and a pair of flip-flops, he looked perfectly at home on the beach, especially with his tousled hair and green eyes. And every time she paid him attention, more details stuck with her. How considerate he was. How attentive. She tried not to admire how good he looked in his tanned skin: cut with muscle, his arms powerful. Although not bashful by nature, Beth's heart skipped when she noticed Will's gaze lingering on her, too.

"Do you surf?" she asked, trying to distract herself.

"I do," said Will, pulling off his singlet. "I even started up kite surfing. This is a fantastic place for it, especially in the afternoon when the sea breeze gets going."

"I never learned to surf," said Beth, another legacy of Richard, who'd always pointed out the dangers of the sport. But she was again distracted by Will. Oh, the man had a wonderful body, and that tattoo set off all the muscle in his shoulders.

Beth leaned behind him to study the work … and maybe a little as an excuse to be close. The angel was exquisitely drawn, every feather of her wings rendered, her face the melancholia of eternal loss. An ache pulsed in Beth's chest. She gently touched the angel's robes. "Is this for your mum?" she asked.

Will shifted under her hand. "Something like that." He smiled. "Race you to the water?"

The quick swim turned long. Will didn't hover, instead swimming out further than Beth was comfortable with, and she soon lost sight of him. She couldn't help a little disappointment, even though she'd been the one to tell him she wasn't interested. She floated through the breakers, lulled by the water, looking forward to doing this again tomorrow, her first Christmas at the beach. She only dragged herself away when she was afraid her sunscreen was depleted. She retreated into the shade and lay on her towel, admiring the strip of perfect sand. Even the Pilbara's beauty couldn't replace the natural high of the coast whispering to her soul.

Beth was dry by the time Will came back. He stretched on his towel beside her, dripping sea water, a grin splitting his face.

"You look better," she said.

Will ran a hand through his salt-stiffened hair. "So do you." Then he pointed up the beach, where a rainbow arc stood out against the sky, bobbing with the breeze. "Kite surfer," he said. Beth watched the acrobatic surfer directing the kite as Will tried to explain the principles.

"So, how long have you been doing it?" Beth asked, fascinated but having to bend her mind to follow his descriptions of power zones and wind directions.

Will saw the look on her face. "Sorry, I was going on, wasn't I?" He stood up, offering his hand. "Probably enough sun for today? I've got a much better idea."

Will unlocked the apartment with an uneasy feeling. He had done this many times before: sand between his toes, returning from the surf to shower and change and return to life as it was. But always before, he'd been alone.

Having Beth here was tripping all kinds of pleasant ideas in his head. He wondered if he'd been crazy to bring her here — he'd never shown anyone where he lived, not even Sarah. They'd always met at a hotel; he'd wanted to keep his own place private. And he was supposed to respect Beth's wishes.

As she went to the shower, he bent for the remote and flicked on the big screen. *Sky News* was coming to the end of its cycle. A cricketer was being interviewed about the upcoming test match, saying absolutely nothing of interest. The bureau was monitoring a low-pressure system off the Western Australian coast. The story changed to preparations for the Sydney to Hobart yacht race, but Will was struggling to concentrate. He could hear the shower running, so Beth would be in there, naked. He rubbed his mouth, wondering how she'd react if he just wandered in and asked if she needed company. Then who would be a jerk.

Will pressed mute and pulled open the television cabinet. Tucked in the bottom were Beth's two confiscated textbooks, and an album of his own. He sat on the couch and turned through the yellowing pages, reminding himself how much things had changed.

He'd intended to put it away before Beth came back, but, silent on her bare feet, she startled him. Her dark hair had dried in waves and she'd tucked one side behind her ear. He couldn't stop his eyes running over her white singlet and sarong.

"What's that?" she asked, sitting down beside him.

He dropped the album on the arm of the couch. She smelled good, too. "Nothing important. Now, do you want original eight-bit Mario on the Super Nintendo, or do you want

Wii?"

Beth's eyes lit up. "Original. Prepare to be defeated."

"Ha!" said Will, glad for distraction. "One game, then we need to make a run out to collect the food. But one game will be enough to change your attitude."

"That's what you think," said Beth, grabbing a controller and easing into the corner of the couch. She looked at home there. Will sighed. Such a perfect day.

By the time the sun was going down, Beth was trailing in a best-of-twenty-seven contest. The heat had been incredible, so after the shrimp had been installed in the fridge, they'd stayed in the air-conditioned unit, Will giving Beth a lot of room on the couch. Now Beth put the controller down firmly. "I have to stop," she said. "My eyes are melting."

"You're just saying that because I'm winning," declared Will. He retreated to the kitchen with their empty water glasses, conscious of the luxury of the whole weekend. When he came back, Beth had taken up his photo album and was thumbing through the pages.

"Oh, wow ..." she said.

Will looked over her shoulder. His chest tightened. She'd found his only picture of that honey-stone farmhouse looking down a long, golden plain. Home. And long ago.

Beth glanced up at him. "Is this Ryders Station?"

"Yeah."

"Looks lovely." She lingered on the photo, her fingers caressing the lines of the house. Longing gripped hard and Will couldn't smile.

Beth turned over the pages. "Is this you?" she asked.

Will caught his breath. In the photo, he was in jeans and a checked shirt, wide belt and a cowboy hat, and lounging against an old farm truck. At a rodeo, probably eight years ago. It was the same truck that had been written off in the accident.

"Now, that's more like the car I thought you'd own," Beth said, smiling up at him. Will sank onto the couch beside her and did his best to smile back. Dozens more photos followed, from truck rallies and balls. Beth kept her eyes on the pictures, but slowly leaned into him, asking questions he barely heard.

She closed the album. "Will, did I say something wrong?"

Will jolted to attention, aware of her warmth against his body and not wanting her to move. "Not at all. Why?"

She met his gaze uncertainly. "You've gone very quiet."

Will looked down into Beth's eyes and couldn't form any words. He was right up against the edge of his past wrongs. He ached for reassurance. Slowly, he leaned towards her and let his lips rest on her hair, hearing his heart thrum in his ears. Man, he wanted her.

"Do you remember what you said before, about not being sure of yourself?" he said softly. Under his lips, her head moved in a nod. "Well, I'm not either most of the time. But sometimes … I get a sense of when things are right."

He pulled her up and led her by the hand to the balcony. The air was balmy; the twilight was nearly blue. All around, he could hear the murmur of celebration on every balcony, locals and holidayers all toasting Christmas Eve. And for the first time in five years, he had someone to share it with. Christmas – this Christmas – made anything seem possible.

Will's head screamed that this wasn't a good idea. But with each passing second, he dug himself deeper. He was keenly aware that she was no longer pushing him away. With her hand still in his, he whispered in her ear. "Does your camera have a timer?"

She gave him a quizzical look, but went to fetch it, showing him the archaic dial on the front of the housing. "You push that lever around, then press that little button." Suddenly, she seemed nervous.

Gently, he extracted the camera and sat it on the window sill, facing the railing towards the beach, and wound the arm around. He pushed the tiny button and as the timer buzzed down, she tucked into his side, smiling into the convex lens glass. The shutter captured them.

Will handed back the camera, his heart light and caught in the moment. Beth returned it to the safety of her bag. When she came back, Will slipped his arm around her. Anticipation turned his legs to jelly.

Below, the kite surfer was packing up on the beach. The path along the shore was thick with evening walkers pushing prams and leading dogs. "Stay here," he said, and disappeared inside the flat. From the fridge, he took out a bottle of Bollinger, an indulgence he'd bought the day before on a whim, and which was supposed to be saved for tomorrow. He didn't have champagne flutes, or even wine glasses; he had to settle for regular water glasses.

"Merry Christmas," he said, handing Beth a glass and pouring. "Sorry about the glassware, but I thought these were better than coffee mugs."

"They're perfect," said Beth, her smile brightening.

Will set the bottle gently on the tiles. The horizon was rimmed in pink cloud, but the rest of the sky was clear, the evening warm and full of good cheer. Beth's eyes sparkled. He ached to kiss her again. Then they heard a knock on the apartment door.

Beth raised her eyebrows. "You expecting someone?"

"Probably the neighbors looking for ice or something. Don't go anywhere." Will put his glass down reluctantly.

He paced to the door, the apartment air cooling his skin. On his doorstep was a man in a suit, a stranger.

"William Walker?" he asked.

"Yes."

The man handed him an envelope. "Merry Christmas," he said, then disappeared back down the stairs.

Will stared at the plain white envelope in confusion. It wasn't sealed; he unfolded the paper within, and reality crushed him like a steel band around his chest as he read.

Will stared into the now empty stairwell as his elation condensed into dread.

It was the subpoena.

Chapter 21

As she waited for Will to return, Beth felt more alive than she could ever remember. Her heart beat in time with the breakers. The breeze lifted her hair and licked her skin. She felt light and happy, and her soul was brave.

Will reappeared, silently taking up his glass. She shifted back to where she had been before: tucked against him. He smelled clean, of soap and sand.

"This is nice," she said softly.

His arm moved around her. She sipped the champagne and it danced on her tongue as she made her decision, the first she'd been sure about in a long time. She would take the leap.

She led him inside, putting her glass on the coffee table. Will's glass joined hers, and they sank onto the sofa, Beth sliding close. With no lights on in the apartment, his skin was tinted blue.

Beth remembered how it had felt when his lips touched hers – just two weeks ago, but it seemed so much longer. Back then she hadn't been ready, but now she'd glimpsed a new life. Maybe Will was just what she needed. It was his admission of being uncertain that had pushed her forward. No, she wasn't sure, but she was brave enough to try.

She ran the backs of her fingers down his jaw, her face mere inches from his. He closed his eyes briefly and his chest rose with a deep breath. She sensed his tension but she hoped she'd show him he didn't need to keep his distance.

"Do you remember the plant in East Ang?" she murmured against his lips.

A soft groan escaped him. "Yes."

She kissed him softly, letting her arms settle around his neck. Will hesitated, then pulled her against him until Beth could feel his heart thundering against her skin. His mouth caressed her, capturing her upper lip, then her lower, before his tongue slid gently between her lips. Beth lost herself to his embrace as his hands slid under her singlet, his touch hot against her flesh. Every concern she had, every doubt, fell like a shed skin. Her defenses were gone. The last act of trust.

And for a few glorious minutes, he was everything she'd hoped. Exciting and strong, gentle and perfect. Nothing like Richard had ever been. An unmatchable passion.

Then Will broke away, his face dark and changed. He held her at arm's length, his breathing heavy. "Beth, this is a really bad idea."

Beth found this impossible to process. Her hands still rested against the flat muscle of his chest. Slowly he shifted out of reach and sat on the coffee table facing her. Beth's hands fell into her lap. "I don't understand," she said, bewildered.

"It's not you," said Will. "I really like you. But this can't happen. Not now."

"Why?" Beth's chest ached with rejection.

"I don't want to hurt you," he said weakly.

Too late. The hurt had sprouted the moment he'd pulled away, and now it grew on its own. Had she misread him? She'd been sure he wanted this as much as she did. She took a breath. "Two weeks ago you kissed me. I know I said I didn't—"

"I shouldn't have done that either," he said, his voice now steady. "I can't get involved with you, not now."

The pain pushed inside her lungs, as if it could rip her open. She didn't believe him; she expected him to say he was joking. But slowly, she understood he was serious. He was not going to hold her again. This perfect day in this perfect place was going to end in the worst possible way.

"I still don't understand," she said desperately, hating that she felt weak, the shreds of her dignity falling around her.

"I just want to be friends," was all he offered. He reached out to squeeze her hand, but Beth moved it. Her breaths trembled. He was backing out, leaving her stranded like an island, impassable water all around.

She leapt up, mortification flaming in her cheeks and burning all the tender parts of her heart she'd exposed to him. The pain was more than she could bear. She waited for him to say that it was all a joke. But no. This was real.

Her bag was by the door. She grabbed it and didn't look back. In a few moments, she was down the stairs. She strode along, rubbing the tears from her eyes, not knowing where she was going.

Somehow, she caught a bus that dropped her near town. Its back seat was full of drunken partiers wearing Santa hats. Then she took a taxi the rest of the way to the hotel. It was only when she opened the door to the cold, dark room that she remembered her precious textbooks, confiscated by Will to ensure she didn't do any work. Abandoned on Christmas Eve, just as she now was.

Chapter 22

Fourth swing

Beth was back in Iron Junction on Boxing Day. The medical center was officially closed, functioning as an emergency room only, but Maxine was spending the day reorganizing the rooms, placing orders and cleaning out old stock, so she welcomed Beth's presence.

With few words, Maxine set her to work. But by noon, when they'd started on the drawers in the eye-room cabinet, the silence became overbearing. "So, you came back early," commented Maxine, scrutinizing the expiry dates on tubes of fluorescein.

"Yes," said Beth.

"Is Mr. Walker responsible for that?"

Beth stared at Maxine. The woman shrugged. "One of the patients was gossiping about it with Jennifer. They spotted you at the festival."

"And assumed," said Beth, crossly. Her embarrassment had transitioned to anger, which she found exhausting. But there was no point in denial. "Yes," she said shortly.

"I didn't mean to pry," Maxine said.

Beth rummaged in a disordered saline stack with renewed vigor. "It's fine," she tried, but soon, the whole story poured out. Richard and Sydney. Meeting Will when her battery had gone flat. The mine sites. Christmas Eve. And finally, how Beth had spent Christmas Day alone in her hotel room, only escaping to the movies in the afternoon where she'd eaten her way through a bag of caramel popcorn and a box of Maltesers.

Maxine listened to it all, surprising Beth with her patience. Finally, she asked, "Beth, why did you really come up here?"

Beth worried her forehead with her fingertips. "I wanted to be out in the world … and because I'm too much of a coward to tell my fiancé why I left." She tried to summon a screw-the-world attitude, but after the confession, the broken pieces of her heart were more jumbled than ever.

"Are you losing your faith in men?"

"In specific men," she said.

Maxine grunted. She tipped rejected tubes into the bin, then restarted on the stock. "Optimistic of you. I gave up long ago."

Beth paused. "Oh?"

Maxine sighed, as if considering what to say. "Beth, I come from a violent country. I don't know what you know about South Africa, but you would not believe the things I saw there working as a doctor. Horrific things that men do when they think they have a reason, or can get away with it. I tried for the longest time to make a difference. It's a patriarchal culture. And some of those ignorant men took it upon themselves to show me my faults."

Rage flashed through Maxine's features. "After what happened to me, I couldn't stay there. But it killed me to leave, and I was never the same again."

Beth was thrown into turmoil. "Can I ask—?"

Maxine held up her hand. "I'm not going to talk about it. I may never. I survived and I escaped, that's all you need to know. I came here because it's different, and yet so familiar. Don't forget, this is still a man's world. Count the women around town. We're outnumbered and marginalized, and if you're a black woman, it's worse again. I just want to be left to do my work here. I've got no illusions left; my enthusiasm has gone. But I was impressed you stood up to Dale King. It takes someone who knows themselves to do that. Who's still got the fire. Good for you. This won't be the end of you."

Beth heard these words, and yet they seemed false. The idea that she knew herself? What a joke. She hardly knew what she was doing at all. Just wavering in a vague land of unmade decisions.

Maxine got up and stretched her legs. "Doctor Gregg is apparently going to be discharged this week."

Beth stopped restacking the sheets. "Really."

"He might make it up here before that storm comes in."

"What storm?"

"The one they're tracking off the coast. It's not a cyclone yet, but we're overdue for one this season."

"I should call the agency," said Beth idly.

"I'll miss having you here. Think about coming back sometime."

Surprised, Beth looked at Maxine, with her short-cropped, no-nonsense hair, the lines around her eyes and mouth. The stare that hid her bitterness and hurt under brusque directness. Beth could only guess what had been done to her, and it made her sick to think about it. But Beth liked Maxine's strength. She realized she would miss the prickly older physician, too.

But could she really imagine coming back to Iron Junction, with the memory of Will Walker hanging around?

"I'll think about it," she said.

The week sped past. Maxine had the Christmas decorations taken down promptly, so that the holidays seemed past even before New Year. Beth heard nothing from Will. She told herself that this was a good thing; he still made her angry — how could he have shown such clear interest, only to reject her? But she missed him, especially in the quiet times when she wanted someone to talk to. Instead, she rang Tom, until she felt she was intruding too much on his time. She didn't mention she'd agreed to go home for Victoria's engagement party, Maxine approving the leave due to the New Year weekend.

In the face of imminent travel, she was restless on Thursday morning, until she looked down her appointment schedule and saw Caitlin Murray's name.

Caitlin seemed well as she sat down in the patient chair, but she didn't have the energy about her that Beth had seen at Karijini.

"How have you been feeling?" Beth asked.

Before she could answer, Caitlin had a coughing fit that left her breathless. Grimly, Beth collected the sputum and ran through the usual tests. Although Caitlin's spirometry was down and she was using oxygen more frequently, she wasn't running a temperature, and Beth let Caitlin show her several pictures from Karijini before she got into the medical stuff.

"Did Mack print these?" she asked.

"Yeah, they just came in," she said. "And I have one for you." She pulled a thin plastic ziplock from her bag. Inside was a sheet of card, keeping a photo flat. Beth caught her breath: it was the shot of Will from the pool in Karijini, as if she needed a reminder of that day.

"Thanks," Beth managed, even as her heart was in freefall.

Caitlin coughed again, taking Beth's attention from the photo. "You're coughing more than usual," she said with concern.

Caitlin made a face, then, after a moment's silence, she admitted, "Aunty's not well. She does my physiotherapy, so I've missed a day or two."

Beth got to her feet. "Well, we can try to get that sorted now. What kind of not-well is she?" Beth worried more for Caitlin if there was an infection going around.

"Not sure."

"Does she need to come in?"

"She's okay."

Beth looked at her. "Caitlin, I'm only filling in here for Doctor Gregg, and he's going to be back soon."

Caitlin's expression remained fixed. "Yeah, I know," she said. "Where you going?"

"Wherever someone needs a doctor next."

Caitlin played with the photos she'd brought, pushing the edges of the stack into straight lines. "Not going home?"

Beth thought about trying to explain. She understood that for Caitlin, home was where her soul was tied to the earth, but Beth felt her own soul floating free. She didn't say what she'd been thinking: she'd probably go back to Sydney, or even Brisbane. Finally, she said, "My sister's getting married. I'm going to Brisbane for her engagement party this weekend. I'll be coming back here next week, but after Doctor Gregg comes back ... I'm not sure."

"Time to wander, then," Caitlin said.

Beth thought on *wander*, such a serene word. It didn't capture the tumult that now spun around her future.

She cleared her throat. "Right. Well, let me try to give you a round of physio."

Beth's technique at the chest physiotherapy was unskilled, but nonetheless, Caitlin's cough improved.

"I want to see you again next week," finished Beth. "To make sure you're not coming down with another infection. And if your aunt's still sick, you'll need some more pummeling. Bring her with you if she's not better."

Once Caitlin had left, Beth went to make tea, fortifying herself before the afternoon antenatal clinic and the long drive and flights ahead of Vicky's engagement party.

She found Jennifer in the kitchen, intently listening to the radio.

"What's going on?" asked Beth.

"Shh."

" ... *expected to track east towards Broome. The bureau is monitoring the system, which is currently a category-one cyclone but is expected to intensify over the next twenty-four hours. And now to sport. Connections of Sydney-to-Hobart race winner—"*

"They just called it," said Jennifer, switching the radio off. "Cyclone Fletcher. First one of the season. It's still way off the coast, though."

"Do we really have to worry about that here?" asked Beth. She knew they were several hours' drive inland.

"If it's big, it could still be blowing by the time it gets here. The biggest problem for most places is the flooding, but we're okay – the creek's on the other side of the ridge. I was in Port Hedland for one a few years ago. That was fun. Don't worry, though, they always give us plenty of warning."

Cyclone Fletcher quickly slipped to the back of Beth's mind. She was facing her first drive back to Paraburdoo alone, and tonight, once she reached Perth, she was on the midnight red-eye to Brisbane. Her shoulders drooped just thinking about it, and she wondered, after everything that had happened this week, how she could convince Vicky she was having a good time.

Chapter 23

Beth stepped out of the Brisbane domestic terminal just after six in the morning feeling like death in a skirt. The party didn't begin until eight that night, and wouldn't end until after the New Year's fireworks. She wondered how she'd stay awake that long.

As she approached the taxi queue, Beth tried to push memories of last New Year's Eve aside, but she was aware her emotional shield was as thin as an eggshell. Her heart lay in shards, her direction lost. Coming home felt like defeat.

A slug of humid air struck her cheeks when she pulled herself from the taxi in town. She was used to the heat from Iron Junction, but the humidity was like a smothering blanket. Grimly, she wondered if a thunderstorm would roll in this evening and put a dent in the fireworks.

At the hotel, she tried to sleep, finally drifting off twenty minutes before she had to get up again. She caught a taxi back to her mother's house, where she, Victoria and Anne were getting ready.

As Beth squeezed into the bathroom beside Vicky's and Anne's open make-up cases, her mother called out from down the hall, "Is that Beth?"

"Yes, it's me," she answered, nervous about her reception after not coming home for Christmas, and only handing over her gifts when she arrived.

But all Meredith called back was, "You'll have to wait for the shower."

Beth pulled Vicky aside. "Is Mum mad?" she asked.

"Maybe a bit at first," said Vicky. "But Christmas was lovely and she was really relaxed after all the orders went out. She's enjoying the new ensuite. And we have a surprise for you later."

"What kind of surprise?"

"I don't want to spoil it. What?" she asked, when Beth glanced away.

"I don't like surprises, Vicky. Not right now."

Vicky wouldn't be drawn. She was in a golden mood, she and Anne cavorting around to music like they had as teenagers.

In a nice moment, Victoria slipped in behind Beth and gave her a hug. "I'm so glad you're here," she said. Beth felt the tears gather in her throat. She hugged Vicky, saying how happy she was for her. Next thing, Vicky had turned Lady Gaga up to full volume and was speeding down the hall away from Anne, who was trying to stick ice down her shirt. Beth grinned, trying to cover up the black marks under her eyes, and avoid spilling powder on the black cocktail dress she'd paid an outlandish sum for in an airport boutique. But the atmosphere was heavy; she couldn't shake the feeling of gathering clouds. Maybe it would storm after all.

The heat had not abated by the time the women were piling down the stairs and into a taxi van, which then crawled in the traffic crush towards town. Beth sat in the front, cut off from the merry party in the back, which swirled with her mother's perfume and wedding talk. Everyone seemed to have forgotten Beth had ever been engaged. Perhaps that was a good thing, but it seemed ominous that no one mentioned Richard.

When they reached Riverside, the sidewalks were thick with people jostling into position for the early fireworks. Watching them duck down alleyways and scramble for the riverside seats, Beth felt an urge to hitch up her party dress and escape to a seat on a wall, her legs dangling over the water. And that made her think of Karijini.

Will came into her mind. Again. A dozen times today she had caught herself feeling his touch on her skin, his kiss on her lips. Beth sighed, exasperated. Why couldn't she simply banish him? Corral his memory off in her mind behind a velvet rope, like the one her sisters now slipped behind into the restaurant.

Victoria had kitted herself out in a short white dress with a pair of blue sparkly heels. Anne had a longer hemline, her dress green and softly wrapped. They were both in high spirits, and greeted a throng of friends at the door. And her mother – who Beth knew didn't like black – again foxed her expectations, pausing by the door to admire Beth's dress, and asking where she'd bought it. Beth wondered if she'd thought about her family all wrong, even as she hung back while her mother and sisters posed for photographs with Ryan. After the raw isolation of the Pilbara, to Beth all the glitz was crass and fake. She felt more out of place than ever.

But she tried with all the generosity she had left not to let her feelings show. She said a brief hello and congratulations to Ryan, then accepted a glass of bubbles and took herself to the floor-to-ceiling windows where she could see the outline of the Story Bridge, crowned with red lights on the dark snake of the river.

After a few minutes of watching the crowds packed along the riverbank, she turned back to the party, the room a den of bodies and noise. Her gaze skipped across the faces and spotted her aunt Judy at the edge of the crowd. Beth hurried over.

"Twice in one year," Beth said, kissing Judy's cheek, grateful for an uncomplicated friend.

Judy lowered her voice unnecessarily in the throng. "I heard things went south with Richard. Are you doing okay?"

Judy's concern was so genuine, Beth had to pause while emotion surged through her. She tried to smile. "I'm not sure. I went to work in the Pilbara to get away," she said.

"What an amazing adventure!" Judy exclaimed, beaming. "Whereabouts?"

"A little place called Iron Junction."

"Ah."

Beth waited to be asked more about Richard, but instead, Judy quizzed her on her travels, and where she was planning to go next. Beth admitted she didn't have an answer.

"That's all right," said Judy, eyeing an hors d'oeuvre plate that a waiter was bringing out from the kitchen. "You'll find your way. You'll be fine."

Grimly, Beth remembered Will saying something similar. "I'm not sure about that," she admitted, the cold hand of doubt trailing its fingers through her mind. "Anne and Victoria have everything sorted out." She watched her sisters across the crowd. "I don't know what's wrong with me, but I just can't seem to get there."

Judy popped her eyebrows. "Anne and Victoria? Don't let appearances deceive you. Besides, Beth, my dear, you've taken such a different path to them. You are so much more like your father. You can't compare yourself with them."

Beth froze in confusion. She was about to ask what Judy meant when the waiter with the canapé plate appeared before them. "Do you care for salmon?" he asked.

As they both refused, and Beth caught her mother staring at the two of them. Judy touched Beth's arm. "I'm going to go and give Victoria my best wishes. I'll find you for a chat later. But you know you can call me any time if you need to."

Beth took a step backwards as Judy left. From outside, she heard a bang, and the next moment, a brilliant red sparkle lit the room. The party surged towards the windows to watch the nine o'clock fireworks. Beth couldn't help remembering the music festival, the last time she'd seen fireworks. And so her thoughts again drifted to Will. She slipped further along the windows to stand alone.

Even so, when someone stepped in next to her, for a

moment she thought it was him. Enough, she thought. Really. Enough. Then, she glanced up and her heart froze.

"Hello, Beth." Richard looked down at her with a tight smile, his face lit with reflected fireworks.

"H-hi," she stammered, struggling for composure. Here was the moment she'd been dreading. The time apart had transformed Richard into an abstract concept in Beth's mind. Now, he was suddenly and confusingly real again. The details flooded her senses. The way his dark hair curled at its ends, the curve of his lips. The scent on his skin, which pulled up memories of their beach apartment, of the sun-warmed bed on a lazy Sunday morning. His shirt was crisp, one she'd ironed for him many times. Some part of her longed for this familiarity. He seemed … safe. A point of reference in the uncertainty of everything else. She was terrified about what he would say.

"You look well," he said.

"What are you doing here?" Beth turned the almost-finished glass in her hand, round and round.

"Let me take that," said Richard, extracting the glass. "Can I talk to you?"

Beth allowed him to lead her away from the windows into the back of the restaurant where they could hear each other.

"I didn't expect to see you," she said, feeling so awkward.

"Vicky invited me. I didn't think it was such a good idea at first, but she said your job was ending soon, and I wanted to talk to you in person. Is it so bad to see me?"

Beth swallowed. This must be Vicky's surprise. She regretted mentioning that the Iron Junction job was winding up. But now, with the dreaded moment of meeting Richard again behind her, it appeared less awful than she'd imagined. He seemed genuine, eager and hopeful.

She allowed herself to remember the positive things, which wasn't difficult. "No … it's not so bad."

"So," he began, then looked down at his feet. "Look, Beth. It's been two months. You were upset when you left, I understand that. But not why. Can you give me that much?"

Beth found her words drying up. Richard always had this appearance of steady, calm understanding, the perfect cover for his very fixed ideas. She felt the familiar urge to give him an answer he'd find acceptable and avoid a conflict, rather than what she really thought. "I'm not sure I can."

"Try," he said, earnest. So, Beth thought of Maxine and her no-nonsense approach. She pulled him outside to sit on the back steps of the restaurant. Everyone was down at the riverside, so it was comparably quiet. Richard finally, after dusting the step with his hand, sat beside her.

"Okay." Beth paused, struggling to assemble the sentences. "I like you, Richard. I loved you. I probably still do. But I don't know that we ever really had much common ground. We want different things, and I knew that was going to make me miserable."

"You never told me," he said.

Beth sighed. "Not explicitly, I suppose not."

"If this is about working away—"

"It's not just about that," she said quickly. "It was everything from what movies we saw, to what we planned for the next five years. You wanted to stay put. I wanted to travel. You wanted me to settle for regular hours. I knew it wasn't what I wanted. You wanted a dog, I didn't. I tried to tell you I needed something else, but you never heard me. I changed to please you, and then I didn't like myself. When I realized it was always going to be like that ... I had to leave."

Richard was silent for a few seconds. "So, we were on different pages, I guess."

Beth nodded. "I suppose, but more than that ..." She fished around for the right word. "I wanted a real connection between us. Real engagement. And it never felt like that."

"We got engaged," he said in confusion.

"Not rings on fingers! I mean I wanted you to be interested in my life the way I wanted to be interested in yours."

"I don't understand."

Beth took a breath. "I felt … alone when I was with you. I needed to be able to be myself, not be someone you approved of."

Here, Beth had to stop. Because she realized that the only time she'd felt valued for herself was when she'd been with Will. And he didn't want her. It hurt so much she closed her eyes, wishing to be somewhere else.

Richard was silent again for a long while, then he rubbed his face. "It's hard to imagine what things were like a year ago, isn't it?"

Beth swallowed. A year ago, he'd proposed to her, by the harbor in Sydney, boat lights twinkling on the water. She looked away. He was being so conciliatory. Maybe they could part on good terms. "Yeah."

"But what about when you come back from Western Australia? Do you think it will be out of your system then?"

Beth frowned. "What do you mean, out of my system?"

"Look, your mother might worry you're like your father and have trouble sticking around, but I don't think you're like that. We had five good years. I just want to know how long it will take for you to do the things you want, so you can settle down."

Beth's thundering pulse was back. "When did she say that?"

"When we spoke last week," he said tightly. "I'll tell you what I think. You think you want something different to what you have. Lots of people do. It's just green-grass syndrome. Then you'll go after it and find that it doesn't work out. Then it'll be another thing, and another. I don't want you to have that disappointment, of being so superficial, of not sticking at it. There's nothing wrong with what we have."

Beth scrambled up, her cheeks burning. "I'm – that's not – I'm not …"

Richard's gaze was steady. The same look he'd always adopted when he'd seen her find some truth in his words. "How is it going out there?" he asked. "Be honest."

"It's just fine," said Beth. But she couldn't help sounding tight as Caitlin, Dale King and Will from splashing through her thoughts. She knew that the shock of having Richard voice the same doubts she'd been carrying must have been written on her face.

He watched her with a knowing expression. "Is it really worth it for 'just fine'? You gave up on a good job and a good life."

"That's none of your business," she whispered.

He stood with an exasperated sigh. "It used to be. And I'd like it to be again. I can wait, Beth. You'll get over this. I do love you."

Fear and shame were simmering in Beth now. She was so close to saying he was right. She rubbed a hand across her face, in despair, and took a last look at Richard, her emotions tangling. She imagined her mother and Vicky waiting to hear how things had gone with him, expecting them to patch things up. "I have to go," she said.

She rushed down the stairs, and away from the restaurant, feeling as though there was nowhere to go; aware she was running again, just as her mother thought she would.

Chapter 24

Will had been relieved to find plenty to do when he arrived back in Iron Junction on the Tuesday after Christmas. Handling the pressure of the mine work running behind schedule, coordinating deliveries and staffing the shifts kept him in the office far beyond his allocated hours. The only problem was, it wasn't enough. No matter how much he worked, five days crawled past with painful slowness; and he lay awake when his head hit the pillow. His mind ran in circles. For only the second time in his life, he considered seeing a doctor to get something to knock him out for a few nights. But he couldn't show his face in the Iron Junction medical center.

The only upside was that, as good as his word, Dan came to the site. Will signed him in as a visitor and, aided by Matt's eagle eye, kept him out of King's sight as they scrutinized the plant. He waited until after dark, when King was sure to be off-site, before he took Dan to see the stage-two earthworks.

"I can't thank you enough," Will said the next morning as Dan climbed into his car for the drive back east.

"Don't. You did an outstanding job with what you had. Management's failed you. They've got too much happening and not enough controls in place. There's only so much subordinate engineers can do." He massaged the wheel. "Like you said, the two stages weren't planned to run parallel. But they are now and there's contracts involved. I'll make some enquiries. In the meantime, keep your head down."

Will nodded, then dropped his voice. "Dan, how'd it go with your wife?"

"Ah, not good." The older man shrugged. "Can't blame her, really. I'm never home and I don't listen. But I've been through it before. I can do it again."

"Geez, Dan. That's shit."

"That's life, Will. What are you gonna do? Talk soon." He waved as he pulled away.

Dan's news sat heavily. Will had almost reached the site office when his mobile rang, an unfamiliar number on the caller ID. Holding a faint hope it might be Beth, he turned around and headed for a nearby awning.

"Hello?"

"Will. Been a long time."

Michael Hodges.

An invisible hand punched Will in the gut. "Hi, Mike," he managed. They'd been good mates, right up until the accident that had killed Mike's girlfriend.

"So, since your lawyer gave me your number, I assume you know what's going on," said Mike.

"Why's it happening, Mike?" Will asked. "There weren't any charges before. Why are her parents suing you now?"

"Isn't it obvious? Because all the reports say I was the driver."

Despite the hot sun, Will's stomach turned to ice. They both knew it wasn't true. "So?"

"They're angry," Mike went on. "Come on, Will, you know they thought I wasn't good enough for their girl. They were never satisfied with the investigation. They think I'm lying and the cops didn't have enough evidence."

Will had to concentrate just to keep breathing. "You did. We both did."

"The truth doesn't help anyone," Mike said, his voice hard. "So just stick to the story, right?"

Will felt faint. After the accident, they'd both been in shock. Will had liked Mike's girlfriend, liked her a lot. She'd been his sister Cat's age. He'd grieved for what had happened. But now they were talking about being under oath, in a court. He knew he should ring Bruce and tell him the whole truth, ask how it could be dealt with. But that would involve dragging up the whole affair again and nothing he said could bring her back.

"Yeah," he said finally. "Same as ever."

After he ended the call, Will felt the most wretched he ever had in his life. Neither of them had said Mike's girlfriend's name. Caroline. But everyone had called her Kaz.

He walked back to the office on weak legs. His desk was crowded with drawings. Through the window's tint, the sky was drab, the clouds like pencil smudges.

Will started at the figure waiting for him. Dale King leaned against the desk, his arms folded. Will felt as though someone had him lined up in their sights, and was having fun dropping one problem on him after another.

"Walker, we need to have a talk."

A shot of heat coursed through Will.

"I thought we understood each other," said King. "If you had issues or problems, you should have come to me about them. Isn't that what we agreed?"

Will kept his mouth shut, sensing the anger behind King's words. "You brought an unauthorized person to this site. Into the plant. You showed them confidential documents. That's a very serious breach of company policy."

Will pressed his fingers onto the desk. "We both want the same things, Mr. King. I'm a junior doing a senior's job. My supervisor's a company engineer and I needed his help."

"I'm your supervisor here," King said. "And no one from off-site is certified to look at those documents. Your actions are unacceptable and they'll be going on your record."

A bubble of amusement suddenly lodged in Will's throat. He glanced out the window at the plant, at all the sheaves of papers. His hard work and sweat was out there, not in this kind of bullshit. He'd worked in a dozen places; there were a dozen more to go on to. He looked King in the eye. "Fuck it, then, I quit. You can find someone else to push around. And I'll be reporting your shoddy management to my superiors."

Color flooded into King's cheeks, his eyes narrowed, his voice soft. "Well, I'd think carefully if I were you. A lot of important managers in the company listen to what I say. Your performance hasn't been great from the beginning. Failing to check in after you arrived, accepting defective shipments, botching a tie-in process." King shook his head. "I've had a great deal of trouble keeping you in check, really."

Will's amusement transmuted into rage, a primal reaction that urged him to solve this with his fists. "There's nothing wrong with my work here. Everything you just said is out of context."

"I'll be the one making that judgement. And you haven't exactly been candid. Do you think the company would like to know you're involved in a dangerous-driving case? I think you're supposed to disclose that kind of thing."

Will's confidence evaporated like a desert mirage. Too late, he realized his reaction showed on his face. King had an unmistakable look of satisfaction, eyes shining, lips curved.

"You've got thirty minutes to get off-site," he said. "And you'll leave camp tomorrow. Walk away, keep your mouth shut and suck it up, there's a good boy."

Ten minutes later, when Will was clearing his locker, he found the lawyer's letter still inside. He ran his fingers over the combination lock and glanced up at the security camera in the corner. So, that explained it. King must have searched his locker. The violation made Will's skin crawl, but at the same time, he was powerless. He didn't want anyone to know.

Will spent the evening packing and blankly watching *Die Hard* on the cable feed. In the morning, he plucked up the courage to call Dan.

"I quit yesterday after you left," he began when Dan answered. "Although I'm pretty sure I was about to get fired. King found out you were on-site."

Dan's response involved a volley of creative swearing. Finally, he said, "Resignation not accepted. You can come back under me until this is sorted out. Though I'm not surprised."

"Why?" asked Will.

Dan paused. "I finally found the senior engineer who was there before you, though he wasn't keen to talk. He confirmed stage two's not supposed to be started until the dry season. But King signed contracts and the whole project got away. The engineer was being asked to sign off on schedule changes and short cuts. Some changes were signed off in his name without his knowledge. He left pretty fast.

"Anyway, King can't keep it under wraps much longer, so let it go. I'm sitting in on a risk-assessment meeting for the Dampier port next week. It's a big project and I could use your help with it."

Will took a breath and blew it out. It wasn't like he'd wanted to come to town in the first place, but now the idea of leaving again was unpalatable. Business was unfinished here, as bad as leaving Ryders had been all those years ago. "I guess I don't have a choice," he said.

"Guess not. I'm driving up tomorrow. Come back to East Angelas and we'll go together."

Beth welcomed her return to Iron Junction. The New Year weekend had felt like two journeys bookending a very bad night out. She found the missed calls from the medical agency only when she reached Perth, but couldn't get them on the phone. Only when she walked into the medical center Monday morning did she guess what they'd been calling about.

Maxine was in the kitchenette talking to a man Beth didn't know. He had a thick moustache, thinning dark hair and meaty hands, but a friendly and obliging expression. Skin hung loose around his jaw, as if he'd recently lost weight.

"Ah, Beth," began Maxine, "This is Doctor Gregg."

The man extended a hand. "Very pleased to meet you, Doctor Harding. Thanks for holding the fort."

"You must be glad to see the back of the Royal Perth," Beth said, but the blood thinned in her veins. Her job here had been the only touchstone she had after the weekend, and now that was being yanked away.

"He's taking back his patients from the day after tomorrow," said Maxine.

"I'd better make arrangements, then," said Beth.

It took a long while for Beth to get the agency on the phone at lunchtime. "Sorry it's a short-notice end," apologized the agent, seeming busy. "But you'll be paid till the end of the contract regardless."

"What else have you got for me?" asked Beth.

"Well, um. I'm not sure we can offer you anything else at the moment."

"I thought you were always short-staffed," she said, confused.

"Well, ah, yes, I suppose …"

When it became obvious the agency was keeping something from her, Beth asked to speak to the director, who was far more candid.

"I'm sorry, Doctor Harding, but we received a poor evaluation from your employer there. I can't give any details, but until we've resolved the issue, I can't put you forward for another role. You're welcome to contact another agency—"

"What do you mean, a poor evaluation?"

"I'm sorry, confidentiality means that I can't …"

Beth mentally cursed Dale King. "So, you'll allow someone

else to make unsubstantiated claims against me but you won't allow me to defend myself?"

The director apologized but could not be swayed, and Beth gave up when she realized that her anger was only adding to whatever poor feedback had been given about her. She hung up, her blood now boiling, at a loss for what to do.

The afternoon appointments went by in a daze. Tomorrow would be her last day, and she didn't have the faintest idea where she was going next. As Beth left at closing time, Jennifer pushed two packets across the desk. "Mack just dropped these off. He said they came back Express Post today."

Beth took the photos numbly, as if this were indeed a sign of the end of things here. She tucked the packets into her backpack, her heart blue. She had no wish to stay and work near Dale King, but tears caught in her throat anyway. He was only a tiny part of this town; she couldn't imagine leaving after tomorrow and never seeing Mack, Maxine or Caitlin again.

Instead of going to her flat, she walked down the main street, past Iron Junction Auto, Mack's convenience store and the Re-Bar. After a few minutes, she passed the showground, still bearing scars from the music festival. The mine's temporary housing camp was dotted with lights on the far side. She had no desire to linger in a place that reminded her of Will Walker, so she circled back down the main street and saw a light still on in the medical center. Using her key, she found Maxine at her desk, leafing through a stack of journals.

"Did you forget something?" asked the doctor briskly, glancing up.

"Not exactly," said Beth. "Maxine, do you remember me telling you about Dale threatening to give a bad report to my agency? Well, it seems he did."

The older doctor pushed back in her chair. "I see."

Briefly, Beth relayed the details. "But why would he bother?" she asked finally. "You'd be able to tell them that things have been fine in the clinic."

"Because he's one of those people," said Maxine. "It's

about him, not you. He wants position and power, and he knows how to exploit every system and rule for himself. I told you I've seen men like him before." Maxine's indignation was so strong, Beth could almost smell it. "I might be an old recluse, but I'm not without contacts. Leave it with me," she said finally, in a quiet, dangerous tone.

Beth only had to wait until she'd circled the main street and arrived back at her flat for her phone to ring.

"Ah, Doctor Harding. I'm sorry for calling after hours. My name's Walter O'Donnell. I'm a locum manager out on the coast. Are you able to talk? Good, good. I've just been speaking with Maxine de Wet. I understand you're looking for a new position. Can I persuade you to consider Karratha?"

Beth closed her eyes, silently thanking Maxine even as the feeling of being uprooted made the world spin. She knew nothing of Karratha. But she was out of options at this point, unless she went back to Sydney.

Walter pressed on. "Of course we'll pay for your time to come out for an interview. You could fly into Karratha without having to go back to Perth. It's on the coast."

"I'll have to think about it," she said finally.

"Fine. Please do. Anything I can do to tempt you, let me know. The coast is lovely. Great travel spot. Sparkling water, white sand, endless sunsets. Any of that strike your fancy?"

"Sure does," she said. But her heart was a lead weight.

The pieces fell together too easily. Beth said goodbye to Maxine and Jennifer at the medical center on Tuesday afternoon, trying not to make a big deal and promising to drop through at some point. In her heart, she wasn't sure she would.

On Wednesday morning, she drove to Paraburdoo, where a tiny fixed-wing plane, dwarfed by the Perth-bound jets, was waiting. The pilot, a jovial man with short bleached hair and a deep tan, introduced himself as Troy, as he loaded her bag into the cargo hold. Beth eyed off the cabin, which held six seats and had only a low partition to separate it from the cockpit. On the floor, she spotted a wrapped candy wedged against a seat support.

"You're not the pilot who dropped sweets over Iron Junction, are you?" she asked.

Troy gave her a mock salute. "The same. Uh-oh, you don't look pleased."

"I'll tell you all about it," said Beth. "Don't worry – I suppose it's funny now."

"Do you want to sit up front, then?" he asked, giving her a winning smile.

Beth quickly agreed, and climbed into the co-pilot's seat. Two other passengers arrived in high-vis orange site clothes, but settled into seats at the back, their heads together over a sheaf of papers. Beth waited for Troy to return, peering at all the switches and resisting the urge to touch anything.

Soon, they were underway. The small plane rattled down the runway and lifted into the sky, heading north across the afternoon sun.

"So, you been down in Paraburdoo for business?" asked Troy through the headset.

Beth shifted it on her ear, the drone of the plane's engines humming through. "I was a temporary doctor in Iron Junction for a while."

"I see. Got a new job in Karratha?"

"Maybe."

She leaned forward to peer through the windshield. From up here, the view didn't do the land justice. It seemed deserted and brown, its richness lost with altitude. As they flew, Troy pointed out a few landmarks: Tom Price, where Will had taken her up Mount Nameless, and later Millstream National Park. As they approached the coast, clouds bunched on the far horizon, the ocean a perfect blue arc. Excitement finally stirred inside Beth.

"Hmm, look at that," said Troy, pointing out a smoke

plume from some kind of burn-off, the gray cloud billowing strangely along the ground.

"What?"

"Smoke's not rising. Going to be some weather coming in. Might want to keep an eye on the forecast. There's that cyclone out there," he said.

"Oh, right. Fletcher," said Beth, who'd caught the news in the Paraburdoo airport. "But they said it was moving away."

"Sure. But forecasts are just educated guesses. And sometimes, not so educated." He laughed.

Moments later, the plane was descending on the runway. Beth listened to Troy's radio calls with the tower, imagining she was the co-pilot, and when they touched down with a bounce, she wished she could do it again. Beth farewelled Troy, collected her bag and picked up the hire car, another four-wheel drive. The monster size didn't faze her this time. As she maneuvered the vehicle out of the airport, the news on the radio confirmed the cyclone was nearly stationary off the coast but expected to move north. The bulletin moved on.

She followed the airport road to the highway turn-off, a crop of palm trees bending in the stiff breeze. Across the road, an endless line of iron-ore wagons shuffled on the roadside tracks, heading for the dump stations further north. She gritted her teeth: she knew this only because Will had explained the process to her, and she didn't want to think about him now. She just had to limp on.

She passed into the town proper where she'd been put up in one of the camps, too like the one in East Angelas. Only then did she allow herself to cry over Will Walker. She would never see him again.

Thursday, 0730 hrs, Perth

The next morning, seven hundred miles south, Captain Aiden

Bell sweated up the Swanbourne beach dunes, his thighs burning, his feet sinking in the sand. Breathing hard, he halted at a crest, looking down on the pale azure water darkening the sand. He'd already done the loop twice and was considering going again to burn off his restless energy.

Deep down, he knew why he was twitchy. Cyclone Fletcher had parked its ass somewhere off the northwest coast and was steadily spinning up its power. Category three, now; he'd seen the overnight bureau data. He dropped to the sand and pumped out thirty push-ups, making his arms burn like his legs; good to share the love around. Another thirty. Another.

Finally, he collapsed on his back, pulling his phone from his pocket. He'd had this same feeling before cyclones Larry and Yasi had screamed through Queensland, leaving a massive clean-up and weeks of sleepless nights as he coordinated the recovery. On his phone's small screen, he watched Fletcher's swirling mass on the BOM satellite image.

Stay away, he thought. No one needs you here.

Fletcher vanished as the phone rang. It was the call he'd been waiting for, the one that commanded him to jump on a transport plane north, to prepare for the worst.

Time to get to work.

Chapter 25

Beth slept late the next morning and had to rush to make it out to Walter O'Donnell's office for her interview. Walter, a short man with graying hair and a Father Christmas beard, greeted her with enthusiasm. He took his time, going through her career history and reminiscing about his days managing suburban family medicine practices before he'd moved into the locum agency.

"The job's in the hospital," he continued. "Bigger than Iron Junction, but not what you'd be used to in Sydney."

Beth silently was thankful for both those things. "I'll set up a meeting for you there tomorrow," he finished.

Afterwards, Beth made her way back to the camp, wondering what to do with herself until the next day. Clouds had rushed across the sky, further dampening her spirits. She took her camera and drove through town, until the houses ended and the road became a ribbon through the green grassland, which ended in a sandy bay, the tide lapping at the shore. Beth didn't get out. Instead, she drove back to the main road, past the rail yards and the airport, all the way down into Dampier. Along the esplanade, the water touched the rocky coast, and behind it, a wide sandy strip was dotted with shelters. The sky was slate gray now, the wind bending the palm trees and paperbarks along the road. She pulled over as the route wound into an industrial complex. In the distance, she spied massive ships. The road ended. She turned the car around. Weary, she went to bed early.

The next morning, when Beth entered the mess in search of breakfast, the atmosphere had shifted. The queue for hot food was abandoned and a group of workers were clustered around a radio. She drifted over, trying to listen in and heard the name "Fletcher".

"What's going on?" she asked. Two men turned towards her.

"Cyclone turned around overnight," one said. "It's heading south now. They reckon if it keeps on it'll make landfall here."

"It's up to a category four, too," put in the other guy. "That's bad."

Beth stayed to listen, but the radio had moved on to other news. She grabbed an apple and ducked outside. Both the men seemed unperturbed by the idea of a cyclone bearing down on them, but Beth immediately called Walter. "I just heard about Fletcher," she said. "What should I do?"

"I'm just waiting on an update, myself. These things are hardly predictable. Happens a lot round here. I'm supposed to have another doctor flying in today, but there's some issue with the airport. Can I call you back?"

So, Beth waited, unsure whether she should still go to her interview at the hospital later that afternoon. Cyclone Fletcher seemed a sign: this job probably wasn't meant to happen. It was time to think about getting out while she could. She was packing her bag when Walter called back.

"They don't really know yet what's going to happen," he began. "If it does come this way, it's not expected until tomorrow morning. I'm sorry about the inconvenience. The interview will have to be rescheduled."

"Should I see if I can get a flight out?" asked Beth. "You know, before it gets here."

"Sorry, I should have explained. They've closed the airport. That's why my other doctor couldn't get in. The army is evacuating all the patients from the hospitals and they're using the runways."

"Oh," was all Beth could say.

"Look, if it does come across, all the buildings here are rated for it," Walter continued. "Anyone who's in a camper can go to a public building, even the hospital is used as a shelter. In the camp, everyone will go to the mess hall if they need to."

"If it's so safe, why are they clearing the hospital?"

Walter's brief pause reminded Beth she wasn't from around here and how little she understood. "They're talking about it going to category five, and there's a spring tide. If it hits us bad, we'll flood and it could be hard to get people out afterwards. Could be days before power and water work again. It's safer this way. Keep a radio on," he added. "And check with the camp desk. They'll tell you if you need to go to the hall."

Beth ended the call and sat numbly on the bed. She managed to watch television and clear her inbox for a few hours, her frustrations crawling to the surface, until she could bear it no longer. She couldn't sit here waiting for things to happen. She had to find something to do, some way to help. Taking out her phone, she thumbed through the maps and found directions to the hospital.

Outside, she looked into the mighty sky and had a sense of foreboding. Cyclone, bearing down; a monster of air and water coming to test the dry red country, and hold her back from moving on. Beth scowled at the gathering clouds. As the wind caught her car door and rocked it open on its hinges, she cursed the storm for all it represented.

"Leave me alone!" she shouted. Then she shut herself inside and tore out of the car park, the wind chasing her down the road.

A pale-blue sign showed the location of the hospital, the

buildings set back behind a stand of eucalypts. Rain fell steadily. Beth pulled in to the front and looked around. Nothing moved, just a slick of dirt in the emergency entrance evidence of recent activity.

She jogged through the rain, and pushed inside in the ER. Empty. She checked her watch: it was just after five. The lights were on in the reception area, but further down the hall they blacked out.

"Hello?" she called. She stuck her head into the main hall. "Hello?"

Backing into the reception area, she nearly collided with a woman coming around the desk, her arms full of plastic bags. "Oh, sorry!"

"Can I help you?" the woman asked. She had gray hair in a short bob and glasses on a chain around her neck. Beth noted her uniform shirt, complete with upside-down watch, and the assortment of pens hanging from her name badge.

"I'm Beth Harding," explained Beth. "I'm a doctor and I was supposed to be coming in for a meeting about a position."

The woman's harried expression softened. "Ah. I'm sorry, but everyone's been evacuated. It was very sudden. The other on-duty staff went with the patients to Perth, so I'm guessing your meeting's not going to happen."

"I came hoping to help out with the evacuation."

"You missed it. But you can still help." She handed Beth the bin liners. "We have a doctor on-call, and one of the off-duties is meant to be coming in, too. We have to be ready if the storm hits. But things are in a bit of a mess after the exodus. I can find plenty for you to do. I'm Barbara."

Beth quickly discovered that Barbara knew every inch of the hospital, and everything that had been moved, displaced or disrupted during the army-led evacuation. She trailed after Barbara, clearing bins, righting upended furniture and gathering refuse.

"Where did you work last?" Barbara asked as they worked.

"I just left Iron Junction," said Beth. "A doctor there was

sick for a couple of months."

Barbara brightened. "My husband's from Iron Junction. Is Mack still running the store?"

Beth smiled. "Certainly is."

"Well, I haven't seen him in years." Barbara then told Beth about her days out east, where she'd met her husband, their time running cattle and sheep on various stations, and finally settling in Karratha where she'd gone back into her nursing profession. "I wanted to stay today," she said finally, gesturing around the empty hospital. "They had enough other staff to go with the patients, and I didn't want to leave my husband here to go through the storm by himself."

Beth tied back the emergency-bed curtains and glanced out the window. The sun had long set behind the clouds. The rain had stepped up, striking the glass in waves. Through the droplet-dotted darkness, Beth saw headlights.

Barbara straightened. "That must be the on-call doctor now," she said. "He's very late."

But the man who came through the door, rain-soaked and miserable-looking, was not the elusive on-call doctor. He was a gray-haired, portly man with a red, round face and a biker-style moustache. Beth recognized him instantly but couldn't remember his name.

He paused in the doorway, out of breath. "Hi," he said, coming in a few paces, a grimace on his face. His left arm held his ribs. "I've got some pain."

Barbara steered him towards a bay and Beth hovered nearby, conscious it wasn't her hospital, but Barbara made no move to exclude her so she stepped in.

"I've forgotten your name ..." Beth said apologetically. "But I met you in East Angelas."

"Dan Beecham," said the man. "I remember you, too. Will was driving you around. He's just parking the car."

Beth wanted to die in that moment. He heart hammered, her thoughts split between anger and despair. Why couldn't

Will still be in bloody Iron Junction, where he was bloody well supposed to be? She tried not to peer out the window. "Where's this pain and how long have you had it?"

Dan cupped a hand over his solar plexus. "There, started about half an hour ago."

Barbara set up a pulse oximeter and wheeled out the equipment trolleys. "I have no idea where our regular is," she said to Beth. "Fancy sticking around?"

Beth glanced towards the glass doors, at the dark night, the rain and the wind. It wasn't like she wanted to go out there.

Will Walker chose that moment to push open the door, rubbing the rain out of his hair. The air stretched taut as their eyes met. Beth allowed herself one beat of pure aching hurt for him before she yanked the bed curtain closed.

She focused on the problem. Dan's pain was near his chest, so this could be a cardiac emergency. But the ECG looked normal.

"Have you had this pain before?" Beth asked.

Dan looked sheepish. "A few times, not as bad, though."

"Does the pain ever travel up to your jaw, or down your arm?"

"No, never."

Taking the history, Beth soon discovered that Dan had a penchant for drinking as well as eating, and that because his knees were bad, he took a lot of painkillers, too.

"What sort?" Beth asked.

"Just supermarket stuff, you know. Panadol. Nurofen."

"And what were you doing right before you felt the pain?"

"Sitting in the car, waiting for Will," said Dan. "That boy's got talent, I have to say. He's going to go far. But he's still got half his head in the tools; he took a lift up the port to help with the tie-down before the storm. Lots of equipment there you don't want to flap around ..."

Clearly, Dan had a penchant for talking, too. Beth rubbed her temples, letting him bang on before hauling him back on topic.

"What else were you doing?" she asked. "While you were waiting?"

"Ah, eating. A burrito. A big burrito. They have good ones at that truck stop on the Dampier road."

Beth started the examination while he chatted on. Dan's lower lids were pale, and his stomach tender. She frowned. She wanted to repeat the ECG, but now she had gastric complaints on her differential diagnosis list, including a bleeding ulcer and gall stones. The man certainly had risk factors for all three. But they weren't exactly in a position to give him a referral for an endoscope or exercise stress test right at this moment. Beth thought about what else they could do, and turned to ask Barbara where occult blood-stool tests would be.

Barbara had her ear to the desk phone. "The on-call doctor's still not answering," she said, putting the receiver down. "He comes down from Dampier. Should have been here hours ago."

Wearily, Beth hauled herself up and pushed the curtain back. Across the waiting area, Will stood and walked forward.

"Dan's fine for now," Beth began, desperate to speak first, and on her terms. "But we'll keep him here until the storm's over and we can organize some other tests."

"See, mate, what did I tell you?" said Dan, clearly forgetting his earlier discomfort. *"We're going to the hospital.'* Christ. We could have been back at camp, enjoying a few cold ones."

Will gave Dan an exasperated look, which only earned him a lopsided grin in return. Beth turned away, not able to soak in any of the humor, and paced down the hall.

"Beth, wait."

Will jogged after her. Beth screwed her fists closed, then tucked her arms across her chest.

"What are you doing here?" he asked, his voice amazed.

Beth sighed and folded her arms in defense. But she saw Will's usual assurance was gone, his expression haggard. For a second, Beth imagined that he would tell her how wrong he'd been, that he wanted her after all. That meeting here was surely a sign of fate. But that flash of hope soured as soon as he spoke.

"I'm sorry," he began. "Just give me a chance to explain. It's not you—"

"Don't you dare," she shot at him. "Don't you *dare* do the 'it's not you, it's me' thing."

He put his hands up, shamefaced. "All right. But you can't get involved with me. There's something you don't know."

A barb bit its way into Beth's heart, drawing tears that she just managed to hold back. "Well, I was trying to get to know you. Thanks a lot for your trust."

Helplessly, he gripped his elbows, as if he were trying to stop himself from reaching for her. "I didn't mean to hurt you. I hate myself for it."

"Didn't mean to?" she asked, narrowing her eyes. "That's why you led me on with Christmas and champagne? And then backed out so fast you almost fell over yourself? Give me a break."

She pushed past him, back towards reception, hoping some disaster had brought patients to the waiting area so she could distract herself. But there was only Dan.

Barbara had her ear to the triage-desk phone again, a deep frown pulled on her brow, eyes searching as she listened.

"Say again, Alex? North of the salt pans?"

What? mouthed Beth. Barbara shook her head, then after a quick glance at the receiver, palmed the hang-up button and dialed three numbers: 000. Beth listened in disbelief as Barbara relayed what she knew: the on-call doctor, Alexander West, had had some kind of accident.

"Still with the car, I think," said Barbara, as the dispatcher quizzed her. "I couldn't hear everything. The wind noise is pretty bad and he was slurring."

"Shit," said Barbara grimly, as soon as she hung up. "All units are out at other emergencies, and they don't know how much longer they can respond in these conditions. They're going to try their best, but they might not go at all."

Beth forced herself to breathe steadily. The storm was getting inside her, the wind's moans fanning the helpless anger she carried like an infection. "Where did you say he was?"

"Just north of the salt pans, off the road, I'm guessing. But I don't know how far off. He wasn't making much sense."

Beth knew the salt pans, on the road from Karratha to Dampier. She'd driven over them several times yesterday when she'd been burning time. She glanced down the hall, which was now empty. A gear shifted in her head. Screw it. One moment, she was waiting, passive. The next, she dug the keys from her pocket and paced to the mobile kits in the store room. She had one in her hand in a second and headed for the door.

"I'm going to find him," she told Barbara.

"You can't go out in this!" called Barbara in dismay.

Chapter 26

As Beth fought her way to her vehicle, fear crept in. She was trusting the forecast that said the full force of the storm wouldn't be here until the early morning, a few hours yet; and that she could even find Doctor West in the driving wind and rain.

She hauled the white Prado out of the hospital grounds, flicking on the strobe for what it was worth. Rain strafed across her windshield in sheets, and she heard the wheels graunch through deep puddles. Airborne twigs and leaves pelted the car as she finally found the highway turn. It couldn't have been more different from the dry, dehydrating day at Iron Bluff, but pitching herself against the raw elements was just the same, and was consuming every inch of her courage. Please god, she thought, let's get this over with before anything bigger starts flying around. And let the paramedics be there already.

Beth peered over the wheel as the wind buffeted her driving. She found the turn towards Dampier, but the road seemed much longer than she remembered. Then the lights of the airport turn erupted from the night, and she pushed out over the low, dim land of the pans. The wind was at its worst now, and Beth tightly held onto her wheel. As the country rose on the other side she slowed, searching the verges for signs of Doctor West. When she began to wind around the low foothills, she knew she'd come too far. Cursing, she threw a U-turn and headed back, crawling along the road's edge. She'd just spotted a fleck of white through the rain when another vehicle came up the hill. When it left its path and cut across in front of her, Beth had to jam on the brakes.

"What the f—"

The driver's door flew open and Will appeared in her headlights. A second later, he yanked open her passenger door. "Are you out of your mind?"

"What do you care?" she shouted over the wind.

"I do," he returned, stabbing a warning finger in her direction. Some part of Beth's righteous anger quailed, but what did it matter now? "Someone's out there and needs help," she said. "I wasn't going to sit there and wait to see if the paramedics were coming. And I saw something down there." She pointed off to where the fleck of white was now lost in the rain.

Will thumbed towards the Pathfinder. "Come to my car."

Heart in her mouth, Beth hauled the mobile kit from the back seat and climbed out. Once she'd shut the door on his cab, he hooked the steering off the verge and crept through the thick grass and mud, wheels catching, suspension rolling. Neither of them spoke as they peered through the darkness. The speck jolted in and out of view until finally, it steadied and grew.

Yes, it was a car. One that had left the highway, plowed across the land and into the boulders. The failing headlights made dim puddles of light against the rocks. Will pulled up and Beth jumped from the cab. She stumbled towards the wreck, the rain pushing against her. Twice, she slipped on muddy banks, but finally she reached the vehicle.

And that was where she found Doctor Alexander West, slumped in the front seat.

He was conscious, but only just and was obviously in pain, his face as white as the ID tag hanging around his neck. He had a bleeding laceration on his forehead, which matched the curve of the steering wheel. Both his arms were folded limply in his lap. The cabin appeared intact and made a small pocket of calmer air, but the rain was soaking through and the man was already shivering. Beth quickly checked his vitals. Strong pulse, rapid breaths. She slapped on an automatic blood-pressure cuff, thankful she had it; she could never have taken it the old-fashioned way with the wind screaming around them. Will held the door open, waiting for her assessment.

In ordinary circumstances, it would be best not to move him. Wait for the professionals so they could carefully extract the injured patient in as controlled a fashion as possible. But there was no way they could stay out here. Beth bit her lip, wondering how long to wait. The ambulance could be just around the corner.

Then again, it might be half an hour away, or more.

Or it might never come.

She leaned into the car so the injured doctor could hear her. "Alex, we've got to get you out of here before the weather gets any worse. I'm going to give you a shot of morphine, all right? Then we're going to figure out how to move you."

The doctor nodded weakly, grateful as the opiate charge smothered the pain. As swiftly as she could, Beth eased on a neck brace and splinted his arms, using a rolled medical journal she found on his front seat, the stiff handle of a tendon hammer, and bandages from her kit. Beth grabbed Will's collar and pulled him in close. "We need to make a stretcher," she said.

Will dragged Beth back to his Pathfinder. The rear faced straight into the weather, so they crawled into the back seat to inspect what he had, which turned out to be depressingly little. A tool kit. A tarp. The jump-start battery that Beth well remembered. Nothing to make a pole. Beth knew that the limited trees nearby were twisted and short; no good for poles.

"How are we going to get him out of the car?" asked Will.

"We'll figure that out," said Beth.

Will's hand was strong on her shoulder, holding her back. "We're going to struggle to carry him," he said. "Everything's wet and the ground is all mud."

Beth hated that he was right. "Can you move the car in closer?"

"I'm not sure I can get it out now," he began. Then he saw the look on her face. "I'll try. And if we get stuck, we'll have to bring yours down from the road for a tow."

Progress seemed to take forever. Doctor West's injuries were mostly to his head and arms, and his left ankle, so they were able, with a lot of strain, to help him out of the car onto his good foot. Will had brought the Pathfinder in as close as he dared, parking it with the rear door in the lee of the storm.

They supported his weight between the two of them, then Will gathered Doctor West's legs until they had him in a fireman's chair. Beth's breath emptied with the effort. She wasn't strong enough to carry this man, and she knew Will was trying to take more of the weight. Their feet slipped and sucked for the fifteen paces it took to reach the Pathfinder, Beth terrified they would fall and never rise again. By the time they'd hauled Doctor West across the back seat, her stomach was screaming with the pain of too little oxygen. She gasped, moving with aching slowness to carefully bend up Doctor West's legs, while keeping his injured ankle from further damage. When Will closed the door, water ran down the inside, and she propped the doctor's foot on the door's arm rest; Doctor West grunted, but he was only semi-conscious, lost to the pain and morphine fog.

Will hauled himself into the driver's seat and set off through the deluge, guided by Beth's strobe, just visible on the road. Crouched in the footwell, Beth watched his control, correcting each slip and skid. For a terrifying moment, they came to a halt, and Beth heard a wheel spin. Then the tires bit and they lurched on.

When they finally found the highway again, Beth's fears amplified. Seeing ahead was nearly impossible. She didn't know what Will was using to navigate. As she worked, all she could see was each cat's-eye creeping into view as they left behind her Prado, its tiny strobe disappearing into the swirling rain.

Beth worked automatically from the moment they arrived back at the Karratha hospital. With Barbara, she was able to fully evaluate Doctor West's injuries. One arm definitely broken; the other and the ankle probable. Bad gash on his forehead requiring stitches; concussion. While Will spoke to emergency dispatch to call off any rescue, and Fletcher lashed the hospital, Beth and Barbara straightened Doctor West's arm and re-splinted all three limbs. For an hour, while the howling wind amplified, she watched his vitals like a hawk, but he showed no signs of a worsening head injury.

She kept up his pain meds and stitched the cut with leaden hands. She was grateful to have something to do, because Will hung around as a powerful reminder that her heart was fractured like the limbs before her. She gritted her teeth.

"That's enough," said Barbara, close to her ear, when Beth had tied off her last suture. "You're cold and wet through. I can finish here. Go and have a shower while we still have hot water, and put some scrubs on."

Beth obeyed, staggering past a clock that proclaimed half past one in the morning. The shower thawed her, but the storm's noise had reached an unbearable level. She was exhausted, physically and mentally, and the storm was doing its best to rub those raw nerves to meltdown.

When she emerged, dressed in dry scrubs, she avoided Will. She didn't know what was going on with him, but it wasn't her problem; he'd made that abundantly clear. Besides, under the shower's spray, she'd finally made the decision her mind had been circling since Christmas. She didn't want him getting in the way of it.

Barbara had settled Doctor West for the long wait until the storm abated, and having moved away from the windows they worked out a watch roster. Beth lay down to sleep on a waiting-room couch, but she persisted in a strange half-waking state. She began to hear crashes and thumps as loose debris hit the hospital's walls and roof. It was amid this noise that she heard her phone beep. She turned the glowing screen in the darkness. A message from Victoria. The reception symbol was struck out now; one text had snuck through.

Mum in hospital, it read. *Looks serious :(:(where r u???*

Beth flew off the couch. Her mobile was no use, so she tried Vicky on the desk phone, and went straight to voicemail. She tried again; nothing. She returned to the couch. Trapped by Fletcher, panic ran cold through her, stretching her frayed emotions. God, she should never have come here. She clutched her ears as Fletcher howled agreement. But for now, there was nothing she could do. She lay in the dark slipping towards sleep with tears on her cheeks.

What seemed like a few hours later, Beth woke to an eerie calm. Dim light brushed her senses, and she eased her feet to the floor. The roar of the previous night made the morning silence huge and ominous. She paced down the hallway. Out the front doors, nothing moved. The air hung with a mist, softly glowing in the early light.

She slipped outside and across broken leaves and twigs. The gums ringing the hospital floated like an enchanted wood, buried in fog.

Will stood at the corner of the hospital's paving, his thumbs in the waistband of borrowed scrubs. His head tipped towards her as she stood alongside him. Beth was suddenly very unsure she was even awake.

"The eye," he said, his voice barely a whisper.

Beth surveyed the white world. Her emotions levelled. She wasn't angry, now, just resigned and sad, waiting for escape.

Her hand settled on Will's forearm, his skin a cool shock, like the mist.

His hand covered hers. Warmth grew where he touched her, and a deep well of emotion threatened to rush upwards and spill down her cheeks. She was ashamed of how deeply she'd fallen for him. And she knew that the only solution for shame was to own its cause and move on, however much it broke her.

"I don't blame you," she said softly. "I made a mistake coming here. I have to go back to Sydney when this is over, while I still have a chance." There, she had said it, made the decision real.

"Don't go back," he said.

Her courage held, even while her heart crumbled. "There's nothing for me here."

"Of course there is."

But she couldn't stand to hear more. She could bear no more disappointment. She could hear how Will's breath caught; knew there were tears in his eyes she couldn't afford to see.

"Goodbye, Will." Slowly, she withdrew her hand. She had no tears left, now, just the heavy air in her lungs. He couldn't change her mind; but perhaps Richard would forgive her, and she could forget she had ever been to Iron Junction. She would give up on the idea that the world held something better than what she'd had in Sydney. The world was what it was: brutal and kind in turn, without reason or justice. She had no right to expect more.

So, when Beth finally retreated inside the doors, she prepared for the final hours in the roar of Fletcher. A last trial as she let all her hopes go.

Chapter 27

By late afternoon, the second phase of Fletcher beat itself out, and the radio broadcast announced it was safe to go outdoors again. Beth tried and failed again to reach Victoria. Barbara and Beth both spent time on the hospital's radio, trying to organize an evac for Doctor West, who needed surgery. Through the broadcasts, they heard that flash flooding had damaged large parts of the town, but it wasn't until patients began to arrive – some bringing stories of coming part of the way in boats – that Beth appreciated the extent of the impact. Finally, one of the ambulances managed to make it through and load Doctor West for the trip to the airport. Will offered to drive behind, and take Beth back to where she'd left her vehicle the night before.

Out the ambulance's back window, Beth could hardly believe what she saw. Water lapped the street edges, and in some places, the four-wheel drive crept through foot-deep flood. People floated by in small boats and canoes. She winced as she spotted waders in bare feet.

The airport seemed undamaged, and debris from the runway had already been cleared, like a freshly mown lawn. Beth spied two gray, heavy-looking planes on the tarmac, and as the ambulance pulled into the terminal, she could see a bunch of uniformed men moving around inside.

So, the army really was here.

A man in camouflage with two pips on his chest approached them, the name Rogers stitched over his right chest pocket. "Afternoon," he said. "You're here for the evac?"

Beth let the ambulance officers do the hand-over. Will had pulled up beside them now and climbed down from the cab to watch the goings-on. Beth turned away.

Instead, her attention snared on another man in fatigues, standing in the doorway of the terminal, a phone pressed to his ear, a pen in his hand. Beth counted three pips on his chest. He stood out from the others: commanding, focused, exuding authority well beyond his years. Dark hair cut short, lean face, wide stance, powerful-looking shoulders. Beth knew nothing about ranks, but she was sure this man was in charge. A moment later, he ended his call, took a sheet of paper from the waiting subordinate and strode over. Beth read the name on his chest: *Bell.*

"Rogers," Bell began, handing over the paper. His gaze fell on Will with a start of recognition.

Will stepped forward, an incredulous look on his face. "Aiden?" he asked.

The man offered his hand. "Captain Aiden Bell," he said slowly. "And you look familiar too … Walker?"

"Will, yeah. I'm Mark's older brother. And you're Daniella's brother. I've only ever seen you in photos, but Mark mentioned you'd been posted to Perth. I'm FIFOing out of there."

Beth finally made the connection. Will had mentioned Daniella Bell, his brother's fiancée and fellow doctor.

"Right. I move around a lot. Haven't seen Dani in ages, but you look a lot like Mark." He glanced at Doctor West's stretcher, now being maneuvered towards the terminal. "Look, I'm sorry, Will, but we're pushed here. Is there anything I can do for you?"

Will shook his head. "I'm just giving Doctor Harding a lift."

Doctor Harding. The casual distance Will injected between them cut Beth's heart like a razor.

"When this is all over, we should catch up in Perth," Aiden said, then vanished back inside the terminal.

Beth turned to stare at Will. He shifted uncomfortably, then walked to his vehicle. Reluctantly, Beth followed him. Silence was the soundtrack as he drove back to the highway and then north towards Beth's Prado. The edge of the road had crumbled in places and debris littered the tarmac.

"I don't like the idea of you driving through this," Will said at one point.

"That's not your problem," she said softly, and stared out the window.

Beth's vehicle was where she had left it, on the slightly higher ground, unobstructed by water. She noted the slowly spinning strobe, which she'd deliberately left on this time so the Prado could be seen. Another flat battery, another jump-start.

Will administered the electric charge as smoothly as before. As the engine ran, he said, "You should drive around for a bit before you turn it off. Make sure the battery's charged up."

Beth reached for the door handle, and as she pulled herself into the cab, Will said, "So, I guess this is it, then."

Beth said nothing. All she could think of was the first time she'd had a flat battery, and the land had been hot and dry, the town a remote oasis she'd wanted to reach, and Will had been the one to take her there. Now, the world was sodden, the town within reach, and Will was leaving. The finality of it was too much. She hated being defeated; hated that she was going back to her old life. Tears prickled her throat. "Guess so," she said. Then, with great effort, she pulled the door closed.

In the rear-view mirror, she watched him drive away, heading north towards Dampier. She had never wanted someone to turn around so much in her life. Tears silently etched tracks down her face.

Beth drove slowly, her exhaustion knocking. Picking her way through the streets made her all the more weary. The road was like an apocalyptic landscape, a real one this time, not the one she'd imagined when she first drove to Iron Junction.

It seemed her life was running in reverse; that Iron Junction had been nothing but an aberrant dead-end loop. She'd soon fly east, back to the start.

Will only went a few miles down the road to Dampier before he swung a U-turn and headed back. The hollow sensation in his chest was unbearable. He felt like throwing himself off a cliff, and not only because Beth had been so obviously heartbroken. It shredded his heart to know he was the reason she was giving up and going back to Sydney. It wasn't right for her. He'd seen her determination, her decisive and uncompromising capability, even in a frightening and unforgiving situation.

It had certainly scared the life out of him when he'd come back from the hospital bathroom to find she'd taken off into the night. Those gut-wrenching seconds when he couldn't see her car ahead, didn't know if she was all right.

But her fire was also the reason he had to walk away. He couldn't saddle her with his problems, and there wasn't any better reminder than the wreck of Doctor West's car across the field. He pulled to a stop on the side of the highway and stumbled out. The crumbled metal leaned against the boulders, burrowing inside his mind and waking uncomfortable memories.

As he slogged across the sodden ground towards it, the images of that night trickled back, ones he'd worked so hard to suppress. He leaned against the mangled body, light-headed amid the details. Crumpled bonnet. Water pooled in the footwell. Blood on the seat.

The trickle became a flood. Will felt a lurch. He was back in *a traveling car. Night-time. Dark. His head spun. He was pissed, he knew that. Wedged in the middle of the front bench seat. They were sliding around a corner. Kaz laughing. He didn't like this. Even with his hammered senses, he knew the car wasn't in control. This had been a good joke, but it was time to pull over. He straightened up to say it, moving slowly. Man, he was so drunk.*

And that was when he saw the eyes.

Green pairs, all over the road.

Oh shit.

A kangaroo was right in front of them. A swerve. They weren't on the road anymore. He felt the suspension bounce as they hit the grass clumps, and then the tree was rushing up to meet them.

Will stumbled backwards, blinking in the sun, tears in his eyes, humid air filling his throat, and dug out his mobile with a shaking hand. Down in Karratha, reception had become patchy, probably a damaged mobile tower. But here there seemed no problem. He searched through his phone's log, wincing at a text from Sarah telling him she was moving back to Adelaide. He'd never answered it. Finally, he found Mike's number.

The phone seemed to ring for a long time. "Will," Mike finally answered.

"Mike, look, I'm really not comfortable about any of this," said Will. "We get in a court and it's perjury. And what if they've got something new?"

Mike didn't answer for a while. "Will, she was my girl. I did it for her. You owe her to keep quiet. It's going to get a whole lot worse if we start changing the story. You can't back out now. Don't do that to me, too."

Will sucked in a breath. Mike had been a good friend back then, right up until the point where Will had wanted to tell the truth. Between Mike's grief and Will's shame, they'd never repaired the friendship.

"Think about it," Mike was saying. "You're a smart man. They haven't got anything to go on. The cops never took enough evidence. It'll blow right over. Then you can forget about it."

Will barely registered this. He was back there again, standing on the side of the road, in a daze. Flashing lights, red and blue and white. A copper was asking him what had happened, and someone else was trying to clean blood off his face. All he could see was Kaz, being loaded into an ambulance and taken away. He couldn't form any words. Will knew he was the one who could have prevented it. And then Mike was there beside him, giving his version. *Roo on the road*, he'd said. *I swerved and we went off.*

"How'd you fare in the storm?"

Will shook himself back to the present. "Survived it," he said bleakly. But he didn't want to talk to Mike anymore. Surviving the storm seemed the least of his worries.

He ran back to the Pathfinder and took off towards town, driving around debris and water. Twice, he found people in the streets attempting to shift rescued belongings to higher ground in overloaded boxes. He stopped and loaded them into his vehicle, ferrying people and dogs and framed photos from their sodden houses to the evacuation center. All day he kept at it. The effort was cathartic, but the more he did, the more he realized how much cleaning up would come later. The flood had made everything muddy. Most of the buildings were still standing, but many were compromised and no longer weathertight. The rain closed in again, falling softly.

When he finally made it back to his camp room, he found it amazingly unscathed. The temporary buildings remained in their rows on the hill above the Dampier shore, only covered in leaves, the ground sodden. A bunch of workers sat in a ring of plastic chairs, sharing a slab of beer.

As he passed, a guy Will vaguely knew brandished a can in his direction. "Want one?"

"Nah, thanks anyway," said Will, in a hurry to get inside.

"There's no power, they're just getting warm!" called the guy after him.

Will shut his door and leaned his shoulder into it. He didn't know what to do with the awful guilt he carried. He'd been wrong to go along with Mike back then.

But the truth wouldn't bring her back.

And Will knew in his heart he wasn't just thinking of Kaz, but of Beth. Nothing he did could bring her back, either.

Beth couldn't face the idea of going back to her room just to bear boredom and irritation alone. So she made her way to the hospital, where she found Barbara directing a clean-up, and a team of army guys up on the roof, applying tarps.

"What happened?" asked Beth.

"Part of the roof came off," said Barbara, ushering Beth back inside. "We didn't notice because it was down the back corner. But it shorted out some of the cooling system, so we need to get that fixed. Patients are starting to come in."

Beth noticed the half-dozen patients waiting in the ER. She spied an army man with a red cross on his arm helping a resident who had his arm in a sling.

"The army's lent us Captain May – he's a doctor," said Barbara. "We still have no idea where our reliever is – probably stuck somewhere with the highways cut. If you want to pitch in, be my guest."

Beth soon found herself in a curtained space with a man called Ricky, who had hobbled in with a shirt wrapped around his foot. Beth opened it to find a deep, three-inch gash running from his big toe down through the pad of his foot.

"How did this happen?" she asked him.

"Didn't want to get my shoes wet," he admitted. "I don't know what was in the water – might have been some metal sheeting, maybe. Or glass. I couldn't see it."

Tiredly, Beth set about finding local anesthetic and sutures, plus a tetanus booster.

All through the afternoon, she listened to the radio updates:

the water was going down, at least in Karratha where there wasn't a river to keep feeding water from higher ground. Reports hinted at a much bigger problem inland, where flash floods had swept through some creek systems. The highway might be open again in the morning. Beth sent several more texts to Victoria, worry mounting over her mother. She saw another two patients with injuries from unseen objects in the flood water, a man who'd dislocated his shoulder trying to catch a box thrown from the roof of a house, and another man with cuts from flying glass when a tree branch had gone through his window. She was amazed she didn't see anything more serious.

In a rare lull, Beth stood around the triage desk with Barbara and Captain May, drinking strong black tea made with a kettle boiled courtesy of a generator outside. Captain May appraised the case list. "This isn't too bad," he said.

Barbara nodded. "People up here are used to it. They're pretty well prepared. Although—" she raised her eyebrows at the latest man with a cut foot, "—that doesn't apply to everyone."

"What happens now?" asked Beth.

"We make sure this place is up and running, and get the staff back," said Barbara.

"And we test the water, to make sure there's no sewerage," said Captain May. "We don't want an outbreak of waterborne infection. That would be a disaster."

Beth was impressed to see the way the organizations had swung into action and were putting the town back in order. The army and State Emergency Service were out in force, patching roofs, supplying clean water and food, and the town council was keeping the evacuation centers running smoothly. But her heart had still sunk lower than the debris under the flood.

The next day, in the early evening, between the army and a

holidaying doctor who'd turned up to pitch in, the case load was under control. Beth escaped to the couch in a waiting area down the hall.

For the tenth time, she tried Victoria, and at last, her sister picked up. "Beth, finally!" she declared.

"Is Mum okay?" Beth asked, breathless with worry.

"Of course. Why?"

"Because you sent me a text saying she was in hospital!"

Vicky laughed. "Oh, yeah. It turned out it wasn't serious at all. Just a panic attack, they said. But I was so *scared*. I thought she was going to die. I needed you. What took you so long to ring back?"

"I tried," Beth began, clutching her head. This seemed absurd after everything that had happened. "Vicky, haven't you been watching the news at all? I've been busy."

"What, the cyclone? Why on earth would you be busy?" she said.

Beth hung up, at the end of endurance, and acutely aware how different she was from her sisters. She scrolled through her contacts, trying to decide which friend to call, trying not to want it to be Will. She paused when she saw: *Judy.*

Beth rarely called her aunt, but now her words from the party in Brisbane pushed themselves forward.

"Hello?"

"Aunt Judy. It's Beth." Beth's voice wavered, threatening tears. She had to bite her lip at Judy's delight, and her concerned questions after she learned Beth had just been through the storm.

"Are you shaken up by the whole thing, love?" she asked. "You don't sound too steady."

Beth plowed on while she had the courage. "It's not that. It's just … I wanted to ask you about something you said at Victoria's party. You said I was like my father, but I don't know what you meant."

"Well," began Judy, letting out a sigh as she settled into the story. "David Harding was a very clever man, and a good fixer. He had testing jobs – difficult sites, impossible projects and finding ways to make things happen. But he had purpose, got the best out of people. I always thought you were like that. Plus," she went on, "he had to be out in the world. He would have gone mad in a desk job. And when you went to Sydney on your own, I could see the same thing in you."

Something settled inside Beth, both sweet and bitter. "But he left," she said. "I guess he liked that more than he liked us."

Judy paused. "Yes, his job took him away from you, and he hated that."

Beth's throat prickled with tears. "Hated it so much he never wrote or called."

This time, Judy's pause stretched. "I'm sorry, Beth," she said at last, "Do you really not understand what happened?"

"What do you mean?"

"You know that it was your mother who left him, not the other way around?"

"No, that's not what happened—"

"Yes it is. She decided he was no good anymore, and she cut all ties. He wrote to you, always. I know because he wrote to me, too. I can't say for sure what happened to his letters, but I think you can guess."

Beth screwed her eyes shut, remembering calls in the evening she was never allowed to pick up, and her mother hanging up the phone, always saying it was telemarketers.

"It turned ugly after a while. Meredith accused him of some dreadful, untrue things. She's my sister, and I love her, but I'll never understand why she did that. He didn't want to put you girls through courts, and his work was at risk, too. In the end," Judy went on, gently, "he gave up. Sometimes patience ends. I'm so sorry, I thought you knew."

When Beth ended the call, she felt as though her mind and body had been worked over with a sledgehammer. She sat still for a long time, the information barely processing, her phone softly bleating its low-battery warning. As she lay down to try to sleep, her disbelief gave way to sinking acceptance.

What seemed like hours later, she opened her eyes to find light streaming in through the blinds. Her back had stiffened from the couch's lumpy seats, and her phone was ringing.

Beth fumbled on the floor for the handset and took a stab at the answer button. "Hello?"

"Doctor Harding?" A female voice. Vaguely familiar.

"Yes," said Beth, pushing up and rubbing her eyes.

"This is Doctor Forrest at the Prince Harry. It's about Caitlin Murray."

Beth was instantly awake. "What about her?"

"We've been trying to reach her and can't make contact. We were hoping you might know where she is."

Beth's phone made another bleep. Desperate, she said, "Hang on, my battery's going." She jogged towards the doctors' offices. She'd seen a charger somewhere in here. She found it and plugged it in, hoping the generators would hold.

"I haven't seen her," she then had to admit to Doctor Forrest. "But I haven't been in town for a few days. I'm out in Karratha. What's this about?"

"We have a donor match. A good one. But we need to find her in time. I know things aren't in a good way up there ..."

Beth's heart rate spiked. "Have you tried Maxine de Wet? She's the doctor in charge at the Iron Junction medical center."

"Of course, but I can't get through there at the moment. I don't have to tell you time's short. I'll keep trying but soon they'll have to move on to another match."

"Let me try to find her," Beth pleaded. She couldn't get around the idea that Caitlin had a chance. She was somewhere out there.

A pause. "Do you think you can do that in time?" asked Doctor Forrest.

"How long do I have?"

"Well, look. The donor's in Perth, which helps. But we can't sit on it. I'd need to hear from you in four hours, tops.

And she'd need to be on a flight then. We'd still have to do a work-up once she got here."

"Four hours?"

"Yes. We might have more time if we knew she was coming and could coordinate at this end, but so far, for all we know she could be in Queensland, and that's just wasting time for someone else."

Beth stepped into the hall. Through the window, the sun shone bright blue on the stripped eucalypts and the muddy earth. "Give me the four hours. I'll call you."

Beth hung up and dialed the Iron Junction medical center. The phone rang out. She tried again, with no success.

She cast around for another option, then remembered she had Maxine's private mobile number.

The phone rang and rang, and then, finally, Maxine picked it up. "Hello," she said briskly.

"Maxine, it's Beth Harding."

"Beth! How did you fare in Karratha?"

"We're still here. But I need your help – have you seen Caitlin Murray?"

"Not since last week. Why?"

Beth tried not to think that Caitlin might have skipped town and headed back to Karijini. "Her number's come up on the transplant list. They've got a match, but we've only got a couple of hours to find her."

Maxine paused. Beth could hear her moving, the muffled sound of her hand cupping the receiver. Beth suddenly felt sick. "Beth, the community was wiped out here," she said. "A flash flood came right through town. The water took everything on the low side, right over the roofs. There's still water through the town, and over the highway all the way to the mine. The medical center was spared, but our phone line's gone. The place is full of refugees – and she's not here."

"Has anyone seen her?"

"We're overrun, but I'll see what I can find out," said Maxine. "I'll call you back."

Beth was left with the hollow line. She paced, her thoughts spinning, until finally, her phone rang.

"Nancy saw her going into Mack's yesterday," said Maxine abruptly, without a hello. "That was just before the water came through. But no one has anything more recent. They're worried."

"It's not that big a place," said Beth in frustration.

Maxine's laugh was short and humorless. "You haven't seen it yet. As soon as we can get in again, we'll check the community area, I promise."

"I'm coming back," said Beth, but Maxine had already hung up.

Beth put her phone down on the bench. A sense of purpose welled up within, as it had on the night of the storm. Doctor Forrest wasn't hopeful; Maxine's report on Iron Junction was frightening. Ex-Cyclone Fletcher had dumped all its rain, making a red sea of the Pilbara.

But some part of Beth refused to accept defeat. All her exhaustion, her bruised heart, her doubt were shoved aside. She ran for the front desk.

Beth re-emerged into the ER to find Barbara scrutinizing a medication chart. The nurse took one look at her face and asked, "What's going on?"

"I need to—" Beth began, then she spotted Captain May's camouflaged back inside a patient bay and an idea struck.

Chapter 28

A commotion at the airport terminal door dragged Aiden Bell from deep thoughts on supply movements. Clearly, his subordinates were trying to keep someone out and weren't having much success. He sighed, wondering if this was the first desperate resident come to beg or vent.

"If I could just have five minutes," he could hear in a firm but exasperated voice.

Aiden leaned forward so that he could see the back of Rogers' head wagging back and forth as he attempted to dissuade the woman at the door. Aiden stood, and caught her profile: the doctor who'd been here yesterday with Will Walker.

He mentally filed a stop point on his task list and strode across the terminal. Good with faces and names, he'd remembered hers. "Doctor Harding," he said. "That's fine, Rogers," he added.

He faced the woman – her eyes bright, cheeks flushed, mouth set in a determined line. He'd seen this look before: the hopeful gaze of someone who believed he could give her something she needed. She reminded him of his sister, who'd served him a similar look many times. Aiden groaned inside, wondering what tall order he was about to be presented with and most likely have to refuse. "What can I do for you?"

"I'm looking for my patient. She's a young woman with lung disease and she just got a match for a transplant. She needs to get to Perth."

Aiden's brain moved unbidden into planning – if he had to make another evac, what could he scramble and how soon? What other movements could be put back to make room—

Then he registered her first statement. "What do you mean, you're looking for her?"

Beth knew she'd reached the point at which she could easily blow the goodwill she'd glimpsed in Captain Bell's eyes. She was sure, had Caitlin been here in Karratha, that there would be no question of a flight to Perth. But what she was asking was entirely different. Help finding someone she wasn't sure was lost, for a purpose she wasn't sure would even be available if she succeeded. And he was clearly a busy man with a whole host of other priorities.

"I need to make it to Iron Junction," she said. "And once I find her, she'll need to be evacuated to Perth."

"It's an emergency case?"

"Well … not exactly." It wasn't truly an emergency, compared with someone who was at risk of dying in the next few hours. "But if we don't find her, she might not get another chance at this, ever."

Captain Bell searched her face, no doubt looking for signs of madness, then paced back inside, beckoning her to follow. A large map was pinned up on a rolling board, multicolored pins stuck in various points. Beth had to wait while he took several messages and a short phone call, but he began again as if they hadn't been interrupted. "Here's us," he said, pointing to Karratha on the map, by the coast with a number of pins stuck in it. "And here's Iron Junction." His finger traced a good arc of the map, resting on the smaller text. "And this—" he looped his finger around the whole region, "—is where we have serious flooding. There's so much water out there, we're having to go off satellite photos for where we can put supply drops down. But wait a few days, and the level will stabilize, then it'll start to go down. It'll be easier to get in then."

"I've got three-and-a-half hours," she said bleakly.

Captain Bell paused with a raised eyebrow, which Beth suspected he didn't do very often. He sighed. "Iron Junction's three hours' drive from Paraburdoo, and that's when the road is in good condition," he said. "Iron Junction has an airstrip, but I haven't got a plane available that could land there, and certainly not one to take off inside three hours. It's forty minutes' flying time."

Beth's hope ebbed. Captain Bell regarded her with sympathy, but she knew that it wasn't his problem. She stepped towards the windows, unable to accept it. But, as she looked out over the airstrip, her hope sparked to life.

"What about those planes?" she asked, pointing across the runway.

He followed her finger to where, tucked down the tarmac, three small planes were still tied down from the storm. "Those are commercial planes," he said. "Nothing to do with us." But he gave her a sidelong glance with a boyish smile, and in it Beth saw a man who knew that sometimes bending the rules was possible, when it was necessary and daring.

"But ... ?" she asked, hopeful now.

Captain Bell tipped his head. "But ... if you find a pilot, I'll talk to air-traffic control and have you on your way, fast."

Beth's heart surged even as she glanced at her watch in despair. Time was running out. She remembered the pilot who'd flown her into Karratha – the engaging Troy – but she had no idea if he was even in town. She eyed the low charge on her mobile. "Don't suppose I could borrow a phone?" she asked, before Captain Bell could get back into his routine.

Less than a minute later, Beth was plonked on a desk at the side of the room with a phone and a dog-eared antique telephone book, open at listings for local regional airlines.

"Hello, Red Dirt Air," came the first answer.

"Hi, my name's Beth Harding and I'm looking for a pilot

named Troy. Yes, Troy. No, I don't know his last name. Actually, any pilot would do—"

Beth was then briskly told they weren't open for business. With a mounting panic, she heard the same story from every operator. Then someone tapped her shoulder.

She looked up to find an Aboriginal man in army fatigues, a Pilbara Regiment patch on his arm, *Hudson* stitched above his pocket. "You looking for pilot Troy?" he asked.

"Y-yes I am. Do you know him?"

"Yeah, I know him. We go fishing," he added.

Beth scrambled up. "Do you know where he lives?"

"Dampier, up the hill a bit."

"Can you give me an address?"

"Nah, but I could show you. It's ten minutes' drive."

Beth glanced towards Captain Bell, who looked sufficiently harried at this moment that she didn't dare ask the man for anything. But Beth's courage was buoyed. She had three hours and five minutes. Could she ask to relieve him of one of his men for half an hour?

Two minutes later, Captain Bell stared at Beth Harding's departing back. In truth, he wished her well. From an operational standpoint, his hands were tied, but that didn't mean he didn't admire her spirit. Lieutenant Rogers came alongside. "Briefing in five, sir," he said.

Aiden shook his head. "That woman was in here twenty minutes, and she managed to extract a favor, and now she's making off with one of the local regiment." He glanced at Rogers. "They're trouble, these medical women. My sister's a doctor. When we were kids, she got me tied up in bandages once, and I couldn't move. Dad had to cut me out."

"That right, sir?"

"Yes," said Aiden, thoughtfully. He hadn't seen his sister Daniella in a long time, and he missed her. His encounter with

Beth Harding had only reminded him of the fact. And he felt something like the same anticipation of trouble he'd had as a child, when Daniella had suggested he act as her bandaging guinea pig. "Rogers," he said. "Let's get the RAAF boys in the tower on the line. I want to speak to them."

"Right away. Any reason I should give?"

"I've got a funny feeling she's coming back with a pilot."

Chapter 29

"Run that by me again?"

Beth smiled. "I want you to fly me to Iron Junction. Right now."

They stood on the porch of Troy's house near the Dampier foreshore, having found him piling storm debris out the front. A bank of clouds had run across the sun, but the air was muggy with rising damp. Beth could feel the warm slick of sweat, part panic, part excitement, running between her shoulder blades.

He shook his head. "The army's got the airport."

"It happens they've promised to give us passage," she said, nodding in Hudson's direction.

"You don't know what condition the Iron Junction strip's in."

"Captain Bell said it wasn't flooded, on their last information."

"That doesn't mean it's landable."

"It doesn't mean it isn't," Beth fired back.

"And you don't know where this girl is," he countered.

"Not yet, but that's my problem, not yours."

"And what do I do about the fare back?"

"If she's there, you can take us to Perth," Beth said. "If not, you can bring me back here."

Troy flexed his arms, and put them up behind his head,

clearly enjoying himself. He eyed her curiously. "You've got an answer for everything. Who's going to pay for it?"

"Can we work that part out later?"

He laughed. "Nice try." But just as Beth's hopes were falling, he stood up. "Let me get my gear. You pay for the fuel at least. Anything else, we'll talk about it later. We'll do a pass on the runway and if I say we can't land, we're coming back here. Deal?"

Relief struck Beth dumb. She stuck out her hand, which he shook. "You know, I could get in a lot of trouble for this," Troy said but with a big smile.

Half an hour later, after pre-flight checks that seemed to go on forever, Troy taxied a four-seater light plane down the Karratha runway, which Captain Bell had duly cleared. Sitting alongside Troy in the cockpit Beth checked her watch. Two-and-a-half hours to go.

At first, as they lifted above the city, Beth fretted about the time, but as they moved further inland, her attention was arrested by the view. "Oh, god, look at it," she whispered.

Below them, great swathes of red water covered the country, only the ridges lifting above it. The highway emerged and dove back under the water like huge gray snakes. Beth saw no evidence of people, though at one point they passed a knot of cattle, stranded on an island amid the red ocean. "Poor buggers," said Troy. "Hope those army blokes are going to drop them some food."

The trip sped by, and finally, the familiar landscape of Iron Junction, cradled against the ridges, grew in their forward view. The sky was darker out here, tendrils of bad weather retreating south. Already, Beth could see the stain of flood water marring the town, a great yellow streak that stretched from the mine and down the bowl in which the town nestled. In some places, she saw it was over roofs, just the tops of white gables visible like wave peaks. On the other side of the bowl's hills, the creek was swollen into a giant puddle. Troy angled their approach, descending towards the runway, unflooded on the high northern side of the bowl. "Running that pass," he said.

The plane angled down, and Troy tipped his head as they sped past the red strip. "Yep, reckon that's good," he said. "You must be lady luck."

Five minutes later, after a banking turn, he set them down with one bounce. As soon as they'd stopped, Beth could smell the mud in the air, more fetid than it had been on the coast. She whipped her phone from her pocket, hoping the charge she'd given it back in Karratha would be enough. "Away from the plane with that," said Troy, twirling a cigarette between his fingers. Beth raised an eyebrow, but jogged away to the edge of the red dirt.

"You're where?" demanded Maxine a moment later.

"At the runway. How about a lift in?"

One hour and fifty minutes. And five of those ticked by while Beth and Troy waited. Then ten, then fifteen, until Beth began to wonder if Maxine had decided to abandon them. Finally, they spied a mine vehicle flying down the connecting road. A moment later, it pulled up, its sides thick with mud, the tires dripping.

"Are you crazy?" said Maxine through the open window.

"Certifiably," said Beth, jogging round to the passenger door, where she paused to shout back at Troy. "You coming?"

"Nah. Enough excitement for me today. Plus, I gotta get turned around and ready for when you come back."

As they drove towards town, Beth understood Maxine's delay. She was taking the longer route, the high road that looped around the western edge of town. As they approached the streets, Maxine said, "Hang on … this bit's slippery," before the borrowed four-wheel drive dipped down a low point before the train tracks and into a half-foot of mud. "The town's still under," said Maxine, steering them back on the high road. "But the community took the full front of the flash. All their places are on the low side. The water came through like a pole driver. People had to climb onto their roofs.

"Practically the whole community's at the medical center, now. It's hot and we're running low on supplies. People are angry, and Dale King's been hanging around making it worse."

"Why's that?"

"The water came down from the mine. They all want to know why. But even with everyone there, no one's seen Caitlin. I'm sorry, Beth."

Beth didn't like Maxine's tone. "I'm going to find her. She's here. I know it," she said, wishing she felt so sure.

Maxine hooked the vehicle onto the back street, and for the first time, Beth glimpsed the main drag through the building gaps. Every business was under water, halfway up the windows.

And silent.

The water didn't run, it pooled heavily, and she spied a small boat moving on it.

"Stop the car," said Beth. Before Maxine could protest, she was out the door running down the alley between Iron Junction Auto and the produce store. Halfway down, her feet hit the flood, and she slogged on, thinking to hell with her shoes, until the water was up to her thighs and the main street spread out before her, a still, red river.

"Mack!" she called. She saw the small boat do a pirouette in the water.

"Doctor Harding?" Mack leaned forward, maneuvering the craft towards her, using a spade as a paddle. As he came closer, Beth saw how ashen his face was, how the despair had pinched the life from his eyes. His bad leg was folded under him.

"Have you seen Caitlin?" she asked desperately.

"Most people are over at the medical center," he said, looking vacantly towards the remains of his shop, so deep in flood. "But I just wanted to wait here." Beth's heart broke for him; all the town history, all the photos, ruined beneath the water.

"She's not there," Beth said. She felt the water wicking into her shirt, filling her nose with a damp, slick smell. "Nancy saw her in your shop two days ago. Is that right?"

Mack dragged his eyes back to her. He seemed not to register the question.

"Mack … where did she go?"

Finally, he answered. "She dropped off files for printing. She was heading out with her camera. The rain had just stopped then. She was going to take shots from Iron Bluff."

Eighty minutes.

Beth put her hand to the side of Mack's boat, feeling a chill. She thought about the land between the town and the mine, the way it scalloped together to make a basin, and how the flash flood had come straight through there.

"Iron Bluff," Beth whispered. "Mack—" she reached out a hand to him. She wanted to find some comfort for him, as he watched his life soaking under the flood. "Stay strong. I'll be back," she said finally.

She waded away, then scrambled up the alley in her sodden shoes to where Maxine was waiting. Beth hauled herself into the cab, Maxine pointedly scrutinizing the water pooling in the footwell.

"Mack said she went to Iron Bluff, so let's go."

"Can't do it," said Maxine, pulling away from the curb and heading towards the medical center. "The highway's still closed. The medical center's on a local high point, but the water's right across the road, all the way up to the mine, from what we've heard." Maxine stared straight ahead. "Beth, if Caitlin was caught in the water … I don't have to tell you that even a strong person would have struggled. With her lungs … no chance."

"I'm going to look anyway; there must be a way," said Beth belligerently. She buried the fear deep, though she could plainly see that anything on the low side of town, towards the creek, was still under. "What about a chopper?" she asked.

"Ha! You might find one out on a station, but you won't make it through to those either. And unless that plane you flew in on has water skids in a storage compartment, it can't go anywhere near the place."

"Mack had a boat," Beth said. "Take me back down to the main street and we can use that."

Maxine gave her a hard look. "That was practically a canoe, and he was also using a spade to paddle it," she said. "Iron Bluff's a few miles away. It would be faster to swim."

Beth sagged. It was too much, this constant up and down.

As the mad part of her gave the idea of swimming some room, she became aware the vehicle was slowing. A pensive frown creased Maxine's brow.

"What is it?" asked Beth.

"You remember I told you people climbed onto their roofs to escape the flood, and they're now in the medical center? Well, they said someone picked them up in a boat."

"A fast boat?" Beth's hopes surged.

Maxine accelerated again. "Let's find out."

Just over an hour remained.

As they pulled into the medical center car park Beth could see that the place was overrun with refugees. Not only was nearly the whole Aboriginal community here, but many of the mine workers, too. Tents had sprung up on the edge of the car park, and knots of men sat on the curb, passing around a packet of cigarettes.

Beth followed as Maxine strode through the center's doors. Inside the air was humid and dank – the emergency generators were providing lights and essential power, but no air-conditioning. People were propped against every wall. Workers came and went through the front doors, gazing out on the water and retreating inside to the shade.

Maxine's rapid queries pointed them towards a familiar man in company site clothes, who was leaning back in a chair, wearing a cap that read *I'd rather be fishing*. Beth recognized him as one of the men who'd been there the night Grinner broke his arm.

"Are you Matt?" Maxine asked.

"That's me," he answered. Then his eyes shifted between Beth and Maxine. "Is there a problem?"

"I hear you have a boat," said Beth.

As far as Beth was concerned, Matt's boat was the chariot of the heavens. They found the sleek fishing cruiser where Matt had left it – tied to a street sign post, water lapping the underside of the hull, on which her name – *The Off-swing* – was scrolled in blue letters. To Beth's surprise, Maxine came along, leaving the medical center to Jennifer and the volunteer paramedics. The older doctor quickly showed she knew her way around boats. After releasing its tether, the gutsy Mercury engine roared to life, and they were soon creeping through town.

"Have to be careful around here," said Matt, gingerly maneuvering down the center of the street. "Can't tell what's down there. Don't wanna snag the prop and have to use those." He nodded towards two oars tucked down the side.

As soon as they cleared the outskirts, Matt let the engine have it, carving a wake across the red-dirt water. Beth checked her watch; she was down to forty-five minutes.

Matt slowed briefly when they crossed the highway – or at least, where he guessed it was – then cut the water towards the bluff. As they approached, Beth could see that the car park was just high enough to be dry, the bluff rising bluntly towards the scattering gray clouds.

"This is as close as I can get," Matt said, pulling them up five meters out.

Beth didn't hesitate; she leapt into the water, which reached her thighs. *Please be there, please be there.*

Her legs burned as she hauled herself out of the water and started on the upward path. As she neared the top, the Pilbara stretched before her, an orange, featureless sea, punctuated by rises: the western part of town, the ridge above, a few tree tops. A haze smudged the horizon, where distant flood and watery sky were indistinct. Alien. And beautiful.

Beth scrambled around the bluff columns. At first, she saw nothing, and the energy left her legs. Then she spotted a shoe, and a shin, and a different panic thrust into her heart.

Caitlin lay on her side in the shelter of the rock, her eyes closed, her lips pale. Her body was curled around a black shape – her camera – and an open rucksack. Beth saw in it boxes of medication, and three water bottles: two empty, one down to an inch. The oxygen cylinder was tucked against her cheek, the mask dusty.

"Caitlin!"

Caitlin's eyes fluttered. "Hi," she said vaguely, but nothing more came.

Beth cleared room and assessed her status. Her breaths were shallow and labored. Beth pressed the oxygen mask in place and opened the cylinder. A bare hiss came out. And although Caitlin was still conscious, it was clear she wouldn't be able to walk down the bluff. Beth scrambled back to the car park.

"She's up there!" she yelled across at the boat. "I need the kit, and some help to bring her down."

Maxine swung into action, wading across with the kit, then two oars and a tarp. "What's that for?" asked Beth.

"Stretcher," explained Maxine as they scrambled up. "Old trick I learned once." When they reached Caitlin, Maxine laid out the blanket, aligned the poles on top, then tucked the blanket edges under and around the oars. Beth looked Caitlin over. "Dehydrated," she said. "She could drop fast. We need to get a line started and get her out of here."

It was murder lifting Caitlin down the hill; in fact, if Beth had thought they had the option, she'd have stayed put and waited for a helicopter. Even though Caitlin was a slight woman, the extra weight made the descent tricky. At the end, they had to rest the stretcher while each of them stepped over the final drop, then picked it up again from below. Beth had stuffed whatever she thought she'd need of the kit in her pockets and tucked the precious camera in beside Caitlin, and left the rest of the kit at the top. For the final slog, Maxine and Beth, panting and exhausted, waded into the flood, the stretcher just above the water.

"Bloody hell," said Matt, grabbing the ends with his strong hands as the *Off-swing* held steady. Then, finally, Caitlin was on board, and Beth and Maxine hauled themselves up via the tiny ladder fixed to the back of the boat.

"Back to town," Beth gasped, shaking as the adrenaline burst faded.

Maxine gripped Beth's shoulder. "She can't go on a commercial flight. She needs oxygen support. And that plane you came in is too small."

Beth glanced up and caught Matt's eye, who reached for the *Off-swing's* radio. "India Juliet, India Juliet, India Juliet, this is the *Off-swing*, over."

A second later, Jennifer's voice crackled on the radio. Matt passed the radio handset to Beth, who pushed the button. "We need a medical evac to Perth asap for Caitlin Murray. And meet us at the water's edge with the ambulance." Beth glanced at her watch. "And call Doctor Forrest at the Prince Harry, and tell them we found her."

Beth knew the arrangements could take a while. She had less than five minutes left. *Please be enough.*

Four minutes later, Jennifer came back on the radio. "We got through. Doctor Forrest says you owe her a strong drink."

Beth leaned back on her seat as the *Off-swing* cut towards town. Caitlin opened her eyes above the oxygen mask and blinked in Beth's direction. A giddy smile broke through the sweat-salt on Beth's lips.

As they reached town they spotted the flashing ambulance lights. Caitlin was looking better as she was loaded, and they had fresh oxygen and all the meds they could wish for, but Beth knew that this was far from over. Beth and Maxine settled Caitlin and waited to hear how long it would be before they could leave for the airport. Beth had a sinking feeling it could be a long time.

Finally, Jennifer rushed down from the center. "They'll touch down in about forty-five minutes. Head to the strip now; you don't have time to unload and reload again."

"You mean *an hour* and forty-five?"

Jennifer shook her head. "No. Forty-five. Karratha's been taken over, but some army guy on the radio said they were scrambling something for you out of Paraburdoo. Does that make any sense?"

Beth tipped her head back, blessing Captain Bell with all her heart. Satisfaction glowed inside her, warm and without qualification. She felt … right. She had no idea what to do with such a tender, new feeling, so she tried to enjoy it, afraid it would disappear like magic.

"Beth?" said Jennifer, her face drawn with concern. "Make sense?"

Beth realized her whole body had tensed around the spark of excitement within. Slowly, she relaxed and smiled. "Yes," she said. "Yes, it does."

Chapter 30

Will kept himself busy for two days until the highways were open again: roofs were leaking, windows were broken, cars wouldn't start. With his hands-on skills, he never had an idle moment, from giving the touch of life to flooded generators to helping the emergency services personnel with the tarps. In between, he visited Dan, who'd been discharged to the camp and was spending time coordinating resources and telling stories to anyone who'd listen. Neither of them had seen any TV – power was still a limited commodity – but the radio had been clear. The Pilbara was swimming. People were stranded everywhere, many losing everything. The army was deployed all over now, dropping food, retrieving remote medical cases. But even occupied, Will couldn't make the emptiness go away. The pain of losing Beth deepened with each hour.

It wasn't until Will and Dan were both rolling out of Karratha, heading for home in East Angelas, that a special report broke the news about Iron Junction. The sun was coming up, glancing beams off the dust arcs on the windscreen. They listened in disbelief. A flash flood had lanced right through town, leaving over ninety per cent of buildings damaged and water trapped in the low parts within the ridges. The mine was shut, its dam burst, the pits flooded.

" *... although road access to the mine is still limited, company* *investigators have arrived to begin enquiries into the flash flood. Local residents are pulling together in the clean-up but the company is refusing to comment until the investigation is complete. This is Warren Booth, from Iron Junction."*

Will turned the radio off. The men sat in thick silence, measured only by the growl of the Pathfinder's engine along the highway. Will's fingers turned white against the wheel.

The older engineer cleared his throat. "Stage two," he said. "They were big earthworks, Will. Neither of us are civil engineers, but those walls would trap a lot of water. And if they weren't finished, and one of them failed, that's a tidal wave right through the town."

Will's gut turned. "Yeah, the reports mentioned the risk of water-course alteration, and recommended the work avoid the wet season." He shook his head. "But it's more than that. I saw the drawings. They were meant to build levee walls to push any water around the mine and the ridge, down the creek. But they weren't there. Never got built."

As the highway rushed towards them, and the sun lifted up and up, Will and Dan talked the whole thing through.

Finally, Dan pressed his fingers together. "So, King runs a parallel construction program with two stages that were meant to run in series. He pisses off key people by trying to go too fast or just because he's a bully, and they leave, so he ends up short-staffed in management. The work's not being properly checked, so mistakes are made, and rework gets expensive. So, now, he's got a cash-flow problem and a timeline problem; the whole thing's got away from him. Does that about sum it up?"

"Yeah," Will said. "He was committed to contracts he'd awarded. And he changed the program – took out witness points in the plant tie-in, changed the earthworks drawings. The thing I don't understand," he said, slowing as he spotted an intersection in the distance, "is why he let it go so far."

"Will, for a man like that, there is no problem. He'd never admit it, let alone ask for help. I guess if the cyclone hadn't happened, it would have limped on like that."

Will mulled on this as the intersection grew closer, and the sign for Iron Junction pointed south. Without needing to ask Dan, he took the turn. Something was smoldering inside him, a restless energy that needed to see the town or what was left of it. That wanted to put an end to all this.

Dan seemed to sense it. "It wasn't your fault, Will, remember that. King was in control. You weren't even on that part of the project."

But the coals within Will only flared, a metallic taste filling his mouth. Whatever he'd done, it could have been different.

"What's that?" he breathed. A speck had materialized in the road's mirage. Dan leaned forward. Will peered ahead, on the lookout for stranded travelers or wandering livestock. Then he cursed in amazement. Two plodding camels appeared, with the trailer made from an old Kombi van. A man swathed in khakis and a fabric-skirted hat steadily led them towards the coast. Just the same as they'd been that day with Beth.

Will pulled over and clambered down, his legs suddenly unsteady. The man raised a hand in greeting, his skin tanned and covered in red dust. "G'day."

"You okay?" Will asked.

"Yeah," said the man. "Lots o'water, eh?" The words tumbled like mud in a mixer. A voice that kept its own company.

"You need anything? Food? Fuel?"

The man barked a laugh. "Nah, mate. Everything's 'ere." He gestured to the trailer. One of the camels rotated its neck, jaw slowly working. Without a word, the man restarted on his road. A moving island in the desert.

Will watched them go with an aching sadness. He didn't want to wander alone like that.

Dan stuck his head out the window. "Finished communing with the wildlife?"

Will hauled himself back into the Pathfinder. He didn't know what the new start was, yet, but he knew he'd find it in

Iron Junction.

Half an hour later, Will and Dan coasted into the full force of the devastation. Will headed for the medical center, thoughts of Beth contrasting with how much the place had changed. Company marquees had been set up in the undamaged car park and alongside, a sea of tents had formed a temporary shantytown, from which grill smoke rose skywards. He also spotted five news vans parked behind a red-and-white tape.

"Cavalry's here," Dan said, nodding towards one of the vans. "That's the guy we heard on the radio. Hot shot from Channel Nine. The one who got punched by that politician last year."

Will grunted and watched people coming and going from one of the marquees, collecting generators and returning pressure cleaning rigs. He parked and left Dan in his wake, stalking towards the information tent. A man he didn't recognize stood behind a table, wearing a company shirt, and reading down a clipboard.

"I want to talk to the investigator," Will began.

The man's eyes fell on Will's work shirt. "And you are?" he asked warily.

"Will Walker. I was the engineer on the plant upgrades." He flicked out his old ID.

The man ushered Will into the medical center's kitchen, where a balding man sat across the table with a younger man, a laptop and piles of note paper. The balding man introduced himself as the company investigator. "We're just starting to collect information about what happened here," he said, with a small smile.

"I'm happy to tell you all about it," said Will.

"Good, that's good."

Will laid it out, from beginning to end, everything he knew, and his theory about how the flood had happened. The note-taker's fingers flew, but the investigator's face was unreadable.

"So, you weren't actually here when it happened?"

"No," said Will. "But everything was being pushed ahead, cutting corners. Stage two included."

"Do you have any proof to support your theories?"

"There were documents," Will said. "And any of the contractors will tell you what happened."

The investigator rubbed his eyes. "Mr. Walker, the flood destroyed all the office buildings, including records. And for now, none of the workers are willing to talk."

"What about off-site back-up?" Will's thoughts were flying, thinking of other options.

"The back-up center was also inundated. Of course, we'll attempt to recover the data, but even if we can it will take time. For now, the site will be focused on clean-up and repair. But thank you for the information, and your details. We may need to speak with you again."

Will pushed his chair back, deflated. He found it hard to believe that no one else had told this story. "Who else have you spoken to?" he asked.

"I'm sorry, I'm not able to discuss those details. But I assure you, we will be making a thorough and complete investigation."

Will walked back into the hall, and nearly ran into Dale King, who was striding towards the investigator's room with a coffee mug in his hand. King pulled up, surprise sending a jolt through his features. He recovered quickly.

"So, Walker, you're back in town." They stood for a moment in stand-off, neither of them moving. Then King stepped in close. "I thought I was clear last time."

Will struggled to maintain his temper. "I had to come back," he said tightly.

"Creature of strong convictions, aren't you, Walker?" said King, his voice flat. "And I suppose you've told the investigator some story. But everyone knows this was a terrible accident, a force of nature. And let's be honest. Your conduct in the project was questioned long before this incident, and you have no proof. Whatever you say will sound like a wild story to cover your own ass. And I won't have such allegations derailing the investigation."

Will stared at King. "You're running the investigation?"

"Local site coordination, really," said King, straightening his cuffs. "They need someone who knows their way around, who understands how to talk to the workers. Who can coordinate data recovery. And media spokesman, of course. We have a public face to maintain."

The fire inside Will became a furnace. His fists bunched.

King's eyes glittered and he stepped forward, until he was nose to nose with Will. "Well, Walker. Are you going to do it? Or are you a pissweak coward as well as incompetent. Come on," he hissed.

Will was coiled, ready to erase King's smug expression with his knuckles. He remembered that once, when he was ten, his father had hauled a station hand out and struck him, the only time he'd seen his father lay hands on another man. The man had been caught whipping the horses for sport and Will had seen the rage on his father's face. The man had been sent off with a fat lip and a bad reference. Sometimes, country justice was done that way.

Will had that feeling now, as if his father had uncurled inside him. But something stopped him. This was wrong; too easy. King wanted him to do it. Will's mind spun; King had tried to hold ransoms over him before – a poor report, the court case, and he'd done the same thing with Beth. Will was sure he'd love to add assault to Will's damaged record.

Slowly, Will unclenched his fists. He laughed. "Nice try," he whispered. "But you've got nothing on me. And I'm going to take you down."

Then he pushed past King, a solid shoulder connecting as he passed. Will stalked out into the glare of the morning sun, searching for a solution.

He spotted Dan picking through the equipment under the marquees. An older woman with a cast on her arm checked supplies on a clipboard. Behind the tape cordon, the reporters and cameramen leaned on their vans.

Will paused, his attention intent on the vans, an idea turning in his mind.

"Whatcha doing, Will?" Dan's hand landed on Will's shoulder.

Will turned. "There's a problem. A big one."

"I know it's a bit damp," began Dan, then he looked at Will's expression. "Shit, what?"

"King's chaperoning the investigation, trying to call it an accident. I told the investigator my version, but King's questioned my record, and he's going to keep it locked down."

"So, why are you looking at those reporters?"

"The investigation needs scrutiny, Dan. You said there was a hot-shot reporter over there."

"Will, wait," said Dan, his hand squeezing. "You can't go in front of someone's camera. Soon as you do, the story's about you and King will smear you. That's what happens to whistleblowers. I've seen it before."

"Then I'll give them something off the record."

"Like what?"

Will clenched his jaw. "Shit, I need those documents. They were all on-site, and under water now. Even the remote back-up flooded," he said in frustration.

"What about hard copies?"

"Anything I have is for the plant, not stage two. I wasn't on that part of the project—"

Then, abruptly, Will stopped. He and Dan looked at each other. "Site copies," said Will.

"Who was the foreman on stage two?" asked Dan.

"From what Matt said, King was overseeing it himself. But," said Will, fumbling for his phone, "They were all contractors. Someone was supervising."

He punched Matt's number.

Twenty minutes later, Will was standing with Matt and a crowd of workers on the muddy floor of the sports hall. Two pressure cleaners lay abandoned to the sides, and some ruined chipboard was piled in a wheelbarrow.

"Here he is now," said Matt, as a burly, graying and vaguely familiar man pushed his way to the front. Will took a moment to place him: the man who'd been arguing with King, weeks ago at the beginning of the job in Iron Junction. The one who'd been demanding work orders in writing.

"Yeah, I've got paperwork," the man said, after Will had explained the situation. "Fucker wasn't paying his invoices, so I made sure it was in writing after that."

"Signed by King?"

"Nah, signed by the tooth fairy. Of course signed by King."

"What about drawings?"

"They were in my camp room. All under water. But …" The contractor boss looked around. "Any of you blokes get your cars out in time? Yes? Check your toolboxes, gloveboxes and lunchboxes."

He turned back to Will. "Let's see what we can find."

The crowd dispersed to find their vehicles, and soon, site drawings and work orders were turning up, mud-splattered and coffee-stained. Will scrutinized the documents. Some were illegible, but it was something. "It's not a complete set, but we can prove King ordered the work, and that at least some short cuts were taken on the original designs."

"Do you really think you can get around him?" asked the contractor boss. "He's a slippery bastard."

Will spun his keys, knowing there was one cog left. "Come to the next briefing and see for yourself."

At one o'clock, Will watched King calmly position himself in the shade of the medical center to give the latest company briefing. The press held up their microphones as Will, Dan, Matt and the mud-splattered workers hung back. King appeared at ease, charming the journalists and ensuring they were satisfied with the sound quality before beginning. Will folded his arms, nerves tumbling inside him, wondering how this would go.

"It's still unclear what occurred prior to the inundation," King was saying. "But we are investigating the circumstances thoroughly and completely. In the meantime, I am ensuring the town is cleaned up and rebuilt where necessary." King gestured across to the workers.

Then, from nowhere, a strong voice cut above the press pack.

"Warren Booth from Channel Nine News. Mr. King, what do you say to allegations that you yourself made key changes to the works at the Iron Junction Mine, which then led to this flooding event?"

"Well, Mr. Booth, I'd say any such allegations are baseless," said King without hesitation. Will stopped breathing. The rest of the press were frantically scribbling.

"Isn't it true, though, that you changed the works schedule, and began earthworks that were allocated to only occur in the dry season?"

"This was an unfortunate accident and these scurrilous—"

"Are you now pre-empting the findings of the investigation?" asked the reporter. "And how is it appropriate that a person of interest, such as yourself, is involved in organizing the investigation?"

Three seconds ticked by, punctuated by camera flashes. King held up his hand, for the first time appearing wrong-footed and out of depth, his lips compressed. But he waited for quiet before going on. "Let me make one thing clear. We won't be having any conspiracies or unfounded nonsense speculated about this incident. The company will view such accusations as defamatory."

King caught Will's eye across the crowd, but the irrepressible Warren Booth plowed on, holding up a fistful of curling papers. "This reporter has personally sighted documents that support your ordering work and altering documents. Will you answer these questions, Mr. King? What are you hiding?"

Soon, all the reporters were clamoring with questions. King braved them for five seconds with a stony face and threats of lawyers before he stormed back inside the center. The press were kept out by company security, but Will's heart lifted. They had their story. And that would keep pressure on the investigation.

"Mr. Walker."

Will turned to find Warren Booth standing before him. The man had a hard face with prominent brows and a broad, twisted nose. Will suspected that nose made a good target.

"Thank you," Will said.

"No, thank you," said Warren, handing back the documents. "We've been stonewalled for a day and a half. Might have some action now. I'll have my researcher follow up with you. Never know. Might be a Walkley in it for me."

As he stalked away, Dan clapped Will on the shoulder. "Nicely done," said Dan, watching the reporters frantically making calls and recording introductions with their cameramen. "Now, if you'll excuse me, I want to have a word with the company reps."

"What for?"

"Giving my account, of course, assuming that the path to the investigator is now clearing up," said Dan, hitching up his trousers. "I also thought I would offer my services. You'll be going back to the clean-up, but I'm supposed to take it easy until I get the ticker checked out. And this place is going to need a decent manager."

Will gripped his hand. "Good luck."

Much later, Will found himself in a group with Matt and Grinner – his arm in a cast – who spent the last of the day going through the inside of Mack's shop. As the sun went down, they sat, exhausted and muddy on the windowsill, cracking open bottles of tepid water that the army had dropped down the street. A generator hummed out the back, and the radio played through the early news.

With his bottle finished and the news coming to a close, Will stood, looking for work. The weather report was for more fine, sunny days. Then the serious tone of the female announcer lightened. *"And now, a good-news story from the midst of the Fletcher devastation. It seems a local doctor has gone the extra mile for a patient trapped in the flood-affected region. Doctor Beth Harding was in Karratha when she heard her former patient, a local of Iron Junction in the Pilbara's mine country, had been matched with a donor for a lung transplant in Perth. When no one knew how to find the patient, Doctor Harding found a willing pilot and flew to the tiny town inundated by a flash flood. Undaunted, Doctor Harding found a boat and powered across country to locate her patient, who is now in the Prince Harry Hospital awaiting her transplant. Doctor Harding spoke with our reporter a few minutes ago from Perth."* Will's heart gave a great kick. *"It's a miracle, really,'"* came Beth's voice over the radio. *"'I want to thank Captain Bell and the army for their help in the evac, and Troy who flew me in, and Maxine, Matt and all the folks in the Junction who helped us out. It was a real team effort.' And that's the bulletin …"*

"You hear that?" demanded Matt. "I'm a national hero!"

As the boys all cheered, Will tipped his head back and laughed. He would bet any money that the team effort had been Beth, doggedly pulling others into the plan she had to see through. God, he loved her.

Will's laughter ran out as the ache collapsed him. He stood up and stumbled around the corner, where he could press his face against the bricks, sucking for air, tears spilling down his face.

Shit, what a mess he'd made. He hadn't been protecting her at all. She'd let him in and he'd covered himself. He didn't deserve her; that much had not changed. But he'd been a coward not to return her trust.

He thought about the camel man, out on the highway. You could hide out here in the vastness, disappear in it. Lose yourself, and everyone around you, too. But sometimes, in the isolation, you found things that mattered. He watched the people working in the street, piling debris, helping each other. Contractors and townies and the army, all together. Then he thought about Dan, two marriages down and still working here, still doing the same things. He didn't want that fate, either.

He wiped his face and found his keys in his pocket. Matt still sat at the window.

"It's all right, sunshine. Mum says the dirt comes right out," teased Matt.

Will gave him a crooked grin, not caring. "Matt, there's something I have to do."

Chapter 31

Beth was contemplating whether she could get away with staying at the hospital for a third night. Doctor Forrest was currently off-shift, but Beth couldn't bring herself to leave. After the tense flight to Perth, rehydrating and coaxing Caitlin to an improved condition, all the final work-ups had been completed and the transplant had gone ahead. Caitlin had been in the ICU for two days, and right now, rounds were assessing if she could come back to the regular ward tomorrow.

Beth hugged herself, unable to be still. Things up north were still awful, so she'd avoided watching the news; she'd only had one brisk contact with Maxine when Caitlin had been in surgery.

So, Beth was surprised when the older doctor called.

"I suppose the worst is over now," she said. "I hope it goes well."

"So do I," yawned Beth. "How are things up there?"

For a while, they discussed the town, the anger over the flood. But with the water going down, people were taking stock, throwing out the irreparable, and starting again. Beth glanced down the hall. In a funny way, it was almost exactly what a transplant did.

"We had some excitement today," Maxine went on. "It seems one of the reporters took Dale King to task, and the company's had to stand him down while they investigate." She paused. "Beth, I wanted to say something to you. I've been in this job a long time, and after things that happened to me, I'd lost my drive. I told you that before. But you've reminded me why I got into it in the first place. Not that I want to be tearing off across country looking for lost patients like a mad woman, but I'm inspired again. I think everyone is. Caitlin's aunt's on her way down there, but we all want to see Caitlin back here. And I hope we'll see you again, too."

When the call ended, Beth slumped in a chair, bone-tired, the glimmer of satisfaction tempered by reality. After the six-hour operation and time in the ICU, Caitlin still had a long way to go. And in these quiet times of waiting … that was when the ache came back.

So Beth kept busy. For the third time, she paced around Caitlin's empty ward bed. The precious camera sat perched on the side table, and Beth couldn't help but see the room as Caitlin might. So stark.

She rummaged in her backpack looking for color and came up with the photo packets she'd stuffed in there the day she left Iron Junction. They had taken a battering around the edges, but when she slid them open, the photos were crisp and unscathed. She flipped past a few blurred shots. Reaching the images of Karijini, she shuffled past them, not wanting to deal with the feelings they would evoke. Then, right at the end, she found the photo from Will's balcony.

In the frame, she and Will were off to one side, the rest of the image given over to the beach and the horizon. But what shocked Beth were the similarities with another shot. Fumbling in the backpack pocket, she pulled out the creased picture of her and Richard from Sydney. It could have been the same photo; pictures from different universes, different versions of herself. But the one from Perth had life in it. The color in her cheeks, the smile reaching her eyes. The right version. Beth put her face in her hands, tears gathering. This was too cruel, the universe taunting her with should-haves and could-haves. She closed her fist, ready to destroy the evidence, when in the window's reflection, a figure appeared.

No, it couldn't be. She whirled.

Will stood in the doorway, wearing a beaten pair of jeans and a worn blue shirt, looking tired and thoroughly unsure of his reception. Beth had no idea what to say. At the one time he was the most appealing sight she had ever seen, and also the one that tied her in knots.

"Hi," he said.

"Hi," she returned.

Silence.

"I heard what happened, on the news," he said. "I also heard you claiming it was a team effort." His grin briefly flashed over his lips and Beth felt the anguish of wanting him while fearing he would only hurt her again.

"It was," she said.

He glanced heavenwards. "Of course it was." He fixed his gaze on her. "Come on, I know it was all you."

"Many people helped …" she said with a small smile. "Just some more willingly than others."

"Ah," said Will. "How is she?"

"Probably out of ICU in the morning," said Beth.

"Is that good?"

"It's excellent," she said, with genuine relief. Until this moment, Beth hadn't been able to share the good news with anyone close to her. She longed for Will to make it clear why he was there, to stop toying with her hopes.

Will shifted. "Beth … can we talk?"

"About what?"

"About what an ass I've been."

"That depends …" she said.

"On what?"

She glanced towards Caitlin's camera. "I have an idea. You help me out, maybe we can talk."

"What do you need?"

Beth reached for the camera and ejected the memory card. "I'll tell you about it on the way."

The mighty Mini Moke was waiting for them in the hospital car park. Beth turned the memory card over in her fingers, hoping that this idea was a good one.

"So, where to?" asked Will.

"I want to go to a copy store. We need to print some pictures." Beth noticed that the green tinsel was still on the dash, and tried to avoid thinking about the last time she'd seen it. "I want to make them big. On canvas, on paper, whatever."

"Then what?" asked Will, starting the engine and heading out of the car park.

"Then I want to put them up in her hospital room. She told me last time she was here that it didn't feel like home, so I want to put something up from up north, you know – her pictures, through her eyes."

Will made no comment. Beth glanced at him. "What?" she challenged.

"Nothing. That's a really good idea."

Beth sat back. "Well, all right, then."

Later, when Beth and Will finished their handiwork in Caitlin's room, they stood back to admire the effect. The barren walls had been transformed into a great Pilbara window. Beth had found shots on the card from Karijini, so she'd put those right at the foot of the bed, the soothing rock pools washing the red rock in direct view. Around the side of the room, she'd hung some of the incredible shots they'd found of the flood. Caitlin had captured the leaden sky, the mine swallowed by water while the tiny dip of land and the town faced the roaring front of the flash flood. They were confronting pictures, images of devastation and of loss. But also of the raw power of the country Beth knew that Caitlin loved. To balance this, she'd added a few shots of her own, texted from Maxine, of the miners and the community clearing the houses in town. Downtrodden and muddy, but proud and strong and brave.

Will bent his head towards her. "I hope she likes it."

"Me too. But mostly, I just want her to get well again so she can keep doing her work." They stood close, now, enough for Beth to feel the warmth from Will's skin. Buried hope stirred, and she looked up. "Thanks for your help."

He glanced down into her eyes. "What do you think about that talk? If you're too tired—"

"No, I'm fine."

She took him down to the empty patient lounge, with its shelves of books, comfortable couches and soft blue walls.

Beth lowered herself onto a sofa, and Will sat carefully beside her. "I made a complete hash of it," he began.

"You did," agreed Beth. "It hurt."

"I know. And I know it was the worst time to do it. But please don't go back to Sydney. I know you don't really want to."

Beth took a breath. "I don't know if I can trust you."

"That's a fair call, but last time had nothing to do with you." He reached for her hand, and she let him take it. Comforting warmth spread through her. "I want this. I really do. And I will explain, I promise. Give me another chance?"

Beth looked into his green eyes through the lens of her pain, wavering. She released his hand.

"I kept your textbooks," Will plowed on bravely. "Do I get points for that? Safe on my nightstand."

Suddenly Beth cracked a smile. "God, you haven't been reading them, have you?"

Will grinned back. "I had to get to sleep somehow."

She laughed, then her voice became serious. "But I'm not in Iron Junction anymore, and neither are you."

"I know," he said. "And there's a lot of stuff to work out,

but I want to try."

Beth considered for a long moment, leaving him hanging as she looked around the room. Patient lounges were scenes of both joy and suffering. Family gatherings happened here. Bad news was given here. Where this conversation led wasn't yet clear. "There's one thing I want to know. How did you even get down here? Karratha's tied up and every plane seems to be in use for something else."

Will ran his hand through his hair. "I drove to Paraburdoo. And I happened to find a pilot there, refueling, by the name of Troy. He remembered you, so I put on my best charm."

"Oh really?"

"Well, it might not have been altruism, or my superior negotiating skills. He said you owed him some money."

Beth smiled to herself.

"Beth," said Will finally. "I've never met anyone like you. I love you. If you say no, I'll deserve it. But I'd rather try and deserve you."

Will offered her his hand.

Beth was aware of the turn of this moment, the potential for all to go wrong again. But maybe that was what made adventures. Exhilaration and reward came with risk, and neither doubt nor hope could change what would happen. She'd learned that from Caitlin. There could only be courage, action, and what would come.

Will's flat at Cottesloe was exactly as he'd left it. As he and Beth climbed the stairs, he let his hand drift, capturing her fingers. Not a word was said, but the electric shock of the contact drove him faster. He fumbled with the keys.

Inside, he avoided the couch, the scene of their awful confrontation on Christmas Eve, and drew Beth towards his bedroom. He half expected at any moment that she would turn him down; would pull away and tell him he was dreaming.

But the tension never broke. As they crossed the threshold, she turned and pressed against him, slipping her arms around his neck, and kissed him. Her lips were soft, her mouth caressing him, making him tremble with desire. She unbuttoned his shirt and slowly pulled it off his shoulders, allowing it to drop to the floor. She ran her hands over his chest, then down his back. He groaned softly.

Then he realized. She wasn't going to stop him, wasn't going to push him away. She was braver than he was, taking the chance that he'd hurt her again but wanting him all the same. He wasn't worthy of her, truly he wasn't.

But he knew he wanted to be.

So, he gathered her closer. Stopped his second guessing, and enjoyed the moment for the honesty it was, slowly kissing her neck and collarbones, then sitting on the side of the bed so he could kiss from her throat to her belly.

"Beth … I think we have a problem," he said roughly.

"What?" she answered. A flicker of concern. And he loved that she had no reason for it.

"You have too many clothes on."

And he pulled her down onto the covers so he could kiss her again while he slowly removed all her clothes.

Midnight was nearing by the time they were quiet again. Beth lay tucked against him, her fingers drifting over his stomach, one each side of his board-shorts tan line. Will's hand was cupped against her hip. He very much wished this night would not end, or that if it had to, he could repeat it again tomorrow, and the day after. And the day after that.

Later, when the early hours of the morning were still dark over the beach, Will left Beth sleeping and paced out to the lounge room, where he could hear the surf on the shore. He flicked on the TV, the volume at a whisper, and waited for the news bulletin. He was shocked a moment later when the picture behind the newsreader flashed to the Iron Junction town sign.

"Revelations today in the Pilbara flood disaster," began the grim anchorman. *"There are more damning reports surfacing around the Iron Junction Mine manager in the wake of the devastating flash flood."*

Will stood and watched as the reporter detailed allegations of accounting irregularities, and safety breaches raised by employees, former and current. Halfway through the report, a warm hand touched his bare shoulder, leaving a trail of goosebumps. Beth. Will trapped her hand and squeezed.

The report cut back to the anchor. *"Acting mine manager Dan Beecham says the community is devastated but pulling together, grateful for help. He added he hoped justice would be swift and the town could move on to a bright future. Accused manager Dale King continues to deny any wrongdoing."*

Will flicked off the television, an uneasy truth surfacing. What a shit it was to deny responsibility for things you'd done. He sank into the couch. He didn't want to be that man, not anymore.

"It sounds like interesting things are happening in the Junction," Beth said carefully, sitting beside him.

"Yeah," said Will. "I might have had something to do with that."

He pulled her down next to him, smoothing her hair back from her face, and told her the whole tale: driving back with Dan, the investigator, facing all the contractors and his conversation with Warren Booth. Beth listened, astonished. "So, the reporter got stuck into Dale in front of everyone? Isn't that the guy who got hit by that politician last year?"

"Yeah. King probably tried to have the lawyers jump on the footage, but there's too much momentum now."

Beth gave him a coy grin. "I love you."

"You do?"

She snuggled against him. "Yes."

Will felt the smile fading from his face. Now or never. "Beth, there's something I need to say."

"I wasn't snoring, was I?" But one look at his face and she stopped joking.

Will paused. His plan had an unknown outcome. He had to warn her he was walking into trouble.

"It's what I promised to explain. All I can say is that it's serious. It's to do with an accident I was in a few years ago. I've been running away from it for five years and I need to end it."

She squeezed him tightly. "This what you didn't want to talk about?"

"Yeah. You might have to prepare to hate me again."

Will plunged on before he lost his nerve. "This goes back to when I was living in Queensland," he said. "You remember I said how I was into cars in school? Well, I was crazy about them. And I had this friend, Michael, who drove the demo circuit. He got me into it too, and I drove his cars, we had a few sponsors. And then this one weekend, he brought his girlfriend out for a truck rally. And that's where it all went wrong."

Beth listened patiently while Will related the whole story. Though her shock was evident, she never made a move to leave.

"I have to make a trip to make it right. Will you come with me?"

"Yes," she said, so simply. He knew that other women would have left, but here was Beth, sticking by him. "Where are we going?" she asked.

"Mackay, in Queensland," he said.

Chapter 32

The Mannings' house was a modest brick place in an estate a few miles from the center of Mackay. Bruce Turner would have been horrified to know that his client was taking this action, so Will hadn't bothered to tell him. He hadn't told Michael Hodges, either. What he had done was call ahead, asking if they had time to talk to him. He'd heard the surprise in Mrs. Manning's voice, but she didn't question it. So, now, here he was.

He left Beth at the hotel and took their hire car, feeling bereft as soon as he'd driven away. He steeled himself. What he was doing was without doubt the second-stupidest thing he'd ever contemplated in his life, but one in which he no longer believed he had a choice.

His knock was answered by a woman in her fifties with straight, shoulder-length hair. Her mouth was lined, her eyes watery, but Will could see the resemblance in the bone structure. His stomach tightened. "I'm Will Walker. I called earlier. You must be Mrs. Manning?"

"Yes, come in," she said. A man appeared in the hallway. Will offered Mr. Manning his hand; he wondered if the man would want to shake it again after he heard what Will had to say.

"Through this way," he said.

They sat in a living room on plain, pale-gray sofas, facing

each other across a low wooden table. Will refused their offers of a drink. Now he was on the cusp of action, he felt courage deserting him, and couldn't contemplate further delay.

"Mrs. Manning, Mr. Manning," he began. "You don't know me, except that I imagine you've seen my name on papers for the case, and on earlier ones from the accident. But I wanted to speak with you before court. Everything I'm going to tell you I'm sure my lawyer would advise me not to, but I'm going to anyway. Is that okay?"

Mr. Manning glanced at his wife. "We were surprised to hear from you," he said. "But I want to know what you have to say. And if I can keep our lawyer out of it for now, that's better. The man costs a bomb."

Will nodded. "I can't begin to understand how awful it must have been to lose Kaz. And I think you deserve to know what happened. That's why I'm doing this." He swallowed. "All the accident reports are pretty much right. We did lose it going around a corner. We got straight again, but then there were roos on the road and we swerved and went off. But the reports say Michael was driving." Will looked both of them in the eye. "And that isn't true."

Mr. Manning sat back in his seat and sought his wife's hand. "Go on."

"I was responsible for everything that happened," Will said. "I liked Kaz. Everyone did. She was Mike's girlfriend, but that didn't stop me being an idiot trying to impress her. She liked my car. The truck rally was on and I'd been doing demos, so I'd been showing her burnouts and circlework. We were at the pub most of the afternoon. Mike was playing pool, keeping his eye in. When we went to leave, I was trashed. I knew I shouldn't drive. But Kaz had only had a couple, and she grabbed my keys."

For a long, awful silence, no one said anything.

"I don't believe it," said Mr. Manning, getting up. "She didn't drive."

Mrs. Manning's lips twisted. "That's right. She wasn't licensed," she said. "She'd never bothered. Her friends drove her everywhere."

Will nodded miserably. "Yeah, I didn't realize at first. I thought … well, she *was* twenty-one. We learned to drive young out on the stations." Will took a sticky breath. "It was my car. She wasn't a good driver, that much was obvious, and she admitted it after a few minutes. But I let her keep going. I had plenty of opportunities to shut it down. And I didn't."

"I suppose Michael was in on this? He knew she couldn't drive," said Mr. Manning.

Will swallowed. Mike had been beside him on the bench seat, thinking the whole thing was hilarious, and egging Kaz on.

"It was my car and I was sitting next to her," Will said carefully. "I wish I could tell you I'd been driving. Maybe if I had, she'd still be here."

Mr. Manning made a frustrated sound and sat down again. "Bloody Michael," he hissed. Then Mrs. Manning spoke. "I want to know what happened afterwards."

Will took a breath. "We were all in shock. We sat there for a long time. Kaz hadn't put her belt on, but she seemed okay at first. She just said she was sore. Then we had to wait to flag someone down. It took ages for the ambulance to get there, longer for the police. And then Mike told them he'd been driving. I thought he was confused, but he wasn't. He loved her and he didn't want her to end up being charged: driving unlicensed, and over the limit, too. We thought that would be her biggest problem. We … didn't expect her to die."

Will broke off. The room was silent, save ticking from a wall clock. "I've thought a lot about whether you'd want to know," he said finally. "But it's the truth, and in the end, I don't think it's right to hold it back from you."

For a long time, neither of them said anything, their faces masks of shock and agony, until Will wondered if he should just get up and leave. But then Mrs. Manning spoke, her voice rough. "We always knew there was something not said about what happened. Michael was so wild. I didn't think he was good enough for her. He promised to look after her. But I shouldn't have let her go on that trip." Her face crumpled.

Mr. Manning gripped his wife's hand. "It's not your fault," he corrected. Then he returned his attention to Will. "I don't really know what to do with what you've said. We got into this case because we were never satisfied. There wasn't enough evidence for a criminal trial, and we thought this would be it. Of course, it doesn't feel that way. Just lawyers and court dates and no one really cares about Caroline. But we kept going because we wanted some justice for her. She was our only—" He broke off, then fixed Will with a hard stare. "How do I know you're not just shifting blame onto her? It would be very convenient, wouldn't it?"

Will slowly nodded. "I can understand how it might look. But I've got no reason to lie to you. Mike and I haven't been friends for years now, and I'll probably be looking at charges for obstructing police if nothing else. So will he. It's terrifying to be sitting here. But I don't feel I can do anything else."

The Mannings looked at each other, and Will's chest ached with their anguish. He hated that he'd been part of the injustice they'd suffered. He stood slowly. "I don't imagine this changes anything about how you feel, and I'm sure you don't want to spend more time with me. But I'll leave my number and I'll do whatever you need to make this right. She was—" Will found the tears slipping down his face now. He imagined what it would have been like for his own mother, if his sister had died like this. "She didn't deserve what happened. She should have had a long life. I'm sorry I had any part in it."

The Mannings didn't move. Then, Mr. Manning looked Will in the eye. "We'll have to think about all this."

Will drove back to the hotel feeling lighter, but with a new terror inside him. Now he'd acted, all the potential futures he had dreaded – in which he was prosecuted for obstruction of justice – were now possible.

He found Beth sitting cross-legged on the bed, staring at the television in disbelief. "Guess what?" she said.

"What?"

"A gallery in Perth saw Caitlin's pictures on the news – the journos tried to interview her after the operation – and she's agreed to run an exhibition of her shots for the relief effort."

"That's fantastic," he said, though his enthusiasm was forced.

Beth picked his tone immediately and shut the TV off. "How did it go?"

He rubbed his hair and sat down beside her. "I'm not sure, yet. I told you I could be looking at charges. Michael, too. I'll just have to wait and see what the Mannings do."

Beth nodded solemnly. "Are you scared?" she asked him.

Will thought about it. "Yes," he said softly. "But I was done with it haunting me all the time."

"I have to ask – did the accident have anything to do with you leaving home?"

For the first time, a pulse of emotion hit Will behind the eyes. He blinked and looked away, but Beth snared his hand. "Yeah," he admitted. "Though no one knows about that. I meant it when I said I love Dad and I respect him. He was always the straight-talker. He would tell you what he thought, no matter what. I knew I'd disappoint him, leaving farming for the mines. But after the accident … I knew I hadn't done right, and I couldn't stand myself. He was a constant reminder of what I hadn't done. He would have been ashamed of me."

"He never found out?"

Will shook his head. "I'd been taking my car to trade, so I just came back with the new one, no questions. It didn't make the news. There was a lot going on that weekend."

"How did you explain—"

"My injuries? They were minor, really. That was one of the

hardest things: Mike and I walked away. We thought Kaz would be fine, too. I said I'd been in a bar fight. That was the end of it … Dad went on and on about the right way to conduct yourself. That the Walkers were better than that sort of thing. Mark looked up to me, and I couldn't stay. I knew I didn't belong there anymore. I took my bag and walked out. I've never been back. Mum was …" Will paused, struggling to continue. "I think she knew that something had happened. But even when she was dying, I couldn't tell her. It hurt such a lot to lose her. But it was worse that she'd raised me better than I'd behaved. I got the angel to remind me." Will tapped his shoulder. "She was supposed to look over me, motivate me to put things right. But I couldn't quite get there."

"Wow," Beth said slowly.

Will held his breath, a horrible weight in his guts. Then Beth pulled him down beside her on the bed, taking him into her arms as they lay close together. "I wish that had never happened to you," she said slowly. He felt her lips on his forehead. "But you did get there. You've started to put it right. You can only keep going. And it doesn't change how I feel about you."

Will turned to nuzzle against her neck. "See, I knew you were too good for me," he mumbled.

"Nah, I just want something from you."

He shifted to look at her lovely face, wanting nothing more than to kiss her for the rest of the day. "What's that? Name it. And I'm into all kinds of stuff. No judgement here."

She punched him softly in the arm. "Will you come to Brisbane with me?"

"What's in Brisbane?" he asked.

She rested her cheek against his chest. "Family drama."

Beth wasn't sure whether to be optimistic about the trip or not. Her last visit home had been awful, but after her experiences with Caitlin and her time with Will she'd glimpsed a direction forward. So, now she wanted to repair things with her family. She felt rude about how she'd left Victoria's engagement party and even though Vicky inviting Richard still stung, she wanted to be the mature voice – apologize and move on.

"Oh, it's all right," said Victoria, again foxing Beth with her forgiveness. "If you're coming to town, you should both come and have dinner. I want to meet William and show you the designs for my dress. I'm so glad I didn't buy that awful thing in Perth."

So, Beth had agreed. It was only when she and Will had left for Victoria's apartment that her mobile rang.

"Where are you?" asked Vicky.

"Nearly at your place."

"No, no. Come to Mum's! Didn't Anne call you? We're all here."

"What?" asked Will.

"Change of plan," said Beth. Will raised his eyebrows but said nothing.

As they pulled up outside the house, Beth tried to think happy thoughts as butterflies flew around her stomach.

"You all right?" Will asked, squeezing her hand.

"Fine," she said brightly.

They got out and mounted the stairs. Her sister Anne answered the door. "Hi, Beth," she said, pulling Beth into a hug. Behind her, Beth could see the big dining table laid for a fancy dinner, complete with crystal and the good cutlery, which Beth had never seen used. Anne wore a midnight-blue cocktail dress, and glanced up and down Beth and Will, both clad in jeans. "You didn't dress up?"

Beth was thrown. "I'm sorry, no one said we should—"

"It's all right, come in. You can always borrow something. Mum's gone to a lot of effort. She was really looking forward to you coming."

"She was?"

Anne shut the door and gave Beth an exasperated look.

"Of course. Why wouldn't she be?"

Beth felt Will's arm protectively around her shoulders. Briskly, Anne looked up at him. "Pleased to meet you," she said, then drifted back to the kitchen. Beth smelled a roast. She drew Will into the lounge room, where she found Victoria and Ryan. Still no sign of their mother.

"Hi, Vicky. Hi, Ryan. This is Will."

"Beth!" Her younger sister jumped up and embraced her, then quickly steered Beth to the opposite couch where she'd been poring over a bridal magazine.

Beth lowered her voice. "What's going on, Vicky? You said it was pizza at your place, and now it's a big dinner here?"

Vicky shrugged. "Mum insisted. You know what she's like. She said she missed you at the engagement party, and she wanted to meet Will. I really thought Anne called you. Sorry."

Beth saw Will and Ryan shake hands and strike up a conversation; a moment later, Ryan disappeared to the kitchen and came back with a beer for Will. "What'll you have, Beth?" he asked across the room. Beth shook her head, feeling light-headed enough as it was. Even when her mother finally appeared ten minutes later, disaster did not strike. Meredith had done her hair, and was wearing a wrap dress in soft green, the same one Anne had worn to Vicky's party.

Heart dancing in her mouth, Beth introduced her to Will. "Welcome home," she said. "Hello, Will. Please call me Meredith."

Beth tried not to show her surprise – perhaps she really had imagined everything. "How was your flight? Vicky said there were delays at the airport earlier," her mother went on.

"We flew in yesterday, no delays," Beth managed. "How's the business going?"

"Slow after Christmas. But that's fine. I'm glad I could have some time to do this while you're visiting." She smiled, her tone playful. "You should have let me know you were coming earlier."

"It was last minute," said Will smoothly. "But it smells wonderful."

Her mother turned a bright smile on Beth. "Well, would you like to serve for us, Elizabeth? Anne will help you, won't you, Anne?"

Beth felt intensely uncomfortable that they hadn't brought a bottle of wine, or cheese, or anything at all. She apologized, expecting some remonstration, but all her mother said was, "Well, you're here now."

From the kitchen, Beth could hear Ryan telling Will about his work; he was on the management track at a big accounting firm. Beth had never really warmed to Ryan. She found it hard to make his work – which seemed like endless meetings and client maneuverings – into interesting conversation. Beth knew that to her mother, however, Ryan was smart and secure and settled; the same reasons Beth found him of little interest. But Will was making an effort, and now was telling Ryan about his own jobs on mine construction sites, from Mount Isa to the Pilbara. Beth's mother listened to this keenly, her head tilted, a hand at her chin.

"What's left?" Beth asked, watching through the kitchen doorway.

"Salad," said Anne, pointing to a large crystal bowl full of greenery, which Beth carried out.

Soon, Ryan was carving the roast as they passed around salad and potatoes. Anne filled their mother's wine glass. The lamb was nicely done.

"This is really good," Beth said.

Her mother's expression flickered. "Well, you don't have to sound so surprised," she said. But there was a tiny flash of humor in her tone, and Beth counted it as a win. "I wanted to make something nice. Having everyone here. The marinade has been one of our best sellers."

In between praise for the meal, Victoria monopolized most of the dinner conversation with wedding plans. Under the table, Will's hand found Beth's. "How are you doing?" he asked in her ear.

She smiled at him. "I'm great," she said honestly. The talk of engagements and weddings passed over her easily; she felt whole and healed, and happy that Will was here with her.

Then, when the plates had been cleared and the kettle was boiling for coffee, Ryan leaned back in his chair. "So, Beth. I heard you had an exciting adventure."

All eyes turned to her.

"Come now, Ryan," her mother scolded playfully. "No one wants to hear about that again." Beth heard the irritation.

She shot Ryan a silent appeal: drop it, leave it alone. But he seemed oblivious. "No, no," he persisted. "It was all over the news. Commandeering pilots and screaming across the flood in a boat. Being interviewed by journalists. You're quite the star."

Beth instantly hated the fact that she'd spoken to the journalist and that so many people had heard about what she'd done – it was ten times worse than when she'd walked across country that first week in Iron Junction. Quickly, she said, "I was just doing my job."

But Ryan wouldn't let her off and he was still talking about Cyclone Fletcher and the flood as the party shifted to the powder-blue couches in the lounge room with coffee in the best china cups. Beth headed back to the kitchen with the empty milk jug, listening to the swell of conversation: Victoria's and Anne's laughter, the murmur of Ryan and Will's exchange. She reminded herself that soon the evening would be over and she could tunnel back into Will's embrace. Beth opened the fridge, her eyes falling on the trifle with its perfect layers in jelly green, red and custard yellow, beads of condensation under its cling-film cover. She reached for the milk bottle.

"Don't stand there with the door open."

Beth turned with a start. Her mother stood in the kitchen doorway, wine glass in hand. "You're letting the cold out."

"Sorry," Beth said.

Meredith took a sip from the glass, her nose wrinkling. Her eyes were steel-hard. Beth felt the fridge's escaped cold air curling around her.

"You must be pleased with yourself," said Meredith. "Getting on television."

"I didn't care about that," Beth said quickly. "I just wanted to make sure my patient was okay."

"Your *patient*," her mother drawled. "You must think you're so much better than the rest of us. Turning up in jeans, not bothering to bring anything."

"I really didn't know—" Beth began, but her stomach felt liquefied and her voice quavered.

"I went to all this effort, and look how you repay me," her mother went on. "I sacrificed for you. I had to work hard when your father left, providing for all of you. Giving you every opportunity to make your life better. But you turned out just like him, didn't you?" Her words were slurring now, but Beth felt none of the usual emotional collapse at her mother's mention of her father. Her aunt Judy's words replayed in her mind. For the first time, Beth thought: this is not normal.

Beth's lungs pushed against her breastbone, her heart drummed. Her voice came as a whisper. "Please, Mum. I know it didn't happen like that. I know you kept him away."

Meredith's full temper unleashed. "Oh, you know about it, do you? Now that you've found one of your own. I can't believe the gall of you, bringing him here so soon after you up and leave Richard. People are talking about you. It breaks my heart thinking about what you threw away."

Beth finally found her voice. "It's my heart that was broken, Mum. It was *my* choice."

"Well, it was a stupid choice," her mother hissed. "You should—"

A shadow appeared behind her mother, and she glanced around. Will, streaked with light from the hall. Beth sensed the rage within him from ten paces, his body coiled as it had been that night in the bar fight. He must have heard it all.

The difference was so plain to Beth. Richard would never have reacted in her defense; he'd have ignored it and later patiently explained to Beth why her mother was the way she was, and why Beth should cut her some slack. Now Beth had the momentary worry that Will might charge through with his shoulder.

Instead, he tipped his chin. "That's enough. Let's go, Beth."

Meredith cracked a smile, her wine sloshing in the glass. "Happy to run away. What did I tell you."

Will stepped around her mother and Beth felt his hand under her arm. Suddenly, Beth could move again. She allowed Will to guide her out and down the stairs, until they had escaped the yard and stood on the street in the pale moonlight.

He faced her.

"I'm so sorry," she stammered. "She shouldn't have said that about you."

Suddenly, Will's arms were around her. He shook as he held her in a tight hug, part rage and, she realized a moment later, part laughter.

"What?" she asked bewildered.

He pulled back and kissed her wrinkled forehead. "You don't get it. I don't give a shit what she thinks of me. But she doesn't think much of you, and that makes me crazy." His hands cupped her face, thumbs stroking her cheeks as he grew serious. "Were you just going to stay there and take it?"

Beth felt a tear roll down her cheek. "I guess," she managed. "But ..."

"But what?" he demanded. Beth opened her mouth to explain, to say *but they're my family*. That she needed her mother to see she was really okay. That family excused everything.

But instead, nothing would come. Reflecting a sad truth.

She looked back at the house. She remembered laughing with her sisters. Christmas mornings. Birthday cake. She remembered early curfews. Confiscated books. Hearing the phone ring and that she wouldn't be allowed to answer, and now knowing it had been her father calling. Good and bad and indifferent … but she didn't see home. Just a place she'd been, once. A still frame in time, like a photo. And the meaning was only a habit. A pattern written into her thoughts.

"Beth," Will said softly, his love patient in his eyes.

"It's never going to change," she said.

He kissed her hair and said nothing, but Beth didn't need him to. She thought of all the energy she'd spent cataloguing the ways she was responsible for her mother's behavior. And yet, nothing had ever changed.

But still, her heart squeezed. She'd held the idea of a happy family. One that plainly did not exist, except as a hopeful idea. Tears flowed down her face now, her hands clenched against Will's arms. Silently, he held her against his chest, rocking until her body relaxed.

"Let me tell you something," he said against her hair. "You're talented and clever and beautiful … and sexy. And I don't think you should have to put up with people who want to drag you down for it. They may change, but the onus is on them."

Beth smiled through her tears. She had never known comfort like this. His embrace was more home than anywhere else had been.

Beth looked up at him, into those green eyes. "Maybe it's time for a change."

"Letting go?" he asked.

She shook her head. "More like a new plan."

Chapter 33

Will and Beth talked long into the night.

"You know," Beth said carefully at one point, when she'd relayed the conversation with her aunt Judy, "I used to write my dad letters, and Mum told me she'd post them. I wonder if she did."

Will hugged her closer and Beth snuggled into his smooth skin, naked under the crisp hotel sheets. "Do you think he's still out there?"

Beth pushed herself up on her elbow. "Honestly, I have no idea. I wonder if it's too late."

"Do you want to find him, if you could?"

Beth bit her lip. Her father now seemed very much like an abstract concept, an incorporeal thing absent from her life. She had no idea what it would be like to have him take form again. "I don't know." She was silent for a while, thinking, tracing her fingertips across Will's stomach.

"I like that," he murmured.

She smiled in the darkness. "What about you, though?" she asked seriously. "Do you think you'll see your dad again?"

"I've been thinking about that," Will said.

Beth glanced up. "You have?"

"Yeah." He settled back against the pillows. Then a moment later he spoke again, this time playfully, "But I've been thinking about other things too."

"Such as?"

He pulled her up on top of him, his hands slipping down to her hips. "I think you know," he said with a cheeky grin.

Beth woke the next morning to a mobile phone ringing. Sleepily, she reached for her bedside table, but her phone was dark. Will stirred beside her. "It's mine," he said, reaching out a lazy hand. Beth admired the smooth muscles in his arm and chest. When he saw the caller, he stilled. Instantly, he got up and paced over to the window in his boxers.

"Hello, Will Walker," he said, his voice weary.

Beth watched him as the caller at the other end spoke. "Yes?" he was saying. "Yes. Okay. I understand. Okay." It went on a long time, and finally, Beth went to shower to give him privacy, a rush of concern flowing through her.

When she returned, Will was sitting on the edge of the bed, the phone in his hand, rubbing his hand across his mouth.

"What is it?" asked Beth, bracing herself for bad news.

"That was Mrs. Manning," said Will. "They're dropping the case."

Later Will and Beth walked along the Brisbane River as Will tried to make sense of it all. The events of that night five years ago had dogged him for so long, and the decision to come clean had been hard. He'd been ready to face the consequences. Now, it was the Mannings who were asking him to step back.

"I can understand their position," he said at one point, as they sat near the red-brown river. "They don't want the statements corrected. They don't want her name dragged through another case; they're tired of lawyers and courts. None of it brings her back."

"But you wanted it done with, and now you have to keep

quiet."

Will nodded. "It doesn't seem like enough. I thought it was going to be harder to confess. I never imagined I'd have to keep it quiet. I think it might send me crazy."

Beth seized his hand. "What are you going to do?"

Will knew he'd righted what wrongs he could. He'd already called Sarah to apologize and wish her well in Adelaide. But now, he couldn't help thinking of his family. Beth's experience had shocked him. He knew she would carry the scars for the rest of her life. He felt an immense sadness that his own wonderful mother was already gone; he could only imagine how much she would have loved Beth. And Will wanted her to feel she had a home somewhere.

So, as they left the riverbank he made his decision; one he had never thought would happen.

Will pulled Beth to a stop. "How do you feel about another trip?"

"Where?" she asked.

"Home," he said. "Can you give me a minute to make a call?"

Her eyes searched him. "Sure. I'll walk down to the Goodwill Bridge and back."

As she turned away, he sat on a bench beneath the spreading boughs of a fig tree. Sunlight dappled the grass, still damp from an overnight shower and on the water below, yachts bobbed against their moorings.

The phone seemed to ring for a long time. Then Mark was on the line. "Will, good to hear from you. Are you still caught up in the flooding?"

"I got out of Karratha," said Will. "The region's hit bad, though. As soon as I can I'm going back."

"That girl you mentioned – Beth Harding? – I saw something about her on the news. Daniella's been riveted," said Mark.

Will smiled, feeling proud. "Yep – and ... well, we worked

things out. We're together now."

Mark laughed. "Good on you, mate. When are we going to meet her?"

Will paused, then pushed the difficult words out. "Actually, Mark … can you put Dad on?"

Will heard the intake of breath before Mark, clearly bursting with curiosity, said, "Sure. He's in the office. Wait a sec while I walk over."

Will's heart thundered, and his stomach fizzed with the old dread. He hadn't dared to rehearse this conversation. The silence on the line was broken by rustling as the phone changed hands.

"William Walker." The familiar rumble cut straight into Will's center. He sounded well … even happy.

"Dad," Will said, and then couldn't continue.

"Will? You're breaking up a bit."

Will struggled for a steady voice. "I'm here," he managed, a bit louder. "Is that better?"

"Yes, I can hear you. How are you?" The words still carried authority, but Will did not hear judgement now, as if the memory of the last time they'd met had mellowed and faded like an aged photograph.

"I'm okay. How's the station?"

This was the real test. Will steeled himself. But William said, "We're doing well. Did Mark tell you we're part of a national study? Never thought I'd see it, but we've got satellites tracking the herd."

"Is that right?" said Will, even though he had heard about it from Mark.

His father went on a bit longer about how the project was going, how many head they had now, and the weather. Will couldn't follow most of it – he'd never been engaged by the practice of running the station – but he listened because he felt hopeful.

"So, you survived all that cyclone drama?" his father asked eventually.

"Yeah," said Will. "I was in Karratha, and it was pretty wild. I'm in Brisbane now."

Will took a breath. There would never be a better moment. "Actually, Dad, I wanted to ask you something."

"What's that?"

"I met a girl over in the Pilbara. She's … special. Anyway, I was wondering if I could bring her to the station."

A pause came down the line. It was only then Will realized that they were both playing the same game: both locking themselves down, keeping their defenses up while hoping that this time, one of them would take the risk.

His father's voice was not altogether steady. "Of course. I want to meet her. Can we pick you up?"

Will had to swallow a sob, and push his response out in one breath. "No, it's fine. We'll drive from Isa. I'll call from there."

When the call ended, he leaned back, his heart clear and lofting. He didn't need anyone to tell him what his father had not said. *You're coming home, my son.*

Coming home.

They boarded a flight for Mount Isa the same day, and before Will really knew what had happened, he was taking the turn off the highway in the rental car. The road felt as though he had never left. He knew every bend on the long driveway out to the homestead. The sun was setting and throwing pinks and reds across the golden grass heads.

Beth sat with her hands pressed between her knees in contained excitement. Will loved her eagerness, but his chest was like a riot of flapping insects, which only got worse as they crested the last ridge and he saw the homestead for the first time in five years.

The house looked exactly the same: honey stones beneath a wide veranda and a pale roof that was touched with the last glow of the sunset. Will noted changes in the peripherals – a new shed, and another had been re-roofed. But the gathering of buildings still looked a perfect arrangement on the spur of land, facing down the expansive paddocks. He felt a great sadness in his chest. The last time he'd been here, his mother had still been alive.

But now, Beth was beside him as they climbed out of the car. "Oh, it's lovely," she said, walking a little way around the house where she could see the yards and horses, who flicked their ears in her direction. As Will watched her he saw a figure come around the house veranda.

"Will!" exclaimed Mark, striding over. Will hadn't seen Mark since the year before, when Mark had come to Mount Isa, devastated when his relationship with Daniella had gone south, and then later in Brisbane after he'd been involved in the chopper crash. Mark had been a mess, then, and now Will could see he was back to his old self.

Mark threw his arms around his brother. "Good to see you, mate." He held him tightly for a moment before he broke away. "And this must be Beth." He embraced her like a sister. "I want to hear all your adventures," he said, with a wink. "And my fiancée is going spare waiting to meet you, too."

"Daniella's here?" asked Will.

"Yep. She's slaving over a sticky date pudding and won't let anyone touch it."

Mark stepped back, and Will became aware of the man standing quietly at the edge of the veranda. William Walker had aged since that last pyrotechnic argument they had shared. Gray had crept into his hair, and he was thinner. But as his father stepped down from the veranda and approached them, Will could see an energy in his bones that had never existed before.

"Will," he said. "Welcome home."

Will had to pull Beth to him to stop himself breaking down. Not a word of remonstrance was spoken. William simply offered his hand, his voice mellow and measured, as if time had worn the edges off his anger. Will took his father's hand, bridging a divide so long between them. "It's so good to see you," his father said, still holding on.

"Dad, this is Beth," Will said proudly, to keep the tears at bay.

Beth stuck out her hand. "Mr. Walker, thanks so much for having me. You have a beautiful property."

"Thank you," he said smiling at her. "And you're most welcome. We're cooking a feast."

"So I heard," she laughed. "How many horses do you have?" she asked, pointing down the hill.

And like it was the most natural thing in the world, William stepped across to point them out. "Five you can see – that's Buttons, there. And Rocket. Then Trooper, Ziggy, Tommy."

Then his father glanced back at Will. "The light's fading, so why don't you show Beth round? We'll eat when you come in."

Will watched his father's departing back as the day sunk to an end. Animosity was gone, as if lost on a distant highway. Beth was with him. He'd come home.

Open loops, now closed and done.

Beth soaked up the earth's radiant heat as the light slipped away. She'd imagined this place many times after seeing Will's photo, and her mental images had been a bit American-cowboy-western, with lush green grass and rocky hills in the distance. But the reality – the weathered land that was gilt by sun and grass, the low hills and endless sky – was far more beautiful, more restful and more raw than she could have dreamed. And looking into Will's face now, she could see how much it had meant to him to come home, how grateful he was that he was welcomed.

And how much he loved her.

Will took her hand. "Come on. Let's walk down the ridge. There's a good spot there to watch the stars come out."

And so they went, past the sheds and through the thicket of

trees that dotted the ridge top. Then, he led her to a patch of thick grass, where the sky opened overhead.

"I see Venus," she said, pointing to the first twinkle.

Will followed her gaze. "Nah, that's Sirius. Venus is over there." And he pointed at another spot where a brighter sparkle hung near the horizon.

"Smartass," she teased him.

"It's all right, you like my smart ass," he said, pulling her down to lie with him on the grass.

"You're happy now, aren't you?" she said, as he lay out with one arm around her and the other behind his head.

"In a way I'd never thought I could hope for. I don't think I deserve it," he said. He glanced at her. "If I admit something to you, will you promise not to laugh?"

She gave him a slow grin. "I think I asked you that once."

"So you did. And didn't I make a mess of it. Well ..." He looked up, as if embarrassed. "I boarded for high school. And I had all these grand fantasies of finding a fantastic girl and bringing her back here for the holidays. Take her riding. Kiss her in the stables. I had a very keen imagination. Of course, nothing like that ever eventuated. But now you're here, I feel like I finally made it happen."

Beth bit her lip, trying not to laugh.

"Hey – you promised," he protested.

"I'm not laughing," she said seriously. "But I'd better watch out for you in the stables."

Will winked. "Why wait?" He kissed her for a long time before speaking again. "Look, Beth. This place is beautiful, and it's where I grew up. It'll always be special because of the people who were here. Mum, and Mark, and Cat. Even Dad. But I'm not made for working here. I've been thinking about it a lot."

Here was the point, thought Beth. They had avoided talking about what would come next.

"Me, too," she admitted. "After everything that happened, I don't know if I'm made to sit in a clinic. I think I want something … bigger."

Will looked down at her with interest. "What are you going to do?"

Beth sighed. "I don't know yet. Do you?"

"No, but I'm thinking something similar. All that flood recovery was tough, and sad for the people who lost so much, but helping them was really satisfying."

Beth smiled, but she didn't know how to ask him her next question.

Instead, Will saved her. "Mark and Daniella have a largely long-distance relationship. She's training in hospitals, doing rotations. But they're separated a lot. She's in Townsville, or Brisbane, and he's here. Somehow they're making it work, though."

Beth tried not to hug him too tightly as she looked him in the eye. They both understood what they were to each other, how the complement couldn't function at a distance. "I can't do that," she said.

Will nodded. "Me either. So, that's why I need to know what you're thinking of doing next."

Beth thought about the positions she'd held in hospitals, jobs she'd done well but were nonetheless about marking time, waiting for life to start. And what the past few months had taught her about herself. "I think I have an idea."

"Might this idea allow a man with skills to find a job in the same place?" he asked with a grin.

"Oh, you're a man with skills now?"

He laughed. "You bet your ass."

She wriggled to escape as he tried to steal a kiss.

"Nope. Not so easy," he said, finding her ticklish rib.

"Stop!"

"You haven't answered my question," he said.

She smiled at him, feeling alive amid the land and sky. "It might. It just might."

Soon after, when they went up to the house, Beth found

the kitchen in a merry state of activity. She met Kath, the wiry housekeeper, who was ferrying dishes to the table, and finally, Daniella, Mark's fiancée.

"I'm so glad to meet you," said Daniella, who looked relaxed with her light brown hair over her shoulders and an apron daubed with caramel sauce.

"Me, too," said Beth. "And I met your brother in Karratha."

At this, Daniella's eyes lit up. "Oh, I wondered after I saw him mentioned on the news. I haven't seen Aiden in so long. Will you tell me all about it at dinner? Please?"

And so they went in to eat, the conversation easy and enjoyable. Beth was relaxed with Will beside her, soaking in the history of this place and marveling at how the circle had closed to bring her here. She had never enjoyed a meal with family like this, never felt welcomed like this. And she was certain that wherever she and Will went, they would find a home together.

Six months later

Beth dropped her cabin bag at her feet and stared up at the departures screen. Five a.m., and still thirty minutes until boarding. She rubbed her eyes and sank into a chair where she could see the long arm of the terminal stretching away, dotted with monitors and full of early-morning passengers. Nearby, she heard the hiss of an espresso machine and the scent of roasting coffee drifted past. But her attention was on a television screen.

The early news was still occupied with the devastating earthquake in India. She watched the images of ruined houses and field hospitals, her legs twitching impatiently.

"We'll be there soon."

Beth smiled as Will sat beside her, offering a takeaway coffee and putting his arm around her shoulders.

"Last chance to say you don't want to go," she said to him.

"And have you run off without me?" Will nudged her playfully. "Not a chance. I want to go as much as you do."

Beth leaned into Will's shoulder, sipping the strong coffee and feeling she was in exactly the right place. After the Pilbara flood, she and Will – when they'd returned from their Queensland trip – had spent a mad month pitching in as Iron Junction pulled together. She'd shifted around, relieving other doctors, while he'd gone back to work for Dan, helping to recover the mine's operations. Captain Bell had even come to town personally, overseeing the troops assisting the clean-up. Dan had proved himself as the interim manager. Under his direction, they'd had some success recovering the water-damaged records, and Caitlin's photographs of the mine had proved critical in showing the configuration of stage two. Newly returned after her transplant, she credited her zoom lens and joked that the paparazzi would have been proud. Beth was gratified to see her taking on more and more, organizing the fundraising exhibition and making full use of her celebrity status to benefit everyone. Just before the exhibition opened, Beth had seen Dale King on the news, again fending off Warren Booth and other journalists as he left a preliminary hearing in Perth. She and Will had toasted the moment with Maxine, Dan and Mack.

But as normal life was re-established, Beth knew it was time to move on. She'd sold her share of the Sydney apartment to Richard. She kept in touch with Vicky, but on her own terms, trying to maintain a healthy distance from her family. Even so, something was still missing.

Then one night, Will had brought home printouts from Médecins Sans Frontières, Engineers Without Borders and RedR, and soon, they were both taking courses in international emergency relief. Among this, Beth had been putting out feelers, applying to the Emergency Physicians college and even eyeing off the army reserve after her dealings with Captain Bell, of whom Will jokingly complained he was jealous.

Then, the earthquake had struck and neither of them had hesitated. Now, here they were, ready to go.

Beth looked at Will, with his long legs stretched out, sipping his coffee with a small frown between his brows. She grinned.

"What?" he said, sneaking a quick kiss.

"Nothing. Just thinking this is so right," she said.

He raised his eyebrows at her. They'd spent yesterday in a briefing and now they faced a flight through to Delhi before meeting coordinators who would send them where they were needed. It was a daunting prospect; an unfamiliar place in the midst of a terrible event, but Beth reckoned she was ready.

"It's going to be tough," Will said, as if he'd read her thoughts. "We may not see much of each other while we're there. Long hours, not much sleep. Real danger." He squeezed her hand.

Beth nodded. "We'll need a break when we get back."

Will's eyes lit up. "How about a cruise?"

"Where did you get that idea?"

"Well," said Will carefully. "A ship's captain has special powers in international waters."

"Do they?" she said.

He wrapped his arms around her. "Yes. What do you say?"

"About what?" she teased him. He'd been doing this for the past week, and she'd been parrying back. Now, he looked at her, serious. "Beth Harding. I want to be with you forever, wherever that is."

Beth felt the blood rush through her body. "So do I," she said. "Your brother's wedding isn't far away though … do you think we ought to wait until that's over?"

"We can wait as long as you like," he said. "The important thing is we're together."

Beth slipped her fingers between his. She couldn't believe the way life had opened around her; the world was a big place, full of experiences, and work that gave her days meaning. She thought of her album, carefully packed in a box in Will's apartment. She didn't need it, now. These experiences were in her heart. The last entries she'd made were postcards from Caitlin, proudly sent with her magnificent photos on the front, evidence her career was just taking off. Beth hoped her travels would one day take her back to the Pilbara to touch base with Caitlin and Maxine under happy circumstances. Until then, she'd learned how her soul worked, and that there would always be a new page to turn. The airport PA announced their boarding call, and Will looked down at her with a grin, and love in his eyes. Beth squeezed his hand, excitement in her heart, knowing that for all these adventures, Will would be with her.

Thanks for reading!

I loved writing Will and Beth's story: all the exciting rescue action, bringing Will home again, and giving them a new and exciting future together. If you'd like to leave a review for other readers, please head to Goodreads, or Amazon, iBooks, Kobo – wherever you found this copy.

For more books in this sweet romance series (an excerpt of the next, *Crystal Creek*, follows this section), please visit charlottenash.net. If you enjoy stories with horses and a sexy hero, there's *The Horseman*, a stand-alone sweet romance with a hint of crime, set in the mountains. If you enjoy women's fiction with a romantic subplot, you will also find *The Paris Wedding* and *The Lucky Escape* there.

If you'd like to hear when new books are out, or be in the running for giveaways, you can sign up for my newsletter at charlottenash.net. Happy reading!

Aiden Bell has a past of his own …

Read on for the first chapters of *Crystal Creek*, the next installment in the Walker-Bell series. Get to know Daniella's brother, Aiden, and aspiring doctor Christina. Are they prepared to heal their pasts and find a future together?

Crystal Creek: Chapter 1

"And what is your differential diagnosis?"

Christina Price stood against the wall in the stark hospital hallway, in the middle of the most important exam of her life. She tried to take a deep breath, but her ribs were panic-stiff, the clack of the nearby nurse's keyboard too loud. Her phone vibrated in her pocket yet again, distracting her. She had to *think*. "Uh, cirrhosis. And liver cancer," she said.

The examining doctor peered over the top of his glasses. "You need to expand on that."

She squared her shoulders, fingering the knot of scarred skin on her right palm for motivation. She'd had fifteen minutes with her patient. Surely she could think of something else.

"Um, there could be a primary liver tumor. Or a metastasis from another site." She tried to picture the anatomy in her mind, but her attention kept sliding back to her phone. It had been ringing for the past half-hour, and only one caller would be that persistent. Something bad must have happened.

The consultant tapped a pen on his clipboard, bringing her back to now. "Where else could a tumor be?" he prompted.

Her thoughts moved like sticky mud. "The pancreas?"

The consultant made a note and sighed. "Go back to your second idea. Which neoplasias could have metastasized to the liver, in this patient?"

A nurse with a phlebotomy trolley rattled past. Christina averted her eyes, trying to remember the page from her textbook. "Ah, stomach, breast, ovarian, ah … lung and kidney."

"In *this* patient."

The blood drained from Christina's face. Oh god, had she just suggested breast and ovarian cancer for a male patient? "Umm … lung and kidney."

"And what about your physical examination findings? Did you find evidence to support your diagnoses?"

"Um." She looked at her notes, her handwriting blurring. She knew this stuff. Why couldn't she remember? Her phone buzzed again.

"Like in the abdomen?" prompted the consultant. "Ascites?"

Christina shook her head. She hadn't remembered to check, and her thoughts were too hopelessly muddled now. Her face was burning, her stethoscope pulling the fine hairs on the back of her neck. She knew she'd done terribly, as she had all term. Really, as she had for the past two years, especially on the ward. At the beginning, she'd thought getting into med school was the hard part; it had certainly taken her long enough. But it turned out that she was hopeless at practical skills. *See one, do one, teach one* was the motto, but Christina could never pick things up that fast. All the other students seemed so much more confident. Maybe it was because they were younger.

"All right." The doctor checked his watch. "Please summarize your findings."

The thought of failing tore something in her soul. She forced a deep breath; maybe she could still recover.

"Grant Reading is a fifty-five-year-old man who initially presented with jaundice and, um, right-upper-quadrant discomfort …"

When she finished, she realized she'd failed to ask Grant about any family history.

The consultant grunted, plainly unimpressed, his hands clasped behind his back. "That will do. You may go."

That was when reality crashed in. She hadn't recovered. Not even close.

Christina turned away, limbs sluggish with despair. She pushed through the ward's big double doors and trudged down the stairwell, then along the corridor towards the student common room, checking her phone as she went. Her heart froze when she saw five missed calls from the care house number. How bad was this going to be?

Other surgical students had collapsed on the old couches. Christina skirted them, and sank into a hard chair by the window, plucking at her shirt, which had stuck to her cold-fear sweat. She braced herself for the coming conversation.

Lena, one of the care staff, answered on the second ring. "Christina, I'm sorry, I know you have exams, but there's been a problem today."

"What kind of problem?"

A pause, as if Lena was considering where to start. "Your mother – she went missing."

"What? How could that even happen? She's partly paralyzed."

"She came back a few hours later. But she's been drinking again. I'm so sorry. One of the carers was sick and we were short-staffed."

Christina cursed, though it wasn't Lena's fault. Across the common room, she could hear a group of students from her class – Toby, Sean, Sarah and Katie – commiserating, giddy with post-exam relief. Katie was talking over everyone else, going over details no one wanted to discuss, until Toby threw his notes at her. Soon they would go out to drink beer and celebrate. Christina had never been part of that circle. Her life was taken up with responsibilities and obligations.

"I'll come now," she told Lena. "But I have to be at work in an hour." She ended the call and grabbed her bag, doing the math in her head. Thirty minutes to drive to the care house, time talking to her mother, another thirty to get to work. To revive herself, she splashed water on her face from the kitchen tap.

"How'd you go?" called Katie. "Hey, Christina, I said how'd you go?"

Christina glanced warily at Katie Prior, who was dressed impeccably in a crisp pale-blue shirt and black pants, her artfully streaked blonde hair pulled into a perfect bun. Katie was the only student who knew where Christina had come from. Her older brother, Sebastian, had been in Christina's high-school class. And the less said about both those things, the better.

"I don't want to talk about it," Christina said, heading for the door.

"Bye!" called Katie with a laugh.

Toby followed her into the hall, panting as he tried to catch up. "Hey, wait. Was the exam really that bad?"

"That bad," said Christina, not slowing even as she felt rude. Toby had tried to help her study, his efforts always interrupted by work or her mother. He was quiet and soft-spoken, the kind of study partner she'd have liked if she could. "Sorry, but I have to go."

She didn't look around. All she could think about was what might be waiting for her at the care house.

She pulled her ancient Corolla into the care house driveway twenty-five minutes later. Lena met her at the door, her dark eyes apologetic, her uniform blouse rucked from the day. She went to speak, but Christina cut her off. "Don't apologize again. Tell me the whole story."

When Lena was finished, Christina was aghast. She turned towards the lounge, the weight of what had happened sinking in. Four months ago, when the residential care package had first been granted, Christina had thought that the days of dealing with her mother's destructive habits were over. The care package was supposed to allow Christina to step back, to be only her mother's guardian – ensuring her finances were sorted, making medical decisions if needed. Not giving lectures.

She paused before she went in, carefully putting up her mental barrier.

Rita sat in one of the electric-lift chairs, a *New Idea* crooked against her weaker arm, her blonde hair shot with gray and tucked behind her ears as she stared at the pages. No matter how hard Christina pulled her emotions back, she always felt the gut strike when she saw the sunken cheeks, dotted with spider nevi, the red flush across her mother's palms – all medical signs of the addiction that had taken over her mother's life and nearly destroyed Christina's. She could smell the sour fumes in the air as she sat down in the opposite seat.

"What were you thinking, Rita?"

"What, no *Mum* today?" Rita said with a slight slur, not looking up from the pages.

Christina ignored this. "Where did you go?"

"Nowhere."

"This nowhere have slot machines?"

"So what if it did?"

Christina rubbed her forehead, wondering how much of this month's disability payment was gone. "How did you get there?" she asked quietly.

"I walked."

"No, you didn't."

"I took the bus."

"No, you took the house car. You took the keys and you drove."

"Why are you asking, if you know so much?" said her mother, folding her good arm across the other one, and keeping her attention on a spread of Kate and Wills.

"Jesus, Mum. You have fits. Your arm is paralyzed. You're not allowed to drive. And you were drinking. What would have happened if you'd hit someone?"

"I wasn't going to hit anyone. I'm a good driver."

"You know you can't drink with your medication."

"I had one beer. That never hurt anyone."

Christina's heart sank. Her mother's denial was powerful. Intractable. One beer had never been enough.

"I just wanted to get out, spread my wings," Rita said now, plaintive. "Eating up the miles, free as a bird. You understand that, don't you, Chrissy? You always loved road trips. You're my one baby, the only one who understands me. We were always so alike."

Christina abruptly stood. *So alike.* The words struck her emotional barriers like heavy fire, reviving her worst nightmares – of failing, of ending up where everyone had said she would: poor and dependent, just like Rita. She paced to the window and looked out into the backyard. The grass needed mowing and a paling had come loose from the fence. She had to remind herself that there had never been any road trips. That was her mother's fantasy. But it was harder to dispute the claim that they were alike, especially when she was close to failing out of medical school.

"Aren't you going to sit down and talk?" Rita demanded.

Christina didn't look around. "I have to be at work soon."

She found Lena in the kitchen, counting out the residents' medication into weekly pill boxes.

"This can't happen again," Christina said. "The keys have to be secure, all the time."

"Of course. The director is reviewing the procedures tomorrow. We'll call you."

Christina sighed. Lena did her best, but the house was always short on staff, and the agency that ran it had three other houses on their books.

"Lena, if this happens again – call the police. I mean it. She'll hurt someone."

Christina hurried out the front door, cursing as she checked her watch. She was twenty minutes late to work, where she shuffled around the hospital emergency room with her survey question sheets until nine thirty, doing the research legwork that a doctoral student hadn't wanted to do themselves. The department was quiet for a Friday evening, the rush of cases not due for at least an hour when the end-of-week partying turned serious. She scanned down the cases on the computer system, looking for suitable candidates, and managed four in three hours. Not her best effort.

By the time she reached home, her feet were throbbing and her back ached all the way down into her tailbone. Her rented room was upstairs, in a share house behind the freeway, which emitted a constant low roar. Even as she walked up the driveway, she could hear music. When she pushed open the back door, she found her housemates in the kitchen amid sizzling pans and a radio cranked to eleven. The air smelled of tacos, and charred onions.

She avoided them, climbed the stairs and pushed her door closed, which at least muted the music. She sat on the bed and tugged off her shoes, stretching out her toes on the threadbare carpet. Breathing in … and out. This wasn't forever. Things would get better. She just had to get through the next eighteen months, finish her degree, and her life would change.

But she'd never had less confidence in that vision.

It wasn't just the exam. Maybe it had been seeing Katie Prior, reminding her of home. Or maybe it was Rita's reference to road trips, evoking so many other broken promises. Or just that when her mother had gone into care, she'd thought her life would improve, too. … No, focus, she told herself. Breathe.

Her lecture notes were stacked in piles across her desk, her ancient laptop on screensaver. The muscles pinched between her shoulders as she pulled out her phone, deleting Lena's missed calls and messages.

Wait. What was this? Another missed call earlier in the day, from a number she didn't recognize. Frowning, she dialed voicemail.

"*Oh, Christina*," began a vaguely familiar voice. "*I'm so sorry but Dr. Winterbourne's had some unfortunate news. I'm leaving you my home number. Please call me when you can. It's …*"

Christina's insides twisted. It was the receptionist at the family practice for her next rotation. The one she'd organized weeks ago. She dialed the woman's home number, not caring about the time.

"Is Dr. Winterbourne all right?" she asked as soon as the receptionist answered.

"No, it's terrible." The woman's voice shook. "He has cancer. Quite out of the blue, and they're still running tests. He's about to have surgery. I'm really sorry, but there's no chance you can start on Monday week. We have a locum coming in, but he'll be flat out. I'm sure you'll find something else."

When she'd hung up, Christina let the phone fall into her lap. How awful for Dr. Winterbourne. She'd only met him twice, a kind elderly man with a shock of white hair and half-frames on a chain. She couldn't imagine him facing surgery, or chemotherapy. Then there was the fact that she'd lost the placement. Don't panic, she thought. But she knew that by now all the practices would be full. Space was at a premium, and all the students were expected to organize their own placements. Music pulsed under her feet, starting up a corresponding throb behind her eye.

She thumped the bed with her fist, and allowed herself five minutes of cursing, releasing her frustration. Then she curled into a ball on the covers, thinking madly. She'd overcome so much to be here; there had to be a way through this. She just had to find it.

Late the next morning, dark circles under her eyes from a

sleepless night, Christina slumped at her desk amid the crossed-out and discarded sheets of the medical school's approved practice list. She'd called every number; they were all full. The medical school's receptionist refused to take any more of her calls. They were seeing what they could do, she said.

So Christina stewed in miserable suspense. She did her laundry while listening out for the phone, carefully hand-washing her thin work shirts to coax another week out of them. She went to a meeting with the agency who ran her mother's residential care, numbly listening to their reassurances that it wouldn't happen again. She'd heard that before.

And still no one called. As the clock crept towards five, Christina began to imagine what the school would say. Her grades were poor. Classes missed. Maybe they would make her repeat the year. Or maybe it would be worse: they would tell her there was no longer a place for her in the school.

At one minute to five, when she had given up hope, her phone finally rang.

"I have a solution," the school's placement coordinator began, without preamble, and with a distinct tone of relief. "There's a place available right near your home address."

"How is that even possible?" asked Christina, the reprieve running warm in her veins.

"Another student dropped out. You'll need to do the tutorials by remote, of course, but there'll be another student doing the same thing, so you can buddy."

Christina frowned. "But home's only a few minutes from the campus. Can't I do the tutorials there?"

A pause. "I mustn't have been clear. This place is in Townsville. On the base."

"What?"

"The home address we have for you is in Townsville."

Christina froze. She'd listed the Townsville address when she first applied to the medical school, after someone had told her a regional address would give her a better chance of acceptance. Never had she imagined it was still on file.

"Christina?"

"I haven't lived there for more than ten years," she croaked.

The coordinator cleared her throat, plainly exasperated. "Look, I've spent all day on this and exhausted all other avenues. You're welcome to keep trying yourself, but this is the best I can do. The school expects you'll have to travel for rotations now and then. If you can make it happen, I'd advise you to take it."

"Where in Townsville?" Christina asked reluctantly.

"A clinic on the army base. It works just like a regular practice. They often take students. I understand you'd have to organize accommodation. The school can help with the transport. But don't think too long. Let me know tomorrow morning."

Christina felt as though the stuffing had been knocked out of her body. She'd promised herself she was never going back. Not to the town she'd escaped from … and where Harriet still lived.

But after an hour, then two, distractedly stacking her notes and books into neat piles, straightening her bed and listening to the rumble of her housemates downstairs, she had to face facts. What else could she do – tell the school she wouldn't go?

Christina rubbed a hand across her mouth, considering. She didn't even know yet if she'd passed the current rotation. If she didn't, some kind of remediation might follow, throwing out the rest of the year.

But what if she passed?

She twitched aside the curtain and looked down on her Corolla under the streetlight, its sun-damaged bonnet covered in dropped leaves. No way would the car make it eight hundred miles to Townsville; she wouldn't reach Brisbane's city limits before it overheated.

Grimly, she pulled out a notepad, wrote down her tiny bank balance, and began a list, just to convince herself this couldn't work. *Take leave from job,* she scribbled. *Pay for flight.* That would use up most of the balance. But at least the school had said they could help. The bigger issue was: *Find somewhere to stay.*

Christina chewed her pen.

This should be where it ended. Harriet was only one option. Which she couldn't contemplate, could she?

Exhausted after staying up late studying the night before, her mind still swirling with thoughts and calculations, she went to bed, hugging the blanket close around her.

When the first lorikeets shrieked past her window Christina gave up on sleep and woke her computer. Results would be posted by now. She dragged the blanket over her lap as the school portal loaded.

The practical mark was first: forty-nine per cent, a terrible mark if at least a conceded pass. Christina groaned; that would earn her another caution on her record. Any more and she would repeat. She heard her mother's voice in her mind: *We're so alike.* With a surge of panic Christina flicked to the written exam result.

Ninety-two per cent.

"Oh my god," she whispered, reloading the page just to make sure, double-checking her name. She'd actually done it. Despite everything – her mother, her housemates, her job – she'd managed to do one thing right. The first time she'd ever earned more than a scraping pass.

In disbelief, she ran her hands over her crowded bookshelf, where two and a half years of notes were carefully arranged in folders alongside her textbooks. She'd done all of that in the past two months, converting her disorganized scribble into meaningful summaries, desperate to turn around her performance. Hard work. It hadn't been for nothing.

That boost made her decide to call Harriet.

She waited until eight. The number was still in her memory,

but her fingers trembled as the phone rang, and rang. Perhaps her aunt had moved, or changed her number? Eventually a machine picked up. *"You've reached Harriet Reed. I can't take your call ..."*

When the beep sounded, Christina had to force out the words around fifteen years of anger and regret. "It's Christina," she said. "I, um, have to come to Townsville. And, um —"

Click. "Christina?" Harriet's voice was suddenly alive on the line.

Blood rushed to Christina's face. She could still picture her aunt as clearly as on that last day in Townsville: an imposing woman, broad in the hip and shoulder, with a stern stare that could soften into the kindest smile. Her mother's face, but unmarred by years of drink. But the relationship had soured all the same.

"Yes," she managed.

"Long time," said Harriet. "How are you?"

Christina tried to speak and found that tears had gathered in her throat.

"Well, I didn't expect to hear from you," Harriet said, her own voice cautious. "What's this about you coming up?"

Christina gripped her blanket. "My medical school rotation placement fell through. The only one I can get is on the base up there ..." She very nearly hung up. She couldn't ask.

"How long is it for?"

"Two months."

A tiny pause. "Well, you're lucky you called today," said Harriet briskly. "I was about to leave on a trip. I asked the neighbors to look out for the place, but if you want the job instead ..."

The shaking in Christina's limbs subsided. "You're going away?"

"Thought it was about time. Thomas died last year."

"Oh. I ... didn't know," said Christina. Thomas was Harriet's husband, a man Christina hadn't known and yet who had so changed the relationship between them.

Harriet, never keen on sympathy, made a dismissive noise. "We had a long time to prepare. But the house is there if you want it."

"Where are you going?"

"Oh, Kokoda, if it works out. Then who knows? I've always wanted to see Italy. Be gone a couple of months. So, are you taking the house?"

"Yes," said Christina, not believing her luck.

"I'll leave the key in the usual spot."

Christina put down the phone, her aunt's words still ringing in her mind. *In the usual spot.* As though she were thirteen again, and coming home from school, to Harriet and a new life, one that would end too soon.

And now, after all that had happened, she was going back.

Chapter 2

Eight hundred miles north the next morning, Captain Aiden Bell shook salt water from his short dark hair and dropped his dive mask onto the boat deck as Travers, his best mate and diving buddy, straightened up from inspecting the outboard.

"Is it fucked, then?" Aiden asked, checking his watch.

"Yeah, it's fucked. Won't start."

The runabout barely moved on the water, the sun two thumbs above the horizon, the ocean a flat gray slate. They were only a few miles offshore, near a bommie perfect for an early-morning dive. The unmistakable knobbly peak of Castle Hill marked the way back to Townsville. Aiden stripped his wetsuit to the waist as he appraised the situation. Two main problems. He was due on base before eight, the fervent pace of his latest assignment requiring constant attention. And that would have been easy, if the outboard hadn't just died. That was problem one.

Travers muttered, muscles tensing in his broad shoulders as he cranked the motor again, the air tense. This was problem two. Aiden let the silence stretch out as he stowed their fins and tanks. Whatever it was Travers had dragged Aiden out here to hear, Travers would have to spill soon.

Aiden had begun the day with a bad feeling, a tiny ripple of foreboding that was pressing into the back of his skull. The feeling had intensified as Travers remained silent and evasive through the half-hour trip out, ten minutes of prep, a forty-minute dive and now ten minutes screwing with the engine.

They had a long history together; they'd met as teenagers, fresh off the bus at boot camp. Since then, they might have served in different corps but they'd been through more together than most friends did in a lifetime. They were brothers. They'd seen each other at their worst, knew all each other's secrets. After the past two years … Aiden didn't think there was anything worse to know. But now, sensing Travers struggling to find words, he wondered how bad this could be.

He checked his watch again. "You going to let me look now? Travers?"

Travers finally gave up and slid down onto the runabout's curving side. "Shit."

"Let me look." Aiden stepped around him, fixing his attention on the engine, his mind running through potential problems. "You checked the prime, right?"

"Yeah. It did this last week too. I knew I should've brought some beers." He fell silent again, frowning.

Aiden focused on the motor. "You want to tell me what you did last time?" *You want to tell me what's up?*

"It just came good. I should've had it checked out."

Aiden grunted. Another five minutes ticked by as he inspected the engine. When he could bear it no more, he glanced around. "In about twenty seconds, this motor's going to be running again. So for all that's holy, Travers, spit it out."

Travers laughed. "Don't know what you're talking about. I just wanted to dive."

Aiden threw up his hands. "Fine then." He turned back to the motor.

"I'm getting out."

Aiden paused, mid-reach to the engine cover. Slowly he turned back. "Out of the army?"

"No, out of the boat. Of course, out of the army." Travers

made a face. "My shoulder operation has been scheduled. Once it's done, that's it."

Aiden sank down on the bench opposite Travers, hoping that if he sat, his stomach would stop falling. He'd known this day was coming. Travers had little option left. But after sixteen years in the military together, the sense of loss knocked him sideways. "That's big news," he said carefully.

Travers fixed his blue eyes on Aiden. "I'm okay with it. Really. You don't have to worry."

"I'm not worried." No, it wasn't worry. It was much deeper than that.

"I'm still going to be kicking around," Travers went on. "So you're not going to get out of me dragging you away from that office of yours."

"What are you going to do?" asked Aiden. Travers was from a military family; his father, his father's father. He'd already been removed from active service to a medic's position. This was a much bigger deal than he was letting on.

"This." Travers flung his arms wide. "Diving. Easier on my joints, and I have a lead on some work with the university. Underwater survey, that sort of thing. Start with that, then move into salvage. It'll take a bit of setting up, but I reckon it's solid."

"Sounds like a plan," said Aiden. Relief chased the anxiety away. But a different emotion came heavy on its heels. His best mate was leaving the job they'd started together. Nothing would be the same again.

This time it was Travers who checked his watch. "Well, reckon you're about five minutes over on that engine fix ETA. Typical brass."

Aiden threw a mask at him as he stood up. "As opposed to the grunts, who screwed it in the first place. Didn't think they taught engines in sniper school."

"Bet you don't even know what's wrong with it."

"Safety fuse is gone. Going to bridge it, then we'll be sweet," said Aiden. And just to prove it, twenty seconds later, the outboard roared to life.

Travers laughed. "I knew I kept you around for a reason."

"Yeah, to save your ass from the MPs."

A moment passed, the outboard chugging. Aiden sat on the crossbar, his attention on the coast, now painted in golden early sunlight. "Travers …"

"Yeah, mate?"

There was so much he could say, but none of it was needed now. "If you're going to go into diving, you need a better boat."

Just after eight a.m., Aiden walked into a familiar maelstrom. The Solomon Islands recovery operation had only been official for two days, but he already felt right at home. The command center occupied temporary buildings at the back of the base, a warren of interconnected offices that faced an open bitumen square flanked with sheds. The place smelled of diesel and dust, and hummed with the activity of a new operation.

Aiden's office opened into the main hall, where boot steps and the constant murmur of voices kept him company. He didn't get far into his messages before one of the voices appeared in his doorway. "Bell, you good for this meeting?"

Two minutes later, he was in a conference with the major in charge of the operation. The walls were covered with satellite photos and projected timelines.

"Where are we on the equipment?" asked the major.

"All slots filled, except two," Aiden began, immediately in stride. "We need another two backhoes. But the drivers are a bigger issue. I'm still trying to find personnel. And the readiness of the equipment isn't confirmed."

"How long?"

"Give me twelve hours, I'll have it done."

"Good man," said the major.

Aiden's pulse was racing as he left the room. Shit, twelve

hours. And as the ops officer he had another pile of orders for an upcoming exercise to review. Okay, he could take those home. And the reports from the fires out west last month? Those too. He'd have enough paperwork to start his own bonfire.

"Here's the figures you asked for, sir."

Aiden glanced up to see a clerk holding another sheaf of papers. "Thanks, Corporal."

He plowed on. When he stopped at two to shove a sandwich in his face, he checked his personal mobile and saw two missed calls from his sister. Damn, he'd promised to call her back twice already.

"Dani," he said. "I know, I know, I saw your calls."

"Aiden, it's fine." She laughed, that lovely warm sound. "I know how busy you are. Just as long as you're still coming to the wedding."

"I haven't forgotten." His baby sister was marrying a cattle farmer she'd met working out west. As hard as *that* idea was to process, it was harder to know that it was all happening without his having seen her in an age. Separated for most of their adult lives, they were serendipitously both now working in Townsville, he on the base, she as a surgical registrar at the hospital. But despite their proximity, they hadn't yet managed to meet.

"You must have everything sorted," he said.

"Pretty much. I wouldn't mind going through a few things with you, though. I'm suddenly nervous about some of my choices!"

Aiden leaned back in his chair, a smile spreading across his face. "And you think *I'm* the person to ask? You've seen what I wear to work. Your bridesmaids will end up in camouflage."

"But you always back me up," she said, laughing. "I need you. Dad's become impossible. Every time I mention it, he starts reminiscing about when I was three. It's sweet, but irritating."

Aiden cleared his throat. "How about dinner ..." he

scrolled through his calendar, "Wednesday week? You said that was your night off, right?"

"Good memory. All right, yes." She sounded excited.

"I'll swing by the ward and pick you up after your shift?"

"Perfect!"

Aiden was soon deep in a tactical movement plan as trucks rumbled past outside. "Corporal," he called, spotting the clerk near his door. "I need a copy of the exercise area map. And can you find out if the CO is back from HQ yet?"

Two minutes later, boots stopped at his door. "Well, that was fast —" Aiden broke off. Standing in the doorway was a gray-haired man with a major's crown insignia on his chest and crosses stitched onto his lapels.

Aiden was instantly on his feet. "I'm sorry, Padre, I thought you were someone else."

"I get that all the time," said the padre with a warm smile, stepping forward to shake his hand. "Probably they wish I was. How are you, Aiden?"

"I'm good. Been to Perth since we last met."

"I heard. And now you're here. It's like a reunion."

"More than you know," said Aiden. "Travers is here, too, at the clinic these days." Their eyes met for a fraction of a second, silently acknowledging what had happened just eighteen months ago, when they'd all been posted in Victoria. Aiden searched for the right words. "It'll be good to catch up before things get serious," he said at last.

The padre nodded, then glanced around at the piles on Aiden's desk. The corporal was hovering near the door. "You've a lot on your plate. I'll see you in the mess."

As the corporal handed over copies of the map he'd asked for, Aiden listened to the padre's departing steps. He hadn't seen Major Dunning in more than a year. After the morning's boat trip revelation, maybe it was a sign.

"Sir?"

Aiden snapped his attention back to the room. "I'm sorry,

what?"

"There's one more thing. Word is there's a fire ban …"

Aiden groaned. "You're not serious? We can't have a preparation exercise without rounds."

"Yes, sir. No firing anywhere until it rains. You have a briefing with the CO in ten minutes."

Aiden cleared a space in his piles of paper. There were signs and there were signs. And this one meant he had to go back to the start.